Too Much

Blood

Also by Jane Bennett Munro

Murder under the Microscope
Published by iUniverse, Inc.

Jane Bennett Munro

author of *Murder under the Microscope*
a 2012 IPPY Award winner

Too Much

Blood

A Toni Day Mystery

iUniverse, Inc.
Bloomington

Too Much Blood
A Toni Day Mystery

iUniverse books may be ordered through booksellers or by contacting:

iUniverse
1663 Liberty Drive
Bloomington, IN 47403
www.iuniverse.com
1-800-Authors (1-800-288-4677)

Because of the dynamic nature of the Internet, any web addresses or links
contained in this book may have changed since publication and may no longer be
valid. The views expressed in this work are solely those of the author and do not
necessarily reflect the views of the publisher, and the publisher hereby disclaims
any responsibility for them.

Any people depicted in stock imagery provided by Thinkstock are models,
and such images are being used for illustrative purposes only.

Certain stock imagery © Thinkstock.

ISBN: 978-1-4759-2918-8 (sc)
ISBN: 978-1-4759-2919-5 (e)

Printed in the United States of America

iUniverse rev. date: 7/11/2012

For my Poo sisters: Rhonda, Teala, and Lita, with love

Introduction

The inspiration for this novel, as with the previous one, comes from thirty-plus years as a pathologist in a small rural town. This is a work of fiction: all the characters in it are figments of my imagination, and any resemblance to any real persons is coincidental.

Some of the places in it are real; however, Perrine Memorial Hospital, Southern Idaho Community College, and the Intermountain Cancer Center are completely fictitious, as are all the characters. The Twin Falls Bank and Trust building is real, but the bank itself no longer exists.

My heartfelt thanks goes to my dear friend, Dr. Semih Erhan, who would not let me give up. Without his incessant encouragement, my first novel would never have seen the light of day.

Thanks are in order for many other people as well:

To Janet Reid of FinePrint Literary Management, whose advice has been invaluable. She read several versions of my first novel, and although she ultimately rejected it, without her input Toni Day wouldn't be the kick-ass character she is.

To Dennis Chambers, formerly of the Twin Falls Police, currently County Coroner, for information on police procedure and introducing me to the police lab; I'm still using the book he gave me twenty years ago.

To my good friend Marilyn Paul, Twin Falls County Public Defender, for getting me into the courtroom and giving me essential information on courtroom procedure.

To my BFF, Rhonda Wong, who read the first draft and pointed out all my egregious errors.

Finally, to all those people at iUniverse, without whom this book would not exist: Jamie Mitchell, the check-in coordinator who got me started; George Nedeff, editorial consultant and my go-to guy for questions; Christine Moore, my editor from whom I learned so much; Shawn Waggener, publishing services associate, who guided me through the actual publication process; Daisy Morgan, who provided me with books for book signings; Dayne Newquist, senior marketing consultant, who advised me on ways to market my book; and Kelly Ferguson, senior marketing services representative, who hooked me up with my publicist, Jessica Kiefer at Bohlsen PR, who has done a terrific job at getting the word out; and Brittani Hensel, who guided this clueless senior citizen through the bewildering maze of Facebook and Twitter, et al., and taught me how to blog effectively.

Any anachronisms, medical misstatements, or other errors are entirely mine.

Friday, December 12

Chapter 1

There's a sucker born every minute.
—Phineas T. Barnum

The phone rang.

Normally this would be no big deal. But I'm a pathologist, and it was one o'clock in the morning. And I was on call.

For a moment, I felt completely disoriented. My husband, Hal, picked up the phone. I tensed. Phone calls in the wee hours are never anything good.

"Oh, for God's sake!" he snapped and handed the phone to me.

Shit. Couldn't it be a wrong number, just this once?

"Hello?" I croaked. My voice wasn't awake yet either.

I heard the deep voice of Roland Perkins, local funeral home owner and county coroner, and my heart sank. This could only mean one thing.

"Hello there, Dr. Day."

I've known Rollie for thirteen years and have done numerous autopsies in his establishment, Parkside Funeral Home; yet he still insists on calling me either "Doctor" or "young lady" when he knows I prefer to be called Toni.

"For God's sake, Rollie, you're calling at one in the morning. Couldn't you call me Toni just this once? What's up—as if I didn't know?"

"Well, I don't know how you would know," he said. "We just found him an hour ago."

"Found who?"

"The estimable Jay Braithwaite Burke, Esquire, sitting in his car in the middle of the interstate, without a mark on him. He was even wearing a seat belt."

"Dead?" I realized as soon as I said it what a stupid question that was. Of course he was dead, or Rollie wouldn't be calling.

"Of course he's dead," said Rollie. "That's why I'm calling. I need an autopsy. When do you think you can do it, Doctor?"

"Since you saw fit to wake me at this ungodly hour, do I assume you want me to jump right out of bed and do it now?" I knew the answer to that, but I figured it wouldn't do any harm to let Rollie know that he really didn't need to call me in the middle of the night for an autopsy, again. Still, I knew it wouldn't make any difference this time when it hadn't for the last thirteen years.

Sure, I knew he had to schedule services around it, but did he really think I was going to go downstairs, get my purse, and haul out the damn Day-Timer to see if I could squeeze it into my busy schedule and give him a definite time? Hell no. I was going to just go right back to sleep and deal with it tomorrow, same as he was.

"No, no, it doesn't have to be done now. I just need to know because we have services tomorrow, and I need to work around them."

"I'll have to let you know. Until I get to work, I won't know myself what kind of a day I'll have."

That's the usual, pointless kind of conversation we have in the wee hours of the morning, where no decisions are made and people lose sleep for nothing. Actually, Hal and I lose sleep for nothing. After all, the cops who found the body were awake, and Rollie was awake, so why shouldn't the pathologist also be awake? And why should Rollie care that my husband was awake when his wife was too?

We said our good-byes and hung up. I looked at Hal. I knew exactly what he was about to say, because he always said it. He might as well have a sticker made up, to plaster across his forehead for these occasions.

"Why the hell do those guys think they have to call you in the middle of the night for an autopsy you're not going to do until the next day? The guy's dead, for God's sake! Now I'm not going to be able to get back to sleep for hours!"

Join the club, I thought. I knew he'd be snoring again long before I got back to sleep. He always was, damn him. His anger had every bit as much to do with keeping me awake as the phone call did—maybe more—and I wished he would just keep it to himself and shut the fuck up about it. It wasn't going to change anything except the speed of my getting back to sleep any time soon.

And the more I thought about that, the madder I got.

The name Jay Braithwaite Burke calls to mind (to my mind, anyway) a portly, red-faced, sixtyish individual with a mane of silver hair and a vest with a pocket watch and chain adorned with a Phi Beta Kappa key. He would have a sonorous voice with a Southern accent, and as he spoke, he would hook his thumbs in his vest pockets, stick his belly out, and rock back on his heels.

That pretty much described the grandfather, now deceased, of the Jay Braithwaite Burke that we knew.

Our Jay—a small, beige man of about forty, with a slouch and a caved-in chest, thick spectacles that made his pale blue eyes look huge, and sparse, wispy, colorless hair—had a large hooked nose that dominated his otherwise unremarkable face and actually looked out of place there. The Nose was one of two things that Jay had inherited from his grandfather that, along with his concave chest, made him look rather like a buzzard in profile.

The other thing Jay inherited from his grandfather was The Voice. Plummy and rich, it vibrated with evangelical zeal when addressing his favorite subject, money, and his favorite audience, clueless doctors with lots of it to invest.

Our Jay had quite a long history with the doctors of Perrine Memorial Hospital, where I worked. He had managed to talk nearly the entire medical staff into giving up their nice, safe profit-sharing plans to invest in a hedge fund guaranteed to earn at least ten percent per year. Jay's magical hedge fund, elegantly named Sentinel Elite Advantage, had been one of the numerous feeder funds for a much larger and more elegantly named fund, Fairfield Greenwich Sentry, which had investors all over the United

States and Europe, and allegedly included English and French royalty as well as the Russian Mafia and some South American drug cartels. It had turned out to be a Ponzi scheme, and all his investors had lost their shirts. They also wound up owing years of back taxes, interest, and penalties to the IRS.

A physician in California, who ended up owing the IRS nearly a million dollars, promptly sued Jay Braithwaite Burke. Jay Braithwaite Burke promptly declared bankruptcy and left Idaho. He didn't take his family with him. They were still here, dealing with the fallout.

He also left us with unanswerable questions. Was he really bankrupt? Did he vanish to escape taxes and liability from lawsuits or a prison sentence, or to escape the wrath of the drug lords and Russian Mafiosi, who take a dim view of anyone messing about in their investments?

Or all three?

And why had he left his wife and family hanging out to dry?

And where did he go?

Nobody knew.

Not until he showed up two months later, sitting in his cream-colored Mercedes in the middle of the median on I-84 on that snowy December night.

I got up early and went to my aerobics class to work off some of my wrath. Hal was still in bed when I got back. I'd just walked in the door and started the obligatory pet-greeting rites with our dogs—Killer, the hundred-pound German shepherd, and Geraldine, the ten-pound terrier mix with the coloring and disposition of a tiny

Rottweiler—when the phone rang. I raced them across the room to catch it before it woke Hal, but I was too late. I heard his voice as I picked up the receiver.

"For God's sake, Elliott, do you realize what time it is?"

"Yes, I do, Shapiro. But I don't want to talk to you. I need to talk to your wife, the pathologist."

"I'm here," I said.

"Do you know one esteemed attorney, name of Jay Braithwaite Burke, Esquire?"

"I know he's dead," I said as I handed out Milk Bones. "Rollie wasted no time in letting me know he needed an autopsy."

"Yeah, he called at one o'clock in the morning," Hal said. "I just got back to sleep."

Big fat lie, I thought.

"What I'm saying is, did you know him when he was alive?" Elliott asked. "Do you realize who Jay Braithwaite Burke is?"

Well, of course we did. Our favorite person, he wasn't.

Even though I'd been the only member of the medical staff not to get roped into Jay Braithwaite Burke's investment scheme, the effects on the rest of the medical staff had had an adverse effect on the fortunes of a private, doctor-owned hospital like Perrine Memorial. This in turn had had an adverse effect on Hal's and my bottom line, even when the economy was good.

And the economy was sucking right now.

There would be no shortage of persons who might have wished Jay Braithwaite Burke dead.

Including Hal and me.

Chapter 2

We are not amused.
—Queen Victoria

"Of course I know who he is," I told Elliott. "Why are you calling me about him before breakfast?"

"Because you're doing the autopsy today," Elliott said. "A lot of people stood to gain by his death, and they're going to be royally pissed off about it if this turns out to be a freakin' homicide. Everything'll be held up until it's solved. So the sooner you know what killed him and the sooner you tell me, the better."

"Gain what?" I asked. "I thought he was bankrupt. Are you telling me he wasn't?"

"Supposedly he was, but his will mentions several sources of money, some of them offshore. Bankruptcy wouldn't affect those funds. Neither would a lawsuit."

"Wouldn't his wife know about those?"

"I have no idea," Elliott said. "He was in the middle of a divorce and was having an affair with his secretary."

"And I suppose those offshore accounts won't be part of the divorce either?"

"Right."

"So who inherits what?"

"Maybe nobody," Elliott said. "You and I both know that if there's anything left in all those offshore accounts, the IRS will probably grab it all."

Too true, I thought. The IRS was pretty damn grabby, in my personal opinion, but that's another story altogether. "But can the IRS tax an offshore account? I thought that was the whole point of having it offshore."

"It is," Elliott said. "But the minute his wife tries to bring any of it into the country, it instantly becomes taxable. She puts it into a domestic bank account, and the IRS can attach it and empty it out until they have all that's owed to them."

Well, that just gave me the heebies *and* the jeebies. "So what are the terms of his will?"

"I can't divulge that. Confidentiality."

"The police are going to have to know," I objected. "So they'll know who to suspect."

"Then they can get a freakin' subpoena, just like everybody else."

The instant I hung up, the phone rang again.

"Toni? Bernie Kincaid. How are you today?"

Speak of the devil and he calls you on the phone. Bernie Kincaid was a detective lieutenant with the Twin Falls Police Department.

"Hi, Bernie. I'm just fine. May I assume you're not calling just to say hello?"

"Always the smartass, aren't you? You may assume that. You want to try for Double Jeopardy?"

"Okay. Jay Braithwaite Burke."

"Bingo. When are you doing the autopsy? Pete and I would like to be there."

"Are you actually going to let me do this one?" I inquired. "Don't you want to send it to Boise so the *experts* can do it?" Like he did the last time a possible homicide involved the hospital, three years ago.

"You're never going to let us forget that, are you? No way. We learned our lesson the last time."

It wasn't really all Bernie's fault; I'd actually been a suspect at the time. One can't really put one's faith in an autopsy done by a known suspect, even if it was me. I could have fabricated all sorts of things to divert suspicion from myself, and the cops and lawyers would never know the difference.

Unfortunately, the forensic pathologist in Boise had been recovering from open-heart surgery at the time, and the autopsy had been done by a locum tenens who had no more forensic experience than I did.

"Well, I don't know yet, Bernie. I'll have to call you back."

By this time Hal was up and dressed for work. He came downstairs and poured himself a cup of coffee. "You ready for coffee?"

"Not yet. I have to get out of these sweaty clothes and take a shower before the phone rings again."

"Can't you talk to those guys and tell them not to call you in the middle of the night?" he asked, as he opened the sliding glass door to let the dogs out.

Here we go again, I thought with resignation. I was so sick of this particular conversation that I could spit; but Hal didn't care. It was all about him these days.

"I have been," I said, showing what I considered admirable restraint by not actually strangling him. "For the last thirteen years, I have been, and you can see for yourself how much good it's done." I wished I could find a way to make Hal quit bugging me about it, short of actually solving the problem, which wasn't going to happen anytime soon; but when something bothers him, he *never* quits bugging me.

I mean, I didn't like the situation either. I could never understand why it couldn't wait for morning and normal working hours. What, did they think I was going to just pack up and go on vacation in the middle of the night if they didn't pin me down quick enough? The body wasn't going anywhere, as Hal pointed out.

"It'd be one thing if the patient was alive and needed immediate attention," Hal said, "but these are dead people, and you don't need to be called at all hours of the night about it!"

"Sweetie, you're preaching to the choir here …"

He overrode me. "Don't they realize it wakes up everybody in the house? I have to teach in the morning. How am I supposed to do that when I'm half asleep?"

"I have to read out surgicals and Pap smears and do frozen sections when I'm half asleep," I countered.

"*Well?*" Hal gave an exaggerated shrug. "All the more reason to tell those guys off. I'm not kidding, Toni. You need to deal with this, because I'm not going to put up with it."

He'd been saying that for the last thirteen years—no, wait, seventeen years, because I'd had to take calls as a resident too—but things were a lot better now, since autopsies had decreased so much, and besides, now I had a partner.

So why was he still hammering at me about it?

Something snapped. I jumped to my feet, hands on my hips, and glared at him. "*You're* not going to put up with it? What are you going to do about it, Hal? Move out? Divorce me? What?"

Hal stared back at me for a long minute before he replied, very softly, "Don't tempt me."

I stared at him, aghast, feeling the blood drain from my face. I had never challenged Hal like that before, and his reaction shocked me. It felt like a physical blow to the solar plexus. I couldn't seem to get enough air into my lungs, and I could only imagine what my face looked like.

Abruptly I turned away from him and headed for the stairs, needing to escape his nagging and hide my undoubtedly shocked expression. I really hadn't expected Hal to react that way. I thought he'd back down and apologize to me. Now I wondered if he expected me to back down and apologize to him; but I'd be damned if I would. *To hell with him*, I thought, but in spite of my mental bravado, I was still unwilling to aggravate him further and find out what his feelings really were. For instance, did he really want to divorce me and move out? Or was that just bravado on his part, just big, tough-guy talk?

Maybe it was simply an expeditious way to shut me up. It'd worked a treat, hadn't it?

I decided against saying anything more to Hal. Experience had taught me that we both needed time to cool off before that would accomplish anything.

Only maybe this time that wouldn't be enough.

Over the last few months or so, Hal had changed. Things that used to bring a shake of the head, a sympathetic comment, or an indulgent smile now seemed to truly piss him off. I wasn't sure exactly how long this had been going on, but I thought it had been since around the time school started in August. I had absolutely no idea what had set him off, and even less of an idea what to do about it.

I had asked him on occasion what was wrong, but he denied that there was anything, and if I persisted, he asked me to please get off his case.

Was whatever was bothering him enough for him to threaten divorce over such a minor matter? What on earth could change a man's feelings to that degree?

I took a quick but very hot shower and hurried into a pair of pants and a turtleneck sweater, shoved my feet into boots, blew my hair dry, and stared at myself in the mirror, trying to arrange my face to not show any hint of the turmoil going on inside me. I applied minimal makeup with shaking hands.

In the kitchen, I filled an insulated cup with coffee, screwed the lid on it, grabbed my coat and purse, and headed for the door. Hal continued to read the paper and ignore me just as hard as I was ignoring him. *Screw him.* I could get breakfast in the cafeteria, and he could just go perform impossible physical acts of a sexual nature upon himself.

Outside, the sky had just begun to turn pink, but it didn't make me feel any better. As I crossed Montana Street, I tried not to think about possible reasons for Hal's behavior. I failed. How the hell do you actively not think about something without thinking about it?

Three years ago, when that surgeon who had been harassing me at work was murdered and Bernie Kincaid threatened to arrest me for it, I'd had Hal solidly behind me, supporting me, comforting me, and loving me. Now, I didn't have that comfort, because this time *Hal* was the problem.

Was it me or something else? Something at work, perhaps? He wouldn't talk to me about it when I asked. If it was something unrelated to me, he'd talk about it, I was sure. If he'd recently been diagnosed with a terminal illness, he'd tell me. So it must be me.

Had I done something that pissed him off? Other than get phone calls about autopsies in the middle of the night, that is? I couldn't think of anything in particular. Again, Hal would tell me if that was what was bothering him. He always had.

Until now.

What could it possibly be that he couldn't talk to me about?

As I crossed the hospital parking lot, I knew that I had to get my mind off my personal life and onto work. Mike was on call, but I still had to sign out all those goddamn surgicals before all those goddamn doctors started bugging me. This was not the time to dwell on Hal and the state of my marriage.

I checked my face in the ladies room before going to my office, just in case repairs were necessary, but they weren't. Rage had given my cheeks a healthy flush, and my eyes were shining. I looked positively triumphant: a much better look than that droopy, tearful, woe-is-me-I-had-a-fight-with-my-husband look.

Professionals don't let their personal problems interfere with work, I told myself. They don't let their emotions show.

You go, girl.

Chapter 3

Where the telescope ends, the microscope begins.
Which of the two has the grander view?
—Victor Hugo

I found my partner, Mike Leonard, in Histology, hunched over the cryostat, working on yet another unscheduled frozen section. Mike, who towered over my diminutive five foot three by several inches, had joined me three years before. "Morning, Mikey," I greeted him, pasting on a smile and endeavoring to act normal. "How's it looking?"

"Hey!" he responded. "Got a lymph node here. Jeff's doin' a routine choley and found big nodes all over the place. Wants to know if it's carcinoma or lymphoma."

Two different types of cancer, requiring totally different treatment and totally different surgery. If it was a carcinoma, it would require extensive resection and debulking; but a lymphoma required only removal of enough tissue for the pathologist to make a diagnosis. I hoped that it wouldn't turn out to be one of those undifferentiated tumors that required a battery of immunostains in order to even identify it as lymphoma, carcinoma, or melanoma. That would have to wait until the next day, and it would put the surgeons in the position of having to do a possibly unnecessary debulking procedure for which they might not get paid, which would put everybody in a bad mood—even Mikey.

Mike's sunny personality was a welcome change from Hal's grumpiness. I wondered how Mike's wife, Leezie, coped with being awakened in the middle of the night. It would be worse for them; they had a baby.

So I asked him.

He laughed. "Oh, yeah, it pissed her off, I tell you what. She'd threaten to divorce me or kill me or worse; but not anymore."

"How come?"

"I keep my cell phone in my pajama pocket on vibrate," he said. "She never hears it, and I go into the bathroom to answer it."

Sheesh. How simple. Hell, I could do that. How come I never thought of it? Maybe it was because I didn't have a pajama pocket. Maybe I could keep it under the pillow. If that didn't work, I'd start wearing Hal's pajama tops.

Of course I'd have to first make sure everybody who was likely to call knew to call the cell phone and not the home phone. Hal and I hadn't yet joined the ranks of those who no longer had a land line.

If that was all there was to Hal's problem with me, it was fixed. If not, well, then, I guess we'd just see what else happened. Because surely there was more to this than me getting phone calls at night.

"Where are the girls?" I asked.

The girls to whom I referred were our histotechs, Lucille and Natalie.

"On break," he said. "Your slides are on your desk already."

"Cool!" I headed for my office. A stack of slide trays sat on my desk, along with a pile of requisitions and my typed gross dictation. I could easily sign these out this morning and leave the afternoon free for the autopsy. I called Rollie Perkins and let him know, asked him to pass it along to Bernie, and then got to work on the surgicals. Since Mike was on call, all the interruptions would go to him, and I could work undisturbed.

At two o'clock, I headed for Rollie's establishment, Parkside Funeral Home, to do the autopsy. Perrine Memorial doesn't have a morgue, at least not one that's usable. When they recruited me, they bought an autopsy table and set aside a room in the basement but made no provision for ventilation, running water, or drainage, and over the years, everybody just forgot about it.

My erstwhile autopsy suite was now a storage room, and the gleaming, once state-of-the-art autopsy table was buried under boxes of toilet paper, Chux, and the like, and I still have to do my autopsies in funeral homes.

Which means I have to (a) call Hal and ask him to come get me so that I can drive him back to work and keep the Cherokee, (b) lug all my stuff out to the car, (c) drive to the mortuary, and (d) lug all my stuff into the embalming room. Then after I do the autopsy, I do the whole thing in reverse, and then try to remember to pick up Hal from work. Of course we could avoid the whole thing by just getting a second car, but we haven't because I only have to do this maybe ten times a year—no, actually five, because sometimes it's Mike's turn—and if I didn't walk to work I'd weigh five thousand pounds.

Besides, we only have a one-car garage and consider ourselves lucky, because most of our neighbors have no garage at all. In the central and oldest part of Twin Falls, most of the hundred-year-old Victorians like ours don't have garages, and the rest have only rickety carports added on.

In the last couple of years, we've arranged for all our autopsies to be done at Parkside, and we keep the stuff there; so now all we have to do is keep track of the consumables, such as scalpel blades, needles and syringes, blood tubes, and specimen containers, and carry the specimens back to the lab. In addition, I can usually borrow Mike's car, so I don't have to bother Hal. So it's a lot better than it used to be.

I was still pissed off, though, about not having my own morgue. Surely in thirteen years they could save up enough to build me a proper morgue. Mitzi Okamoto, the radiologist, only has to say she needs a new six-hundred-thousand-dollar CT scanner, and they fall all over themselves to get it for her and build a place to put it, complete with lead-lined walls, for at least another hundred grand. But if I need a fifteen-hundred-dollar automatic slide stainer for frozen section slides, oh, golly gee, do I really need it that bad? Because they can't afford any more capital expenditures in this fiscal year.

In the world of durable medical equipment, fifteen hundred dollars is pocket change.

So that's the way it is; radiology is the queen, and the lab is the poor relation. I can't even claim sexual discrimination, because Mitzi is a girl too.

Still, I owe Mitzi big time, because when I wanted to get my lab accredited by the College of American Pathologists back in 1997, the medical staff objected to the cost. Mitzi mentioned that her mammography unit had to be accredited by the American College of Radiology in order to get Medicare and Medicaid reimbursement, and maybe someday the same thing could happen to the lab.

As if by magic, out came the checkbook, and we got our accreditation—after a rigorous inspection, that is.

Of course there was a lot more to it than money; I think I run a damn good lab, and we've always done everything according to CAP requirements, whether we were accredited or not. To my techs, it's a matter of pride. It's good for morale. Physicians who aren't pathologists just don't get it.

Detective Lieutenant Bernie Kincaid was already waiting for me at Parkside Funeral Home along with Detective Sergeant Pete Vincent, their cameras and rape kits, and various other police-type paraphernalia.

Bernie and Pete looked like a cop version of Mutt and Jeff. Bernie was of medium height, dark-haired, dark-eyed, compactly built, and irritable. Sandy-haired Pete towered over him and was as laid-back and easygoing as Bernie was uptight. Pete had grown up in Twin Falls and played football for Twin Falls High School. Hal and I had known him since he was a student at the college where Hal taught chemistry.

As a college student, he'd watched me do autopsies on several occasions and had put on gloves and gotten his hands right in there with mine. The gangrenous bowel that made Bernie sick the first time I ever met him didn't affect Pete at all. I'm not sure Bernie's ever really forgiven me for that.

Bernie and I first met three years ago when a surgeon at our hospital was murdered. Bernie, a recent transplant from California, had insisted on sending the body to Boise, where there was a forensic pathologist. In California, apparently, forensic pathologists grow on trees, but the only one in Idaho was on extended sick leave after a heart attack and a coronary bypass. The locum tenens, or substitute pathologist, had left some important information out of his report and confused everybody.

Then, as if that wasn't bad enough, Bernie decided that *I* had murdered the surgeon, based on nothing more than the facts that (a) I had threatened to resign if she became a permanent member of the medical staff and (b) her body had been found in my office. Of course, I'd been proven innocent, and Bernie had ended up saving my life, so we've got a much better relationship now.

Rollie Perkins, rotund, bespectacled, and balding, came out of the embalming room. "Well, good afternoon, young lady and gentlemen," he greeted us, smiling and rubbing his hands together. "He's still in the body bag. Is that right? We're handling this as a homicide?"

"Seriously?" I asked. "You've already decided that this is homicide? Not just an accident?"

"No, no," Rollie assured me. "We just want to handle it that way so we don't overlook anything. I wouldn't have even asked for an autopsy if there'd been obvious injuries. I would have called it an accidental death and let it go at that."

Well, that made sense.

"That's right," Bernie said. They unzipped the body bag, and I got my first look in two months at Jay Braithwaite Burke. He hadn't changed much, aside from being dead. He still looked beige. The only touch of color was the bright red blood around the nose and mouth, some of which had trickled back across his cheeks into his ears. In the fluorescent light from the ceiling, it had a magenta cast. Without The Voice, he seemed really insignificant in contrast to his illustrious grandfather, Joseph John Braithwaite Burke, whom I had autopsied upon his death from a heart attack shortly after my arrival in Twin Falls.

J. J. Braithwaite Burke had looked imposing even in his coffin.

"So exactly where was his car found, and which way was it going?" I asked.

Pete consulted his notes. "It was between the US 93 exit and the first Jerome exit, and sort of crossways in the median with the back end down in the bottom, and the front end facing north, toward Jerome. The interstate had a snow floor on both sides but no skid marks. They hadn't gotten around to sanding yet. And if there *had* been any tire tracks, the snow had covered them up by the time we got there."

"So there's no way to know which direction it came from?"

"No," Pete said. "The car was covered with snow too, and it's a white car. It'd probably been there for hours. It was a wonder anybody could see it at all, especially in the dark in a snowstorm."

"Who did see it?" I asked. "I mean, who reported it?"

"The state cops."

"Were the lights on?" I asked.

"No."

"Was the engine running or had someone turned that off too?"

"The ignition was on," Bernie said. "But it had run out of gas."

"Were the keys still in it?"

"Yes."

"Fingerprints?" I didn't really need to know that for the autopsy, but I was curious.

"Don't know yet. It took a while to get a tow truck out in the middle of the night. We got it into the garage at three this morning, and a tech's been working on it all day, so we should know something this afternoon."

"That doesn't make sense," Rollie said. "Why turn off the lights and leave the engine running?"

"Maybe he was trying to commit suicide," Pete suggested. "Or maybe he was just trying to keep warm. The muffler was buried in the snow. We've had that happen to kids who park in the snow to make out, leave the engine on to run the heater, and die of carbon monoxide poisoning."

"Could it have been sitting there that long without being seen?" I asked.

Pete shrugged. "Maybe. Who knows? The state cops didn't report it until ten o'clock, and it's dark by five."

I felt a flash of anger and glared at Rollie. "So how come you waited until one in the morning to call me?"

"Hey, don't look at me," Rollie said. "I called you as soon as I knew."

I decided Hal didn't need to know that, after the way he acted this morning. But Bernie answered the question I didn't ask.

"Well, for one thing, that section of interstate's in Jerome County. So the state cop reported it to the Jerome County Sheriff, but they turned it over to us as soon as they ran the license number and found out whose it was," Bernie said. "All those things take time, especially after hours."

"Even with computers?"

"Even with."

Jay wore a brown tweed suit, a tan shirt, and a brown-and-green striped tie. His hair, what was left of it, wasn't even messed up. I pointed out to Pete and Bernie the absolutely clean soles of his polished brown wingtips so they could photograph them before removing the shoes and bagging them. We removed the bags on his hands so that I could clean under his fingernails and put the material obtained in evidence bags. I found some blood, but no obvious chunks of skin, or anything like that.

We turned the body first on one side and then the other to look for any marks or trace evidence on the clothes. I found some blood on his shirt front and a few light-colored hairs on the back of his suit jacket, which Pete collected and put in an evidence bag.

"And I suppose if you couldn't see any skid marks or tire tracks, you couldn't see any footprints either?" I persisted.

"Footprints!" exclaimed Pete. "Why would there be footprints? Oh, you think there was someone else in the car with him?"

"Was he sitting in the driver's seat?"

"Yes, he was. What are you getting at, Toni?"

"Because I don't think he was driving," I said. "Look at his shoes. They're clean, even on the soles. He wasn't wearing a coat or gloves or boots. Here he is, out driving in December in a snowstorm, and all he's wearing is a suit—and his shoes aren't dirty? I don't think so. They should have been soaked. His pant legs should have been too. Was there a coat or boots in the car?"

Pete and Bernie looked at each other and shook their heads.

"Somebody else had to be driving the car," I persisted. "Somebody had to put him in the car without getting his soles dirty, drive him here, move him into the driver's seat, turn the lights off, leave him in the car with the engine running, and then disappear."

"So," Pete said, "this really is a homicide. Is that what you're saying, Toni?"

"I don't see what else it could be. Do you?"

"Oh, I agree," said Pete, "but how? There aren't any gunshot or stab wounds or ligature marks that I can see."

"I guess we'll find out," I said, "when we get his clothes off."

Rollie removed the suit jacket and pants, and Pete bagged them. We turned the body again to look for evidence or marks on the tan shirt but found none. Grossly bloody, foul-smelling stool stained the undershorts. I collected a sample of it and put it in a small specimen container.

Next, we removed the shirt and the underwear. Pete, with a grimace, bagged the shirt and the undershorts separately. Again we turned the body to examine the back. Postmortem lividity, the purplish discoloration of the skin that occurs after death when blood pools in the dependent parts of the body—in this case, the buttocks, backs of the thighs, and the feet—was magenta rather than the usual purple. I noted this with detachment, not really attaching any significance to it at the time. At that time, the only thought I had was that Jay had died sitting up.

Jay Braithwaite Burke looked like a starved orphan without his lawyerly clothes. His ribs and hipbones protruded, as did his Adam's apple and his ears. His left pupil was "blown"—that is, fully dilated in contrast to the right, indicating a severe brain injury—but there were no bruises on the scalp to account for how he got it. Perhaps he'd been shaken, like a baby. His skin looked too tight for him. Large reddish-purple patches stained the skin of the chest, arms, and backs of the hands. Examination of the face showed a line of hemorrhage around the edges of the lips, and the lining of the mouth and the tongue appeared to be encrusted with blood. It was hard to hold the mouth open because of rigor mortis, but Pete and Rollie managed to hold it open long enough for Bernie to get a shot of it.

"Why does he look so bruised?" Rollie asked. "Do you suppose somebody beat him up?"

"I don't think so," I said. "This looks more like he's been on anticoagulants or steroids. Or maybe he's got leukemia or something, and his platelets are low. These aren't bruises, they're purpura."

"What's purpura?" asked Bernie.

"It's this patchy hemorrhage under the skin that people get when they're on blood thinners, or who have other bleeding disorders, or just because they're old and their skin is so thin."

At this point, we decided to do the rape kit before we messed anything up—a thoroughly disgusting procedure. It was just routine; we really didn't think Jay had been raped, but one never knows, and it's better to be safe than sorry. I swabbed the mouth, the armpits, the groins, and the anus; and put the swabs in separate, labeled containers; and combed the pubic hair and put the combings in an evidence bag. Pete took combings from the head hair too and put them in a separate bag.

Then I had to wipe the blood off the tongue to make sure he hadn't just bitten it, which was even more disgusting; but the tongue wasn't the source of the blood in the mouth. I did notice an unusually red color of the tongue and mucous membranes, however. He must have been really well oxygenated, I thought, to have such red blood postmortem. Or maybe Pete was right about the carbon monoxide.

At this point I became aware that Bernie Kincaid was standing extremely close to me, restricting my range of motion. I looked up at him, intending to tell him to move his ass out of my way, when his dark eyes met mine, and the expression in them made my mouth go dry.

"Detective Lieutenant Kincaid," I said, still looking into his eyes, "do you know that you're in my way?"

"Do you know that you smell really, really good?" he murmured back.

Whoa. That was completely un-Bernie Kincaid-like behavior. I reached around him, picked the cardiac needle out of my tool kit, and attached it to a syringe. I held it in front of me, point up, rather like a shield. "Back off," I said. "Now."

He backed off.

Next, I collected body fluids. With the cardiac needle, I drew blood from the heart. To my relief, it flowed freely into the syringe without any clots to get in the way. It looked unusually red for postmortem blood. I began to wonder about how long the car engine had continued to run after Jay had been moved into the driver's seat. I also did a suprapubic aspiration above the pubic bone into the bladder to obtain urine, which was bloody too.

Next, I removed the brain. I found a large subarachnoid hemorrhage on the right side, which had caused a right-to-left shift, squeezing the right parietal lobe underneath the *falx cerebri*, the fibrous membrane that separates the right hemisphere from the left. I found a smaller hemorrhage on the left side, and pressure cones on the sides of the cerebellum. This occurs when increased pressure inside the skull pushes the brain backward, squeezing the brainstem into the *foramen magnum*, which leads to the spinal canal and is way too small for it. That accounted for the blown pupil.

"Are you finding something there, Doc?" inquired Rollie, looking over my shoulder as I lowered the brain carefully into a bucket. It would have to fix in formalin for two weeks to make it firm enough to cut.

"I think I've found a possible cause of death," I replied. "See how the brainstem is compressed? Those hemorrhages forced it into the spinal canal, and that could have caused him to stop breathing, because that's where the respiratory center is."

Rollie seemed satisfied with that answer, but I wasn't. "Problem is, I can't figure out what caused the hemorrhage," I told him. "I don't see any bruising on the scalp to indicate a blow to the head, so the smaller hemorrhage on the left probably isn't a *contrecoup* injury."

"A contra-what?"

"A contrecoup injury," I explained, "is a hemorrhage caused by the brain bouncing off the other side of the skull cavity after a blow on the head. But I don't see how anybody managed to hit him over the head without leaving a big honking bruise on the scalp."

Rollie shrugged. "Don't look at me. I haven't a clue."

I didn't either. I gave up on the head and turned my attention to the body. I looked forward to getting into more familiar territory, neuropathology not being my forte. No, that didn't quite cover it. I *hated* neuropathology with a passion.

During my residency, I had always dreaded the weekly Wednesday morning brain-cutting sessions with one or the other of the two visiting neuropathologists from the University of California at Irvine—both women, both brilliant, and each one bitchier than the other, at least to me. They always made me feel stupid and incompetent.

I never understood why female physicians had to be so nasty to each other. We'd all had to struggle to get where we were back when females were in the minority. You'd think we'd all be trying to support each other, not tear each other apart. But no, it was all about competition. Were these gals afraid that I'd grow up to take their jobs away from them, or what? Did they find me, a mere resident, that threatening?

Huh. How about that? Maybe they *had* been afraid of me. Now there was a thought. It made me smile right out loud. I wished I'd thought of it back then; it might have saved me a lot of grief.

I hauled the organ block up and out of the body cavity and arranged it on the cutting board. "Wow," I remarked as I scissor-crunched my way down the aorta to the iliac bifurcation. "This guy's got really bad arteriosclerosis for such a young, thin person. He's hardly any older than I am and look at this!"

Rollie, Pete, and Bernie gathered round and peered at the pile of viscera in front of me. "Maybe he had a heart attack," Pete said. "Can you tell?"

"Maybe," I said. "And then again, maybe not."

They watched in fascination as I dissected the coronary arteries, the carotids, the aorta, and the iliac and femoral arteries, all of which were clogged with calcified plaque. In fact, he had the beginnings of an aortic aneurysm.

Pete gestured at the mess on the cutting board. "But look at all that stuff," he said. "How could he not have had one?"

"Well, just hang on until I cut the heart."

I opened the heart, starting with the right atrium and going down through the tricuspid valve into the right ventricle, and then up through the pulmonic valve into the pulmonary artery, being careful to check for any clots; there weren't any. Then I opened the left atrium, went down through the mitral valve into the left ventricle and then up through the aortic valve into the ascending aorta. After rinsing all the blood away and weighing the heart, which was of normal size and weight, I began to section the ventricles, looking for any discoloration that might indicate an infarct or dead tissue. There wasn't any.

"So," Pete said. "No heart attack, right?"

"Not necessarily," I said. "If he'd had a heart attack and died right away, I wouldn't see anything. It takes twelve to twenty-four hours even for *microscopic* changes to show up. Gross changes wouldn't show up for forty-eight hours or more, assuming he survived that long. I'd have to find an actual coronary thrombosis, an actual blood clot in the coronary artery, to make that diagnosis, and I didn't."

"So we'll never know?"

"Not unless something shows up in the slides," I said.

"Huh," Pete said. "I always thought you could tell right away."

"Well, you can," I told him, "if the patient lives long enough for the dead tissue to turn all yellow and mushy, which would be several days. If the infarct is large enough and goes all the way through the ventricular wall, it can even rupture. There's no mistaking *that* at autopsy."

Pete whistled. "Does that happen often?"

"I've only seen it once."

The normal-sized liver and spleen indicated that he probably didn't have leukemia.

Blood filled the lungs and bronchi, as well as the esophagus, stomach, small intestine, and colon. As I slit open the bowel and evacuated its tarry-black, malodorous contents into the sink, Bernie Kincaid, with his hand over his mouth, fled the room to get away from the overpowering stench. Rollie turned on the fan.

Few things in medicine smell worse than decomposing blood, especially in the GI tract where bacteria, stomach acid, and pancreatic enzymes break it down.

Gritting my teeth, I collected samples of stomach and small bowel contents, and washed the rest of the blood away. The esophagus had a longitudinal full-thickness tear with hemorrhage into the posterior mediastinum, which contains the thoracic aorta, superior vena cava, and a whole lot of lymph nodes.

With an inward smile, I recalled the "five birds of the mediastinum," a silly trick we'd used in medical school to remember its anatomy: the esophagoose, the vagoose, the azygoose, the hemiazygoose, and the thoracic duck.

In this case, the esophagoose had ruptured. "That's called Mallory-Weiss syndrome." I had to raise my voice to be heard over the noise of the fan. "It usually results from forceful vomiting. This looks like he vomited blood and aspirated it. Was there any blood in the car?"

"Nothing obvious," replied Pete, "but it did smell like somebody'd been sick in it. Maybe if we look for it, we could find some traces. Where's all that coming from?"

Good question; it seemed to come from everywhere. The mucosa lining the stomach showed diffuse hemorrhage without any ulcers or other lesions, as did the mucosa of the small intestine and colon. I saw no big ulcers or tumors anywhere to explain the bleeding. It just oozed from everywhere—all of it bright cherry-red.

Maybe the brainstem herniation wasn't the cause of death after all. "I think we need to get a carboxyhemoglobin on this blood," I said.

"You think he died of carbon monoxide poisoning?" Rollie asked.

"I do; and therefore he had to be still breathing when the car went off the road, which should narrow down the time of death for you."

"So, if he was still alive," Rollie persisted, "how do you know he didn't just lose control of the car and die accidentally?"

"I think he was still alive but unconscious," I replied. "I don't think he could have been conscious with that subarachnoid hemorrhage and brainstem herniation. Maybe someone lost control of the car, but it wasn't him."

"How can you be so sure?" asked Bernie, who had come back into the room.

"You'll know for sure if his fingerprint is on the light button. He wasn't wearing gloves."

"What would that prove?" Bernie asked. "It's his car."

"But what if it was someone else's fingerprint? Or what if there aren't any at all?"

Bernie nodded. "I see. Pete, you better get on the horn and make sure that Corey checks that," he said. Pete obligingly hauled out his cell phone and did so.

The body of the once-powerful Jay Braithwaite Burke was now an empty shell. We took a chunk of liver tissue to add to the blood, urine, stomach, and small bowel contents I had already collected. Just out of curiosity, I had filled a purple-top and a blue-top tube for hematological and coagulation studies, and a green-top for the carboxyhemoglobin, which the hospital lab could do.

I put samples of the organs into buckets for transport back to the lab, and Rollie began to sew the body back together. Bernie and Pete collected their stuff in preparation to go back to the police station. Pete started out the door, but Bernie hung back.

"Want me to come by the lab and let you know about the fingerprints?"

I looked up. He had that same look in his eyes again. What was up with that?

"No, I'm just going to drop this stuff off and go straight home," I said.

"Need any help with that stuff?"

"No, thanks, I can handle it." I carefully avoided looking into his eyes.

"Okay, see you later." He left.

What the hell was going on here? I hadn't even seen Bernie Kincaid for the last three years, and back then he'd acted as if he couldn't stand me. And now, after all this time, he's all … what? All over me like a lovesick schoolboy. What had changed in the last three years? I wondered. Back then he'd been going through a divorce. Now I … oh jeez … might I be too? Did Bernie know something I didn't? And if so, how?

With difficulty I wrenched my attention back to filling out the death certificate. Under *Manner of Death* I put "Homicide."

"You'll have that report pretty soon?" Rollie asked me.

"Next week," I assured him.

Back at the hospital, I got the autopsy tissues into formalin, the blood tubes and other samples to the lab, and dictated the gross autopsy findings and the provisional gross diagnoses for the police and Rollie.

Then I went home, uneasily recalling what had happened between Hal and me that morning. The day's happenings had kept it out of my mind for the most part.

34

Now it all came roaring right back into my consciousness, not to mention the pit of my stomach.

Would Hal still be mad? Or would he have forgotten about the whole thing? Would he even be speaking to me? Or would he give me the silent treatment all evening?

What would I do? Apologize? Beg for forgiveness? Cry?

Wait a minute. What was I thinking? No way. *Gawd, Toni, you're such a* girl.

If I asked Hal straight out if he wanted a divorce, what would he say? Would I be prepared for his answer? How would I feel if the answer was yes?

If he asked me the same question, what would I say? No, of course not? Maybe?

I guess my answer to his question pretty much depended on how he answered my question.

My honest answer was, no, I didn't want a divorce. I wanted Hal to be the way he was before things changed.

If I couldn't have that, then I guess I didn't know. I would not beg him to stay in this marriage if he wanted out. If he didn't want to be with me, I'd let him go.

I prayed that I'd walk in the door and Hal would greet me the same way he always did, having totally forgotten the whole thing. He'd never have to bitch about being awakened at night again, since I planned to follow Mike's advice.

But maybe being awakened at night wasn't really the problem.

Maybe it was just a symptom of something bigger.

I climbed up on the front porch and let myself in the front door with trepidation.

But Hal wasn't home.

Chapter 4

The vow that binds too strictly snaps itself.
—Alfred, Lord Tennyson

I didn't know whether to be relieved at the reprieve or pissed that I'd have to wait, after getting myself all worked up, to face Hal and get it all over with—whatever "it" turned out to be—and put it all behind me and move on.

I let the dogs out and fed them. Then I went upstairs, changed out of my work clothes, and got into the shower. We still had a party to go to that night, and I needed to wash the autopsy stink off me and out of my hair. As I luxuriated in the feel of the hot water coursing down my body, rinsing off the shampoo and soap, I considered what could be bothering Hal and why he couldn't, or wouldn't, talk about it.

There was only one thing I could think of that he couldn't tell me about.

What if he was having an affair?

Of course he is, you idiot. What are you, blind or just stupid? It was as if the scales had fallen suddenly from my eyes. Furthermore, it had to be with someone from the college, because he wasn't going out at night or on weekends; it was someone he could be with during the work week.

Maybe that was why he'd acted so cavalier about divorce this morning. He had someplace else to go.

Maybe that was why he never seemed to want sex anymore. He was getting it elsewhere.

I then proceeded to torture myself by wondering how and where they managed to have sex with each other during the work day. Students did it in the shrubbery at night; but where the hell did teachers do it during the daylight hours? In their offices? Empty classrooms? Broom closets? Stairwells? Library stacks? Here in the house while I was at work? In our *bed*? Oh, no. Hal wouldn't do that to me. At least the old Hal wouldn't have, but then the old Hal wouldn't be having an affair in the first place. Anyway, what did I know? The new Hal was a stranger to me.

I wrapped myself in a towel and went into the bedroom, where I stood staring at the king-size bed that Hal and I shared. Tears came to my eyes as I contemplated this comfortable life we'd enjoyed together coming to an end. Goddamn it, we'd both worked very hard to achieve what we had, and now Hal was jeopardizing it all for some little college bimbo who was blonder, younger, prettier, and thinner than I.

Oh, fuck it, now I was sobbing like a child. This had to stop or my eyes would be so puffy that I wouldn't want to show my face at the party tonight. I went back into the bathroom and stared at my tear-streaked countenance, making faces at myself, trying to make myself laugh. It had always worked when I was a child but not so much now. At least I had stopped sobbing. I wrung out a washcloth in cold water and applied it to my eyes, hoping that would get rid of the puffiness.

The doorbell rang. It figured. Here I was, sopping wet with red puffy eyelids and veritable suitcases under my eyes. *Shit.* I hurried into my old black sweats and ran downstairs to answer it, prepared to give short shrift to any door-to-door salesperson who dared to bother me at a time like this; but to my astonishment, Bernie Kincaid stood there. The very last person I'd have expected.

"What are you doing here?" I inquired, my tone somewhat less than friendly.

He responded in kind. "Well?" he said. "Are you going to just stand there, or let me in, or what?"

I stepped back. He stepped inside. I closed the door. "I just came by to tell you about the fingerprints on the light button," he said.

"What about it?"

"It was wiped clean."

"So, that means it really *is* a homicide, doesn't it?"

He stepped closer. "You've been crying," he said, his voice low and intimate. Then, before I knew it, he had taken me in his arms. I stared into his black eyes in disbelief. Oh jeez, there was that look again. I didn't recall having said anything particularly provocative. Then his arms tightened and he kissed me. Tongue and all. Oh, my *God.*

I pulled myself away. "What the hell are you doing?" I demanded, endeavoring to maintain a shred of dignity.

Bernie rubbed his hands over his flushed face as if he were trying to wash it, and wiped his mouth on his sleeve. "Jesus, Toni. I don't know what got into me. I'm so sorry. Christ. Hal would kill me."

"Hal isn't home yet," I said. "You'd better get out of here before he is."

But before he could leave, Hal drove into the driveway.

Luckily, Bernie was a lot better than I at keeping his mind on business. It must be a guy thing.

"I was just telling Toni about what we found in Jay Braithwaite Burke's car," he told Hal. "There were traces of blood on the back seat and on the floor in the back that matched Jay's. And as far as fingerprints are concerned, there weren't any. Not even his."

"So?" Hal said. "Whoever was driving probably wore gloves."

"No," Bernie told him. "The deceased wasn't wearing gloves. Everything, including the light button, was wiped clean. That makes it a homicide, as I was just telling Toni."

After he left, Hal hugged me and gave me a kiss. Then he got a good look at my face.

"Are you okay? You look like you've been crying. Did that asshole Kincaid …"

I shook my head. It wasn't Kincaid, but if I told Hal that, he'd want to know what it was. With this party to go to, was I really ready for this discussion? No. There wasn't time to get into a discussion about the future of our marriage. It would involve more crying. We couldn't beg off this party, either. Mike and Leezie were giving it at their house, and as Mike's partner, I felt obligated to go. This discussion would have to wait. We'd go, and I'd try to act normal.

Hal's uncomplimentary opinion of Kincaid stemmed from the way he'd treated me three years before. It was just as well that he not know what had transpired between us here tonight.

So I said nothing, and Hal went off to take his shower.

Nothing was resolved; it was only postponed.

The Leonards lived in a ranch house on five fenced acres five miles out of town. We could see it from a mile down the road. Red lights outlined the entire fence. An illuminated sleigh and eight tiny reindeer decorated the roof. Multicolored lights covered all the trees around the front of the house, and life-sized, illuminated plastic carolers stood by the front door. When we rang the doorbell, it played the first few bars of "Hark the Herald Angels Sing."

Somebody in that family was obviously a Christmas junkie. I suspected it was Leezie.

Leezie answered the door, pointed out the bunch of mistletoe hanging over our heads, and kissed both Hal and me.

Mike, behind her, said "Hey," and hugged me. Then he shook Hal's hand. "I ain't kissin' y'all," he said.

Leezie, true to form, wore a long, red, sequined, strapless gown and spike heels. Diamond drops dangled from her ears. Mike, also true to form, wore jeans, cowboy boots, and a red T-shirt upon which drunken-looking elves and reindeer cavorted around a leering Santa Claus, who held a half-naked buxom female elf on his knee, with the legend "OFFICE PARTY AT THE NORTH POLE" underneath. He had a beer in his hand. Mike, I mean, not Santa Claus.

Inside the house, huge red poinsettias stood everywhere. Santas, angels, sleighs, wreaths, candles, and miniature trees covered every available surface: a veritable Christmas obstacle course. Christmas songs played softly in the background.

The Christmas tree stood in the middle of the living room, the only place the vaulted ceiling rose high enough. The top four feet protruded into the second story. "You see that?" I said to Hal, *sotto voce*. "That's a real tree."

"So what?" Hal muttered back.

"It looks a lot better than ours," I persisted. "I told you I didn't want a fake tree, and you insisted. Aren't you sorry now?"

"No way. I'd hate to have to clean up all those needles," Hal grumbled as we made our way through the living room to the kitchen.

Mike and Leezie Leonard were both pathologists' children but from totally different backgrounds. Leezie had grown up in the Bay area and was the spoilt darling of two highly successful and wealthy physician parents. Her mother was a plastic surgeon; her father was a pathologist who had filled in for me while I recovered from a car accident three years ago. Leezie had been a debutante, attended private schools, and lived the life of a socialite in San Francisco while Mike did his residency there.

Mike, on the other hand, had grown up on a Texas ranch, with five brothers. He fit right into the small-town lifestyle here, but poor Leezie seemed like a fish out of water, and I had been afraid Mike wouldn't come to Twin Falls because of her. Once here, I feared that Leezie would force Mike to choose between her and his job; but Leezie surprised all of us and plunged right into the social life of Twin Falls, joining the Symphony League and becoming active in the South Central Medical Auxiliary.

She had never changed her style, though, and Mike had never changed his. Over the past two years, they'd learned to accept each other and their differences and go on from there. Mike had been indifferent about children, and Leezie definitely didn't want horses, but now they had both.

The large and informal kitchen had been decorated Santa Fe-style in shades of pale blue, tan, and terra cotta, with southwestern Indian designs. Pale-blue countertops and brick-colored tiles around the sink complemented the pale oak cabinetry. Terra cotta tiles covered the floor. A large trestle table, also of pale oak, filled the end of the room.

The country club had catered the affair, with a standing rib roast and a dizzying array of hot dishes and salads. For once, I wasn't particularly hungry. Facing possible disintegration of life as I knew it might have had something to do with that.

Hal grabbed a beer and disappeared into the family room, where most of the guys had congregated to watch a football game, and proceeded to pretty much ignore me. *Fuck him*, I thought and made up my mind to have a good time if it killed me. I fixed myself a scotch on the rocks and joined the women in the kitchen, but after a while I got bored and wandered out into the living room to contemplate the Christmas tree—or just to breathe in the balsam smell that was so lacking in our fake tree at home. Pine-scented air freshener just doesn't cut it, in my opinion.

"Gorgeous, isn't it?"

Startled, I turned to find Rebecca Sorensen, wife of Jeff, the surgeon, standing behind me. She was tall, thin, blonde, and gorgeous, the opposite of me in oh-so-many ways, the epitome of glamor in a red sequined dress that fit her like a second skin and stopped at midthigh. No way would I get away with wearing a dress like that, I thought enviously. I had attempted to disguise my short, stocky figure in a black pantsuit with a tunic top, which I had accessorized with lots of heavy onyx and silver jewelry to draw attention away from my hips. I looked okay. She looked stunning.

In spite of all that, Rebecca was actually a pretty nice person and popular with the other wives. She was president of the ladies' golf association down at the country club. I wondered why she was out here with me instead of being the center of attention in the kitchen with the wives, like she usually was.

So I asked her.

"Sometimes," she said, "I just get tired of all the girl talk—you know, about the kids and the pregnancies and the illnesses and the husbands and all the dumb stuff they do. Besides, I was curious, so I went looking for you."

"Really," I said. "Why me? About what?"

"You did an autopsy today, didn't you?"

"I did," I said, wondering what she was getting at.

"Kathleen Burke is my next-door neighbor," she said.

"Kathleen Burke? Who's that?"

"Mrs. Jay Braithwaite Burke," she said. "I was just wondering what you found."

Oh, *that* Kathleen Burke. I should have known. No, wait. Why should I have known? It was a coroner's case. The next of kin didn't have to sign the consent. Rollie, the coroner, had done that.

"Oh, you were," I said. "Why?"

"I just wondered if he was murdered," she said. "Was he? I want to know all the details," she added, clasping her hands charmingly under her chin and giving me a beguiling smile. She really did have a pretty smile. It lit up her whole face. But it was wasted on me.

"He died of carbon monoxide poisoning," I told her, hoping that would be enough to satisfy her.

It wasn't. "So it was just an accident after all?" She sounded disappointed.

I wasn't sure how much I should tell her; so I tried to tell her as little as possible. At the same time, it occurred to me that Rebecca might know things that might help me solve the murder.

Wait. Solve the murder?

Since when was it my job to solve the murder? Bernie Kincaid would have my head if I tried to do that.

Only I wasn't sure if that was the part of my anatomy Bernie had in mind these days. But never mind. Rebecca had asked me a question.

"It's possible," I said. "I can't give you all the details, but I think he might have been. Why do you want to know?"

Rebecca sighed. "Okay. I'll tell you. But let's sit down. My feet are killing me."

She was wearing four-inch stilettos. No wonder. We adjourned to the couch. As she turned, I couldn't help noticing a little tummy bulge. "Are you pregnant?" I asked.

She smiled. "Yes. I'm four months along. It's our first."

"Congratulations," I said.

"Thanks. Anyway, Kathleen's my friend," Rebecca began. "I've known her ever since we moved here thirteen years ago. I've been sort of, oh, I don't know, a confidant to her. I'm worried about her. That's why I wanted to know if Jay was murdered."

"You think she murdered him?" I asked.

"Oh, I don't know!" She buried her face in her hands. "I don't want her to have murdered him. I don't want her to go to prison. But I wouldn't blame her if she did. Jay was an absolute asshole and treated her like shit. He treated the kids like shit too. He was a thoroughly nasty person. The world's better off without him, in my opinion!"

Wow. Are you sure you *didn't murder him?*

I cleared my throat. "Exactly what did he do?"

"He cheated on her," Rebecca said. "He'd done it for years. His secretary was the latest. Tiffany. She even had a child by him."

"Goodness," I said. "And Kathleen didn't know?"

"I can't imagine that she didn't," Rebecca said. "But she didn't do anything about it until she came home and caught them in bed together."

I felt a pang. Would I be catching Hal that way too, sometime soon? Resolutely I pushed that nasty little thought right out of my mind. "So that's why she divorced him?"

Rebecca nodded. "Kicked him out of the house on the spot and then divorced him. He rented an apartment over on Washington Street for a while, but when he went bankrupt, he had to move out."

"Where could he go with no money?" I asked.

"Who says he didn't have money?" Rebecca said. "He had money in a Swiss bank. Kathleen set that up back when she worked for him, but that was a long time ago, before the kids were born. He could have spent it all by now, for all we know."

"I didn't know she worked for him," I said.

"That's how they met," Rebecca said. "She went to work there, and they got married, and she kept working until she got pregnant."

"How many kids did they have?

"Four. The youngest one is six," Rebecca said.

"So, what happened to Jay? Where did he go?" I asked.

Dead silence.

"You don't know?" I persisted.

Rebecca cleared her throat. "No. Tiffany doesn't even know."

Now *that* was interesting. "You mean he didn't take Tiffany with him?"

"No, and Kathleen said she was really pissed off about it too."

"You mean Kathleen actually *talks* to Tiffany?" I asked. "I should think she'd be more likely to rip her face off."

"It's funny, isn't it?" said Rebecca. "His running off like that brought them together. Tiffany moved in with Kathleen, and Kathleen treats her like a daughter. They comfort each other. Tiffany helps with the kids. It's really kind of sweet, you know?"

Sweet? That's not the word I'd have used. If Hal was having an affair with a college student, I sure as hell wouldn't be treating the girl like a daughter. And having her move in with me? *No way,* I decided after a moment of thought. *I would rip her face off.* Kathleen Burke was obviously a better person than I would ever be.

"So what's going to happen to Kathleen?" I asked. "Is she going to have to go back to work now, or has she already?"

"I don't know about that," Rebecca said. "But she's sold the house and moved out. I think she had to find someplace cheaper because of the bankruptcy."

"And how about you?"

Rebecca glared at me. "What do you mean, what about me?"

Whoa. Maybe that was a trifle invasive. Maybe I should be more subtle and devious. I tried to appease her. "I mean, how are you doing since you and Jeff lost all that money in Jay's Ponzi scheme. What did you think I meant?"

"Oh, nothing." Rebecca suddenly wasn't meeting my eyes, and I thought I saw a blush working its way up her neck, but maybe it was a trick of the light. "I think we're okay. Jeff handles all the finances, so I don't really know. I mean, if we were in trouble, he'd tell me. Wouldn't he?"

Oh, jeez. Did people really still live like that in this day and age? I thought that sort of thing went out with *The Donna Reed Show.* On the other hand, we were living way out here in the Wild West, the Land Where Time Stood Still.

I wondered if Rebecca was typical of the doctors' wives. Were they all that ignorant of their financial situations? Oh hell, why didn't I just come right out and ask her? Did all their girl talk include household finances?

"Rebecca, do you know if the other wives have the same financial arrangement with their husbands as you do? I mean, the men take care of the finances so the wives don't have to worry about them?

"Certainly. That's the great thing about being married to a doctor. You never have to worry about money."

Yeah, right. Not until they lose it all. "So your husbands all pay the bills and give you allowances for household expenses?"

"Yes. Why are you asking all these questions, Toni? Is there anything wrong with doing it that way?"

Oh, dear God, is there anything *not* wrong with doing it that way? Didn't she realize that doctors are absolutely clueless when it comes to investing? That's why they get targeted with every investment scheme that comes down the pike. And because they are busy doctors with no time to read the fine print and ask questions, an alarming number of them get roped in. Maybe I should tell her about all the phone calls I get at work, about investing in oil and gas futures, or diamonds, or fine art, or cattle ranches; and of course they all want me to commit right now, before the price goes up or the loophole closes. The sense of urgency seems to be a common sales tactic with these people.

I mean, her husband, Jeff, is a decent guy and a good surgeon, but how financially savvy is he? He invested in Jay's Ponzi scheme; what does that tell you?

Sure, I could tell her all that, but would it change anything? The damage had already been done. Sure, I could tell Rebecca and her girlfriends why they should learn to handle the finances in their households, to prevent this sort of thing from ever happening again, but all it would do is piss off their husbands, with whom I still had to work.

But Rebecca had asked me a question, and I hadn't answered it, because I simply could not think of an answer that wouldn't be insulting.

"Oh, I wouldn't say there's anything wrong with it, Rebecca, but I personally wouldn't feel comfortable if I didn't know exactly where Hal and I stand financially."

"You mean you think Jeff's hiding something from me?"

Christ on a crutch. I just kept digging myself deeper into the hole.

Yes, that's precisely what I mean, you innocent babe in the woods. "No, no, of course I don't mean that."

"Oh, I know," Rebecca said, digging me in even deeper. "It's because you're the doctor, and you make more money than Hal does. I get it. So you pay the bills and give *him* an allowance?"

Please, God, don't let Hal come out here and hear this conversation. This is a subject we try not to talk about. "I pay the bills, and we don't invest without discussing it first."

"And that's okay with Hal?"

"More than okay. Hal hates paying bills. It makes him cranky."

"Hmph," said Rebecca. "I like our way better."

Rebecca and the other wives lived in a world that I simply could not comprehend.

My mother, who had been left a widow while still only a girl of seventeen and pregnant with me, told me repeatedly as I was growing up that I should take over the family finances when I got married, so that when my husband died, I wouldn't be a lost soul, not knowing where the money was, or even if there *was* any money, as she had been. So who had taught her to be so smart? Grandma Day, a woman way ahead of her time. Bless her.

What must it be like to be so protected? I felt surreal, like Dorothy in the land of Oz, as if I'd inadvertently entered a fairy-tale world where, yes, Virginia, money really did grow on trees, magically appearing whenever one needed it, without having to deal with the down-and-dirty business of actually earning it and making it stretch until the end of the pay period. So Cinderella married the prince and they lived happily ever after—at least until he left her for his secretary when the kingdom's economy was in the toilet. Only this particular prince had left his secretary too.

"Did Tiffany lose her job when Jay died?" I asked.

"I think she still works there," Rebecca said. "She's Lance's secretary too; with just the two of them, they only needed one. She has to clean up Jay's affairs, transfer his cases to other lawyers, box up his old files for storage, and clean out his office in case Lance wants to take on another partner."

"Lance? Who's Lance?" I asked.

"Jay's partner," said Rebecca. "You didn't know he had a partner?"

I shook my head.

"Oh, well, he didn't get much exposure," Rebecca said. "Jay was such a public figure that poor Lance was completely overlooked. But he's still there, and so is Tiffany."

At that point, the guys started drifting out of the family room. Apparently the football game was over. Jeff came over to us. "What are you girls so deep in conversation about? Solving the problems of the world?"

"We were talking about Jay Braithwaite Burke," I said.

"Join the club," Jeff said. "We were too. Seems like that's all we ever talk about these days."

Jack Allen joined us. He seemed to have had a trifle too much to drink. Weaving slightly, he thrust his flushed face into mine. "I want to know why you never said anything about this."

I recoiled from his alcoholic breath. "What 'this' would that be, Jack?"

"Don't play games with me, Toni," Jack said. "You two were the only ones who didn't get into this. You knew something that the rest of us didn't. Why didn't you tell us at the time?"

"If you're talking about Jay Braithwaite Burke," I said, "Hal and I got the same information you did. Don't put this all on me."

Jack's eyes narrowed and his face grew redder. "Then how do you explain why you didn't invest in this fund along with the rest of us?"

I looked up to see Hal come up behind Jack. "Just plain old common sense," he said.

Startled, Jack whirled. I thought I saw tiny streams of smoke emanating from his ears, but it might have been my imagination. "You can't talk to me like that, Shapiro. Just who the hell do you think you are?"

Eager to avoid the onset of fisticuffs and probable severe injury to Jack, since Hal had six inches and at least fifty pounds on him, I intervened. "We checked with our broker and accountant. Didn't you?"

Jack shook his head, speechless at last.

"We followed their advice," I continued.

Jack now seemed near tears. "Why didn't you tell us?"

I shrugged. "I did. You didn't listen. You said I could roll over and play dead if I wanted to, but you weren't going to. Remember?"

Jack's shoulders sagged. His face, no longer red with anger, now just looked gray. Slowly, he turned and walked away. I watched him go. Sometime during the conversation, Jeff and Rebecca had left too.

I sighed. "Such drama," I said lightly.

Hal put his arm around me. "You're shaking," he said.

I turned my face into his chest. "Jack isn't usually like that," I said.

"He's drunk," Hal said. "You should have heard him in there. If I never hear anyone mention Jay Braithwaite Burke again, it'll be too soon."

I shared the sentiment, but I didn't give two cents for the chance of that happening.

Chapter 5

O, beware, my lord, of jealousy!
It is the green-eyed monster which doth mock
The meat it feeds on.
—Shakespeare, *Othello*

After everybody left, Hal and I stayed to help clean up.

"Toni," Leezie said as she loaded the dishwasher, "just who *is* this Jay Braithwaite Burke person everybody's talking about? I didn't want to ask and look stupid."

"He was a lawyer," I said, "whose specialty was to create ways for people with a lot of money to avoid paying taxes. He set up this hedge fund that was guaranteed to pay ten percent per year and not to drop more than one percent no matter what the market did."

"But that's impossible," Mike said. "How the hell did he manage that?"

"He wouldn't tell us," I said. "He said it was proprietary and had to be kept secret to preserve a competitive edge."

"That sounds like a bunch of bull," Mike said, "I tell you what."

"I don't understand," Leezie said. "How does that avoid taxes?"

"He set it up so that our distributions or salaries would go directly into this hedge fund via an offshore leasing company."

"Leasing company?" said Leezie. "What's that?"

"It's a gimmick," Hal said. "It's intended to create an arm's length between the doctor and his salary by having the hospital pay the leasing company and the leasing company pay the doctors."

"Except that instead of paying the doctors, the money went right into the hedge fund," I said.

"Well, then, how were you supposed to get paid?" Leezie demanded.

"We were supposed to take out 'loans' instead of salary," I said, "and loans aren't taxable."

"These so-called 'loans' were at a really high interest rate," Hal said, "which we could then pay back, to ourselves, and the interest was deductible too."

"Wait a minute," Mike said. "Just how the hell were you supposed to pay back these loans if all your money went into the hedge fund?"

"That's what our accountant wanted to know," Hal said.

"Why couldn't you just have your paycheck direct-deposited into your own offshore bank account?" asked Leezie. "It sounds much simpler."

"Our accountant said that too," said Hal.

"The beauty of the leasing company concept," I explained, "is that the leasing company would manage the pension plans and withhold taxes like any other employer, and they would pay many of the physicians' personal expenses that were normally not deductible by an ordinary taxpayer but were deductible by the leasing company as a business expense."

"And then the money saved went right into the pension plans, which were invested in the hedge fund," Hal said.

Mike looked thoughtful. "Well, I tell you what," he said. "I got me an earful just now from the other guys. It *sounded* good. If I'd been here back then, I probably would have gone into it right along with everybody else."

"Then I'm glad we weren't here," Leezie said tartly.

"What made y'all decide not to?" Mike asked. "If y'all don't mind my askin'."

I shrugged. "We talked to our accountant and our broker, and they advised against it. They both said there was no single fund that could guarantee a ten percent return no matter what the market did and to stay away from anything that was proprietary. To avoid taxes in IRAs and 401Ks, we could invest in offshore funds on our own, if we wanted to, but we'd still have to pay tax on whatever we brought back into the US."

"So why did everybody have to pay taxes on all the money they lost?" asked Leezie.

"Because they invested it offshore to hide it from taxes," Hal said, "so they couldn't very well claim a loss on money the IRS wasn't supposed to know they had, could they?"

"Besides," I said, "they had their pay go directly offshore to avoid taxes, which is apparently illegal, and some of them had been doing that for ten years or more.

So now they owe gazillions in back taxes and interest and penalties."

"Leasing companies are illegal too," Hal added. "As it turns out."

"I don't get it," said Leezie. "If you two could see it, why couldn't the rest of them see it?"

"Hal couldn't see it either," I said. "It sounded good to him too."

"Don't put it all on me," Hal retorted. "You would have gone along too if it hadn't been for Fred and Lorraine."

Defiantly, I put my hands on my hips. "And whose idea was it to check with them?"

Hal thrust his head forward so that he was practically nose to nose with me. "All right, already, you think you're so smart. So whose idea was it to go for that personal corporation thing? I tried to talk you out of that, but oh, no, you just went ahead and did it without me, and look what happened."

I pushed back. "You know perfectly well they were legal at the time. How was I supposed to know they were going to change the tax law before the ink was even dry?"

Hal threw up his hands. "We had to pay five quarters worth of income tax that year! Count 'em. Five!"

Mike inserted himself between us. "Guys, guys, back off! We weren't trying to start a fight. Jesus H. Christ, I tell you what."

We backed off.

"Sorry," I said.

"Me too," Hal said, giving me a poisonous glare. "Toni's got to learn not to air dirty laundry in public."

Furious, I turned on him. "Who aired dirty laundry here? Who mentioned personal corporations?"

Leezie grabbed my arm and pulled me away from Hal before I could get my hands on him. "Stop it, you two! What's the matter with you? Do you both need a time-out?"

I sighed. "Sorry. I'll stop if Hal will."

Hal clutched his head in both hands and turned his back on me. "*Oy gevalt!*"

Contrite, I turned to Mike and Leezie. "I really am sorry. We better go. We're cranky. I think we both need naps."

"It's quite all right," Leezie assured me. "Mike told me what a crazy day you guys had. You must be exhausted."

"I heard something about settin' up another profit-sharing plan," Mike said.

"That's true," I said. "You and I can start investing right away. But the other guys can't start putting anything in until they've paid off the IRS. That could take years."

Leezie shook her head. "Sounds to me like this Jay Braithwaite Burke has hurt a lot of people in more ways than one," she said.

I agreed. But Hal walked out without saying another word.

Chapter 6

Every woman should marry ... and no man.
—Benjamin Disraeli

We weren't done, apparently. As we walked out to the car, we didn't speak. All the way home, we didn't speak. Once we got inside the house, Hal headed up the stairs, still not speaking. In the bedroom, I decided I'd had quite enough silent treatment.

"Hal."

"I don't want to hear it, Toni. I don't want to discuss Jay Braithwaite Burke anymore."

"Neither do I."

Hal turned and looked at me for the first time. "Then what do you want to talk about that can't wait till tomorrow after we've had some sleep?"

I took hold of his hands. He didn't pull away. Encouraged, I said, "I don't want us to go to bed mad. I want to apologize."

He shrugged. "So apologize, already."

I let go of his hands and walked away and then turned back to look at him. He didn't move. "Well?" he said.

I sighed. "I started that argument by saying that you wanted to invest in that scheme and it was my idea to check with Fred and Lorraine. I'm sorry I did that."

Hal sat down on the bed and started taking off his shoes. "Okay."

I sat down next to him and kicked off my shoes too. "I'm also sorry I went into the personal corporation without discussing it with you. I should have, and we should have checked that out with Fred and Lorraine too."

"I'm glad you said that," Hal said. "It's about time. I think I've always been a little resentful that you didn't listen to me about that."

"Listen to you?" I said. "You never said anything about it."

"Yes, I did. You weren't listening. Toni, we've been married seventeen years, and I should think we'd be communicating a lot better than this by now." Hal wouldn't look at me. "But we seem to be communicating less and less."

Oh, the nerve of him! "Oh, right, you're the big communicator," I sneered. "That's why you won't tell me what's been bothering you for the last few months. You just tell me to get off your case."

Hal started unbuttoning his shirt. "That's because there's nothing bothering me, Toni, and I wish you'd stop nagging me about it."

I pulled my tunic top off over my head and threw it on the chair. "If you'd tell me what it is, I wouldn't have to nag."

"Toni …"

"Okay, I'll stop nagging. You don't want to tell me, you don't have to tell me. I can't make you. But just let me say one thing." My voice began to quaver. "I don't want a divorce. I want us to be the way we were."

Hal seemed startled. "Who said anything about divorce?"

By now tears were running down my face and my nose was clogged. I sniffed mightily and to no avail. "You did, this morning."

Hal seemed momentarily bewildered. "This morn—oh, that." His face cleared. "Actually, you were the one who mentioned it."

"And you said, 'Don't tempt me.'" *And if you loved me, you'd be comforting me right now.*

He sighed and got up off the bed. He came over to me and put his arms around me. "Okay, so I was a little upset. But I don't want a divorce either. Now can we go to bed and get some sleep?"

Well, that was a relief. But he still hadn't told me what had been bothering him. We continued to get ready for bed, and when we finally got into bed, Hal leaned over and gave me a kiss. "I love you, honey. G'night." He rolled over and turned out his light.

"Love you too," I said; but I didn't turn off my light. I read for quite a while before I grew calm enough to attempt sleep. Hal might think this discussion was over, but I knew it was just a temporary truce. Hal's and my relationship had subtly changed in ways I couldn't pinpoint. Whatever it was, I didn't like it.

And I couldn't help wondering if the damage Jay Braithwaite Burke had done would include the end of my marriage.

Saturday, December 13

Chapter 7

It's well to be off with the Old Woman
before you're on with the New.
—George Bernard Shaw

Saturday morning found us next door, sampling Elliott's World Famous Christmas Eggnog, which was meant to be served at the party that Jodi and Elliott were having that night. It contained seven different kinds of booze and was so delicious that even I consented to partake.

As a small child, I had refused to eat eggs, so my mother had given me eggnog for breakfast. She made it herself with an eggbeater, so it was always sort of stringy and mucoid, and it wasn't long before I consented to eat hard-boiled eggs just so I wouldn't have to drink the disgusting stuff. But this was different. It was whipped and fluffy, almost like a milkshake, with no strings attached.

Jodi Maynard sighed with pleasure. "Yum," she said. "I love this stuff. It's a good thing we only make it at Christmastime, or I'd weigh a ton."

I licked my lips. "It's a heart attack in a glass," I agreed.

Elliott refilled his glass. "How was the party?" he asked.

"Good," replied Hal, holding out his glass for a refill too. "I never saw so many Christmas decorations in my life. And I thought *Toni* was bad."

"What's so bad about Christmas decorations?" I demanded.

"Nothing, except that you usually put them up in November and then want to leave them up until March."

I was way too old to believe in Santa Claus, and the cost of any presents we gave each other came out of our own pockets; so the magic of Christmas was pretty much a nonstarter, unless I could find something else to ooh and aah over to create the necessary ambiance, and that only left the decorations and the music.

On those, I went all out.

It was important to me. Apparently, in my heart, I was still a child.

For someone raised in a Jewish home, Hal had adapted very well to the observance of Christmas, thank God, and I wasn't too shabby on the Jewish holidays, either. For example, I knew that this year Christmas would fall on the fourth day of Hanukkah, and I celebrated both of them in my unique style.

Up until this year, Hal had always teased me good-naturedly about the lengths to which I took it. His parents were another story.

Shortly after we'd moved to Twin Falls, they visited us during Hanukkah, probably to make sure that their younger son was celebrating it properly and hadn't been totally corrupted by that *shiksa* he'd married; but they were doomed to disappointment. When Ida Shapiro saw the Christmas tree with the lighted blue-and-silver Star of David on top, she started to hyperventilate, and then she saw the *menorah* in the center of the dining room table, with red candles in it, surrounded by holly leaves and shiny red balls.

That did it. As she lay artistically draped over the couch, moaning and clutching her chest, Hal and his father Max hovered over her solicitously, while I called her bluff and an ambulance, in that order; whereupon she miraculously recovered.

Just in time to see Hal's *dreidel* in the center of the mantelpiece between the Christmas stockings.

This year, however, Hal's teasing had an edge to it, as if he was really pissed off about it. I didn't know why. All I knew was that it was spoiling the magic, and that pissed me off, so I attacked.

"And your point?"

Hal glared at me. "You know perfectly well what my point is. I'm Jewish, for God's sake. You might consider my needs once in a while."

Seriously? The man was scolding me for being so insensitive to his *needs,* like I didn't know he was Jewish?

Needs, my ass. "Oh yes, and let's not mention that you ate pork chops and potatoes au gratin over here the other night," I remarked. "Talk about nonkosher! You're a *cafeteria Jew*, that's what you are!"

"All right, you guys, cut it out, already," said Jodi, who had heard this argument before.

65

Hal folded his arms and achieved a martyred expression. "I will if Toni will."

I threw up my hands in frustration. "Oh my God, this is so high school!"

Jodi threw her hands up too. "Oh my God, what is the matter with you two? You're acting like children. Can we just change the subject and talk about the party? Can you manage to do that without killing each other?"

"Hmph," Hal said. "Some party. All they wanted to talk about was that damn Jay Braithwaite Burke."

Elliott clutched his head as if in severe pain. "Don't mention that name in this house," he said. "I hear nothing else all day, day after day. All I did was draw up his damn will. How can one person be so freakin' much trouble?"

"How is he giving you trouble?" I asked.

"Drawing up that will was the dumbest freakin' thing I ever did. And for what? A damn Ponzi scheme that went south and probably has no money in it for anyone to inherit."

I hoped that Jay had at least paid Elliott for that will, but perhaps this was not the best time to ask.

"What's a Ponzi scheme?" Jodi asked.

Elliott explained. "Someone gets everybody he knows to invest in something that guarantees a huge return because it takes advantage of some kind of loophole in the tax code or something, and he tells them they need to hurry up and get in on the ground floor before that changes. So they do, and they tell all their friends, and so on. As long as new investors keep putting money in, the old investors get paid, but if that stops and people start taking money out, it falls apart and all the new investors lose everything."

"So if you really do get in on the ground floor, you should come out okay," Hal said.

"Sure, unless you reinvest your profits. Then you could lose big-time, just like everybody else."

"Ponzi?" Jodi asked. "Wasn't he that guy on Happy Days?"

I giggled. Elliott ignored her. "Charles Ponzi," he said, "made a fortune back in 1919, buying postal coupons in the US and selling them in Europe for a few cents more. He got all these people to invest, and the whole thing fell apart because for everybody to get anything out of it there would have had to be something like a hundred million postal coupons printed, and there were actually only twenty-seven thousand."

"Jesus," Hal said. "If we'd gotten into that fund back when we first moved here and it had already been going on for five years, we'd have lost everything."

"Maybe Jay didn't invest his own money in that fund," I pointed out. "Of all people, he should have known what he was getting into. So maybe there is something to inherit, after all."

"I told you that, Toni," Elliott said. "Remember? Offshore accounts in his will?"

"Just because they're in his will doesn't mean there's any money left in them," I said.

"Maybe," Elliott conceded, "but why the hell couldn't he just leave everything to his wife and children and a few charities, and be done with it? Oh, no, he has to get all tricky and set up all these freakin' trusts. It's gonna be pure freakin' hell to administer it. I keep getting all these phone calls, and I can't tell anybody anything because you, Doctor Toni Freakin' Day Shapiro, called his death a homicide."

Well, hell, I wasn't about to apologize for my autopsy report. "Who were the trusts for?" I asked.

"Now you know perfectly freakin' well that's privileged information. But one of them is that his secretary inherits on the condition that she moves in with the wife and helps her take care of the kids. If she moves out, she has to give the money to the wife. I could go on, but you get the point."

"So that's it," I said.

"What?" Hal asked.

"That's why Tiffany moved in with Kathleen," I said.

"How'd you know that?" Hal asked.

"Rebecca Sorensen said so last night," I said. "She thought it was so sweet. She said Kathleen treats Tiffany like a daughter. She also said Tiffany had a child by Jay."

"That would explain why he set up a trust for her," Elliott said.

"Who else did he set up trusts for?" I inquired, hoping to catch Elliott off guard.

It didn't work. Elliott held up a hand. "Toni, you're not listening. That's privileged."

"You told me about Tiffany," I countered. "You know you can trust me not to spread this all over town. Don't you?"

Elliott knew better than to argue with me. Even my Mum would say I could give any lawyer a run for his money in an argument. Sometimes she'd even wonder why I'd wasted my time in medical school. "The trusts are for some people that make no freakin' sense," he said.

"I mean, they're not related to him in any way that I can figure."

"Hey," I said, struck by a sudden thought. "Were all the other people women with small children?"

"Yes, they were, now that you mention it," Elliott said. "What are you getting at, Toni?"

"What kind of conditions do they have to meet before they can inherit?"

"They have to be divorced from their husbands and not remarried. Why?"

"Well, Rebecca said he'd been cheating on his wife for years. Maybe they were *all* women that he had affairs with and got pregnant. Maybe all the children are Jay's, and he set up trusts to make sure they were taken care of if their parents divorced."

"It's possible," Elliott said. "But one of them was your radiologist."

"Mitzi? Why on earth?" But even as I said this, I remembered Mitzi'd had a baby last year, at the age of forty-two, and as soon as he'd found out she was pregnant, her husband, Dave, left her. They subsequently divorced, and I'd always considered Dave a prize shit for walking out on Mitzi when she was pregnant. Dave and Mitzi had another child, Jeremy, who was ten. But suppose the baby wasn't Dave's? Suppose it was Jay's?

Ridiculous. Not Mitzi. She wouldn't be that desperate. Would she?

"What did all those women see in him?" I asked. "He was such a sleazeball and not the least bit good-looking."

"Jesus, Toni," Hal said, "why don't you tell us how you really feel about him?"

69

"Ah," Jodi said, "but he had The Voice. He could mesmerize you."

"Not me," I declared. "He just turned me off. Sort of like a pushy used car salesman."

Jodi shrugged and turned away. I wondered if what I'd said upset her, but now wasn't the time to ask. Could *Jodi* possibly have been involved with Jay?

No. No way. Jodi and Elliott were solid. She wouldn't have given the likes of Jay a second thought.

"So, Elliott," I continued, "I don't suppose you can tell me who the other women were, could you? Seeing as you've already violated confidentiality by telling me about Mitzi?"

Elliott cleared his throat and turned away from me before he spoke. "I'd rather not," he said.

"Oh, come on, Elliott," I urged. "I'm a doctor. I'm real good at confidentiality."

But Elliott just shook his head. "No, Toni, I've told you enough."

I changed the subject. "I also found out that Jay had a partner. Lance Something. Did you know that?"

"I thought so," Hal said. "I had occasion to drive by Jay's office once, and the name on the sign was Burke, Braithwaite, Burke, Bartlett, and Brooks. It stuck in my mind because it was all B's, and I wondered if that was a prerequisite for partnership, or something. So which one is Lance?"

"Brooks," Elliott said. "The first Burke was Jay's paternal grandfather, Braithwaite was his grandfather's cousin, and they're both long dead. And Bill Bartlett's dead, too. Dropped dead at his desk at the tender age of forty-eight. Heart attack. Happened about ten years ago."

"That's scary," said Hal, who was fifty-four.

"Tell me about it," Elliott said. "*I'm* forty-eight."

"Wait a minute," Jodi said. "If Tiffany's child is three, and Mitzi's baby is only one, if they're both Jay's, that means he was fooling around with Mitzi and Tiffany at the same time. Do any of these women know about the others?"

Elliott groaned, clutching his head melodramatically. "Jesus freakin' Christ, I hope not."

"Were all of these women's ex-husbands involved in Jay's Ponzi scheme?" I asked.

"Yes," Elliott said. "They were. Now do you see why this is one freakin' hell of a mess?"

Not to mention an embarrassment of motives, I thought. Was there anyone left who *didn't* want Jay dead?

Jodi cleared her throat. "Not to change the subject or anything, but does anybody want to guess who's moving into the house across the street?"

Old Mrs. Merriweather, who'd lived across the street in a house older than she was and much too large for her, had died last year on Christmas Eve at the age of ninety. I'd done the autopsy. The house had stood empty and decaying for nearly a year when the For Sale sign came down and the Sold sign went up. I hadn't really given it much thought until Jodi mentioned it, and I wondered briefly why Jodi had chosen to mention it just now.

I didn't have to wonder long. "Who?" I asked.

"Kathleen Burke," Jodi said.

Holy shit, I thought. Rebecca told me Kathleen had sold her house and moved out, but hadn't said where to.

Of all the places in this town she could have moved to, she had to pick the house across the street from me.

Looked like I was going to get involved in this case whether I wanted to or not.

Chapter 8

There's a fascination frantic
In a ruin that's romantic;
Do you think that you are sufficiently decayed?
—Sir William Gilbert

So, while Jodi took time out of her busy day preparing for the party and made a tuna casserole, I made a pan of brownies; and so armed, we crossed the street to make the acquaintance of our new neighbors.

Mrs. Merriweather's house was Victorian, like ours, built at the beginning of the last century, when Twin Falls had consisted of just a few muddy streets. Originally Wedgwood blue with darker blue shutters, the paint had faded and peeled to an uneven, scabrous gray.

In the sunshine, the house would look friendly enough, but against the dark, gray winter sky, it loomed ominously, and the branches of the stark, leafless trees around it looked like skeletal fingers, arching over the roof as if to grab anyone foolish enough to climb up there. One could imagine them closing over the house at night, rather like the closing of flower petals, imprisoning its occupants until morning, when they would open again with the rising of the sun.

I was obviously channeling Hansel and Gretel.

As we climbed the sagging steps to the broad porch, I almost expected that Lurch would answer the door, intoning, "You rang?" But before we had a chance to knock, the screen door opened, and we came face to face with a stocky, dark-haired woman about my age, who took one look at Jodi and exclaimed, "Don't I know you?"

Jodi knitted her brow for a moment, and then said, "You've been in my shop, haven't you?"

Jodi owns and operates a beauty spa called First Resort, which features such things as yoga, aromatherapy, tanning booths, and acupuncture in addition to the usual amenities. Most of the doctors' wives, and even some of the doctors, patronized it. Me, for instance.

Jodi stuck out her hand. "Jodi Maynard," she said.

The dark-haired woman shook it. "Kathleen Burke," she replied.

I stuck my hand out too. "Toni Shapiro," I said. "We brought you some food."

"Oh, thank you," Kathleen said. Her mahogany-colored hair fell in ringlets to her shoulders, and she had liquid, dark-brown eyes with thick black eyebrows and eyelashes like mine. "Would you like to come in? Oh, what am I saying—of course you would, it's so cold out. I'll bet you've been in this house lots of times, haven't you?"

"Actually, no," I said.

"Me either," Jodi said. "But my husband, Elliott, has. He drew up Mrs. Merriweather's will."

And found her body, but I didn't think Kathleen needed to know that. Some people get squeamish about houses someone has died in, particularly when the bed they died in was still there. Kathleen had apparently bought the place furnished.

With an inward shudder, I hoped someone had at least taken the sheets off Mrs. Merriweather's bed.

"Oh, your husband is a lawyer, then," Kathleen said, and she didn't sound too happy about that. A small dark-haired girl tugged at her pant leg and whined, "Mommy, I'm hungry."

Kathleen picked up the child, who wound her small arms around Kathleen's neck and looked at us with huge chocolate eyes that were just like her mother's.

"This is Angela," Kathleen said. "She's six. Honey, these are our new neighbors, Jodi and Toni."

"Hi, Angela," I said. "Do you like your new house?"

Suddenly shy, Angela hid her face against her mother's shoulder.

"Do you have children, Toni?" Kathleen asked.

"No, but Jodi has five."

"That's probably why Toni doesn't have any," Jodi laughed. "Mine are always at her house."

"They like to play with our dogs," I said.

"You know very well that's not it," Jodi scolded. "Toni always says she's not good with kids, but somehow she's the one who ends up with them climbing all over her. Like now." She pointed to a tiny golden-haired girl who had appeared from nowhere and was hugging my leg.

"That's Emily," Kathleen said. "She's three. She's Tiffany's little girl."

"Tiffany?" Jodi inquired.

"Did somebody call me?" A slender twenty-something blonde came out onto the porch, and the screen door slammed shut behind her. "Emily, come here and leave the lady alone. Kathleen, the kids are all hungry. Shall I take them to McDonald's or something?"

"I brought a tuna casserole," Jodi said. "It's still hot."

"Oh, yum," Kathleen said. "I love tuna casserole. I was going to fix peanut butter and jelly sandwiches for the kids, but this is so much better. Please, come and eat with us."

So we followed her into the kitchen, where she introduced us to the rest of her children: Bryan, thirteen, Bobby, ten, and Megan, eight. The gray-haired lady was Kathleen's mother, Mary Reilly, who lived in Boise. All of the children had inherited Kathleen's dark hair and eyes, but only Megan was stocky like her mother.

"Look, everybody," Kathleen said. "Jodi and Toni brought us a tuna casserole for our lunch," whereupon Bobby and Megan made throwing-up noises, and Angela said, "Eeeuuww."

"That was rude," Kathleen snapped. "You guys can fix your own lunch. Here." She pulled a jar of peanut butter and a jar of strawberry jam out of one of several boxes that stood open on the kitchen floor and handed them to Bobby, who said, "Aw, Mom!"

Kathleen was, apparently, wise to the ways of movers, who tend to run on schedules that don't exactly conform to the needs of their clients.

When Hal and I had moved up here from Long Beach, our movers decided to first take a little vacation in Las Vegas that lasted a week—without telling us. We had our houseplants with us but no food or bedding. Jodi and Elliott had rescued us, and we'd been best friends ever since.

Unlike us, Kathleen had packed the kitchen essentials herself and brought them over in her car. Tiffany busied herself dishing up tuna casserole onto paper plates for everybody else. The kitchen table only seated four, so Kathleen sent the children into the living room to eat.

At this point, I heard the front door open and a voice call, "Yoo-hoo! Anybody home?"

"In here!" Kathleen called back.

A round, bubbly blonde about my age bustled into the kitchen with a large baking dish covered with foil. She put it on the kitchen counter and whipped off the foil. Instantly, the enticing aroma of Italian sausage and tomato sauce filled the air.

Kathleen sniffed deeply. "Oh, Ruthie, that smells heavenly!" As the newcomer stared inquiringly at me, Kathleen hastily introduced us. "Ruthie, this is Toni Shapiro, who lives across the street, and of course you know Jodi. Toni, this is Ruthie Brooks, Jay's partner's wife."

Kathleen dished up portions of Ruthie's lasagna, and we all dug in. It was without doubt the best lasagna I had ever tasted, but having already eaten tuna casserole and a brownie, I didn't eat much of it, and neither did Jodi. Ruthie didn't stay; she said she had absolutely *tons* of things to do and she'd see us at the party, and she bustled away.

As I ate, I looked around the large kitchen with its 1950s vintage appliances. The dingy, brownish linoleum had been worn completely through in front of the stove and sink. A round-shouldered Frigidaire wheezed on the opposite wall. Windows over the sink and in the dining alcove, hazy with their decades-old coating of grime, inside and out, failed to provide much light.

At first I blamed the dinginess on the gloomy weather outside, until I noticed the color scheme; the dark wood cabinetry, the dark-red countertops, and the ceiling that had been painted dark red to match. The wallpaper, once cream with a colorful pattern of vegetables and fruits, had been turned a dark yellowish-brown by time and cooking fumes. The overhead fixture held only one fluorescent bulb where there should have been two.

"Would you like to see the rest of the house?" Kathleen inquired as we cleaned off the table and disposed of our plates into a garbage sack on the floor.

The downstairs looked fairly clean and well-kept. Off the living room, a smaller room served as a study. It housed a massive black roll-top desk at least a hundred years old, in addition to Mrs. Merriweather's bedroom furniture. *This must be where she died*, I thought. The rumpled bedclothes were still on the bed and visibly soiled. I wrinkled my nose in distaste.

"Yuck," commented Bryan from behind me. "They could have at least changed the bed." But Kathleen appeared unperturbed, and I wondered if anyone had told her that Mrs. Merriweather had died in there. I glanced at Jodi, and she shrugged.

Dust lay thick everywhere upstairs. The wallpaper was faded, and the baseboards were crumbling. Lace curtains, once white but now discolored and disintegrating, hung at windows with sills blistered from the sun. Cobwebs festooned every corner, possibly with resident spiders.

I wondered if Kathleen actually planned to sleep there tonight and shivered at the thought. She'd need a respirator, with all that dust, unless she wanted a lung transplant in her future.

The children ran ahead down the hall. "This is gonna be our room," shouted Bobby, pointing out a smaller bedroom in which bunk beds had been shoved up against one wall and a dresser crowded a single bed against the opposite wall. "Me an' Bryan. It really sucks, huh?"

"Bobby!" admonished Kathleen. "Don't talk like that!" But privately I had to agree. The room looked no better than the master bedroom. The tall trees shading the equally filmy and cobwebby west-facing windows made it look dark and gloomy. Bryan, behind me, said, "Well, he's right, Mom. This whole house sucks. I bet it's a hundred years old. I bet it's *haunted*."

At this, Angela began to cry and clung to Megan, who said confidently, "Don't listen to Bryan, he's full of shit."

"Megan!" snapped Kathleen, almost automatically. Megan's eyes met mine and quickly slid away before I could read the expression in them, but I got the feeling that Megan, despite her bravado, wasn't too sure the house *wasn't* haunted; and I had to admit, neither was I. I kept thinking I saw movement out of the corner of my eye, but when I turned to look, nothing was there. Goose bumps rose on my arms, and I shivered.

Tiffany picked up Emily, who had also begun to show signs of distress, and said, "Let's show them our room, okay?" Emily nodded and looked happier, but their bedroom, and also the one to be shared by Megan and Angela, looked as bad as Brian's and Bobby's.

The bathrooms looked even worse, with rust-streaked sinks and blackened toilet bowls. As I noted the water stains on the ceilings, I wondered what condition the roof was in.

I suspected Mrs. Merriweather hadn't cleaned or changed or repaired anything up here since her husband died and her children moved away. She probably hadn't been able to climb stairs for years, since she'd been using the study off the living room as a bedroom.

"You guys have really got your work cut out for you," Jodi said.

"I know," Kathleen said. "Thank heavens I've got lots of helpers."

"Whatever possessed you to buy this house?" I asked. "Surely there are nicer houses you could have bought."

Kathleen took her time answering. I wondered if I'd been tactless. But if you don't ask, you don't find out.

Finally she spoke. "Jay declared bankruptcy, you know." She sighed. "Everybody knows. All the same, I'd rather not discuss my finances with someone I've just met. We're entitled to our privacy, just like everybody else. Now if you don't mind, we have a lot of work to do."

I felt as if I'd been spanked. Now I had to apologize, since we still had to be neighbors and be civil to each other. "I'm sorry, Kathleen, that was thoughtless of me."

"Oh, it's okay," she said. "I'm just irritable. This has all been so hard." Her voice quavered, and I put an arm around her and squeezed. She returned the gesture, and we all went back downstairs.

"She may not have had much choice of places she could afford," Elliott pointed out later. "Jay declared bankruptcy.

That means she and her children have to suffer the consequences."

"But don't her debts get paid automatically?" I asked.

"No, not really. What the bankruptcy court does is inventory the assets, make her sell whatever she doesn't absolutely need, and consolidate the debts.

"But surely they don't take your house!" I exclaimed.

"No, and they don't take your furniture, or your clothes, or your car. But if the house is too large and luxurious, or there are nonessential articles, they make you sell them, or they sell them for you and add the proceeds to the funds that the trustee manages."

"So," said Hal, "the bankruptcy court made her sell all her nice furniture and buy this house furnished?"

"What happens when the money runs out?" asked Jodi.

Elliott shrugged. "She'll either have to get a job or go on welfare."

"Has she ever worked?" Hal wanted to know.

"She's a legal secretary," I said, suddenly remembering. "Rebecca Sorensen said she used to be Jay's secretary before the kids were born."

"Is that so," said Elliott with interest.

"Don't you have someone who's about to go on maternity leave?" asked Jodi.

"That's what I was just thinking."

That's what it's like in a small town like ours. Neighbors and coworkers get involved in each other's lives and try to help out when problems arise.

And the Burkes had more problems than most.

Chapter 9

You can observe a lot by watching.

—Yogi Berra

That weekend was a busy one for Christmas parties.
Hal and I went home to get our Saturday chores done and get bathed and changed for the one at Jodi and Elliott's house. And then, since we felt guilty about having taken up so much of their preparation time, we went back over there to help them get ready.

People started arriving at about seven, the men in slacks and Christmas-themed sweaters and their wives dressed in a similar fashion but with lots more bling.

At these parties I was usually the only physician in a sea of lawyers. Hal, as a teacher, was neutral territory, rather like Switzerland.

There were Fritz Baumgartner, the district attorney, and his wife, Amy, and Elliott's partners: Stanley Snow and his wife, Cherie, and Russ Stevenson and his wife, Trish. Jay and Kathleen Burke had originally been invited as well, but I didn't expect to see Kathleen here under the circumstances.

However, Ruthie Brooks was here with her husband, Lance, Jay's partner. Elliott introduced us. Lance, a tall, thin stick of a man with a grayish, unsmiling, American Gothic face, gave me a limp handshake and barely acknowledged me before turning away; but Ruthie was another story. She glommed on to me and got right down to business; and it became obvious with the first words out of her mouth why she couldn't have done so at Kathleen's house earlier.

"Oooh, wasn't it *awful* about poor Jay!" she began. "He's going to be missed by *so* many people."

Like who? I wondered. *All his clients who owed their souls to the Internal Revenue Service?* But Ruthie answered that question before I had a chance to verbalize it.

"I don't know if you're aware of this, dear, but he was quite the *stepper*, you know," she continued, *sotto voce*, as she drew me away from the crowd into a corner of the living room where she could monopolize me uninterrupted. "Of course, one can't really *blame* the man, because dear Kathleen *has* rather let herself go in the last few years, you know. I don't think they've actually had sex since *Angela* was born, and the poor man had to get it *somewhere*; I mean, really, I know men have their needs, but one would think he could have used a *condom* or something and not gotten them all pregnant.

"Anyway, I can't help wondering what's going to happen to the children—I mean the *other* children, not Kathleen's, because of *course* he provided for Kathleen and their children; I'm not talking about *them*. I mean all his *other* children, you know, the ones he fathered out of wedlock, because there's *no* provision for *any* of them in his *will*, you know."

What about all those trusts, I wondered. "Are you sure?"

"Well, of *course* I'm sure," Ruthie asserted. "I should *know* what's in his will; after all, *Lance* drew it up, and Bill and I *witnessed* it, and there's nothing in it for *anyone* but Kathleen and their children. I mean, many of those women's marriages have broken up, at least those who had a child by him, except for Jodi, of course. Elliott still must not know, but really, how can he *not* know, when Cody's the *only* one who doesn't look like him, and one can't *really* expect them to pay child support for children that aren't *theirs*, can one?"

"Wait a minute. Jodi? I don't believe it," I objected. "Jodi wouldn't do that." That little accusation took my mind right off the fact that both Elliott and Lance had drawn up wills for Jay, almost before it had a chance to register.

Ruthie glanced around conspiratorially before she went on. "Well, it was a *long* time ago, but yes, Jodi too. And, you know, it's a funny thing. None of the children look *anything* like Jay. They all look like their mothers."

That made sense. Kathleen's children all looked like her. And Cody was the only one of Jodi's children that didn't look like Elliott. He was stocky and red-haired like Jodi, not slender and dark-haired like Elliott. But he had dark brown eyes. He didn't get those from Jay or Jodi; he had to have gotten them from Elliott.

I decided I would take whatever Ruthie said with an entire can of Morton's iodized salt. The giant economy size, from Costco.

Maybe a whole case. Ruthie beckoned me even closer. "You do know Lloyd Armstrong, of course? He's a *very* wealthy dairyman and has served on the State Legislature. I'm sure you've seen his picture in the paper, haven't you?"

It sounded vaguely familiar. The image of a tall, ruggedly handsome man in a western-cut jacket and Stetson hat, his deep-set eyes shaded by thick black eyebrows, came to mind. It was definitely a distinctive face.

I nodded, but Ruthie sailed on before I could open my mouth.

"Well, my dear, he's *quite* the stepper too. One is *always* running into young people that are the spittin' *image* of him. I even saw one of them in *Boise* last time we were there. You can't mistake them. But poor Jay ... why, one would think the poor man had no genes to pass on! It's almost as though he was on a *quest* to create someone in his own image; I mean, if you didn't know who the *mothers* were, you'd never suspect that the children were—"

I interrupted her. "So do you know who all the mothers are?"

Ruthie clasped her hands together and sighed ecstatically. "Well, I really *shouldn't*, you know, confidentiality and all that, I mean, Lance is *always* telling me I talk too much and might get him disbarred someday, but I can tell *you* because you're a doctor."

It seemed to me that Lance was as good as disbarred already, but I figured that I probably wasn't the first person Ruthie had told this to. I felt no qualms about encouraging her in the process. She cooperated beautifully. I couldn't wait to get away from her, run into Elliott's den for a pencil and paper, and write all the names down. I only hoped I could remember them long enough.

Counting Tiffany and Mitzi and, God help us, Jodi, there were *eleven* of them. Going back all the way to the late eighties. Rebecca Sorensen was there too. Poor Jeff, I thought.

Wait till I tell Hal. He's going to plotz.

Well, Hal didn't exactly plotz, but his reaction was much like mine when I told him what Ruthie had told me.

"Not Jodi," he said.

"Yes, Jodi," I replied. "Ruthie thinks that Cody is Jay's because he looks like Jodi instead of Elliott."

Hal saw the flaw in that right away. "Bullshit. Cody has brown eyes."

Right, I thought, and I'll bet Jodi was relieved when Cody's eyes changed color. "Ruthie says that all Jay's children look like their mothers," I continued. "She said that it was like Jay was trying to create a child in his image but didn't seem to have any genes to pass on."

At this, Hal simply shook his head. "Just wait," he said. "They'll probably all grow up to be swindlers, just like their old man."

We set about the business of getting ready for bed, and I had just settled in with a copy of the newest Dick Francis, when I heard Hal mumble something from the bathroom where he was brushing his teeth.

"What was that?" I called out.

Hal came out of the bathroom and climbed into bed next to me. "I said, do you know who else wanted to create people in his own image?"

I fell right into it. "Who?"

"God."

Well, be that as it may, I couldn't believe that my best friend had had an affair with Jay Braithwaite Burke. She's in the beauty business, for God's sake; one would think she had better taste, not to mention better sense. But she had acted a little odd when I asked what all the other women saw in him.

Not that I'd hold it against Jodi if she'd had an affair; to each his or her own. But it might give her a motive to murder Jay. So I decided that I'd ask her about it next time I got her alone. Like tomorrow, maybe.

Kathleen had been affronted when I came right out and asked her why she'd bought such an old, run-down house, but I'd just met her. Jodi was my best friend whom I'd known for thirteen years. She wouldn't be insulted.

On the other hand, if she had killed Jay, she could also kill me.

Did I need to know badly enough to take that chance?

I guessed I'd wait and see how brave I felt in the morning.

Sunday, December 14

Chapter 10

The jury, passing on the prisoner's life
May in the sworn twelve have a thief or two
Guiltier than him they try.
—Shakespeare, Measure for Measure

"A God complex," I said to Jodi the next morning. Jodi clutched her head. "A what?" she said. "And do you have to yell?"

Elliott, preparing Bloody Marys in the kitchen, didn't seem at first quite as hungover as Jodi, but from the way he avoided looking at her, one would think that the canary-yellow robe she wore hurt his eyes.

"I told Hal about all the women Ruthie said Jay had children by, and that none of them looked like Jay. Ruthie said she thought Jay kept fathering children in the hope of creating one in his own image, and Hal said it sounded like he was trying to be God."

Jodi swayed and went white. "I think I'm going to go lie down for a while. Toni, will you come and keep me company?"

It seemed like an odd request, but I shrugged, grabbed a Bloody Mary, and followed her up the stairs. I sincerely hoped she wasn't going to throw up or anything, but I needn't have worried. Jodi shut the bedroom door behind us. "Don't worry. I'm not sick. I just need to talk to you in private."

She stretched out on the king-sized bed. I put my drink on the nightstand and stretched out next to her.

Minutes passed in silence.

Finally I broke it. "What do you want to talk to me about?"

Jodi rolled over and faced me, propping her head on her hand. "Ruthie Brooks."

"What about Ruthie Brooks?"

"You don't know her, Toni, so you might be inclined to believe what she says. But you shouldn't."

"Why not?"

Jodi rolled back onto her back and stared at the ceiling. "Ruthie likes to hear herself talk. She also enjoys creating a sensation. There's nothing she likes better than being the center of attention, and she's not above making things up to suit her purposes."

"In other words," I said, "she's a gossip."

"She's a stone liar," Jodi said, her voice growing hard.

"And has she told lies about you?"

"She told one last night. I heard her."

"When?" I asked, even though I was pretty sure I knew what she was getting at.

"When she told you that I was one of Jay's paramours and that Cody was his child," she said.

"Oh, well," I said. "I know Cody is Elliott's child. He has brown eyes."

"And you know I wouldn't have an affair with the likes of Jay Braithwaite Burke, right?"

I sat up and piled pillows behind my back. "I keep telling myself that you have better taste than that."

She sat up too, and turned to face me. "Well, I do."

I picked up my drink and took a swig. "That sounds like there's a 'but' coming."

She narrowed her eyes at me. "What do you mean?"

I put my drink down. "Jodi, there's something you're not telling me."

"No, there isn't," she insisted.

"Jodi, I'm your best friend. You know I don't gossip. You can tell me the truth. In fact, I think you *need* to tell me the truth. You *did* have an affair with Jay, didn't you?"

"No, I didn't."

"Then why did you turn white and almost faint when I told you about Jay's God complex just now? Why did you get upset yesterday when I asked what all those women saw in him? If you weren't one of them, why react like that?"

Jodi rolled over on her stomach and buried her face in the pillow. Muffled sobs shook her shoulders. I reached over and rubbed her back. Finally she sat up and blew her nose. "I can't get anything past you, can I?"

I put my arms around her. "Tell me," I urged.

"Okay, okay, it's true," Jodi said. "Elliott doesn't know."

"He won't hear it from me," I assured her, "or Hal. But why? What was the attraction?"

"Oh, I know you weren't susceptible, Toni; you have Hal and all the sex you want. But Elliott and I were having problems at the time, and he hadn't touched me for weeks, and I was horny; so when Jay approached me, I thought, what the hell."

Little do you know, I thought, but even as chronically horny as I was these days, the thought of Jay Braithwaite Burke as a lover still repulsed me. Bernie Kincaid, on the other hand …

"So, was he any good?"

"It was the best sex I ever had," she confessed. "The man had a pecker the size of Texas, and he could keep going for hours. I couldn't get enough of him."

"What made you stop?"

"I got pregnant," Jodi said. "When I told Jay, he dumped me."

"*He* dumped *you*?"

"He wasn't nice about it, either," she continued, her voice growing hard. "He said that now that I was pregnant, he didn't need me anymore."

"Nice guy." I made no effort to keep the disgust out of my voice.

"Elliott was delighted, though. About the baby, I mean, not Jay. So I spent the next nine months wondering whose child I was carrying. Can I have a sip?"

I offered her my glass, and she took a huge swig. "Wait a minute, I thought you said …"

She handed the glass back. "Thanks. I know what I said. But one night we went out dancing at the country club with Stan and Cherie, and Russ and Trish, and it was so romantic that when we got home we—"

"Oh."

"Then, when Cody was born, he looked like me instead of Elliott and the other kids, so I still didn't know whose he was until his eyes changed color."

Just as I'd thought. "What an ordeal," I said. "We were friends back then; why didn't you talk to me?"

Jodi shrugged. "You and Hal had only been here a couple of years back then, and I didn't know you that well. I do now, though. I'm talking to you now, aren't I?"

She certainly was, I had to admit.

I went downstairs shortly after that, leaving my drink for Jodi, so I had to get Elliott to make me another one.

"Is Jodi okay?" he asked.

"Yup. She's getting dressed."

"Good," he said.

Hal came into the kitchen. "We were just talking about wills," he said. "I told Elliott that Lance had done a will for Jay too."

"Hmm," I said. "Which one is the real one?"

"That's a good question," Elliott said. "I wasn't aware of another will. That's fairly important. If there's another will, it could turn the whole freakin' thing upside down. I'll call Lance tomorrow. Did you hear anything else I should know about?"

We hadn't, but Jodi and I weren't about to wait for Elliott to contact Lance on Monday. We went to Jim Bob's and got a box of doughnuts and made our second visit to Kathleen's house.

"We have to ask her about filling in for Betsy anyway," Jodi rationalized.

When Jodi asked Kathleen why Jay had two wills, she looked confused. "I don't know," she said, shrugging. "I had no idea. He didn't tell me. It was a simple enough will. He just left everything to me and the children. What's so complicated about that? Why would he need two wills?"

Jodi and I looked at each other. Now *we* were confused. Kathleen gazed wide-eyed at each of us in turn and said, "What's the matter? Is something wrong?"

I shrugged helplessly. What could I say? If Kathleen didn't know about all those trusts, I wasn't about to be the one to break it to her, especially after pissing her off yesterday. Jodi came to my rescue.

"Elliott said it was a very complicated will," she explained. "But I don't know the details. Maybe you'd better talk to him. And speaking of which," she went on, smoothly and skillfully steering us out of rocky shoals, "Elliott has a secretary that's about to go on maternity leave, and he was wondering if you'd be available to fill in for her? I heard somewhere that you used to be a legal secretary, am I right?"

"Yes," Kathleen said. "I worked for Jay before the kids came along. Why?"

"Would you be interested in working for Elliott?"

"That would be great," Kathleen said. "There's not much money left after the bankruptcy, and I was wondering what we were going to do, with Christmas coming up."

"Perfect," Jodi said. "I'll tell him."

Elliott was jubilant at the news. "I wish everything was that freakin' easy," he said. "So what did she say about Jay's will?"

He and Hal had been outside in the backyard splitting logs for firewood and were only too happy to come back into the warm kitchen for some hot cocoa, which they laced generously with peppermint schnapps, creating something called a Peppermint Patty. By now we'd had so many hairs-of-the-dog that I didn't know whether we were curing our hangovers or just postponing them until the next day.

"Apparently she doesn't know about all those trusts," Jodi commented. "And I wasn't about to tell her."

"We still don't know which one is the legal will, either," I pointed out. "Isn't it supposed to be the most recent one?"

"I don't know," Jodi said. "Elliott's is the most recent, I'm almost sure of it, because he did it just a few months ago, didn't you, honey? I remember you grousing about it even back then. When did Lance do his?"

"At least ten years ago," I said. "Ruthie said that she and Bill Bartlett were the witnesses." And when I said that, another thought came to mind. "Hey, was Ruthie working in that office back then?"

Jodi looked thoughtful. "I think so. Yeah, she did, because she worked for Lance before he joined Jay's firm. Why?"

"Was she there at the same time as Kathleen?"

"I'm not sure," Jodi said. "I think Kathleen quit when Bryan was born. That's probably when Jay made that will."

"I wonder if she knows anything," I mused. "Maybe the cops should talk to her when they talk to all those other women Jay had children with."

"If they can find them," Jodi said. "I'm pretty sure some of these gals on the list have left the area and have probably remarried by now."

"So anyway," I said, "the will Elliott drew up last summer should be the legal will, right?"

"Unless there were extenuating circumstances," Elliott said. "As far as I recall, Jay was of sound mind and not under any duress when he made that will, so it should be the legal will."

"So, if that will is the motive for Jay's murder, we've got a choice between Kathleen and any one of eleven other women," I said.

"Jesus," Jodi said. "It sounds like *Murder on the Orient Express*. You don't suppose all twelve of them were in cahoots, do you?"

"I doubt it," Hal said. "Most of them don't live here anymore, and I imagine most, if not all of them, have remarried and are no longer eligible to inherit."

"Unless they know they're in Jay's will," I argued. "Maybe they all stayed single so they could inherit."

"In that case, they'd have to have known how much money Jay had and how much they stood to inherit," Hal argued back. "It'd have to be a pretty significant amount for a single mother to stay single on purpose, wouldn't you think?"

"I wonder if they know that Jay declared bankruptcy and that there's supposedly nothing to inherit," Jodi said.

"I wonder if they know he's dead," I countered.

"If they still keep in touch with friends from Twin Falls or read the *Clarion* online, they do," Elliott said sourly. "They're probably gonna start coming out of the freakin' woodwork now."

Maybe. I wasn't so sure. Jay might possibly have reassured them that they and their children by him would be taken care of in case of divorce, but what if they had other children? Jay's money wouldn't do anything for them. Not much of a motivation to stay single, unless Jay had been dumb enough to tell them all how much money he had.

And did any of them know about the others? So far, that information had not been made public. And if it was made public, would any of them be moved to eliminate the competition by systematically killing off the others?

Especially if one of them had murdered Jay in the first place to get at his fortune. If that were the case, that person would also have to eliminate Kathleen and her children too. Which brought up, oh God, the children. That person would also have to eliminate the children.

Elliott was right. It would be a freakin' hell of a mess.

I fervently hoped the police would have the sense to keep the terms of Jay's will to themselves.

I sincerely did not want to have to deal with the kind of person who would systematically kill off eleven other women and their children for money.

Such a person would not hesitate to kill off Jodi or me, should we get too close; and I knew we *would* get close. Snooping seemed to be embedded in our DNA. We couldn't help it; we just had to *know*.

Curiosity killed the cat.

Nice kitty. Pretty kitty. Here, kitty-kitty. Here's a nice treat.

I shivered.

Monday, December 15

Chapter 11

Accidents will occur in the best-regulated families.
—Charles Dickens

At four o'clock Monday morning by the illuminated dial of my trusty clock radio, the frantic ringing of the doorbell and pounding on the door woke us from a sound sleep.

The dogs leaped off the bed and raced downstairs, barking. Hal went downstairs, and I burrowed under the covers—but not for long. I heard voices and children crying, and Hal hollered at me to get myself downstairs, posthaste. I jumped into my old black sweats and went downstairs to pandemonium.

Kathleen and the children huddled in a forlorn little group in the living room, wearing coats over pajamas. Kathleen, with her arms around Megan and Angela, was crying, and so were the children, except for Bryan, who was tight-lipped and white. Tiffany carried Emily, who sucked her thumb. A sad little pile of personal belongings sat on the floor by the door, consisting of assorted clothing, stuffed animals, and school backpacks.

Halfway down the stairs, I caught sight of the living room window framing the horrifying spectacle of the old house across the street in flames. Plumes of smoke billowed from the upstairs windows, while the downstairs windows glowed with an unearthly orange light. Flames shot out of the open front door. As I looked, the dry, skeletal branches of the trees overhanging the roof caught fire. This was going fast.

Hal called the fire department. I didn't think they'd be able to save it, but they might prevent it from spreading to any other houses.

I went to the kitchen and made coffee. Hal built a fire in the fireplace.

The fire trucks arrived almost immediately, sirens screaming. Two police cars and an ambulance followed. Everybody went out on the porch to watch, except me. I prepared a thermos of hot chocolate for the children and gave them Styrofoam cups and then poured cups of coffee for the adults, who were all out on the porch watching. I stayed there myself for a few minutes, until I got too cold; then I went back inside and settled myself in a chair by the window with my coffee to watch in relative comfort.

What next? What else would that poor family have to cope with? They'd lost their husband and father. Gone bankrupt. Had to sell their luxurious home and move into that old firetrap. And now the old firetrap was on fire. What would they do now? Where would they go? How did it happen? Was it an accident?

Or was it part of the mystery that seemed to shroud the Burke family with an aura of tragedy? It was beginning to sound like one of those Russian novels where everybody loses everything in the revolution and has to cram themselves into squalid apartments together, forty-seven people to a room.

The house was a total loss. When the sun came up and the fire trucks were gone, only a smoking shell remained. The Maynard children, bless their hearts, came over and diverted the Burke children with a boisterous game of Monopoly on the kitchen table. Jodi came over too, but Kathleen seemed to have vanished, and I asked Jodi where she'd disappeared to.

"Work," Jodi said. "I sent her over to my house to get some clothes to wear. Luckily we're the same size."

Elliott had wasted no time, having interviewed Kathleen on Sunday afternoon. Betsy, Elliott's terminally pregnant secretary, would orient her to the job during the coming week.

I tried to imagine going off to work, my second day on a new job, straight from having my house burn down, wearing somebody else's clothes. I failed. Kathleen really *was* a better person than I could ever be, I decided.

What a mess. And I had to go to work too. Hal could deal with it.

He was off because school was out at the college. But I wasn't in school anymore, so Christmas didn't mean vacation to me and hadn't for years; but I still felt cheated. Just another blow to the magic of the season, to my mind.

My fellow physicians always took a week off for the holidays, but they could cover each other. Back when I was a solo pathologist, I didn't have that luxury. I'd try to work half-days, preferably mornings; but somebody always managed to have a frozen section or something in the afternoon that would require me to be present. So that didn't work either.

But now that I had a partner, I could have an actual Christmas vacation. We had arranged for me to have the week before Christmas off, and Mike the week after. This meant that in only a week, I would actually have a week off. I could hardly wait.

We had the same workload we always had during the holidays: brutal. All the patients had met their deductibles and had scheduled all their elective surgeries before the end of the year.

Also, for some inexplicable reason, we always seemed to get a raft of big, ugly cancer cases at this time of year that presented as emergencies: bowel obstructions, GI bleeds, acute abdomens, you name it. They tended to go to surgery in the middle of the night, which required us to deal with unprepped bowel resections full of you-know-what.

Mike and I would earn our time off, by God.

Since I wasn't on call, I decided to do a little detective work while waiting for my slides.

The electronic medical record revealed that Jay Braithwaite Burke had been our patient. According to his computerized chart, he'd had a long history of deep vein thrombosis—blood clots—and anticoagulant therapy with Coumadin, the most commonly used drug for preventing blood clots. He'd had a completely normal treadmill stress test only six months ago, which was amazing, considering the degree of atherosclerosis I'd found at autopsy. If he hadn't been on Coumadin and cholesterol-lowering Lipitor all that time, he would have died of a heart attack a long time ago.

Or a stroke. He'd had his last prothrombin time, which was within the therapeutic range, on October 31st. Halloween. How fitting—blood-sucking vampires, and all that.

Phlebotomists, those lab personnel whose job it was to draw blood from patients, have been called vampires since the beginning of time. Maybe even before that. It was a cliché so ancient that it had cobwebs on it. But back in the day when I used to draw blood, patients would gleefully tell me, "You know what I call you guys? Vampires!" as if they thought they were the first ones to think of it. I would just smile politely and try really hard not to do an eye-roll.

Jay's former physician, the late Tyler Cabot, MD, had diagnosed him with antithrombin III deficiency, a condition that predisposed him to blood clots, and had placed him on a fairly high dose of Coumadin, a dose usually recommended for patients with prosthetic heart valves. Tyler's replacement, Jeannie Tracy, MD, had maintained him on that dose.

However, I'd ordered lab tests on his postmortem blood to show his prothrombin time and INR, International Normalized Ratio, which made it possible to compare prothrombin times from different labs using different reagents. Jay's were higher than the high end of the therapeutic range, but not by much, so an overdose of Coumadin was probably not the reason for all that bleeding. He'd had severe anemia when he died, though—probably from blood loss—but he had normal platelets and no evidence of leukemia.

Jeannie Tracy, a thirty-five-year-old, petite platinum blonde, had a much more cordial relationship with the lab and with me than had her predecessor. So I had no qualms about wandering down to her office for a little chat, with a courtesy copy of my preliminary report.

Jeannie had no idea how lucky she was to be here at all. After the fallout from that female surgeon who got murdered three years ago, our gastroenterologist and staff curmudgeon, George Marshall, would repeatedly tell me that it was a good thing Mitzi and I had gotten on staff before she had.

"It may be the twenty-first century," he would declaim, "but there are still a lot of chauvinists on this medical staff, by God, and it's going to be a cold day in hell before another female physician gets in!" He did this while pointing a long, gnarly finger in my face for emphasis, while I resisted the urge to bite it off.

But blue-eyed Jeannie had charmed even crusty old George.

While she finished up with her patient, I ensconced myself in the soft desk chair that she had upholstered in a delicate floral fabric. I admired the Christmas wreath on her door, made of flocked Scotch pine boughs and decorated with ribbons and ornaments in shades of blue and silver, while aimlessly leafing through the latest issue of the *New England Journal of Medicine.*

I didn't have to wait long. Jeannie never moved at less than a dead run. After barely five minutes, I heard the pitter-patter of her tiny feet, and she appeared in the doorway.

"Toni! What a surprise. Do you covet my chair?"

"No, I covet your wreath."

"Do you want one? Donna makes them. I could ask her for you. Want me to?"

Donna Foster, formerly the late Tyler Cabot's office nurse, had been overjoyed to be assigned to Jeannie, because she had missed seeing all her old patients. I suspect she found Jeannie a lot easier to work for too.

I handed her the autopsy report and vacated her chair. "I thought you might be interested in this," I told her.

"Oh, thanks," she said, already reading it as she sank into her chair. "Jesus, Mary, and Joseph!"

Sweet, soft-spoken Jeannie looked like Tinker Bell but cursed nearly as fluently as I did.

"Damn," she continued. "This guy was a walking time bomb."

"Exactly my thought," I said.

"I hate to think what would have happened if he hadn't been on Coumadin. Only maybe he was on too much Coumadin, by the looks of this. Do you think … oh, crap … do you think I had him on too high a dose? Because his pro times have all been just fine …"

"No, no, of course not," I reassured her. "He was murdered. If he overdosed, it wasn't on Coumadin. His postmortem INR was not that much above the therapeutic range. This is just an FYI, because he was your patient."

"Well, I'm glad it wasn't anything I did," she said, looking perplexed, "but if it wasn't Coumadin, what was it?"

"Good question. Maybe I ought to get some more tests done," I said. "Was he anything more than just a patient to you?"

Jeannie frowned. "What do you mean?"

"Did you ever get into that Ponzi scheme of his?"

She sighed. "I'm afraid so," she said. "Stupid me. Luckily I haven't been here long enough to lose as much as some of the other docs."

"Did you associate with him socially?"

"Absolutely not," Jeannie said. "You know, maybe I shouldn't say this, now that he's dead, and don't tell anybody I said so, but he wasn't exactly my favorite patient. He struck me as kind of a sleazeball. Quite frankly, he gave me the creeps."

"But you got into that Ponzi scheme of his anyway? Why?"

She dropped her eyes. "Well, he just made it sound so good," she said.

Now I was going to have to piss her off. "I heard that he had affairs with a lot of the doctors' wives and got them pregnant," I said.

Jeannie suddenly got very busy with some papers on her desk. "Really," she said.

"Yes, really. I was just wondering if he limited his activities to doctors' wives, or if he included doctors as well."

Jeannie picked up a chart and flipped it open. "I really need to put a note in here before I forget something," she said.

I refused to take the hint. "Did he ever hit on you?"

Jeannie slapped the chart shut. "Toni, why are you asking me all these questions?"

"Did you have an affair with him?" I persisted.

Jeannie drew herself up to her full height of five-foot-two and came around her desk to face me. "This conversation is over. Was there anything else?"

"No. I'm sorry, Jeannie. I didn't mean to be rude," I said. "But the man was murdered, and I did the autopsy, and I feel obligated to try to figure out who might have had a motive to kill him, that's all."

She put her hands on her hips. "Well, I lost money, but as far as having an affair ... Toni, do you realize what it could do to my career if there was the slightest suggestion that I might have had an affair with a *patient*? I could lose my license!"

Oops. I hadn't thought of that. "Well, don't worry about me," I said. "This won't go any further."

She seemed mollified. "I just wish I'd been as smart as you were and had nothing to do with him."

"Well, I wasn't that smart, either. I let him put me into a personal corporation, but as far as the hedge fund was concerned, no, I never got into it."

She rolled her eyes. "Oh, yeah, don't I know it," she said. "I've heard all about it. Your name has come up a number of times. Jack Allen seems a bit put out that you never said anything at the time."

"I did. They didn't listen," I pointed out.

I let her get back to her patients. I'd found out all I could from Jeannie. She hadn't come right out and denied having an affair. She also hadn't admitted having one. She'd just expressed fear that somebody might report her to the State Board of Medicine. Was she protesting too much? Maybe not. She had a lot more at stake than any doctor's wife. Having sex with a patient was a huge no-no in the Idaho Medical Practice Act, and her license could be jeopardized if it came to the attention of the Idaho State Board of Medicine. It could destroy her career if it ever got out. So she might have had one; all I knew for sure was that she hadn't had a child by Jay, or anyone else, for that matter.

Unless she was pregnant right now. But I decided against going back and asking her that. I could look her up in the computer. If she'd had a pregnancy test done here, it would be in there. Jay'd been out of the area for two months, so Jeannie's affair, assuming there was one, would have had to be pretty recent for her to be pregnant and not showing.

Apart from any other considerations, it might have been a handy little tool for blackmail, for someone who knew. And blackmail is a dandy motive for murder.

Ruthie hadn't mentioned Jeannie as one of Jay's love interests, but that didn't mean she hadn't been one. Maybe Ruthie didn't know. I sincerely hoped not. If she did, it'd be all over town so fast the dust would fly. People would have to hold on to their hats. Still, that would really screw up anybody who might want to use the information for blackmail.

Maybe that could be a motive for murdering Ruthie, just to shut her up.

I found Mitzi Okamoto in her darkened office, looking at films, dictating reports, and eating a candy bar. I had to stifle the urge to slap her silly. I gain five pounds if I just *look* at a candy bar, and she eats them all the time and never gains an ounce.

Mitzi's grandparents, originally from California, had been interned during the war in the Hunt camp at Minidoka. Mitzi's father had been born there. After the war, they settled in Jerome and farmed. Mitzi went to the

University of Washington on the WAMI program, did her residency there, came home to practice, and married her husband, Dave McClure, a CPA, the next year.

They had two children, ten-year-old Jeremy and the baby Stephanie, who may or may not have been Dave's. You certainly couldn't tell by looking at the children, because both of them looked just like Mitzi.

But in any case, Mitzi and Dave were now divorced.

I leaned on the doorjamb until she looked up and saw me.

"Hi," she greeted me, brandishing the candy bar. "Want a bite?"

I refused the candy bar, but accepted the implicit invitation to come in and chat. Mitzi and I—friends but never close—still felt comfortable enough to visit each other's offices from time to time. However, getting information from her now might be problematic, since I wasn't supposed to know about the trusts.

"You missed a good party the other night," I began. "How come?"

"I just didn't feel like it," she said. "I figured everybody would be talking about Jay Braithwaite Burke, and I just didn't want to hear it."

"You figured right," I said. "The boys were all talking about the money they lost, and the girls were all talking about his wife and his four kids. They said that she was divorcing him because she'd caught him in bed with his secretary, and that now the secretary has moved in with his wife and is helping her with the kids. Isn't that weird?"

A spasm of pain briefly crossed Mitzi's normally impassive countenance, but she said nothing.

"That's not all I heard," I went on. "Care to know what else I heard?"

Mitzi's eyes narrowed, but she still said nothing. This was going to be like pulling teeth. Mitzi was so self-contained that her facial expressions rarely gave the slightest clue to what she was feeling. She would be a much tougher nut to crack than Jodi or Jeannie had been.

"I heard that Jay had affairs with a whole lot of doctors' wives," I said. "And also some doctors. Know what that means?"

Mitzi got up and closed the door to her office, came back, and sat down. "We shouldn't be discussing this here where people can hear."

"Definitely not," I agreed.

Mitzi ran her fingers through her short black hair until it stood on end. I had never seen the normally unflappable Mitzi quite so upset. For her, this bordered on hysteria.

I helped her out. "How much money did you lose?"

"Seven hundred and fifty thousand," she replied, eyes downcast. "And I owe the IRS almost that much. How could I be so stupid?"

"You? Didn't Dave have anything to say about this? You didn't get into this alone, did you?"

"Well, no, of course not. Dave went along with it too."

"So did everybody else," I pointed out. "You were in good company."

"I don't know what possessed me," she said. "It was like he hypnotized me or something. I couldn't help myself. Now I cringe just thinking about it. I'm so ashamed."

I knew that the loss of all that money had not upset Mitzi so much as the loss of her self-respect. "Mitzi. You're not the first woman to have an affair, and you won't be the last."

Mitzi stiffened. "What makes you think I had an affair? Just how stupid do you think I am?"

Oops. Between Jeannie and Mitzi, I had my foot so far down my throat that I would have to hop back to my office. What could I say? I certainly couldn't tell her that she and Stephanie were in Jay's will. I couldn't betray Elliott's trust that way. "So, you're crying for the money you lost?"

She wiped her eyes. "Well, it was a hell of a lot of money," she said.

"Come on, Mitzi. You got pregnant and Dave divorced you. It doesn't take a rocket scientist to figure out what the connection is."

She turned away. "Toni, why are you bugging me like this? It's none of your business."

"It is too. I did the autopsy. The man was murdered. How does that make it not my business?"

She got up and began to pace, something I couldn't do in my office; it was way too small. "Toni, please, stop this."

"I will if you tell me the truth," I said. "I promise you it won't go any further. I don't gossip. Come on, tell me. Stephanie is Jay's child, isn't she?"

Mitzi stopped pacing. "Okay, yes, she is. Are you happy now?"

"And Dave knew?"

"Yes, that's why he divorced me."

"How could he be so sure? Did you have a paternity test?"

Mitzi laughed bitterly. "How do you think? We hadn't had sex in a year. There was no way it could be Dave's."

And maybe that made you vulnerable too, I thought. Just like Jodi.

Maybe all Jay's conquests had the same problem. I thought it was just me. But that wasn't enough to make me stoop to have an affair with Jay Braithwaite Burke.

Do all married men get tired of sex with their wives? I wondered. Someone should put out a bulletin. After all, it could get them killed.

Which brought another thought to mind. When a man gets killed for fooling around with a married woman, who's the usual suspect?

The husband, that's who.

Which meant that Dave could have a motive, too.

And if Dave had a motive, what about all the other cuckolded husbands? All those doctors?

Wow. The same demographic that had lost their shirts courtesy of Jay Braithwaite Burke, had also been cuckolded by Jay Braithwaite Burke. It was insult to injury—a murderous mix, to be sure. Follow the money and *cherchez la femme*, all wrapped up in one neat, deadly little package.

"Mitzi, where is Dave now?" I asked.

"Up in Sun Valley," she said. "He got the condo in the divorce. As an accountant, he can work anywhere."

I didn't know Dave very well, having only met him briefly a few times at hospital parties. "So how's he doing up there?"

"Pretty good," she said. "He's got plenty of clients, and he just remarried a couple of weeks ago. She's already pregnant."

If Dave had ever had a motive to begin with, he'd probably already forgotten about it, with a healthy business, a new wife, and a baby on the way. Or maybe the girl had used the pregnancy to force Dave to marry her, and he might be more pissed off than ever. Maybe that baby wasn't his, either. Wouldn't it be poetic justice if it was Jay's?

But it probably wasn't. Not unless Dave's new wife had been previously married to a doctor who was in Jay's Ponzi scheme. Not impossible.

Maybe that was why Mitzi and Dave hadn't had sex in a year. Maybe Dave had already been fooling around with his new love, and Mitzi's pregnancy just gave him an excuse to divorce her and make it look like her fault.

Jesus. What if Hal was messing around with a student and got her pregnant? He wouldn't be that dumb. Or would he? If he was thinking with his dick, maybe he would.

I resolutely pushed that thought out of my mind. "Does Dave have a temper?" I asked. "Was he ever abusive to you or the kids?"

"Dave?" Mitzi seemed surprised. "Oh, no. No way. He was a teddy bear." Her eyes filled with tears again. "I really miss him, Toni. I really do. I really loved him. Don't get me wrong; I wouldn't give up Stephanie for anything. But I sure wish I'd never met that slime Jay Braithwaite Burke. Murder was too good for him!"

Whoa. That was more emotion than I'd ever seen from Mitzi in the entire thirteen years I'd known her.

It occurred to me that if Dave had just gotten married, he might possibly have been on his honeymoon at the time Jay was murdered and would therefore have an alibi.

It would be easy enough to check. All I had to do was Google him, get his office number, and then call and get the information from his receptionist.

I needed to make a list.

Number one: check Dave's alibi.

Number two: check Jeannie's medical chart and see if she's had a pregnancy test lately.

Chapter 12

A jest's prosperity lies in the ear
Of him that hears it, never the tongue
Of him that makes it.
—Shakespeare, *Love's Labour Lost*

By the time I'd finished talking to Jeannie and Mitzi, it was nearly ten o'clock, which was not good. On the other hand, my slides were all done, and so were my typed gross descriptions from the day before.

So I shut myself in my office without speaking to anyone, put my phone on hold so that Mike would get all the calls, and plowed through the whole stack in about two hours. By then it was lunch time.

Normally Hal would walk over from the house to have lunch with me in the hospital cafeteria, but now ...

As if my thoughts had conjured him out of thin air, Hal appeared in the doorway of my office as though nothing had happened. "Ready for lunch?"

We went to the cafeteria, where they had my favorite dessert: hot blueberry cobbler with ice cream on it. I didn't have much appetite, but I knew that if I didn't have a blueberry cobbler, Hal would ask questions, and I didn't want to answer them in the cafeteria with everybody listening. So while he devoured a huge salad, a French dip sandwich, and his own blueberry cobbler with ice cream on it, I picked at mine as the ice cream melted into a soggy purple puddle in my bowl. Hal didn't seem to notice.

"How was your morning, sweetie?" he asked between bites.

I poked listlessly at my ice cream. "Oh, fine," I said. "I wasn't expecting you to come for lunch today."

"Why not? I'm on vacation, remember? Why shouldn't I come have lunch with my wife? I thought that would please you," he said.

"Oh, it does, it does," I assured him.

"Toni," he looked at me severely, "you're a terrible liar. Something's bothering you, and I want to know what."

Why the hell do you expect me to tell you, when you won't tell me? "I would tell you," I said, "but not here."

"Then we'll talk about it tonight," he said, "when you get home. You're not sick, are you?" he asked, as if it had just occurred to him.

Yes, I am sick. Sick at heart. "Never felt better," I assured him.

When we finished, he kissed me good-bye and headed home across Montana Street, while I went back to my office.

On the way, I was waylaid in the hall by Marilyn Sanders, a nurse who used to work in the emergency room at the hospital and now taught in the nursing program at the college. She patted my arm and said, "Nice to see you two back together again."

"Thanks," I replied automatically, and then it hit me what she'd just said. "Wait a minute. What do you mean, back together again?"

Her eyes grew round, and she put her hand to her mouth. "Oops. Oh, dear. I just put my foot in it, didn't I?"

"I'll decide that after you tell me what in hell you're talking about," I said, trying to stay calm and keep my voice down. "Come on; let's get out of the hall."

In my office, Marilyn apologized for upsetting me. "I have a noon class at the college," she told me. "Sometimes I see your husband with a young woman. She's almost as tall as he is, and slender, and she has gorgeous, long, blonde hair almost to her waist."

Oh goody. The exact opposite of me in every way. Another Rebecca.

"I think she's a student," Marilyn said. "She's not in the nursing program, though, so I don't know who she is. He eats lunch with her fairly often, and I've seen him kiss her. I came to the obvious conclusion. I guess I was wrong. I'm sorry."

"Kiss her how?" I demanded.

Marilyn seemed unsure as to how to answer that. "Oh, I don't know, on the cheek, on the lips, you know."

"Does he kiss her like a lover or like a friend?"

"Oh, like a friend, definitely," Marilyn said too quickly, not meeting my eyes.

Translation: like a lover, but I'm not gonna tell you that. "How long has this been going on?"

"Since school started in August. I'm so sorry, Doctor. I wouldn't have said anything, but I thought you knew."

The wife is always the last to know. So I was right. Just a little late. The timing fits, I reflected. That's just about how long he's been unlike himself. How blind could I be? He might as well have been wearing a sign.

"I think I know who that must be, and it's quite all right," I lied. "Thanks for telling me, though."

Now how in the hell was I going to get through the rest of the day? Sitting at my desk, I put my head in my hands, groaned dismally, and then jumped when Lucille, my senior histotech, picked just that moment to come into my office with a tray of Pap smears.

"What's the matter, Doctor?" she asked with concern. "Are you okay?"

I told her I had a headache, which wasn't too far from the truth.

"That's too bad," she said. "Maybe you oughtta go home. I know sometimes when I get headaches, I have to." Lucille had good reason for headaches; three years ago she had suffered a head injury that nearly killed her. It took six months of rehab before she could come back to work.

"Oh, it isn't *that* bad," I assured her, and she went away.

By now all the pathology reports were typed and on my desk, so I could just sign them and go home, which I did. The walk gave me a chance to think about what to do next, now that my suspicions had been confirmed. Should I act normal? Confront him? Try to get him back? Did I want him back, under the circumstances? Should I divorce him? Would he want to divorce me? If he asked me to forgive him, should I?

Wait a minute. What was I thinking? Why was I beating myself up because Hal wanted to have an affair?

Why should he get to have all the fun? Why, the next time Bernie Kincaid comes on to me, by golly, I just might …

By this time I was home, and Hal wasn't. Big surprise. I had no idea what I would do when he got home, or *if* he got home.

Maybe I should talk to my mother, I thought. Why, I don't really know, since Mum has no experience with this sort of thing, never having had her husband be unfaithful to her or ever having been divorced. My father had been killed shortly after they were married, and she had never remarried. So, actually, I had more experience with marriage than she had, for what it was worth, which was apparently not much.

But she was my mother, and she did have seventeen years on me, and she loved me. And she had simply oodles of common sense. But as I reached for the phone, I saw that Hal had left me a note saying that he was next door and to come over as soon as I got home.

Hmmm. That was all it said. It didn't say why. Well, I needed to talk to my mother, and the son of a bitch could just wait.

"Darling," my mother greeted me. "To what do I owe the pleasure of your call? Is everything all right?"

Should I lead into it gradually, or just dump it on her? Oh, to hell with it. "Hal's having an affair," I said.

"Are you sure, kitten?"

"Pretty much," I said. "An acquaintance told me today that she'd seen him on campus with a young blonde who may or may not be a student, and she's seen him kiss her."

"Kiss her how?"

That's what I said. Is this telepathy or genetics? "She said on the cheek, on the lips, and when I asked her if he kissed her like a friend or like a lover, she said like a friend, but she was lying."

"Why do you assume she was lying, kitten? Why couldn't she have been telling the truth?"

I sighed. Mum just wasn't getting it. "Because she started out by saying it was good to see Hal and me back together again, and then she backpedaled all over the place when she realized I didn't know what she was talking about. She thought I knew."

"And what did Hal say when you asked him about it? Because of course you have. One doesn't go around accusing one's husband without more to go on than somebody's casual observation, dear, now does one?"

Oh, wouldn't I? "Mum, whose side are you on here?" I said. "If I ask Hal, he's just going to blow me off. Ask me how I know that. It's because he's been blowing me off for at least three months already, ever since school started."

"Darling, are you telling me that he's been having an affair since school started and you're just now telling me?"

With growing exasperation, I said, "No, Mum, I just found out today. But he's been acting strange since about when school started, which makes sense if this has been going on that long, and Marilyn says that it has been."

"And in what way is he acting strange, dear?" my mother asked.

"He's been distant, preoccupied, and he gets pissed off at things that never used to bother him before," I told her, "and we hardly ever have sex anymore."

"Does he work late a lot, or seem to have more meetings at night, or go places on weekends without you? Does he take more showers or use a different aftershave, like he wants to make himself attractive to someone other than you?"

"No," I said. "I mean, he showers in the morning before he goes to work, which he's always done, and he uses the same aftershave he's used ever since I've known him, and he doesn't go out at night or on weekends at all. But then, if he's having an affair with someone at the college, he wouldn't need to."

"You don't think so, dear?" Mum asked. "I should think that if Hal were having an affair, he would want to spend every possible moment with his new love. He did with you, as I remember. Wouldn't you, if you had a new love?"

Well, I guessed I would. I hadn't thought of it that way. Perhaps Mum had a point. But if I didn't argue with her, she'd think I was sick. "So why is he acting all preoccupied? Why don't we have sex anymore? There's *something* going on, Mum. What else could it be?"

"Any number of things, kitten. Perhaps there are problems at the college. Perhaps he's having problems with a class, a student, a coworker. Perhaps there's some policy change that he objects to. Or maybe he's ill. Had you thought of that?"

"Actually, I did think of that," I said. "But why couldn't he tell me about it? If he's having problems at work, why can't he tell me about that? I ask him what's bothering him, and he tells me there's nothing, and to get off his case. I figured that an affair would be the one thing he couldn't tell me about, and then today when

Marilyn told me ..." At this point I burst into tears and couldn't finish.

"Darling child," my mother said, "I don't think you need to worry about your Hal. Whatever is bothering him, he'll tell you about it when the time is right, and perhaps you should stop nagging him about it. But I do think you need an awful lot more to go on than you have now, to accuse him of having an affair, dear. Oh, I don't mean you shouldn't ask him, but if he says he's not, just let it go at that until you have more evidence."

I blew my nose. "I'll try," I said, "but it's not going to be easy, you know."

"No, kitten," Mum agreed. "These things never are. Do you want me to come?"

Oh, God, do I. But I'm a big girl now, right? Right? "Oh, no, Mum, you don't need to. I'll be okay."

"Okay, kitten. But if you change your mind, let me know and I'll be there posthaste."

After exchanging I-love-yous, we hung up.

Instantly, the phone rang again.

How rude, I thought. Here I was, all weepy and emotional, and I was supposed to deal with some telemarketer as if everything was all right? To hell with that. Whoever it was could just leave a message or call back. I'd deal with whatever it was when I was good and ready and not before.

I let the phone ring until the answering machine picked it up. Hal's voice said, "Hi, honey, it's me. I guess you're not home yet. I left you a note, but in case you don't see it, I'm next door at Jodi and Elliott's. All hell's broken loose. Get over here as soon as you can, okay? Please? See you then. Bye."

Chapter 13

The supreme happiness of life is the conviction that we are loved.
—Victor Hugo

It was the "please" that did it.

When I went next door, I had to ring the doorbell several times before anybody answered. It was Hal himself who finally answered the door. The household was in an uproar. The kids were fighting over the TV remote. They had the volume up so high that I couldn't hear myself think. Kathleen was screaming into the phone, her opposite ear plugged with a finger.

"Where the hell have you been?" he shouted over the din.

"I was talking to my mother," I yelled back. "Anything wrong with that?"

"I've been waiting for an hour. What did your mother want?"

"Nothing. I called her."

"Didn't you see my note?"

"I saw it. I didn't know there was any big rush. So what's the big deal?"

"Tiffany's in the hospital. So's her boss, Lance Brooks. Smoke inhalation. The office burned down."

Well, *that* stopped me in sarcastic midstream. "No shit."

"The office burned to the ground," he said. "Didn't you hear the sirens? The fire trucks had to go right by the hospital."

Obviously I was too busy all day obsessing over my marriage to notice. "Hello. I work in a hospital. There are sirens all the time. Why should I have noticed *those* particular sirens?"

"Because the fire trucks have a different siren, as you know very well. Why are you being so bitchy?"

"That's what we're going to discuss at home," I said. "Any time you're ready. I'll see you there." Then I turned and walked out the door, ignoring Hal, who called after me. "Toni! Come back here!"

So, I thought as I sprinted back across the lawn, Burke, Braithwaite, Burke, Bartlett, and Brooks—the five Bs—was no more. Now it was in the hands of the arson investigators at the fire department.

Unlike Elliott and his partners, whose office was in a bank building, Jay and Lance had their offices in a converted house.

It took Hal barely two minutes to make his farewells and follow me home. When he threw the front door open, I was waiting with my arms crossed defiantly.

"Toni, what the hell is this all about? You do realize we've got another party to go to, and it's already six-thirty. We have to be down at the country club in half an hour."

I felt no obligation to put in an appearance at this party, which was the faculty party for the college. Hal could go by himself for all I cared, or at least that's what I told myself. Whether or not I believed it was another matter. "Fine. If you think your party is more important than our marriage, go ahead." I turned and walked into the kitchen, where I got a clean glass out of the dishwasher and prepared to pour myself a scotch.

He followed me and grabbed my arm so roughly that I nearly dropped the glass. "What the hell are you talking about? What *about* our marriage?"

I put the glass down and faced him. "Marilyn Sanders talked to me today after lunch. You remember Marilyn, don't you? She worked for Dr. Shore. She teaches at the college now, in the nursing program."

Dr. Shore being the surgeon who was murdered three years ago.

"Toni. Sweetheart. Please get to the point."

"She said it was nice to see us together again."

Hal looked bewildered. "I don't understand."

"Don't you? Want me to explain?"

Hal went to the cupboard and grabbed another glass. Then he went to the bar and snagged the scotch. He poured two fingers into his glass and held it over mine. "Want some?"

"Please," I said, and he sloshed the same amount into mine.

We sat at the kitchen table and toasted each other silently, as we had done every night for the last seventeen years. My eyes filled with tears, and I took a sip of my scotch in an attempt to disguise the fact. Hal took a healthy swig of his scotch, swallowed, and grimaced. "Now. What is this all about?"

"Marilyn said she's seen you with a girl. Tall, slender, long blonde hair. She said you kissed said girl. That's what this is all about."

His answer nearly made me choke on my scotch. "Yes. I was. And I did."

Oh God. He admitted it! Somehow, I had held out hope that I'd been wrong about this. And now, Hal had admitted to having an affair. My heart plummeted right into my stomach. I put my head down on the kitchen table and wept.

Hal reached over and stroked my hair. "Toni, honey, please. Tell me."

"I didn't want a divorce," I sobbed. "And now I've got to have one anyway."

"What the fucking hell are you saying? Why do you have to have a divorce?"

"Because you're having an affair!" I wailed. "You just admitted it! Now I have to divorce you. And I don't want to. I love you so much, and you betrayed me. Oh God, oh God," I sobbed, holding on to my stomach, "I can't believe how much this hurts."

Hal pulled his chair around until he was sitting next to me. He put his arms around me and pulled me to him. I struggled. He pulled harder. "Toni, my dearest love, please stop that caterwauling and listen to me." He shook me gently. "Are you listening?"

I gently detached myself and blew my nose. "Okay."

Hal pulled me back into his arms. "I have a lab assistant. She just happens to be tall, blonde, and gorgeous. She also happens to be the best qualified of all the students that applied for the job. You would not believe the razzing I have to endure every day because of her looks. She gets razzed too. Everybody thinks we're having an affair, because how could any red-blooded male resist such a beautiful blonde bombshell? But we're not."

I turned to face him. "Then what about the kissing?"

"Oh, that."

"Yes, *that*. What about *that*?"

Hal sighed. "Well. Her boyfriend thought we were having an affair too. He broke up with her. I tried to comfort her. I guess no good deed goes unpunished."

"Marilyn said she saw you kiss her on the lips."

"Yeah." Hal took my face between his palms and gave me a quick peck on the lips. "Like that."

"Oh. So you really aren't having an affair?"

He put my head on his chest and kissed the top of my head. "No, my dearest love, I'm not. And I never will."

Well, then, of course I started blubbering again, only this time with joy. Hal pushed a tissue into my hand. "Toni, my darling, please stop crying. We have a party to go to."

It took me a while to pull myself together. Getting dressed was no problem, but my face was a mess. My eyelids were so puffy that my eyes were merely slits. For a while I thought I'd have to wear shades to the party.

We were late. They were already getting ready to serve dinner when we finally got down to the country club. We were seated at a large, round table with two of Hal's colleagues in the chemistry department, and their wives, whom I knew slightly. The professors were about Hal's age but looked older, balding and paunchy. They laughed and joked, and I started to feel better within the first five minutes. Nobody seemed to notice my puffy eyes.

Their wives could be counted on to begin quizzing me at any time about why we didn't have children. I knew that children are of major importance to Mormons, Catholics, and Jews alike, but as none of the above, I didn't intend to apologize to anyone for my lack of fecundity.

I wished for someone like Elliott, who could liven things up with his freakin' this and freakin' that, to show up and put us out of our misery, and no sooner had that thought materialized in my head than another couple joined us and filled the two empty chairs. The man was tall and portly with a head like a billiard ball. I found the glare off it from the chandeliers blinding. Did he wax it or what? He clapped Hal on the back as he pulled out his chair and that of his wife, who was right behind him.

"Shapiro, as I live and breathe!" he boomed, causing every head in the room to turn. "Who's that gorgeous little blonde I saw you with at lunch the other day?"

Jesus. One should be careful what one wishes for.

Hal reddened but kept his cool. "This is my wife, Toni," he said, standing and shaking the other man's hand. "Honey, this is Gary Sanders from the math department, and his wife …"

"Marilyn," I finished as I got my first good look at her. She was muttering something to her husband that sounded like "Ixnay, ixnay," and then she cast a commiserating glance in my direction.

"Dr. Day, Dr. Shapiro, how nice to see both of you here," she said a little pointedly. "Or should I be calling both of you Dr. Shapiro?"

"Dr. Day," I said. "I go by my maiden name, since Hal has a PhD and is a doctor too. It's a little confusing to have two Dr. Shapiros in the same household."

"Aw, come on, honey, don't be such a wet blanket!" her husband bellowed. "No need to be so damn formal. It's Hal and Toni, and we're Gary and Marilyn, okay?"

I think everybody in the room now knew who the four of us were, as well as the guys outside doing the valet parking. Whether or not they were okay with it was another thing. The other two couples murmured uncomfortably among themselves and tried to distance themselves from us while still seated in their chairs. I felt pretty uncomfortable myself and was just wondering if there was anything I could possibly do or say to make this moment less embarrassing, when the band started up, and Hal pulled me to my feet.

"Come on, honey, let's not let the music go to waste," he said, leading me out onto the dance floor. The music in question at the moment was Creedence Clearwater Revival's "Proud Mary."

"Hal," I muttered *sotto voce*, "this is a fast one. You don't like fast ones."

"I like 'em better than sitting there having my business broadcast all over the room," he growled.

We stayed out on the floor for the next two numbers until dinner was served. I hoped that the food would keep Gary Sanders quiet for a while, since he looked like the type who would just shovel it in; but as luck would have it, the man was trying to diet and ate very little, giving him ample opportunity to embarrass us further.

"Just trying to shed a few pounds," he explained in answer to a question from one of the other wives, which I couldn't hear. He had turned down the volume considerably, probably to appease Marilyn, who was no doubt as embarrassed as I was, having just told me that day about Hal's gorgeous little blonde. "The doc told me if I didn't get my weight down, I was gonna have a major heart attack. He said my cholesterol's through the roof, and so's my blood pressure," he went on. "Hell, maybe if I get rid of this spare tire," he continued, turning up the volume to almost its original level, "I'll have the girls all over me like Shapiro does. Har har!"

Hal seemed to swell visibly, and I knew he was gritting his teeth. I could practically *hear* them grinding. I noticed that everybody was staring at us again, and I also noticed that although Gary was eating like a bird, he was sure as hell not drinking like one.

"Honey, please keep it down," Marilyn said. "You're embarrassing all of us, and people are staring."

"So what?" Gary returned. "Hey!" he shouted, waving at the closest waiter. "More wine over here!"

"I think you've had enough, dear," Marilyn said with asperity.

"Aw, honey, you're no fun," he complained. "Ever since she started teaching, she's been acting like a prissy old schoolmarm. So whatta you do, Toni?" He was beginning to slur his words.

Marilyn answered before I had a chance to. "I told you she's a doctor, dear."

"Oh, yeah, that's right, she's a doctor," he roared. "Har har! I bet she makes a helluva lot more money than you do, Shapiro!"

Wrong thing to say. That subject was guaranteed to piss Hal off.

He stood up. "Sanders," he said quietly. "Outside. Now."

Gary stared up at him blearily. "Huh?"

"I said, outside. Now." Hal grabbed the man's arm and hoisted him out of his chair. He made it look effortless too. Once on his feet, Gary went meekly enough, but as the two men approached the outside door, he let loose with one more blast.

"So whatta ya gonna do, Shapiro, punch me inna nose? Avenge the little lady's honor? Hah? Yeah, she's little, but I bet she's a tiger in the sack, hah? Or maybe she's not, eh? Is that why …"

The doors mercifully cut off any further diatribe. Marilyn stared at me, her eyes wide. "Doctor, I'm so sorry! Gary's not usually like this. I don't know what got into him. What's Hal going to do to him?"

"I have no idea," I said honestly. "This has never happened before. Shall we go find out?"

Marilyn said, "Oh, I don't know … Do you really think we should?"

I stood up. "Come on," I urged. "You're going to want to get him home now anyway, aren't you?"

"I guess so," she murmured. "Oh dear, oh dear."

She grabbed her purse and their coats and came with me, no doubt dreading the worst, as I was; but when I opened the door, the sight that greeted our eyes was Gary, braced against a tree, puking his guts out. Hal stood next to him with a hand on his shoulder.

"I think you need to go home, buddy," I heard him say. "Do you want me to go get Marilyn?"

"I'm here," Marilyn said. "Gary, honey? Are you finished?"

Gary straightened up, fished a handkerchief out of his pocket, and blew his nose loudly. "Yeah, I think so," he mumbled.

Marilyn took his arm and turned him in the general direction of the parking lot. "Then let's go home," she said soothingly.

"Do you need any help?" Hal asked.

"No," she replied. "He'll be all right now."

"Jesus," said Hal, putting an arm around me.

When I felt the warmth of his body, I realized that I was freezing. "Let's get back inside," I suggested. "Or do you want to go home too?"

"Not on your life," Hal said. "I want to go in there and dance my feet off with my little lady." I looked up into his face, and he kissed me gently. "And you *are* a tiger in the sack, by the way," he added. "Just so you know."

Hal doesn't usually like to dance that much, but on that night he kept me on the floor until the band took its break. Then, after having much more fun than was good for either of us on a week night, we went home.

I expected to go right to bed, but Hal was wide awake and suggested I pour us each a little nip of Drambuie while he got a fire going. We cuddled on the couch, sipping our drinks and watching the flames dancing.

"I wonder if he gets like that often?" I wondered sleepily, and Hal knew exactly who I was talking about.

"I wouldn't be surprised," he said. "I got the impression that Marilyn has handled that situation before a time or two. So," he continued tenderly, his lips brushing mine, "do you really want to talk?"

Well, no, not really, now that you mention it.

We made love on the couch in the firelight, and by the time we actually got to bed, it was one-thirty in the morning.

Now that Hal had relieved my mind about whether or not he was having an affair and explained what had been bothering him since school started, I expected to sleep very well indeed.

Then I could concentrate on finding out why both Jay's office and Jay's widow's house had burned down. It had to be more than a coincidence.

Tuesday, December 16

Chapter 14

She hugg'd the offender, and forgave the offence:
Sex to the last.
—John Dryden

A frozen section was already waiting for me when I got to work, and I had to deal with it before I had a chance to hang up my coat or put my purse away. I hate it when that happens; it makes me feel used and abused. Someone could just walk into my office and steal my purse while I was tied up doing a frozen section. That really would add insult to injury.

I dumped both into my chair and went across the hall, and that set the tone for the whole morning: one frozen section after another until I felt like I was tied to the cryostat with not nearly enough hands.

Bernie Kincaid called me at work and offered to take me to lunch. Since I wasn't expecting Hal, I accepted and got Mike to cover for me. I had to eat, after all, and we'd be in a public place where there'd be no funny business, or so I thought. And maybe I could find out something about the fires.

Bernie had other ideas, however. The dingy bar he took me to in the industrial part of Twin Falls was so dark inside that I could barely make out the other patrons sitting in candlelit, intimate booths. We had a candlelit, intimate booth of our own in a corner where nobody sitting in any of the other booths could see us. It was, as Flip Wilson used to say, the booth in the back in the corner in the dark.

I wouldn't have minded his choice of venue so much before Hal and I had had our big reconciliation; but since we had, I felt a little uncomfortable. However, I figured I could take care of myself if I had to. I could do my Nancy Reagan impression. Just Say No.

"None of the other cops eat here," Bernie assured me. "When I first came up here, before the divorce was final, I used to come in here at night and get plastered. Then it began to interfere with my work, and Ray told me to shape up or ship out. So I quit coming in here. This is a perfect place to come if you don't want to run into anybody you know."

The Ray he referred to was Commander Ray Harris, whom I knew.

"Okay," I said. "And we don't want to run into somebody we know because …?"

"Because we don't want anyone to think we're having an affair."

"And we don't want to do that, do we?" I said. "Because we're just two friends having lunch and talking about murder."

"You'd rather talk about murder?" At this point it looked as though lunch would be over before it began. The waitress arrived and took our order. When she was gone, Bernie reached across the table and took both my hands in his. "Toni," he said softly, "I want you."

I sighed and withdrew my hands. "You know that's out of the question. I want to talk about arson."

"I thought you wanted to talk about murder," he countered.

"I do, but the only one who's been murdered so far is Jay Braithwaite Burke. And since then, Kathleen Burke's house and Jay's office have burned down. So now I want to talk about arson."

He sighed and assumed a businesslike demeanor. "The person you need to talk to is Roy Cobb over at the fire department."

"Would he talk to me? I mean, you guys talk to me, but you already know me. Nobody in the fire department knows me."

"Well, that's easily fixed." He hauled out his cell phone and pressed a button. "Hey. Roy Cobb around? Good. Hey, buddy. Bernie Kincaid here. What can you tell me about the fires at 202 Montana Street and 815 Shoshone Street North?"

He listened, while I thought, *Jeez, I wish this guy was telling me this stuff. Bernie could suppress something if he wanted to and I'd never know. But who the hell am I to be accusing anybody of suppressing information. I'm not a police officer, just a civilian busybody.*

"Huh. How about that," he said. "So does that mean the same person set both fires?" I thought, *Hey, I was right. It is arson.* Then he said, "Thanks, buddy, talk to you later." He hung up and looked at me triumphantly.

"Well?"

"He says both fires are arson. They found an empty gasoline can at both fires with the cap off."

"No chance of that being a coincidence?"

"Gasoline was the accelerant in both fires."

"Well," I said, "I gotta admit, even to me that sounds like arson."

"Roy says it is," Bernie said. "He should know. He's been in this business for twenty years."

"Does he think the same person set both fires?"

"He can't rule it out. If we have any luck getting fingerprints off the cans or the caps, we'll know for sure."

"Okay," I said. "Here's another question. Do you know about Jay Braithwaite Burke's two wills?"

"*Two* wills?"

"Lance Brooks, his partner, drew up one that had Kathleen and the kids as beneficiaries, way back when Jay's son Bryan was born. But Elliott Maynard drew up one last summer that had all these trusts, benefiting not only Kathleen and the kids, but several other women and their children. Most of those women are divorced from their husbands and all of them have had a child by Jay. And all of the ex-husbands were involved in that Ponzi scheme Jay set up back in the day."

"I heard something about a Ponzi scheme," he said. "It was in the paper. But I thought it was back east somewhere, New York or something."

I realized at that moment that not everybody in this town would know or care about Jay's Ponzi scheme. It was of overwhelming importance to the doctors, lawyers, and accountants who were involved but not necessarily to anybody else. Even though the *Clarion* had covered it in depth, that was way back in October and would have been long forgotten by people who had no reason to give a rat's ass about the problems all those rich people were having.

"That's true," I told him. "Jay's hedge fund was a feeder fund for that big Ponzi scheme that was in the papers. Just a smaller version, involving local people. Mostly doctors."

"Ray's had Pete and me going around asking questions of all these people, who are mostly doctors. They're all the people involved in this Ponzi scheme, aren't they?"

"I would guess so. But what I'm getting at is that there may be another motive for murdering Jay besides losing all that money. Some of those ex-wives may be in dire need of money too. Maybe one of them is willing to kill for it."

"So you're suggesting we need to be asking the wives questions too?"

"Ex-wives," I corrected him. "It's ex-wives who had a baby by Jay who are in the will. Oh, and while you're at it, maybe someone should talk to Ruthie Brooks too."

"Is she in the will too?"

"Maybe not," I said, "but I think she worked in that office, and maybe she knows something that will help. I know she was one of the witnesses to Jay's first will, the one that benefits only Kathleen and her children."

"And that would be connected to these fires … how?"

"I'm wondering whether these fires are either to find that will and destroy it or to make sure nobody ever finds it. So that would mean any one of those women would have a motive, assuming they know they're in Jay's will."

"And maybe one of those women killed Jay too." Bernie rubbed his hands over his face. "Jesus. Thanks for making this investigation even more confusing than it was, Toni. I don't know what we'd do without you; I really don't." He looked at his watch. "Shit. I've got to get back. Are you ready?"

While Bernie was paying the cashier at the bar, I glanced around the room and immediately wished I hadn't. Hal was sitting in one of the booths with a young girl. She had long, blonde hair cascading over her shoulders, nearly to her waist, and she was very pretty. She also had a gorgeous tan. An old Beach Boys tune went through my head: *Little surfer, little one, made my heart come all undone* ... She and Hal were holding hands across the table and appeared deep in conversation, looking into each other's eyes. They hadn't seen me.

In spite of having been alerted about Hal and some girl at the college, with whom he'd assured me just last night that he wasn't having an affair, the stark reality of it struck me like a blow. *Damn him.* I debated whether to just withdraw quietly and discuss it at home tonight in a civilized manner, or just charge right over to their booth and rip Hal's throat out with my bare hands.

If I were to ask Mum's advice right now, she would suggest option number one. Much less messy and less likely to land me in jail than option number two. If I didn't want people to talk about me and Bernie Kincaid, having a knock-down-drag-out fight in a bar was most assuredly not the way to accomplish that.

Was this how it had been for Kathleen Burke when she caught Jay and Tiffany in bed together? Of course, for Kathleen, Tiffany had been the last of a long line of Jay's lovers, but without the fleshy explicits, perhaps it hadn't seemed so bad. And I was seeing them in a relatively platonic setting. What if I had gone home early and caught Hal in bed with this girl?

Why ever not? Jay had done it. Why not Hal? Men are men, right?

Tears came to my eyes and rolled down my cheeks in spite of my efforts to prevent it. I tried to hide it from Bernie, but it was no use. In the car, he grabbed my shoulders and turned me toward him. "Toni, what is it?"

Oh, hell. "Hal's in there," I choked. "With a girl."

"You're kidding."

"I wish I were."

"Maybe they're just discussing grades or something."

"Oh, no, I don't think so. They're holding hands and looking into each other's eyes. Just like we used to," and at this I broke down completely, sobbing like a child while Bernie held me and stroked my hair. He rocked me gently, murmuring unintelligible words, while I buried my face in his navy-blue down jacket.

Eventually I stopped crying and tried to sit up, just in time to see Hal and his girlfriend emerge from the bar. The girl was talking animatedly, looking up into Hal's face, her face alight; but Hal wasn't looking at her. He was looking straight at me.

Chapter 15

Beware of entrance to a quarrel; but being in,
Bear't that the opposed may beware of thee.
—Shakespeare, *Hamlet*

After an eternity, they moved on, and I began crying again.

"Oh, shit," Bernie murmured, "I didn't intend for that to happen," and he proceeded to dry my tears by kissing first my eyelids, then the tip of my nose, my cheeks, and then my lips, and I felt myself melt into him. It took a major effort to pull myself away and ask him to drive me back to work.

I had no idea if anyone else had seen us. Maybe, I rationalized, everybody who went to that bar was there with someone they didn't want to be seen with, in which case, anyone who'd seen us after Hal and his girlfriend would keep quiet about it.

Shit. What a mess. What was I getting myself into?

Big trouble, I was pretty sure. What would Hal have to say about it? What could he say? He was doing the same thing himself. Why should he have all the fun? What's good for the goose is good for the gander, or the other way around in this case.

The gander could just suck it up.

When I got back to the hospital I ducked into the nearest ladies' room to repair my face before anybody saw me. One look in the mirror confirmed the worst. I couldn't let anybody at work see me like that. I applied paper towels wrung out in cold water to my flushed cheeks and swollen lips and hoped that would do the trick.

I had no idea how I'd get through the rest of the afternoon, and the next two phone calls I got didn't help.

"Well, young lady," said Rollie Perkins, "I hate to keep bothering you when I know you must be really busy, but your pal Bernie Kincaid has been over here bugging me every day for the last three days. Usually he just calls, but now he comes over and sits and has coffee with me, and all he wants to do is talk about you. What's going on with you two? Anybody'd think he was sweet on you or something. Heh-heh."

Rollie was kidding, but I felt a stab of embarrassment mixed with a twinge of fear and, to my dismay, a thrill of sexual desire. My face got hot, and I felt very glad I was in the privacy of my office where nobody could see me blush. "Rollie, you haven't said that to anybody else, have you?" I asked anxiously.

"Oho, you mean there *is* something going on?" he teased. "I was just kidding."

Damn. "No, of course not," I assured him, with a confidence I did not feel, "but people talk, and I wouldn't want it getting back to Hal." God knows what it would sound like after a few other people had a chance to embellish and distort it. "Please don't say any more about it, okay?"

Yeah, I know, the gander can suck it up, but I had no desire to rub his face in it.

Rollie assured me he had said nothing and would say nothing to anybody else. I should have felt reassured, but I wasn't; especially when the next call came from the police—not Bernie, thank God, because I had no idea what I would say to him, but Commander Ray Harris, who wanted a copy of the autopsy report, or at least the preliminary, since at that point that was all I had.

"Don't you have it yet? I sent it yesterday."

"Well, that's something," he grumbled. "This case is turning out to be a real bitch, excuse my French. We've been tryin' to interview everybody that was involved in that Ponzi scheme of his. There must be nearly a hundred of 'em! It's a damn exercise in futility, so far. Nobody knows nothin'. Nothin' showed up on the toxicology, neither. We're hopin' the autopsy might help."

"Pete and Bernie were there. Didn't they tell you what I found?" *Jesus.* I thought communication at the hospital sucked, but these guys had that beat nine ways to Sunday. "He died of carbon monoxide poisoning and a brain hemorrhage."

The Commander sucked audibly on his toothpick and didn't answer my question. "Maybe now we can get somewhere," he said. "I feel in my bones that all's not as it should be, but dang! There's no evidence pointin' to any of those people, and we've been keepin' an eye on his wife too, since she's the beneficiary of his will and—"

I interrupted him. "You do know, don't you, that there are two wills?"

"Say what?"

I repeated it and added, "Lance Brooks drew one up thirteen years ago with Kathleen and the kids as beneficiaries, and Elliott Maynard drew up another one a few months ago with a bunch of trusts in it for women whose ex-husbands were involved in the Ponzi scheme and who had children by him."

"You wouldn't be joshin' me now, would you, girl?" the Commander inquired when I had finished. I assured him that joshing him was the farthest thought from my mind. I could hear him riffling through papers.

"Here's what I've got," he said finally. "The Last Will and Testament of Jay Braithwaite Burke, Esquire, from the Law Offices of Burke, Braithwaite, Burke, Bartlett and Brooks, dated June 26, 1995. Prepared by Lance Brooks, witnessed by William J. Bartlett and Ruthanne Brooks. Being of sound mind I hereby devise and bequeath—well, there's a lot of legal mumbo jumbo, but the gist is his wife is the sole beneficiary, unless she dies first, and then the kids divide it equally."

"That's the first one," I said. "But Elliott drew up a will too, and Jodi thought it was just last summer."

"Well, we'll just see about that," the Commander assured me. "We can get a copy with a subpoena if we need to. Hell, I should've called you sooner," he grumbled. "Then we wouldn'ta spent the last few days spinnin' our wheels. Your pal Pete's gettin' right testy, and Kincaid …" He paused, and I held my breath.

"Funny thing about Kincaid," he continued, after audibly sucking on his toothpick for a few moments.

"Usually by this stage in an investigation, he's flat-out obnoxious, ignorant, and ugly, in that order. But he's been goin' around with his head in the clouds lately. He must be in love or something."

"Really," I commented, trying to sound normal. My heart pounded so hard that I felt sure it was audible over the phone, and I could feel myself blushing again. But the Commander was through speculating about Bernie. "Well, thanks for the tip, Doc," he said in closing. "I'll give young Elliott a call."

The Commander referred to Elliott that way because he'd known him as a child. Elliott's father and the Commander had been poker buddies back in the day. Small towns are like that. You have to be careful what you say about people, because you could be speaking to someone they know or—God forbid—are related to.

I sat at my desk with my burning face buried in my hands, realizing that I was in an untenable position, what with Bernie Kincaid going around at work acting like a teenager in love and pestering Rollie Perkins with questions about me. How long would it take for somebody to put two and two together and come up with five? How long before someone mentioned it to Hal? Who would he believe: me or the gossipmongers? Especially when the gossipmongers were the police and the county coroner?

Especially when he had already caught me in a police car with Bernie Kincaid's arms around me? Thank God he hadn't caught us kissing. That *would* be difficult to explain away.

I realized that I was now in the same position as Hal—at least his position up until last night. He would assume that I was having an affair with Bernie Kincaid, just as I had assumed he was having an affair with his blonde bimbo. Up until now, I had remained convinced that Hal was innocent, but after what I'd seen today, I wasn't so sure.

Oh, the fur was going to fly tonight! And I was having a real approach-avoidance conflict about that. How I longed for the days when I didn't dread going home at night!

With foreboding, I watched the clock and tried to find things to keep me busy so that I wouldn't have to go home. But eventually, after Mike and all my techs had left and the lab was dark, I knew I had to.

When I got home, the Maynards were there, but the Burkes, Tiffany, and Emily were not. "Ruthie came and took them home with her," Jodi told me. "She's got a huge house, and she and Lance never had any kids, so she's got tons of room."

Excellent, I thought, and noted that the living room had been neatened up considerably, with pillows stacked at the end of the couch and blankets folded neatly on top of them. Too bad nobody had put them away. Obviously this was a job only I could do. Hal was great at folding and stacking things, but he never put anything away.

He did have a fire going in the fireplace, though, and was allowing Jason, Julie, and Cody to toast hot dogs and marshmallows in it. *At least he's not out fucking his college bimbo*, I thought uncharitably.

Christ on a crutch. What next? Jay murdered and Jay's office and Kathleen's house both burned to the ground. I simply couldn't believe that this string of disasters was coincidence. They had to be related somehow. Did I dare start asking questions? Was it any of my business?

Somebody was after the Burkes, and they were now living in Ruthie's house. Would someone come after them there?

"We have to talk about this," I announced, as I settled on the couch with a hot dog, fending off Geraldine with my free hand. With a gusty sigh, she subsided across my lap, ever alert in case of fallout.

"What *this* would that be?" inquired Hal facetiously.

"Oh, very funny," I retorted as the children giggled. "What I want to know is, am I the only one who thinks there's some connection between Jay's murder and these fires?"

Eight skeptical pairs of eyes gazed at me. Nobody said anything.

"I'm serious," I went on. "I think someone wants something, and they think they can get it from Kathleen or from Lance. Now Kathleen's house is gone, and Jay's office is gone, along with everything Jay left there. What if the person thinks the thing they want is now in Ruthie's house where the Burkes are? Should we be worried about fire there too?"

"Honey, you're being melodramatic," Hal said.

"Maybe not," Jodi objected. "I think Toni has a point. You've got to admit, it's a heck of a coincidence for someone to target Jay's office and Jay's widow's house, don't you think?"

"It was a freakin' close thing too, both times," Elliott said. "They barely got out with their lives."

"Kathleen told me they got out of their house with one of those chain ladders—you know, like they advertise on TV," Jodi said. "They've got them at Home Depot. Ruthie said she'd get one tomorrow."

"Terrific," I said. "What about tonight?"

"Toni, for God's sake," Hal snapped. "Lighten up. Nothing's going to happen tonight. Nobody knows they're there except us."

After a bit more discussion, the Maynards went home and left Hal and me in peace. Or so I hoped.

I closed the door behind them and turned to face Hal. He was looking back at me with a watchful expression on his face. I wanted nothing more than to run into his arms; but then I thought of the girl and decided that what I really wanted was to beat him to a bloody pulp. Since neither was a viable option, I did nothing. Striving to maintain an impassive countenance, I waited for him to speak first.

Hal rubbed a hand over his face. "Okay. I know we have to talk, but I don't know where to start."

I folded my arms across my chest and leaned back against the door, hoping to look nonchalant. "Try the beginning," I suggested, a trifle acidly.

"That's just it. Where *is* the beginning?"

Unhelpfully, I remained silent.

Hal took a deep breath, got up, and came over to me. "That girl," he began, "is my lab assistant. I told you that. I also told you that I wasn't having an affair with her, even though everybody thinks I am. I thought you believed me."

"That's before I saw you holding hands with her in that bar." My voice quavered; I gritted my teeth, like that was going to help.

"I also told you that her boyfriend broke up with her. She came to me for comfort. So now she's decided that she's got a crush on me. She made a pass at me today—a

149

pretty unmistakable one. She's a good assistant, and I don't want to lose her now in the middle of the school year. I took her to lunch there to try and talk some sense into her. I took her there because I didn't want to be seen. Or heard. The last thing I expected was to find you necking with Bernie Kincaid in a police car," he almost spat.

"Bernie Kincaid invited me to lunch," I said calmly. "I accepted. What's wrong with that? The last thing *I* expected was to see you holding hands with a nineteen-year-old girl in a bar. You were looking into each other's eyes just like we used to when we were courting. It made me cry. Bernie was trying to comfort me. We weren't necking." *Not yet, anyway.*

Hal looked skeptical.

"If I'm going to believe you, you have to believe me," I pointed out. "It works both ways. We have to trust each other, or our marriage is a sham."

"I haven't had sex with her," he offered.

"And I haven't had sex with Bernie, either."

Hal put both palms on either side of my head and leaned on the door, looming over me. In the shadows, his face looked hooded and unreadable.

Stubbornly, I stayed where I was. Hal leaned closer to me and looked deeply into my eyes. "I love you, Toni; you're the only woman I will ever love. You're the one I want to spend the rest of my life with and grow old with. You don't need to worry about Bambi."

I slipped out from under his arms and stepped away, turning to look at him in disbelief. "*Bambi*? You've got to be kidding. Nobody is named Bambi, for God's sake."

Hal straightened up and turned to face me. "That's really her name, and she's a very smart girl."

"Okay, so she's smart. How smart is it to make a pass at a married professor?"

"Okay. It's not. She's just a kid, and she's lost her boyfriend. She's emotionally overwrought. I can understand it."

Yeah, I could understand it too. Twenty years ago I had been the student who made a pass at a married professor and ended up marrying him. I should be able to forgive Bambi for doing the same thing. But was I willing to forgive Hal for responding to it? "You don't have to encourage her, do you?"

"I wasn't encouraging her!"

"How was taking her to lunch in an intimate booth in a dark bar not encouraging her?"

"Toni …"

"That's two, Hal. Please don't let there be a three."

Wednesday, December 17

Chapter 16

Marriage resembles a pair of shears,
so joined that they cannot be separated;
often moving in opposite directions,
yet always punishing anyone who comes between them.
—Sir Walter Scott

All night I kept dreaming that the house was on fire and I couldn't wake Hal. Then I'd wake up, and realize that there was no fire and that waking Hal was the last thing I wanted to do.

I turned off the alarm before it rang and went to my aerobics class. Hal was still asleep when I got back, so I decided to let him sleep. I dressed in the bathroom and went to work, stopping in the cafeteria for coffee and danish.

Since I was early, I went up to the nurses' station and inquired about Tiffany and Lance. Tiffany had been released. Lance was in ICU.

So I went down the hall to ICU, and on the way I met Jodi, accompanied by a nurse pushing Tiffany in a wheelchair. Tiffany looked pale, and her blonde hair was disheveled and stringy, but Jodi looked shell-shocked.

"What's the matter with you?" I demanded. "You look worse than she does."

"Thank you very much. Nice to see you too," Jodi retorted. "Guess who else is in ICU."

Oh, no. "You don't mean … Did Ruthie's house burn down last night?"

"No, no," Jodi shook her head. "No, they're all vomiting blood. Ruthie said it started last night with Angela having a nosebleed, and then Emily had one, and by morning everybody was sick."

"Is Ruthie sick too?" I wondered.

"I don't think so," Jodi said. "She's here with Lance."

"So how is Lance doing?" I asked. "Why is he in ICU?"

"I don't know," Jodi said, "but he looks awful. You'll see for yourself when you go in."

Jodi had not been exaggerating. Lance did look awful; he looked grayer and even more skeletal than before, if such a thing was possible—except for his swollen belly, which was visible under the covers and no doubt full of fluid. He had a central line in a subclavian vein through which a unit of blood was running, and a nasogastric tube with bloody drainage in it, attached to a Gomco pump on the floor. He was also unconscious, intubated, and on a respirator. His hands lay on the counterpane, jerking rhythmically. The whites of his half-open eyes appeared jaundiced.

Ruthie sat by his bed, crying. "Oh, Toni, he's so sick," she sobbed. "He started throwing up blood yesterday, and then last night he couldn't breathe, and they said he aspirated, and that's when they put the tube down. They won't tell me what's wrong with him, and I'm afraid he's going to die."

When I leaned over him to check his eyes, I was close enough to smell him, and it was like a flashback to medical school and my clinical rotations at the Long Beach Veteran's Hospital.

Upper GI bleeding. Ascites. Liver flap. Jaundice. Foetor hepaticus.

Ruthie was worried with good reason. Lance was dying of liver failure.

He was undoubtedly bleeding from esophageal varices—enlarged varicose veins in the esophagus caused by portal hypertension, which was increased blood pressure in the portal vein caused by cirrhosis of the liver. They can band those endoscopically these days, and I wondered why they hadn't done it.

Was Lance an alcoholic? That's what it usually was, but I felt reluctant to ask Ruthie about such a potentially painful subject. So I changed the subject.

"Looks like you've got your hands full here without having to deal with houseguests," I said. "Do you need some help? They could come to our house when they leave here and save you a lot of work."

She dabbed her eyes, blew her nose, put the tissue in her purse and snapped it shut with a decisive gesture. "Thank you, but that won't be necessary," she assured me with a watery smile. "I enjoy their company. It takes my mind off things to have them around."

I patted her shoulder in what I hoped was a comforting gesture and went to the nurses' station to check on the Burkes.

Kathleen was in the cubicle next to Lance's. I peeked in. She was asleep. She had an intravenous line in one hand and a nasogastric tube snaked from her nose to a Gomco pump similar to Lance's. The contents were bloody. A bag containing bloody urine hung from the lower bedside rail. I stepped closer and checked what was going into her IV: fresh frozen plasma to replace her clotting factors.

I stepped even closer and leaned over to smell her breath. It wasn't minty fresh, but at least it wasn't *foetor hepaticus*.

Back in my office, I fired up the computer and looked at the electronic medical record, which turned up some very interesting findings.

Kathleen's lab work showed a partial thromboplastin time that was slightly elevated, and a prothrombin time and INR that were markedly elevated. Her platelet count and fibrinogen were normal. Perhaps the fresh frozen plasma she'd been receiving had corrected those already, but if so, it should have also corrected the PTT and pro-time. Had they also given her heparin? Or Coumadin? If so, maybe that explained things, but why would they do that?

Not for the first time, I wished that the medical staff would get a clue and give up using the PTT to monitor heparin. It wasn't because I hadn't tried to educate them. There were so many factors that affected PTT besides heparin, and the anti-Xa—a measurement of activated clotting factor ten—was not affected by them and actually correlated with the amount of heparin in the blood. We had offered the test for the last year, and it was very rarely used, but I hadn't yet given up on it.

The pro-time and INR just didn't make sense.

Upstairs in Pediatric ICU, the children were being treated in a similar fashion and had similar lab results.

Toxicology studies had been ordered on urine, and cultures on stool and blood, to rule out food poisoning, drug overdose, and enteric infections. But as far as I knew, none of these caused bleeding, with the exception of *Campylobacter*, which typically caused bloody diarrhea but not hematemesis—vomiting blood—or nosebleeds.

Unless they'd all received an overdose of heparin.

Oh, come on, Toni, get serious.

Where would an entire family get an overdose of heparin? In the hospital? All of them? And in any case, weren't they all bleeding *before* they went to the hospital while they were still at Ruthie's house?

I was obviously hallucinating. So, to take my mind off it, I looked up Lance—and that's where things *really* got weird.

Like his late partner, Lance also had a history of deep vein thrombosis dating back to his early twenties; but instead of affecting the leg veins, as it did in most people, it had affected the portal, hepatic, and mesenteric veins, resulting in a series of hospitalizations for acute abdominal pain due to bowel and liver infarctions. He'd had an appendectomy and several small bowel resections.

Our curmudgeonly gastroenterologist—George Marshall, he of the Gnarly Finger—had been his primary physician for at least twenty years, along with frequent consultations from the University of Utah, where some of Lance's surgeries had been done.

He'd been thoroughly worked up there for his coagulation problems and had been found to have the prothrombin mutation G20210A, a hereditary alteration in prothrombin, one of the major blood coagulation factors, which made him a very high risk for blood clots, and also resistant to Coumadin. So Lance was obliged to inject himself daily with enoxaparin, a low molecular weight heparin that was sold under the brand name Lovenox and could be given subcutaneously.

No wonder he looked so dour. If I had to shoot up every day, I'd be right pissy too.

According to the chart, nobody really knew why Lance had liver failure. He wasn't an alcoholic. In fact, he rarely touched the stuff because of his history of liver infarctions; he didn't want to cause any more damage. They attributed the bleeding to portal hypertension which is usually due to cirrhosis of the liver from chronic alcoholism, but in Lance's case was probably due to scarring from multiple infarctions. The possibility of another hepatic or portal vein thrombosis, or possibly a liver tumor, was entertained.

Usually a cirrhotic liver, or one with scarring from infarctions, was smaller than normal. But Lance's was enlarged, with multiple nodules, which made tumor a distinct possibility. But was it a primary liver tumor— hepatocellular carcinoma—or metastatic tumor from some other source, such as colon, stomach, or pancreas? Or even lung? I doubted that; Lance wasn't a smoker, as far as I knew. And how far had it spread? If they drew off some of that ascites fluid from his belly, would it have malignant cells in it?

George was planning to get an MRI as soon as Lance was stable enough—and possibly a needle biopsy under CT guidance to get a diagnosis—and then start treatment.

He said nothing about paracentesis or aspiration of all that ascitic fluid. I wondered why. Surely all of Lance's abdominal organs were being compressed by it, not to mention his lungs from the diaphragm being pushed up into his chest. He also didn't mention banding of esophageal varices. Maybe he didn't think Lance was stable enough for that either, or maybe he was hoping Lance would throw a clot and plug them all up; but patients never throw clots where you want them to. They're just ornery that way.

George's plan for an MRI and CT-guided needle biopsy was a worthy goal, I thought, and maybe he planned to remove fluid at the same time, but judging from what I was seeing, Lance would never stabilize and most likely would not survive long enough for any diagnostic procedure. In fact, I saw an autopsy in my future.

I mentioned it to Mike. He gave me an eye-roll. "Oh, goody, a lawyer," he groused. "I sure hope he dies soon enough that we can do the autopsy together. Sounds like it's gonna be a bitch, I tell you what. Damn lawyer's wife'll probably sue just 'cause she *is* a damn lawyer's wife."

I pretended to agree, but I was hoping Lance would hang on until the weekend when Mike was on call and I was on vacation. Still, I'd probably help Mike anyway, just out of curiosity. And let's face it, Ruthie probably *would* sue.

Wrongful death. Failure to diagnose. Failure to treat. The possibilities were endless. Here's your list. Check all boxes that apply. Oh, and don't forget *loss of consortium*, that's always good for punitive damages.

Mike was on call today, actually, and wouldn't you know, he didn't get a single goddamn frozen section all day. I, on the other hand, retired to my office, where I spent the next four hours reading out all of yesterday's goddamn cases with all their goddamn frozen sections. Then I spent another hour proofreading them, editing them on the computer, and signing them out. And then I figured I'd better finish up Jay's autopsy before I got any more calls about it.

Besides, maybe it would get Bernie Kincaid out of Rollie's hair, and that would be a good thing, whereas ongoing gossip and speculation would not. Be a good thing, I mean. No matter what Rollie promised me, such things do get around, and this is a small town, after all.

I shuddered to think what would happen if Ruthie Brooks ever got wind of it. It would get around so fast, it'd stir up dust.

After an autopsy, a lot more work remains to be done before it is actually completed and a final report prepared. Most people don't realize that; they think that everything is obvious once the body is cut open, like on TV. Not so. That's just the preliminary or provisional gross diagnosis, which is what I'd sent the police already. Samples of the tissues removed have to be processed and slides made and examined. In that respect, an autopsy is like a great big surgical case with many parts and subparts. It takes several days at best, and several months at worst.

Unlike a medical examiner's office, our practice predominantly involves surgical specimens on live patients, and their cases get done first.

Then the lab work done on the postmortem blood samples has to be correlated with the autopsy findings.

One has to hope they ordered the right tests in the first place to avoid the delay of having to order any more of them—assuming that the specimens are still any good—because you sure as hell can't go back and get more.

Finally, the autopsy findings from the tissue and the blood tests have to be correlated with the clinical picture; in other words, all the clinical findings should be explained by the autopsy findings.

All that takes a lot longer than the gross autopsy examination does.

Jay's autopsy slides were not particularly illuminating. He had severe atherosclerosis in his coronary arteries, but none of them were blocked. There was slight patchy scarring in his heart, but nothing that looked like he'd had a heart attack—at least not forty-eight or more hours prior to death.

His lungs were hemorrhagic, and there was aspiration pneumonia present, manifested by acute inflammation associated with food particles in the alveolar spaces of the lungs. His liver and spleen and all the sections of his gastrointestinal tract showed generalized congestion and interstitial hemorrhage, explaining the origin of all the bleeding thereof.

None of this was unexpected.

His lab tests were much more interesting than his slides.

First, the carboxyhemoglobin was sixty-three percent, anything over fifty percent being lethal. That was the immediate cause of death.

However, his bleeding problems were a contributing cause of death, particularly the brain hemorrhage. In the absence of carbon monoxide poisoning, respiratory failure and/or blood loss would have killed him. The cause of bleeding, however, was another question. What could have caused it?

Once I knew that Jay's postmortem prothrombin time and INR were not that far outside the therapeutic range, I was pretty sure that he didn't die of an overdose of Coumadin. So what made him bleed to death? What else was there?

Rat poison came to mind. Many years ago, rat poison contained arsenic or strychnine, but now many of them contain anticoagulants that are derivatives of warfarin, the origin of the drug Coumadin. In fact, some of them are super-warfarins that are resistant to Vitamin K, the antidote for Coumadin overdose. But this would also cause the prothrombin time and INR to be way out of the therapeutic range, so that was unlikely.

Then there was heparin, which was used for acute treatment of patients newly diagnosed with deep vein thrombosis or pulmonary embolus before they were switched to Coumadin. But Jay hadn't been in the hospital, and heparin pretty much required hospitalization because it had to be given intravenously. It couldn't be given orally because it was too large a molecule to be absorbed through the GI tract, and it couldn't be given intramuscularly because it would cause hematomas or large painful hemorrhages in the muscle. Lovenox, a much smaller molecule, was given subcutaneously.

Lance Brooks couldn't take Coumadin, so he was using Lovenox at home. He could actually inject himself, or Ruthie could do it. Unlike regular heparin, it didn't need to be monitored because it had a longer half-life, so it didn't require hospitalization.

Nothing is perfect, however. Cases of fatal or near-fatal hemorrhage with Lovenox were occasionally reported, and I had actually autopsied a couple of them in the last few years.

So, although Lovenox didn't need to be monitored, it could be, using the anti-Xa. And when I found out that Jay had not overdosed on Coumadin, I'd ordered one.

It was markedly elevated.

Someone had shot Jay Braithwaite Brooks full of heparin. Or Lovenox.

But how? I wondered. Would Jay just sit there and allow someone to shoot him full of some unknown substance without at least asking a question or two? Wouldn't he have resisted? Did the murderer have to hit him over the head and knock him out first? Was that the explanation for the subarachnoid hemorrhage and the contrecoup hemorrhage?

So, assuming that to be the case, how was it possible for the murderer to hit Jay over the head hard enough to cause an intracerebral bleed without leaving a great big honking bruise on his scalp?

And where were the injection marks? Although Jay had had purpura, there were no discrete hemorrhagic lesions such as what would have been present had he received multiple injections of an anticoagulant drug.

So many questions; so few answers. But one question, I reflected, had an answer that was crystal clear.

Who did we know that was likely to have syringes of Lovenox lying about the house?

I could only think of one: Ruthie Brooks.

But how would she get it into Jay without leaving a puncture mark?

Did she also shoot Kathleen and her family full of Lovenox? Is that why they were bleeding? How the hell would Ruthie get two adults and five kids to stand still for multiple shots in the belly? Because it would have to be more than one shot to make them bleed like that.

Too bad there wasn't an oral form of heparin that Ruthie could sneak into their food. That would explain it.

Or was there?

Thursday, December 18

Chapter 17

What other dungeon is as dark as one's own heart?
What jailer is so inexorable as one's self!
—Nathaniel Hawthorne

Last night I'd added a third item to my list: to get on the Internet and try to find out if an oral form of heparin existed. Things had been so crazy that I hadn't had time. So when I got up Thursday morning I had every intention of crossing all three items off my list. Maybe then things would make more sense.

It was a good thing I'd made a list and left it at work, because otherwise I'd have forgotten all about it in light of subsequent events.

Hal got a phone call at seven o'clock Thursday morning and wouldn't tell me who it was from. All he would tell me was that he had to be at the college that night, so he wouldn't be home that evening.

I objected. "You're on vacation. The college is closed for the holidays. What do you have to go to the college for?"

But he just shook his head and said he couldn't tell me.

"Was it Bambi?" I persisted.

He got mad. "Toni, goddamnit, knock it off! You'll know soon enough."

I got mad too. "Fuck you, asshole," I snapped. I grabbed my purse and coat and slammed out of the house to go to work.

I'll know soon enough—yeah, right, I raged to myself. *He's going to meet up with Bambi the bimbo, is what he's going to do.*

My walk down Montana Street in the crisp, cold air cleared my head and calmed me down enough to get into a work mode. After all, it was again my turn to do frozen sections.

I got hammered. I got a colon cancer case in which the tumor had become so large that it formed a palpable mass, large enough to be felt on abdominal examination. Multiple loops of small bowel were stuck to it and covered with tumor implants. Several large, involved mesenteric lymph nodes were visible.

I also diagnosed two new cases of breast cancer by frozen section. One of the patients was only twenty-eight years old.

This was followed by two modified radical mastectomies on two additional patients, a gangrenous bowel, and a leg amputation for gangrene from a patient who was, no doubt, diabetic. Merry Friggin' Christmas.

Plus, there was all the usual small stuff: a truckload of biopsies from the gastrointestinal tract, several gallbladders, appendixes, skin lesions, tonsils, hernia sacs, and the like, and the odd hysterectomy or thyroidectomy. Not too many frozens, but a shitload of work for a thoroughly exhausting day.

By five o'clock, I was so tired I was nearly in tears. When I considered what I had to go home to, the last vestiges of strength I still had vanished. I put my head down on my desk and let the tears come. Luckily, nobody was around to see or hear me.

After a while, I felt marginally better, but I was not ready to go home to an empty house. So I got back on the computer. I found out that Jeannie had not had a pregnancy test—at least not one that had been done here. I also found an oral form of heparin.

It was called rivaroxaban and was a small-molecule, oral, direct Factor Xa inhibitor that was still in clinical development, having entered phase three, or clinical trials. This meant that it wasn't on the market yet because it wasn't FDA approved, but it probably would be if the clinical trials went well and the drug didn't have prohibitive side effects.

Patients who sign up for clinical trials are put on drug protocols and get their drugs for free, which can be very attractive to patients who can't afford insurance. The downside is that for every patient who gets the drug, there's a similar patient who gets a placebo, and nobody wants to be that patient. On the other hand, if the drug turns out to have deleterious side effects, the placebo patient doesn't get them.

I wondered if any of our patients were in clinical trials, but I didn't know exactly how to go about finding that out. I didn't know if there was a database in our electronic medical record program that listed patients on clinical trials, or if the trials were listed by drug. Maybe

I'd have to look up everybody connected with this case and see what drugs they were on. If I found somebody on rivaroxaban, would that be enough to accuse that person of poisoning the Burkes with it?

By now it was nearly six o'clock, and I knew that even if there was nobody home, the dogs would need to be let out and possibly fed, although Hal had probably done that already. In any case, it was too late to do anything about the other item on my list: calling Dave McClure's office in Sun Valley to check his alibi.

So I turned off the computer, dragged myself out of my chair, and went home.

When I got home, I found Hal and my mother having tea and crumpets in the kitchen.

I really should work harder at putting my brain in gear before running my mouth, as my mother reminded me with asperity when I said, without thinking, "What the hell is going on here?"

She stood and drew herself up to her full height of five foot one. "Antoinette. It so happens that your husband called me and *asked* me to come. The *least* you can do is make me feel welcome, and that is most decidedly *not* the way to do it. Have I taught you *nothing*? *Must* I put you over my knee?"

I had to laugh. She looked so fierce. "Mum," I pointed out, "I'm bigger than you."

Mum was shorter than me by two inches, but heavier. As a young woman, she had worn her curly red hair like Susan Hayward, and she had never seen any reason to change her style, even though she was now sixty and mostly gray.

"I don't *care* how big you are, Antoinette. I'm still your *mother*." She grabbed me by an earlobe, ignoring the fact that there was an earring in it, dragged me over to the kitchen table, and more or less threw me into a chair, just as she had when I was a child. "Sit," she commanded. "I'm going to fix you a nice buttery crumpet with marmalade, and milk tea, *just* the way you like it, and you're going to eat it."

"Mum," I sighed. "I haven't used milk in my tea for years. It's fattening."

"Bollocks," she snapped. "You're *practically* skin and bones."

I looked at Hal. He was leaning back in his chair, arms folded, chuckling.

"You're no help," I snapped at him. He only chuckled harder. My mother rather resembled a tsunami when she got angry. One just had to go along with her until she ran out of momentum, which wouldn't be any time soon, by the looks of it. If I knew my mother, she was just building up a head of steam.

I winced as she slammed a plate with my crumpet—actually an English muffin—down in front of me, followed by a mug full of milky tea, which slopped onto the tablecloth, and then plopped herself back into her chair. "Eat," she commanded.

Was I in a time warp or what? It was oddly comforting. Maybe Hal was onto something here. I thought about that while I sipped my milky tea. I'd forgotten how good it tasted, especially when I was little and didn't feel good. The "crumpet" was delicious. Melted butter ran down my wrist, and I licked it up, along with the sticky marmalade on my fingers.

Mum shook her head. "*Really*, Antoinette, your manners. Use a napkin."

To my dismay, I found myself protesting, "Aw, Mum," just as I had as a child.

For a moment I was transported back to those days when I knew that no matter what I did, no matter how naughty I was, no matter how angry my mother got, I had absolutely no doubt that I was unconditionally loved. Why couldn't Hal love me like that? Why did he have to go play with Bambi the bimbo?

Damn. Why did I have to think of that? Suddenly I came back to the unwelcome present and the knowledge that Hal did not love me like that, not anymore. Maybe he never had. What did I know? One day he's all distant and preoccupied, and the next he's swearing that he loves me and only me, and then the next day he gets all secretive on me. What was I supposed to think? Which Hal was the real Hal?

My eyes filled with tears, and I turned away so that he and Mum couldn't see them, but it was no use. I couldn't fool Mum. When I felt her arms go around me and heard her softly murmur, "Oh, my baby," I burst into racking sobs. As she rocked me gently, pressing my wet face into her plump shoulder, I heard Hal say, "See?"

It was just that one word, and he didn't add "what I have to put up with," but that's what I heard, and I lost my temper. I completely forgot who'd gotten Mum up here in the first place. Pulling out of her arms, I jumped to my feet and faced him. "*Fuck* you, Hal. Why don't you just go live with your precious Bambi if I'm such a burden to you? I don't need this, and I don't need *you*!"

Hal sat motionless, staring at me, looking as stunned as if I had slapped him. Mum, shocked, exclaimed, "Kitten, you *don't* mean that. Tell Hal you don't mean that, at once. Hal, love, you *know* she doesn't mean that."

I stared back, tears running down my face, unable to speak. At that moment, I meant every word of it. Hal stood up, dropped his napkin on the table, and said quietly, "I think she does." Before either of us could make a move to stop him, he had gone out the kitchen door into the garage.

Mum shook me fiercely. "Go after him," she hissed.

Stubbornly, I didn't move. I sat, arms crossed, and listened to the sounds of the car door slamming, the engine roaring to life, the garage door going up and back down, and the crunch of the tires on the snow in the driveway.

As the sounds died away, Mum glared at me. "You bloody little *idiot*."

Resolutely I shook my head. "He doesn't love me anymore, Mum. He's got a girlfriend. He barely tolerates me anymore. Well, now he doesn't have to tolerate me at all!"

"You don't know what you're talking about," she snapped. "He's told me all about this *Bambi* person. She's just a student with a crush on him. Students get crushes on him all the time. Didn't you tell me that once? Fairly *bragging* about it, you were. My handsome husband, all the girls lust after him, you said, and he's old enough to be their *father*. And *don't* tell me you've forgotten the crush you had on that biology professor at Long Beach State—what was his name, Tillotson or something?"

"Tillett," I corrected her. "I haven't thought about him in years."

"Right, then. But you cried for him night after night and swore that you'd never love another man ..."

"I did not!"

"Yes, kitten, you did. I heard you. But at least you had the good sense not to tell *him* that. That would have been embarrassing in the extreme." She sniffed. "Thank heaven I brought you up better than *that*!"

She had a point there. Especially since my next crush was the chemistry professor that I ended up marrying—the one who didn't love me anymore. But she wasn't through with me yet.

"And while we're on the subject, what about you, young lady?"

"Huh?"

"What about this Bernie Kincaid that Hal caught you with? That doesn't exactly make you the innocent, injured party here, now does it?"

I sighed. "Bernie Kincaid is a cop. He's working on a case that I'm involved in. He invited me to lunch. That's all, I swear to God." I didn't really want to tell my mother about the kiss, but I should have known she'd worm it out of me.

Mum cocked her head and looked at me, assessing. "Methinks you protest too much, my love. Why do you need to swear?"

Like I said before, Mum could see right through me. I looked right into her green eyes, trying to stare her down, but it was no use. "Come, now, darling, there's something you're not telling me. I can see it in your eyes. Now, what is it?"

I gave up. "Okay, okay, I'll tell you. He wants to … uh, have sex with me." I started to say "fuck my brains out" but remembered just in time that I was talking to my mother.

"And you want it too, don't you?"

Oh God, did I ever. I summoned up all the false bravado I could. "Are you kidding? I don't even *like* Bernie Kincaid. Don't you remember? He was the one who wanted to *arrest* me, for God's sake!"

My mother nodded. "Mmm-hmm. He's not exactly being nasty to you now, is he, dear, taking you to lunch and all that. Why did you go if you don't even like him?"

I put my elbows on the table and my face in my hands. "Oh, Mum, I'm so confused."

My mother put her arms around me, and I put my head on her shoulder. She rocked me gently. "Kitten, you and Hal aren't so different. Looking at it from the outside, as I'm doing right now, you both have *exactly* the same problem. You love each other, I've no doubt. But you both have someone else distracting you. It happens. Now you each have to decide how to handle it."

"Well, I know how Hal's going to handle it," I mumbled into her shoulder. "He's probably fucking her right now."

"*Antoinette!*" exclaimed my mother, aghast. "Your *language!*"

I raised my head and looked at her. She was frowning, but there was a smile in her eyes. "Well?" I retorted defensively. "Don't you think that's where he went? Where else would he go?"

"Perhaps. Perhaps not. He's only a man, isn't he?"

"So why is it okay for him and not for me?"

"I didn't *say* that, now, did I?" Mum argued. "Kitten, our religion and practically everyone else's teaches that sex outside of marriage is wrong. Obviously not everybody believes that, or it wouldn't keep *happening*, what? The problem comes afterward, with unwanted pregnancies or diseases—or what if you *actually* fall in love with that person and want to leave your marriage?"

"Maybe I do," I retorted with a flash of anger. "Hal's been *shitty* to me lately. Who needs it? I have enough problems at work with doctors being shitty to me. I don't need to come home to the same thing."

"Wait a minute, kitten," my mother said reprovingly. "Who was shitty to *whom*, just now?"

Hal's mother had nothing on mine when it came to dumping guilt, I reflected. It didn't help that she was absolutely right.

"Mum, what am I going to do?"

"I'm sure you'll figure that out in time, love, but one thing you're *not* going to do is sit around here moping."

I challenged her. "How about if I go find Bernie Kincaid and get fucked? Huh? How about that? Then I won't be sitting around here moping."

Mum shook her head. "You're a big girl now, Antoinette, and I can't tell you what to do and what not to do, but that would be the absolute *wrong* thing for you to do right now."

"Mum, you don't understand. You haven't had sex in years!" I protested and then clapped my hand over my mouth, aghast at what I had just said.

"You shouldn't make assumptions, kitten," my mother said, her green eyes twinkling. "I may be sixty, but I'm not *dead*, don't you know."

I stared at her, speechless. The mere thought of my mother having sex ... oh my God ... blew my mind. And with whom? Surely she was just pulling my chain. She changed the subject.

"What are your friends doing tonight?" she inquired. "We could all go out to dinner—on me. How about it?"

"Okay, I'll give Jodi a call."

"Before you do that, do you suppose you ought to try to call Hal?" Mum suggested.

"You mean interrupt him in mid-fuck?"

"Antoinette!"

"I'm sorry, Mum, but aren't you the one who's always telling me that if you love someone and you let him go and he comes back, then he's truly yours? Well, I feel like that's what I should do with Hal. Let him come back in his own good time. Then I'll know if he's truly mine. If he doesn't come back, then I'll know he never was mine, and I can divorce him and move on. Don't you agree?"

"Darling," she said, "you're absolutely right. I did say that. Now call Jodi."

I did so. "Fiona's here? Cool!" Jodi said. "We're gonna order pizza. Come on over."

Elliott answered the door, hugged Mum, took our coats, and led us into the family room, where a fire crackled merrily in the fireplace. Their family room was much larger than ours, but then it needed to be with five kids. On the couch, Julie and Renee sprawled with books, while the boys lay on the floor in front of the TV playing a video game.

"Where's Hal?" Jodi asked.

I wasn't ready to get into that in front of all these people. "He had to go over to the college for something,"

I said vaguely, hoping she wouldn't pursue it, and she didn't. For one thing, the pizza arrived just then, which caused a mass exodus to the dining room, where the boxes could be spread out on the table with the paper plates and plastic utensils, and everybody could just help themselves.

The kids vanished once dinner was over, either to bed or to their own activities elsewhere. "I talked to Kathleen today," Jodi said. "They're all going to be released tomorrow."

"Oh, good," I said. "I'm glad they're all okay."

"I'm not sure how okay they are," Jodi said. "But at least they're not bleeding anymore. Dr. Marshall scoped Kathleen and did upper GI X-rays on the kids and didn't find any obvious bleeding points, so there's no reason to keep them in the hospital."

"How come Tiffany isn't here?" I asked. "Is she sick too?"

"I don't know. She went back to Ruthie's house, and when I called her she said she was having really bad cramps and was just going to go to bed with her heating pad. Ruthie offered to fix her something to eat, but she said she wasn't hungry."

"Poor thing," said Mum sympathetically.

Elliott changed the subject. "I got the subpoena today for Jay's will," he told me. "They'll get a copy tomorrow."

They, meaning the police. "Good," I said. "Maybe now the firebug will leave us alone."

"What are you talking about, Toni?" asked Jodi.

I told them about my theory that someone was trying to destroy all copies of Jay's first will.

"So what?" asked Jodi. "If that will was done in 1995, and the other one just this year, doesn't that make the second one the legal will? What would be the point in destroying all the copies of the other one?"

"Whatever the reason, somebody seems to have it in for Kathleen and her family. I mean, the fires have involved them in one way or another."

"Not necessarily," Jodi objected. "Maybe the person who set fire to Jay's office was after Lance, not Kathleen. That's probably how the police see it too: two unrelated fires." Seeing the skeptical expressions on our faces, she added, "Well, it's possible, isn't it?"

"Oh, sure, anything's possible, but what a coincidence that somebody murdered *her* husband and burned *her* husband's office and *her* house. What are the chances that those are all unrelated? Besides which, Bernie Kincaid told me today that both fires were arson, with gasoline as the accelerant, and they found an empty gasoline can with the cap off at both fires. If they can get any fingerprints off them, they'll know if the same person set both fires. I'll bet that's what happened. She and her family are the common denominator in all these things. Can't you see that?"

"Oh, I guess I can see it," Jodi admitted, "but *why?* What do they *want?*"

Elliott interrupted. "Kathleen's copy of Jay's will is in her safe deposit box at the bank; and now there's a copy of the new one there too."

"So, which one's legal? The new one, right?"

"In general, that's true," Elliott replied. "But there may be extenuating circumstances. For example, was the decedent of sound mind when he made that will? He seemed to be, but was he really? Did he make it under duress? I didn't think so, but maybe he was and was just damn good at hiding it. There could be factors we don't know about. That might affect the validity of any will, no matter when it was made."

"Doesn't probate take care of that?" I asked.

"Don't you have to decide which will's going to be probated?" Mum inquired.

"Not only that," I interjected. "But if Jay was murdered, doesn't that have to be solved before probate even starts? Isn't there something about a person not being allowed to benefit from his crime?"

"Then somebody's going to a hell of a lot of freakin' trouble for nothing," Elliott commented. "A murder and two fires. What would be the point?"

"We really don't know that it's the *wills* this person's after, do we?" asked my mother. "I mean, it's *daft*. Didn't this Lance person have a fireproof file cabinet in his office? Or a safe? And how would this nut job get at a will in a safe deposit box? Is he going to start burning down *banks* now?"

"There's a thought," I said. "Which bank is Kathleen's safe deposit box in?"

"Twin Falls Bank and Trust," Jodi said. "The same building Elliott's office is in."

Elliott clutched his head. "Jesus, Mary, and Joseph! Don't say that so freakin' loud! You might give this guy ideas. And in any case, *I've* got fireproof file cabinets. The guy'd have to be a freakin' idiot. Who the hell came up with this freakin' will idea in the first place?"

I opened my mouth to answer that, but Elliott forestalled me. "Don't tell me. Shapiro. Right?"

Jodi said, "My head hurts."

"Mum's got a point," I said. "Were there fireproof file cabinets or safes in Lance's office or Jay's office? Seems to me that would be a dandy place to keep documents you didn't want anybody else to know about. If Kathleen set up that Swiss bank account, she might know if the documents pertaining to it are there. Or maybe we can go down to the fire department and see if they managed to salvage anything like that."

"If they did, they'd turn it over to the police," Elliott said.

Okay, I thought. Number four on the list: call the police station tomorrow and find out.

Friday, December 19

Chapter 18

*Yet who would have thought the old man
to have so much blood in him?*
—Shakespeare, *Macbeth*

Lance died during the night, and an autopsy was requested.

I didn't find out until I got to work Friday morning. For once I didn't get awakened in the middle of the night for an autopsy, and wouldn't you know, Hal wasn't here to see it. Or hear it. Or not hear it. Whatever. Go figure.

Even so, I hadn't slept well, and it wasn't due to visions of sugarplums dancing in my head. Even with makeup on, I looked like a dog's breakfast, as Mum would put it. Mike would be sure to notice and comment on it.

And he did. "Y'all don't look so good," he observed. "What the hell's goin' on with y'all?"

I leaned wearily against the doorjamb. "I'm just a little tired, that's all. I'd hoped it wasn't quite that obvious."

"Well, I tell you what," Mike said. "You look like hell. You don't just look tired, you look sick. Are you sure you're okay?"

"I told you. I'm just tired. Okay?"

"Well, excuse the hell out of me. Y'all don't need to bite my head off."

"Sorry, Mikey. I didn't mean to snap."

"Y'all want to talk about it?"

"Not really."

Mike took me by the shoulders, steered me to a chair, and pushed me into it. He pulled his chair around to face me and sat down so close that our knees touched. "Well, you need to," he said sternly. "Hell, you've been lookin' like dog meat lately."

"Oh, come on," I objected. "I don't look *that* bad."

"All I'm sayin' is, you keep on like this, and then you *are* gonna get sick, and then I'll have to work twice as hard to keep this department going. Somethin's goin' on, and I need to know what it is. It's not me, is it?"

The idea was so ludicrous that I burst out laughing. "What's so funny?" Mike demanded.

"Nothing," I protested, controlling myself with difficulty. "That thought never occurred to me. No, it's Hal. He left me last night. He's got a girlfriend. I really didn't want to talk about all this," I added as tears came to my eyes and I turned my head away. Mike reached out and turned it back, looking into my eyes.

"I'd say that's more than enough," he said gently. "I tell you what. I thought you and Hal were solid as a rock. What happened?"

I didn't want to talk about Hal, but with Mike's gentle urging, I soon found myself telling him about how distant

Hal had been over the last few months, his constant criticism, Marilyn spilling the beans about seeing Hal kissing a student, and me seeing them together at the bar with Bernie. My tears flowed freely, and somehow I found myself sobbing on Mike's shoulder with his arms around me.

"Well, isn't this cozy," observed a caustic voice behind me, and Mike and I jumped apart guiltily to see Hal standing in the doorway. *Oh, fuck. What next?* I stood rooted to the floor, staring at him, unable to speak. Hal stared back coldly and then turned away. By the time Mike and I managed to reach the doorway, he was out of sight. The whole thing happened so quickly that I wasn't sure I hadn't imagined it. But Mike's reaction told me otherwise.

"Damn. I'm sorry, Toni," he said. "Now he thinks you're fooling around with me."

"I've got to go after him," I said. "Did you see which way he went?"

I turned to go, but at that moment, Lucille appeared in the doorway, her round face avid with curiosity. "Sorry to interrupt you guys, but there's a frozen."

Flustered, Mike and I stared at each other. "Whose turn is it?" he muttered. "I can't remember."

"I think it's me," I said. I'd be glad of the opportunity to hide my hot face in the cold cryostat for a while. Also, the decision whether or not to run after Hal had been effectively taken out of my hands. Oh, sure, if I really had wanted to run after Hal, Mike would have been glad to handle the frozen for me. But what would I have said, anyway? *I'm not fooling around with Mike. Oh yeah*, he would have said, *sure looked like it to me. First Kincaid, and now your partner.* And we would be saying all this right out in the hallway with people going by and hearing everything—and then talking about it.

The hole I was digging myself into with Hal resembled the one on the patient's face, once the surgeon and I got done with it. It was a basal cell carcinoma—actually a basal cell marathon—as margin after margin turned out to be positive, resulting in the removal of more and more skin, until the patient would need a skin graft to close the defect.

Finally, after an hour and a half, the excision was deemed to be complete. For that patient, my job was done, but the poor surgeon still had to repair the damage.

And I'd completely recovered from the morning's emotional excesses. In fact, I felt embarrassed, now that Mike knew about my marital problems, and I was reluctant to face him. Not a good situation for professional partners to be in, but Mike solved that problem for me by marching into my office, coffee cup in hand, and flopping into a chair.

"Are you done signing out already?" I asked.

"Done dictating. Just have to wait for the typing. How about y'all tell me about this autopsy? We're gonna do it together, right?"

So we went over the chart and decided on a battle plan that should cover anything Ruthie could possibly come up with to sue us for.

Then Mike went back to his office and I got busy with my list. So far I'd only been able to check off one item: Jeannie's pregnancy test. Next, I'd established the existence of an oral form of heparin, but I still had to find out if anybody involved in this case was taking it.

That one looked like it would be the most labor intensive, so I mentally shuffled it to the back and tackled Dave McClure's alibi next.

I Googled him and obtained his office address and phone number. Then I called the number and got the receptionist, whose name was Carol. Carol was happy to inform me that Dave and his new wife, Jennifer, were on a Caribbean cruise and were not expected back until next week. When had they left? Oh, let's see now. The wedding was on Saturday the sixth, so they left on the seventh, and they should be back on the twenty-first. Could she tell him who called? Was there a message? I said no to both and hung up.

That took care of Dave. If he'd left on a cruise the seventh, he certainly wasn't around to murder Jay Braithwaite Burke on the eleventh. Next, the contents of Lance's office.

I called the police station and asked for Pete. I was reluctant to talk to Bernie; I didn't really know what to say to him. *Thanks a lot, bub. You got me in trouble with my husband. Oh yeah? All I did was invite you to lunch. You could have said no. Why didn't you? Don't put all this on me. It takes two to kiss, you know.*

But Pete wasn't available and Bernie was, so it seemed I had no choice.

"Toni? What can I do for you? Have you changed your mind?"

Oh, for God's sake. "No, Bernie, that's not what I called about. I was wondering if the fire department recovered anything from the fire at Jay Braithwaite Burke's and Lance Brooks's law office, like a fireproof file cabinet or a safe."

"I don't know," he said. "They haven't turned any in to us yet. Why do you want to know?"

"I'm curious about what might be in them. Like wills. Or bank statements from a Swiss bank account. I want to know if Jay Braithwaite Burke actually had any money for anybody to inherit."

"And you want to know this why?"

"I'm trying to figure out a motive for those fires. If there's no money to inherit, why would anybody set fires and nearly kill eight people just to destroy a will?"

"Okay, Toni, now listen to me. We have copies of both wills. Unless there are extenuating circumstances that we don't know about yet, Jay's second will is the legal will. So why does anybody need to destroy copies of the first one? What would be the point? And in any case, Kathleen probably keeps her copy in a safety-deposit box. Most people do. Surely you don't think this scumbag is going to start burning down *banks* now, do you?"

He sounded like Mum.

"If that's not the reason for the fires, what is?" I persisted. "If whoever it was is trying to kill people, he needs to do a better job."

"All right, Toni, you may have a point. Let me call my buddy Roy Cobb and get back to you, okay?"

Hmph. I *may* have a point? I slammed the phone down. "Asshole," I muttered, just as Natalie came into my office with a tray of Pap smears.

"Goodness, I hope that wasn't Hal," she said, smiling as she put the tray on my desk. Speechless, I stared at her. "Sorry. I was just kidding," she blurted, red-faced, and fled.

I had managed to push Hal to the back of my mind while talking on the phone, but now the tears came to my eyes, and I had buried my face in my hands trying to control myself when Lucille came in. "What's wrong with Natalie?" she demanded, hands on her ample hips. Then she saw my face. "Jesus Christ, Doc, what's wrong with *you*?"

"Lucille, please don't say anything," Natalie begged as she came in practically on Lucille's heels. Her face, like mine, was tear-stained. She stopped short when she saw my face, and Mike, right behind her, almost bumped into her. "I'm so sorry, Doctor," she sobbed. "Doctor Mike just told me."

"Told you what?" I glared at Mike, who looked sheepish.

"Now, Toni, don't get all pissy. Y'all shouldn't have to deal with this alone."

"I'm not alone," I started to say, when Lucille grabbed me in a bear hug, practically smothering me in her ample bosom. "Honey, I know what you're going through. I've been there. Three times," she added with a rueful chuckle.

I knew that. I even remembered all of them.

Natalie put her arms around both Lucille and me. "You and Hal were there for Dale and me when we needed it," she sniffled. "The least I can do is be there for you."

Despite my indignation, I felt touched by their concern. "Thank you, I think," I said unsteadily. "But I don't want the whole hospital to know. I don't even want the whole *lab* to know. I don't want to have to keep *explaining* to people ..."

They assured me that they hadn't told anybody else, but I was skeptical. In a hospital, especially in a hospital lab, the walls have ears.

With Bluetooth amplifiers.

Mike and I weren't able to get to the autopsy until four o'clock. When we arrived at Parkside Mortuary, Rollie expressed surprise at seeing both of us there.

"Can't take the chance," Mike told him, brandishing his Nikon. "Dude's a lawyer."

Rollie nodded and looked wise. "I see," was all he said.

It occurred to me that I was about to autopsy the fourth and final member of the firm of Burke, Braithwaite, Burke, Bartlett and Brooks, Attorneys at Law, because, looking back in my records, I discovered that I'd also autopsied Bill Bartlett ten years ago.

I try not to be superstitious. I am, after all, a physician and should not be susceptible to those sorts of things, in spite of being half Irish on my father's side; but I had a very bad feeling about this autopsy.

I'd even talked to Monty, who informed me that he'd already discussed the case with the hospital's legal counsel, who said we had nothing to worry about.

Mike and I had decided to handle this case as a homicide and leave no stone unturned. Well, we didn't do a rape kit, but other than that …

First, we drew blood from the heart for possible laboratory studies. The blood flowed easily into the syringe, and we kept drawing it until we had filled every kind of tube the lab used. We collected all the urine in the Foley catheter bag. It was grossly bloody.

We removed all the intravenous lines. Blood ran from the puncture sites. When we removed the endotracheal tube, the mucus was bloody. The drainage from the nasogastric tube was bloody.

I had a definite feeling of déjà vu. "Mikey," I said, "this is creeping me out."

"How's that?"

"Too much blood. It reminds me of Jay Braithwaite Burke."

The resemblance didn't stop there. When I made my Y-shaped incision, bloody ascites fluid, under pressure within the abdomen, shot nearly to the ceiling. We hastily jumped back to avoid a bloodbath. We had to suction out several liters of it in order to see the contents of the abdomen more clearly. That was a bit of a problem, owing to extensive scarring and adhesions because of Lance's multiple bowel resections. There were no clots at all, anywhere. Liquid blood filled the stomach, esophagus, small bowel, and colon, as well as bronchi and trachea. The lungs showed hemorrhage and edema, and both chest cavities contained bloody pleural fluid.

We collected gastric and small bowel contents, just in case toxicology would be needed, although we didn't really think it would be.

Normally we would have taken a chunk of liver for toxicology too, but we didn't, because Lance's liver was almost totally replaced by grayish-white tumor nodules. The remaining uninvolved liver was dark green. The tumor originated in the head of the pancreas and blocked not only the pancreatic duct but also the common bile duct, causing bile to back up into the liver, which accounted for its color. We were both amazed that Lance had survived this long.

The cancer certainly contributed to Lance's death, but the actual cause of death was a coagulation disorder. Lance had bled to death, just like his partner, Jay Braithwaite Burke.

It was not clear what had caused the coagulopathy. The coagulation factors are made in the liver, so it could have been caused by the condition of Lance's liver.

It could have been DIC, disseminated intravascular coagulation, in which blood clotting is accelerated for some reason, using up all the coagulation factors in the blood. It frequently happens with massive tissue trauma, where tissue procoagulants are released; but it also happens with cancers, and pancreatic cancer is notorious for that. DIC is treated with heparin to prevent further clotting, and fresh frozen plasma to replace the clotting factors.

Or it could have been dilutional. Lance had received twelve units of blood, which was essentially an exchange transfusion. But he'd also received heparin and several units of fresh-frozen plasma, which should have helped but didn't.

The last possibility was an overdose of an anticoagulant drug, but Lance had died in a hospital setting for more than adequate clinical reasons other than overdose for bleeding to death. Besides, the only anticoagulant drug that Lance was on was heparin, and heparin dosage is carefully monitored. Of course his doctor, George, still living in the last century, had used the PTT instead of anti-Xa, but the PTT had been meticulously kept in the therapeutic range, and everything was documented. If someone had snuck in and shot a bunch of undocumented extra heparin into Lance's IV, the PTT would have showed it—unless it had been done all at once and Lance had died soon thereafter, before any more PTTs could be done.

Mike and I documented every step of the autopsy with photographs, and we took more than adequate samples of tissue and blood so that a complete laboratory coag workup could be done.

Maybe that would clear up the mystery, but I was skeptical. The mechanisms of blood coagulation were extremely complex, and lab tests to detect coagulation factor defects were fraught with preanalytical interferences—that is, factors that affect the blood before it gets tested—one of the more obvious ones being that the patient should not be on any anticoagulant drugs at all. And of course most of them were.

Lance being a case in point.

Mike and I lugged the specimen buckets back to the lab, where Mike took charge of them. I could have gone home at this point and probably should have, since Mum was there and possibly Hal, but I had a definite approach/avoidance conflict going on. So I decided to spend a little time trying to figure out who was taking rivaroxaban.

Lance? I didn't remember seeing it in his medical record, but then I wouldn't have known what it was if I had seen it. So I looked again. It wasn't there. I suppose it would be a bit much to be taking oral heparin and injecting Lovenox too. I mean, why would one do both if one didn't have to?

Kathleen and family had been admitted with hematemesis the day after they'd gone from Jodi and

Elliott's to Ruthie's house. So if Lance didn't have rivaroxaban, how about Ruthie?

I looked her up and hit pay dirt.

Ruthie had the same prothrombin mutation that Lance had. Did they meet in a coagulopathy support group, or what? She also had another genetically altered coagulation factor that causes increased blood clotting: Factor V Leiden. So George Marshall had her in a clinical trial on rivaroxaban.

So that's why Lance and Ruthie didn't have kids. Pregnancy itself is an additional risk factor for deep vein thrombosis. Ruthie'd had one pregnancy in her early twenties and gotten DVT, thrown pulmonary emboli, nearly died, and lost the baby. That was when she'd first been worked up. She hadn't been able to take birth control pills either, because they also increase the risk of DVT, so she had a tubal ligation.

The news that she had both prothrombin mutation 20210 and Factor V Leiden had come later, as those mutations were unknown back when Ruthie got pregnant. Factor V Leiden wasn't discovered until six years later, and the prothrombin mutation 20210 two years after that. Ruthie had first been tested for them four years ago.

Unfortunately for her, rivaroxaban hadn't been approved for clinical trials until this year. Up until March of this year, Ruthie had used Lovenox, same as Lance.

Out of curiosity, I pursued the subject a bit further to see just how a hypothetical child of Ruthie and Lance might have fared genetically.

The chances that their offspring would have either one of those mutations were better than one would think: one in fifty Americans is heterozygous for the prothrombin

20210 mutation, meaning the mutation is on only one of two sets of chromosomes; and one in four thousand Americans is heterozygous for factor V Leiden.

Unfortunately, both mutations are inherited as an autosomal dominant, meaning it only takes one mutation for a person to have the condition; so the chance of one person having both mutations would be one in twenty thousand.

Furthermore, the risk of deep vein thrombosis with 20210 would be two to three times that of a normal person. Add Factor V Leiden, and it becomes ten to twenty times the risk.

With a couple like Lance and Ruthie, there's a 75 percent chance that their child would have 20210, and 25 percent for factor V Leiden. Even worse, there's a 25 percent chance that their child could be homozygous for prothrombin 20210, meaning the mutation is on *both* sets of chromosomes, doubling the risk.

On top of that, the child could *also* be homozygous for prothrombin 20210 and heterozygous for Factor V Leiden, making the risk of DVT … well, you do the math.

I didn't want to do the math. Jeez, I thought, any child of theirs would be a walking, talking blood clot—that is, if it ever made it out of the uterus.

So Ruthie had the wherewithal to poison the Burkes with rivaroxaban, but that didn't necessarily mean that she had done it.

How could I find out?

Well, for one thing, none of the Burkes were taking rivaroxaban. Were they? Not the children, surely, but perhaps it wouldn't hurt to check Kathleen. If she wasn't taking it, then all I had to do was check their anti-Xa levels. If any of them had anti-Xa, it would mean there was heparin in their blood.

There was no mention of rivaroxaban in Kathleen's medical history. She had no history of bleeding or DVT—at least not until this past Wednesday.

And we still had blood samples on all of them from when they were in the hospital, samples that were now only slightly over the forty-eight-hour limit. All that meant was that the test might not be accurate, but all I was interested in was whether anti-Xa was present or absent, and the samples ought to be just fine for that purpose.

It was now nearly eight o'clock, and Mum was at home alone, unless Jodi and Elliott had gone over to keep her company. She knew I was doing an autopsy and that I'd be late, because I had called her earlier. By now the tech on call had left, and so had Mike.

In the chemistry refrigerator, I found racks of blood tubes from Wednesday and pulled out the coag tubes for Kathleen and the kids. Brenda had spun down Lance's coag tube when Mike gave it to her earlier, and pulled off the plasma. I retrieved that tube from today's rack. In the cupboard I found requisitions and ordered anti-Xa's on all of them. I put the tubes in a rack together in the refrigerator and left the requisitions on the desk with a note: Do ASAP and call me!

Then I went home.

Mum and Jodi were watching a movie on DVD.

Hal wasn't home. I called his cell.

It went straight to voice mail.

Saturday, December 20

Chapter 19

A man always has two reasons for what he does;
a good one, and the real one.
—J. Pierpont Morgan

Hal didn't come home Friday night either.

Jodi and Elliott came over, and Mum made breakfast for all of us.

Elliott took me to task. "I heard you did an autopsy last night."

I nodded.

"On Lance Brooks," he continued.

"Yes, so?"

"Are you freakin' nuts? Are you aware that Ruthie Brooks is suing the hospital?"

"We thought she might," I said.

Elliott sighed. "You usually call me about things like that. Why didn't you this time?"

"I don't call you," I informed him. "Hal does. And Hal isn't here. Hal knows nothing about this. And furthermore, I didn't do it alone; Mike and I did it together, and we took pictures, and drew lots of blood, and we found nothing to indicate any fault on the part of the doctors. They did everything they could do, and it wasn't enough."

"Are you aware that I'm the hospital's legal counsel?"

Whoa. "Since when?" I demanded.

"Since the beginning of the year," Elliott said. "I thought you knew. Doesn't that stuffed shirt Monty Montgomery keep you guys informed?"

I folded my arms defensively across my chest. "Not very well, apparently. And I talked to Monty before we did that autopsy too. He said there was nothing to worry about, and he told me the hospital's legal counsel also said there was nothing to worry about. So was that you, or was he just talking through his hat?"

Elliott ignored my question. "So what killed him? What was the cause of death? I haven't seen a freakin' report."

"That's because there isn't one yet. For God's sake, Elliott, we just did it yesterday! We always provide a preliminary report within two working days. That's Tuesday. So quit nagging me!" I was on my feet now, and Elliott got up and pushed me back into my chair.

"Toni, for God's sake, take it easy! I'm on your side, remember? I just wondered what the freakin' cause of death was."

"Hey! Quit pushing my wife around!"

Startled, Elliott let go of my shoulders as if he had been burned, and Jodi and I spun around to see Hal, who had just walked into the kitchen. None of us had heard the garage door opening.

Hal took me in his arms and kissed me with emphasis. "Hi, sweetie," he whispered, holding me tight. I was about to whisper back when I saw who was standing behind him.

Tall. Leggy. Tanned. Long, blonde hair. *Oh, no, it can't be. He wouldn't dare.* "What's *she* doing here?" I hissed.

Hal reached out with one long arm and pulled the girl closer. I tried to pull away, but he kept the other arm firmly around me as he announced, "Everyone, I'd like you to meet my daughter Barbara, otherwise known as Bambi. This is my wife, Toni, and these are our best friends, Elliott and Jodi Maynard, and my mother-in-law, Fiona Day."

Daughter?

Shyly, Bambi extended her hand to me and said, "Please call me Bambi. I hate Barbara."

Picking my jaw up off the ground and not knowing what else to do, I took her hand, which felt like ice. Her blue eyes met mine, and in them I saw the scared child underneath the California surfer-girl exterior, and before I knew it, I'd pulled her into my arms, and she was sobbing on my shoulder.

"Hal," I said over her shoulder, "you've got a shitload of explaining to do."

"I suppose I have," Hal agreed. "But I need to have some catch-up time with my wife first."

Betcher ass you do, you bastard.

The three of us went upstairs. Bambi wanted to take a shower and get into some clean clothes, so while she was doing that, Hal and I shut ourselves in the master bedroom and turned on the radio to muffle our voices.

Hal sat on the edge of the bed and patted the bed next to him.

Reluctantly, I perched tentatively on the very edge of the bed. This was a Hal that I didn't know, and I didn't know how to act. However, we had a lot of territory to cover and very little time. I waited impatiently for him to speak. He seemed to take an inordinately long time to formulate exactly what to say.

"*Well?*" I finally said, unable to contain myself any longer.

"Bambi's parents were here this weekend," he began. "Bambi wanted me to meet them. You could have knocked me over with a feather when I discovered that Bambi's mother was none other than Shawna."

Shawna. Hal's first wife. The one he cheated on with me and then divorced to marry me. Once a cheater, always a cheater, Mum had warned me; but after seventeen years without even a hint that Hal had cheated on me, I'd become complacent, thinking that he never would. Had Mum been right all along? Mum, who had told me just the other day that she didn't think I needed to worry about Hal? If Mum had changed her mind and believed that I could trust Hal, why couldn't I? I wanted so badly to be able to trust him. *Please God, let it be.*

Anyway, getting back to the conversation at hand, Hal and Shawna didn't have children, I thought. In fact, their marriage was already in trouble long before I ever met Hal—for that very reason. Hal wanted them and Shawna didn't. So where did this one come from? "Really," I said skeptically. "Shawna's here. How nice."

Hal sighed. "Not really. Shawna and her husband, Marty, and their two sons are here to spend some time with Bambi for Hanukkah."

"Hanukkah's not till tomorrow," I said, just to be obstinate.

"Toni …"

"And she wanted them to meet her new boyfriend," I said sarcastically.

"No, she wanted them to meet the professor she's working for. I told you before, Toni. She's my lab assistant, not my girlfriend."

Oh, right. Why am I having trouble believing that? With difficulty, I managed to keep my mouth shut, but I'm sure my face showed my skepticism.

"Anyway, Shawna informed me that she was already pregnant when she married Marty and that I was Bambi's real father."

"And you didn't know that until now?" I asked. "Did Marty know?"

"No," Hal said. "He still doesn't, and I hope he never finds out, because unless he and Shawna have a stronger marriage than Shawna and I had, this could tear it apart."

"Why didn't she tell you that she was pregnant with your child before she divorced you? Wouldn't you have had to give her child support?"

Hal looked uncomfortable. "Not if she was married to somebody else. I guess she figured that Marty wouldn't marry her if he knew, and since she hasn't ever told him up to now, I'd guess that was the case."

"I suppose Marty has money?"

"More than God. He owns a car dealership in Newport Beach. Mercedes, BMW, stuff like that."

Newport Beach is a wealthy coastal town. Lots of doctors from UC Irvine live there. A Mercedes dealership there would be a gold mine.

I had to ask, even though I already suspected. "So you were still fucking Shawna at the same time you were fucking me?"

"Well, I still had to maintain my relationship with Shawna so she wouldn't suspect anything. It was supposed to be a no-fault divorce. If she'd known about you and me, she could have charged me with adultery and taken me for everything I had and then some. So I kept fucking her right up until we filed for divorce and I moved out."

"Hmph." I wasn't sure how I should feel about that, but it was a long time ago. I decided to let that subject drop. "So what did she do, just take you aside and drop it on you, just like that?"

"Pretty much."

"Why bother?" I wondered. "She could have just let you go on thinking Bambi was Marty's daughter. Couldn't she?"

Now Hal looked really uncomfortable. "I think she was trying to start a fight. She wanted to see how I'd react to finding out I'd been fucking my own daughter."

Aha! Now we're getting somewhere. "So you *have* been fucking Bambi," I accused. So much for trust.

"No," Hal said. "I haven't; and even if I'd wanted to, I sure as hell wouldn't now."

"Did she tell Bambi too or leave that for you to do?" I was pretty sure I knew the answer to that one. Shawna never did anything she didn't need to do. Dumping it on Hal was typical of her, from what he'd said about her over the years.

"It was pretty traumatic for her, finding out about her real father at this late date—especially after making a pass at me the other day. That had to be embarrassing. We spent a lot of time talking. It got pretty emotional. That's why I didn't come home. Obviously I couldn't just leave her there with Shawna and Marty, and I certainly couldn't bring her here."

"You couldn't call me and let me know what was going on?"

"I don't see how," Hal said. "What would I have said? How would you have taken it? Can you see us having this conversation over the phone? With your mother listening? And maybe Jodi and Elliott?"

He had a point there, I had to admit. However, I had one more question. We might as well get it all out in the open while we had the chance, I figured. With all that was going on, there'd be precious little opportunity from now on. "Did you think about having sex with her? Did you want to?"

Hal turned his palms up. "To be honest? Sure, it occurred to me, and sure, I thought about it. She's a beautiful girl, and she's the image of Shawna at that age, so yeah, I thought about it. *Of course* I thought about it; I'm not *dead*, you know." He sounded like Mum. "But I divorced Shawna to marry you. Why would I jeopardize what I have with you just to repeat history? Why would I risk losing everything I hold dear just to have a fling with a student?"

"It *would* be a stupid thing to do," I remarked.

"It would," Hal agreed. "And I didn't do it. Now, what about you and Bernie Kincaid?"

So he doesn't trust me either. The thought made me feel like crying. Did the thought that I didn't trust him make Hal feel that way too? "What *about* me and Bernie Kincaid? Nothing's changed since the last time you asked me that!"

"Calm down," Hal said. "I'm not accusing you of anything. But you did go to lunch with him, and he did have his arms around you. Can you honestly say that it never occurred to you that it could go further? That you thought about it?"

I sighed. "Yes, to be honest, I did consider having an affair with him. After all, I thought you were having one with Bambi. But I didn't."

"Okay," Hal said. "You didn't have an affair. I didn't have an affair. Now can we put all that behind us?" He held out his arms. "How about it?"

Trust is a two-way street. You trust me. I trust you. I moved closer, and we held each other tight.

"I love you, Toni," he said into my hair.

"I love you, Hal."

He let go of me and stood up, offering me a hand. "Good. Now let's go downstairs and try to explain all this to the others."

When we went downstairs, we found that Jodi and Elliott had left. "They got a phone call, dear," Mum said, "and they just left."

"Didn't they tell you why?" I asked.

"It seemed to be some kind of emergency," Mum replied. "But they didn't stay long enough to explain."

"Jeez," Hal said. "I hope it's not one of the kids."

"And there was a call for you too, kitten," Mum said. "You're supposed to call the lab."

"Are you on call?" Hal asked me.

"No," I said. "Mike is. But I think I know what this is about."

"What?" Hal asked, but I had already picked up the phone. "Tell you in a minute," I said, "assuming this is what I think it is."

Brenda answered the phone when I called the lab. "I did all those anti-Xa's," she said, "but did you realize that all the specimens from the Burke family are over forty-eight hours old?"

"I knew that," I said, "but I just wanted to know if they had any anti-Xa at all. Do they?"

"They sure do. A lot of it," Brenda said. "Were they on heparin in the hospital?"

"No. They weren't. That's the point."

"Well, then, how …" Brenda began, and then she said, "Oh. You think they were poisoned."

"Exactly."

"Are you saying," Brenda said, "that you think somebody in the hospital poisoned them?"

"No, it happened before they were in the hospital."

"But how?"

"Brenda," I said. "Sometime I'll tell you all about it, but for right now, keep it under your hat, okay? It might end up in court someday."

"Oh, is it a murder case?" she asked.

"It might turn out that way," I replied.

"Lance Brooks had a lot of it too," Brenda said. "But he was on heparin, wasn't he?"

"Yes, he was."

"So he wasn't poisoned," Brenda said.

That remains to be seen. "Probably not," I said.

What I needed to do now was to go to the hospital and try to correlate all those anti-Xa levels with the amount of heparin it would take to get them that high. There were graphs available with which to do that. Using them, maybe I could figure out how much rivaroxaban each of the Burkes had been given to get them that high. In Lance's case, I would try to correlate his anti-Xa level with the amount of heparin his medical record said he got, and see if it jibed.

If it didn't, then maybe Lance was poisoned too.

As I was explaining all this to Hal, the doorbell rang. Mum opened the door to admit Jodi, who now wore a bright-orange warm-up suit that absolutely screamed at her red hair. I squinted at her; the color combination made my eyes hurt. "Thank God you guys are still here," she said breathlessly. "Have you got some extra blankets and pillows we can borrow?"

Oh, no, not again. This could only mean one thing.

Chapter 20

Mordre wol out, that we see day by day.
—Chaucer

"I'm sure we do," Hal said, "but what do you need them for … oh, no, don't tell me."

"Let me guess," I chimed in. "Ruthie had a fire."

Jodi nodded grimly. "You got it," she said. "We've got Ruthie and all the Burkes, Tiffany, and Emily. We'll take anything you can spare."

The firebug was obviously not done.

"Holy shit," Hal said. "Honey? Can you …?" He gestured in the general direction of the stairs.

He didn't have to say any more. Groaning, I heaved myself off the couch, dislodging Geraldine, who moved to the end of the couch and gave me a dirty look. Killer, who had been lying on the floor next to me, got to his feet, tail wagging. No doubt he expected a Milk Bone, but he was doomed to disappointment this time.

Bambi, who had come downstairs just in time to hear the tail end of this conversation, said, "I'll help you,

Toni," and followed me upstairs to the linen closet, where we found several blankets and quilts and throws and pillows—and even Hal's and my sleeping bags—while Killer and Geraldine danced around us, convinced that they were helping too.

Of course, the reason I had to do linen detail in the first place was that Hal never put anything away, so he never knew where anything was. He was great at folding things up and putting them into a nice neat pile, as I've already mentioned, but never in the linen closet where they belonged. In Hal's world, the linen closet was my domain, where no man dared to venture.

Then, of course, I had to do cat detail. We'd never forgotten the time Spook had gotten into the linen closet while I was putting things away and then hadn't been seen for two days. Hal had said to me, just in passing, "You know, I haven't seen Spook for a while, and his food dish is still full," and I'd said, "Oh my God" and run upstairs to open the linen closet; whereupon one very irate cat had leaped out at me, snarling, and headed like a blue streak right for his food dish.

Then, of course, I'd had to do cat shit detail.

With Bambi helping, it only took two trips to get all the bedding downstairs.

"Is there anything we can do to help?" my mother asked, but Jodi shook her head.

"It's all under control, so far."

Better her than me, I thought uncharitably. She and Kathleen were far better equipped to deal with hordes of distraught children than I was. Bambi helped Jodi carry all the bedding back over to her house and told us that she was going to stay for a while and see what she could do to help. Maybe she knew what she was doing; after all, she did have younger brothers. Anyway, if she got in the way, Jodi wouldn't hesitate to send her home.

I knew darn well that I'd only be in the way. My experiences with other people's children frequently included some thoughtless person saying, "She's a doctor. If you don't behave, she'll give you a shot," which caused the children to shrink from me in terror, and any chance of ever gaining some kind of rapport with them went right out the window.

So I took the opportunity to go back to my office and do a little research. Brenda, on call for the weekend, was working alone and running her feet off between the lab, the emergency room, and the hospital floor—going to draw specimens, bringing them back to the lab to run tests, and then getting called to draw somebody else.

I knew from my own experiences as a med tech that holiday weekends were the pits as far as accidents and sudden illnesses were concerned, and Christmas was the worst. All that stress. All that rich food. All those GI bleeders and heart attacks. The occasional slip of the carving knife. It reminded me of Dickens's *A Christmas Carol.*

An undigested bit of beef, a blot of mustard, a crumb of cheese, a fragment of an underdone potato …

I pulled Lance Brooks up on the computer and reviewed his postmortem lab results as well as his medication history.

His prothrombin time and INR were normal, but his activated PTT and his anti-Xa were sky high.

On the Internet I found a table showing the heparin dosage needed to put the anti-Xa at a therapeutic level in patients of various body weights. Not surprisingly, obese patients required a much higher dosage than those wasted away to skin and bone, like Lance. In the electronic medical record, I noted the heparin dosage Lance had been on.

They didn't correlate.

Not even a little bit.

There was no way that the heparin Lance was documented to have received in the hospital accounted for the anti-Xa level in his blood. Not unless someone had given him a whole lot of extra heparin, off the record.

So, who did we know that had sat by Lance's bedside for days, even before he was taken to ICU? And furthermore, who did we know that had a bagful of Lovenox at her disposal? And who could have injected a truckload of it into Lance's IV when nobody was looking—like an entire boxful of ten syringes? She'd probably had them in her purse.

I went back and looked at premortem records, just in case this had been going on for a while. But Lance's heparin had been monitored with the PTT, and that had been therapeutic or close to it. This meant that Ruthie, or somebody else, couldn't have been giving Lance Lovenox until the day before he died.

Just for the hell of it, I went back to the Internet and looked up rivaroxaban again and discovered that while anti-Xa could be used to monitor it, PTT could not. Ruthie could have been giving Lance rivaroxaban all along, at home and in the hospital, right up until he was intubated, and his physicians, who had ordered only PTTs, would never have known.

What surprised me was that rivaroxaban prolonged the *prothrombin* time. I supposed it made sense in a way. The prothrombin time was affected by the Vitamin K-dependent coagulation factors, prothrombin, VII, IX, and X. Rivaroxaban was an activated factor X inhibitor.

So *that's* why Jay Braithwaite Burke's pro-time and INR were elevated.

The phone rang. And kept ringing. I went into the lab. No Brenda. I picked up the phone. "Lab, Dr. Day."

"Dr. Day?" The charge nurse sounded frazzled. Her voice was raspy. "What are you doing here today?"

"Just catching up on a little work," I told her. "If you're looking for Brenda, she's in the ER."

Not for the first time, I wondered why the on-call techs couldn't carry pagers. We'd asked for them repeatedly but had been told they were too expensive: that poor-relation thing again.

Brenda walked in and put her tray down on the desk. She looked exhausted. I told her the charge nurse was looking for her, and she sagged visibly.

"Brenda, you've been run ragged already. Don't you have someone on standby in case you get hammered?"

"Yeah. Margo."

"Call her," I urged. "Get some help. You keep on like this and you'll make yourself sick."

"Are you sure, Doctor? They're always after us to cut back on call time."

I knew that. I also remembered the time Monty had come into the lab to talk to Margo about that. "Is there any way that you and your techs can cut back on call time?" he'd asked.

"Certainly," she'd answered calmly. "Nothing easier. Which of the doctors would you like us to ignore?"

Monty hadn't been able to answer that question, because it was an unanswerable question. It was the doctors who asked for lab work during on-call hours, and who was going to tell them they couldn't?

For that matter, when were the powers-that-be going to realize that a hospital this size needed three shifts in the lab? It wasn't like I hadn't nagged them unmercifully for the last four hundred years.

"This is only Saturday, and you're half dead," I said in answer to Brenda's question. "So call Margo."

Then I went back to my office and pulled up the records of Kathleen and the children, noting their anti-Xa levels. It took me a while, but I managed to figure out the amount of rivaroxaban needed to get the Burkes' anti-Xa levels that high by comparing them to Lovenox dosages; admittedly an inexact method, but all of their anti-Xa levels were way out of the therapeutic range from either drug, no matter how exact or inexact my calculations were.

I printed off all the lab reports for the police and put them in my purse. Then I called the station and talked to Pete. "I've got some lab results you might be interested in," I said.

"Really? On who?"

"Lance Brooks," I said. "Also Kathleen Burke and the kids. It proves they were poisoned. Do you want me to bring them down to the station?"

"Where are you?"

"In my office."

"We'll meet you there." He hung up.

We? Uh-oh.

Not only that, but now I was stuck there waiting for them to show up. To kill time, I decided that I might as well haul out Lance's autopsy tissues and cut them into sections to be processed on Monday. The sooner I had slides, the sooner I could sign it out, and then it would be ready for Ruthie to sue us.

Pete and Bernie showed up after about fifteen minutes. "Okay, let's see whatcha got," demanded Bernie gruffly.

See what I've got? Seriously? No, he didn't mean it that way. Did he?

I showed them the lab reports and explained what they meant. It didn't take long. I think I was talking extra fast, because I was extremely uncomfortable around Kincaid. Not because of anything he said or did. He was the epitome of propriety. No, it was all me. When they took the lab reports and left, I heaved a huge sigh of relief.

I dumped the tissue cassettes into a container of formalin, labeled it with the autopsy number, and went home.

Hal sat glowering like a thundercloud from his recliner. "Where the hell have you been?"

"At work," I said.

"All this time?"

"Before you start your rant, could you please give me time to tell you what I found? You might want to congratulate me instead of ripping me a new asshole."

"Yes, Hal, dear," my mother said. "I, for one, would like to hear what she's got to say."

Hal folded his arms and looked mutinous.

"I got anti-Xa's on Lance and Kathleen and all the kids," I said. "They were off the chart. All of them. Do you realize what that means?"

"That's a test for heparin, right?" he asked. "Does that mean that Kathleen and the kids had been given heparin?"

"That's exactly what it means," I said. "That's why they were bleeding."

"Wait a minute," Hal objected. "Heparin has to be given IV, doesn't it?"

"Not always. Lance took it subcutaneously. But it's also available in an oral form called rivaroxaban. And guess who takes it."

"I'm thinking it's not Kathleen and the kids," Hal said.

"Well, not voluntarily, anyway. They didn't get sick until they went to Ruthie's house."

"Darling," Mum said. "Are you telling us that you think Ruthie poisoned Kathleen and the kids?"

"I think so," I said. "And furthermore, I think she poisoned Lance too."

"But Lance was already on heparin, wasn't he?" Hal asked.

"Not enough to account for his anti-Xa level," I said.

"Oh, dear," Mum said. "Have you told the police, kitten?"

"Yep. I called the station, and Pete and Bernie came right over and got them."

"Kincaid came to your office?" Hal was back in thundercloud mode.

"Yes, both of them. Hal, don't you dare tell me you think I've been having a quickie with Bernie all this time!"

"Were you?"

"No. Are you kidding? Didn't we talk all this out this morning?" Was it only this morning? It seemed like days ago. And who was this person wearing Hal's skin and acting like Othello? Was this what it was going to be like from now on? Hal going ballistic at the very mention of Bernie Kincaid?

"Hal," I said. "There are going to be times when I have to deal with the police. There will be times when the police I have to deal with will be Bernie Kincaid. Are you going to go off the deep end every time I have to do that? Because this is my job, and if I'm going to do it properly, I can't have that. I'll have to choose between you and my job. Please don't make me do that."

Hal crossed his arms again. "Okay, now that you mention it, what if you had to choose? Which would it be, me or your job?"

I crossed my arms too and began to pace. "I love you, Hal, and I don't want a divorce. But I have to be able to support myself."

"Oh, here it comes," he grumbled. "I don't make as much money as you do. We couldn't have this lifestyle without your income. Well, for your information, we could live just fine on my salary. We've talked about this before."

"I know," I said. "You're right. We could do just fine on your salary. But what if something else happened that threatened our marriage? What if we end up getting

215

divorced anyway? Or what if you get sick or injured and can't work anymore? What if you die? I need my job."

Hal put his hands over his face. "I just can't stand the thought of you and Bernie Kincaid," he mumbled.

I went over and sat on the arm of his chair. "Don't you realize that's exactly how I felt about you and Bambi?"

He removed his hands. "You did?"

"I did. Ever since school started."

"Since *August*?"

"Well, I didn't know about Bambi then, but I knew something was wrong, and you wouldn't talk about it. So after a while, I began to wonder if you had met someone else and might be having an affair, and then Marilyn told me about Bambi, and then I saw her with you in that bar."

"Oh, honey, I didn't know. Why didn't you say something?"

"I did. You got mad. You told me to get off your case."

Hal groaned. "Christ. I've been such a jerk. I'm so sorry. Can you ever forgive me?"

"I already have," I said. "Now let me ask you something. Here you are, all day long, all week long, surrounded by young, nubile, gorgeous college girls, some of whom have crushes on you because you're so goddamn handsome. Have I ever complained about that? What if I made you choose between me and *your* job? Huh? How about that?"

Hal looked at me for a long moment before he spoke. "I'm sorry, honey. I don't know what got into me. You're absolutely right. It's been hard, this week. I'm not sure how to handle all this." He reached out and pulled me into his lap.

I looked around and noticed that Mum had discreetly disappeared. "You mean discovering that you had a nineteen-year old daughter and that your wife might be having an affair with a cop? Hell, what kind of a man couldn't handle that?"

He pulled me close. "One who loves you very much."

The kitchen door slammed, and Bambi rushed into the living room, face flushed and hair flying. She stopped short at the sight of us, hooking long strands of it out of her eyes with her thumbs. "Oh, I'm sorry. Am I interrupting something?"

Hal released me, and I resumed my seat on the arm of the chair. "Not at all. What's going on?" I asked.

"You'll never guess what just happened!"

Chapter 21

A chiel's amang ye takin' notes,
And faith, he'll prent it.
—Robert Burns

Mum came quietly down the stairs and resumed her seat on the couch.

"The cops arrested Ruthie," Hal said.

Disappointed, Bambi flopped into my recliner. "How did you know?"

"He didn't, not really," I said. "But we thought they might."

"But why?" Bambi asked. "What's she supposed to have done?"

"Murdered her husband," I said, "and tried to murder Kathleen Burke and the children."

"Dear me," Mum said. "Are you sure, kitten?"

"I don't believe it," Bambi said. "Who says so?"

"Me, I'm afraid," I told her. "We've got lab tests that prove it."

"But Ruthie wouldn't hurt a fly," Bambi protested. "How could you do that to her, Toni?"

"It's her job," Hal said. "If she has reason to suspect foul play, she has to tell the police. Otherwise, she could go to prison for obstructing justice or suppressing evidence. They could even consider her an accessory to the crime."

"Really?"

"Yes, really," I said.

"But Ruthie just doesn't *look* like a murderer," she said. "She's so … *cuddly.*"

"No," I agreed. "Murderers look like anybody else. You can't tell by looking at them."

"Do you know for sure that Ruthie did it?" Mum asked.

"No, not for sure. What I do know is that Ruthie's husband and Kathleen and the kids were given an overdose of certain drugs and that Ruthie has those drugs in her possession and had the opportunity to use them."

"Blimey," Mum remarked.

"Means, motive, and opportunity," Bambi chanted. "They always say that in murder mysteries. But what was her motive?"

"Money, I suspect," Hal said. "There's a shitload of it involved in this case."

"Do you like murder mysteries, Bambi?" I asked.

"I love 'em," she said. "I'm always reading them, and I love crime shows. I wish I could do some of those things they do on *CSI* and *NCIS*. I'd like to be Abby!"

"Why can't you?" Hal asked. "You're in college. No time like the present."

"I'm not smart enough," she said, eyes downcast.

"Who the hell told you that?" Hal roared.

Bambi cringed. "Nobody. But my grades suck. So I'm not smart."

"Were you smart in high school?" I asked.

"Not really," Bambi said, with a slightly sheepish grin. "My grades sucked there too, but I partied a lot, so I guess I deserved them."

"What are you studying now?" I asked.

"I'm a math major," she said.

Math? *Shit, no wonder*, I thought. "Why math?"

"I got better grades in that than anything else in high school," she said, "so I figured I'd do okay. But I'm not. Professor Sanders says I need to pick another major, because I don't have what it takes."

"Professor Sanders? Gary Sanders?" Hal bellowed. He snapped his recliner into the upright position and leaped to his feet. "That jerk? That overbearing, pompous excuse for a human being? The man is a blithering idiot! How dare he talk to you like that! Why, he can't even—"

"Hal," I said, anxious to prevent further diatribe. I felt pretty sure the next words would be *hold his liquor*, and Bambi didn't need to know that about one of her professors. "We get the point."

Hal paced the living room, fuming, while Bambi dug herself even further into the soft cushions of my recliner. "She's smart, goddamnit! Didn't I tell you she was smart? I interviewed six candidates who wanted to be my lab assistant, and she was smarter than all of them put together. Who the fuck does that dickhead Sanders think he is?"

"Hal, darling, do calm down," my mother urged. "You'll give yourself a stroke."

"Hal doesn't like Dr. Sanders very much," I said.

"Yes, dear," Mum said. "I can tell. Do you know why?"

"Yes, as a matter of fact," I told her. "He said some rather uncomplimentary things about Hal and me at the faculty Christmas party."

Bambi had come out of the cushions and looked at Hal and me with new respect. "Did Hal punch his lights out?"

"Not quite," I began, but Hal interrupted me.

"The man was drunk," he said. *So much for discretion.* "So I took him outside, and he got sick, and then his wife took him home."

"Eeuuww," Bambi said. "Perhaps I shouldn't take what he says so seriously, then."

"I should say not," Mum said.

Hal sat down in his recliner and cranked it all the way back. "You're right, Fiona, I do need to calm down. Bambi, if it's your desire to work in forensics, there are courses at the college. If you don't want to do math anymore, that's something you can try. I can even introduce you to someone on the police force who can help you with that."

"Bet it won't be Bernie Kincaid," I remarked to nobody in particular.

"Definitely not him," Hal said.

"Which one is he," Bambi asked, "the short dark one or the tall blond one?"

"The short dark one," I said.

"Oh good," Bambi said, "because the tall blond one is sooo cute! But he didn't even notice me."

Spoken with the righteous pique of one who *always* gets noticed by guys. I attempted to soothe her ruffled feathers. "Well, I suppose there was a lot going on, and they were preoccupied with Ruthie."

The doorbell rang again, and Mum opened the door to admit Jodi, who made a beeline for the bar. "I need a drink," she announced. Hal started to get up, but she waved him back. "I can get it; I know where everything is."

She fixed herself a scotch and soda and joined Mum on the couch. "Jesus. What a zoo. I had to get out of there for a while."

"I'll bet," I said. "Bambi says the police arrested Ruthie."

"Not exactly," Jodi said. "They wanted her to come to the station and make a statement."

"Did she go quietly?" I asked.

"Not hardly," Jodi replied. "She cried and screamed and carried on and ended up punching Lieutenant Kincaid in the nose."

"Oh, no!" I said.

"Couldn't have happened to a nicer guy," Hal remarked.

"Oh, it was messy," Jodi said. "It bled all over the place. Well, then, of course, they did have to arrest her for assaulting an officer. They took her out of there in handcuffs."

"I hope they don't forget why they wanted her to come to the station in the first place," I said.

Jodi took a healthy swig of her drink and leaned back among the cushions. She kicked off her shoes. "Ah, yes, the statement. And I suppose you know what that's all about?"

"Oh, yes, I do," I said and told her about the results of the lab tests.

She nearly choked on her scotch. "Oh, my God. You've got to be kidding. She poisoned Kathleen and the kids? She couldn't have. She wouldn't have. Would she? Why would she want to do something like that?"

"She poisoned Lance too," I said.

"No," Jodi protested.

"Love or money," Hal said. "It's usually one or the other."

"I'd guess money, in this case," I said. "This case is absolutely swimming in it. Those wills, for example."

"Surely," Mum said, "they've figured out which one is the legal one by now."

"They have," I said. "Jay's second will. But surely Lance has a will, and Kathleen, and Ruthie. Maybe we need to find out what's in those wills … and speaking of that, I still don't know about the safes or file cabinets in Jay and Lance's office. Bernie was going to ask Roy Cobb about that and get back to me, and he never did. Maybe I should call him—"

Then I got a look at Hal's face. "Later," I finished.

"Wise choice, darling," Mum said.

Jodi drained her drink. "Well, I'd better get back over there," she said. "Elliott will be needing a break from all the rug rats."

"Hey," I said, struck by a sudden thought, "did you ever get one of those ladders?"

"You mean the ones for getting out of your house if there's a fire?"

"Yes. Did you?"

"No, not yet. Why? Do you think I need one?"

"Maybe," I said. "You've got the Burkes in your house now, and every house they've been in since Jay died has been burned down."

"Oh, jeez. You're right."

"Home Depot's open till six."

"I'll send Elliott down there right now."

The evening passed quietly. Bambi went back over to Jodi and Elliott's, and Mum and Hal and I watched TV. I couldn't have said what the programs were; I was completely immersed in my own thoughts.

I came out of my reverie when Hal turned off the TV and suggested that we all go to bed, since it had been a hell of a long day and we could all use the sleep.

Hal and I settled into bed and snuggled together as comfortably as if nothing had happened. He put his arms around me and held me tight. I assumed that we'd just go right to sleep, but Hal started talking.

"Toni. Can you ever forgive me for what I've put you through?"

I pulled away and sat up, plumping my pillows behind me. "I already have, I told you. But I'm wondering if there's something I've done to you."

Hal sat up too. "Done to me? What do you mean?"

"Was there something missing in our marriage? Is there something I could have fixed? Or were you just having a midlife crisis?"

Did men really have midlife crises, or was that just a convenient sociological excuse for them to wander? In other words, was this something common to males that had nothing whatever to do with the adequacy of their wives in bed?

Hal looked confused. "Missing? Midlife crisis? Do you still think Bambi and I were having an affair? I thought you believed me when I said we weren't."

"I did. I do. But you said you did think about it. And you were cold and distant with me, and we hardly ever had sex anymore. Was that all because everybody was teasing you at work, or were you really missing something at home?"

Hal slid down in bed and rolled over on his side, propping his head on his hand. "I was distracted by what was going on at work, like I told you; and I didn't want to talk about it. But you kept asking what was wrong, and I didn't want to tell you."

"So that's why you got pissed off at me so much?"

"Well, honey, I'm not the only one who got pissed off, you know. You've been snapping at me a lot more than you used to too. What was bothering you? What were you missing that you thought about having an affair with Bernie Kincaid?"

"Sex," I said. "I was missing sex. You never wanted it. I was terminally horny."

Hal looked thunderstruck. "That's it? Sex?"

"Yes, that's it."

"I had no idea."

"How could you not know? I was practically waving it in your face. I did everything but parade around naked wrapped in Saran Wrap. You completely ignored me." My voice quavered. Tears threatened.

Hal reached for me and pulled me close. "I've been so wrapped up in my own problems that I never noticed yours. I'm so sorry, honey. The fact is that sex was the last thing I wanted to think about with all that was going on at work."

"Including sex with Bambi."

"Including that."

"Then our marriage has been safe all along. I didn't need to worry."

Hal held me tight. "You didn't, and you never will, if I have anything to say about it."

I hugged him back, and he kissed me.

"I really want to make love to you now, honey, but I'm exhausted."

"Me too," I said. "I can hardly keep my eyes open."

"In the morning," he suggested.

"It's a date," I murmured.

A frantic pounding on the bedroom door unceremoniously jerked Hal and me from a sound sleep.

Hal had enough presence of mind to turn on a light, but before he could even put a foot to the floor, the door opened and a distraught Bambi burst in and leaped onto the bed, displacing animals in all directions.

"Hal! Toni! There's a *fire!*"

So much for morning sex.

Chapter 22

There's husbandry in heaven;
Their candles are all out.
—Shakespeare, *Macbeth*

Mum, in her green bathrobe, followed at a much more sedate pace and was nearly knocked ass-over-teakettle by Killer in a mad dash for the stairs, with Geraldine and Spook right behind him.

"My stars and garters!" she exclaimed, clutching the doorjamb to steady herself. "Sorry to disturb you, my dears, but the house next door is on *fire*, don't you know."

Jesus. I squinted at my bedside clock radio. Three-thirty in the morning. A childhood rhyme danced through my mind: *everywhere the Burkes went, fire was sure to go.* In the hallway behind Mum, orange light flickered from the guestrooms that faced the Maynards' house, the rooms Mum and Bambi occupied.

Hal called 9-1-1 from the phone in the hall. "They're on the way," he told us as he hung up, but he needn't have, because I could already hear sirens. I got out of bed and pulled my black sweats on over my pajamas, but not before the doorbell rang. *Here we go again*, I thought. *Hell of a vacation this turned out to be.*

It was déjà vu all over again. By the time Hal, Mum, and I got down the stairs, Bambi had opened the door to admit all the Burkes, Tiffany and Emily, and all the Maynards in pajamas, bathrobes, and snow boots, everyone shivering and pinch-faced from cold. Each child carried an armful of clothing and stuffed animals. Emily and Angela were both crying, and Megan and Julie looked like they wanted to. Killer went up to Angela and licked her face, and she put her arms around him and buried her face in his soft fur. The older kids had their school backpacks, the women carried armloads of clothing and bedding, and Elliott, I was glad to see, carried sleeping bags for the children, including the ones they'd borrowed from us. The fire department had arrived, and firefighters were already swarming over the hook-and-ladder truck, carrying hoses and ladders toward the house.

"That chain ladder worked great," Jodi said, dumping her load on the living room floor. "We even had time to throw bedding and clothes out the window before we got out. There's still some more out there where we threw it."

"I'll get it," Bambi said, and sprinted out the door.

"That child is *barefooted*," Mum observed. "And there's snow on the ground. Shouldn't we …"

"She'll be okay," Hal reassured her. "She'll be back before she has a chance to freeze a toe," and by the time he finished the sentence, Bambi was back with an armload and barely out of breath. "That's all of it," she told Jodi and added it to the pile by the door.

"Hey, Shapiro, we need a fire here," Elliott said, unmindful of the irony. "These kids are freezing."

Together they went out to the garage and brought back armloads of firewood. Within minutes a cheery fire crackled in the fireplace, while I prepared coffee for the adults and hot chocolate for the kids. With everybody helping, the kids—with bellies full of hot chocolate— were soon snugly ensconced in their sleeping bags by the hearth with their own pillows and stuffed animals. Jodi and Elliott took the couch and recliner, while Bambi moved her things into Mum's room, and Kathleen and Tiffany shared Bambi's bed.

We had bedded down a total of eighteen people in this old house and had used up every bit of bedding we had, plus everything the Maynards had.

By now it was after five, and I was just sinking into a nice, warm, soft place somewhere between drowsiness and coma, when an unwelcome thought jerked me awake.

What if the firebug targeted *this* house next?

Shit. Why hadn't I asked Jodi to get a ladder for us too?

So much for going back to sleep.

Sunday, December 21

Chapter 23

*One half of the world cannot understand
the pleasures of the other.*
—Jane Austen

Early Sunday morning I lay on the couch with Geraldine, a cup of coffee, and a book, watching the sun come up, reflecting on the fact that my first Christmas vacation in thirteen years would start the next day, and trying not to act put-out that there were eighteen people in my house for the occasion. If Ruthie hadn't been in jail, there would've been nineteen. Ten of them were spread out all over the living room floor in sleeping bags at this very moment, most of them still asleep.

Fourteen of those folks were homeless. They deserved warmth, shelter, food, hot drinks, and love. They didn't need a pissy, self-centered hostess. Ruthie, on the other hand, if she had actually done what the lab work suggested she'd done, deserved to be right where she was, rotting in jail.

Jodi and Elliott had vacated the couch and recliner and sat at the kitchen table having coffee with Hal, while Mum fixed herself a cup of tea.

Christmas was now three days away. I'd finished my shopping weeks ago, but now I had to think of what to give Bambi. What does one give a nineteen-year-old that one hardly knows? I sounded out Mum on the subject. She joined me on the couch, cup in hand. We talked in low voices so as not to wake the children, because once they were up we wouldn't be able to hear ourselves think, let alone carry on a conversation.

"Just give her money, kitten," Mum said. "That's what I used to do with you when you were that age, remember?"

That brought up another problem. The fires at Kathleen's, Ruthie's, and Jodi and Elliott's houses had destroyed their Christmas trees and all the gifts they'd bought. This meant that unless they all went shopping again, the kids would have no Christmas. I shuddered at the thought of shopping for eleven children three days before Christmas. The mall would be a nightmare.

I thought that God, or whoever saw to it that Hal and I didn't have children, had probably done both of us a huge favor. Acquiring one that was already age nineteen didn't really count. Neither did housebreaking puppies.

Mum must have read my mind. "Aren't you glad that you and Hal didn't have children, kitten?"

I looked around. "I suppose so. But it wasn't our idea, you know."

"I remember," Mum said. "You told me that Hal's first wife didn't want children, and it was some kind of big deal because they were Jewish. But I can't recall what that was all about."

"Well, let me refresh your memory," I said. "Jews don't believe in an afterlife like we do. When you die, that's it. You live on in your children. Without children, there's no immortality."

"Oh, yes," Mum said. "And you went off the pill so that Hal could have his immortality."

She sounded sarcastic, but nowhere near as sarcastic as she'd been seventeen years ago when we'd first discussed it. Back then, it had been an extremely emotional discussion, and Mum and I had had a major argument that resulted in our not speaking to each other for a month. Now I understood that Mum had acted that way because she was scared. She was terrified that I was going to throw away my career to be a mother—after all the work she had done to make sure I wouldn't have to spend forty years doing a job I hated, like she had.

But she needn't have worried. I never got pregnant. Not for lack of trying, though; Hal and I had been busy. Later we'd accepted the fact that we weren't meant to have children, without trying to find out whose fault it was. But now, with Bambi showing up, the fault was obviously mine.

"It didn't work out," I said. "I couldn't give that to him." Tears came to my eyes at the thought, one that hadn't occurred to me till now. "You don't suppose he's subconsciously holding that against me, do you?" I held my breath to keep from crying. "Because there's nothing I can do about it now."

Mum put her arms around me and pulled me close. "No, kitten, I don't think Hal holds anything against you.

He knows there isn't anything you wouldn't do for him, and you and I both know there isn't anything he wouldn't do for you. Both of you are too old now to even think of starting a family. It's a moot point, as they say."

"I suppose we could have adopted," I said, "but it never came up. I didn't suggest it, and neither did he."

"Well, there!" she said. "Surely if he cared that much about having children, he would have mentioned it, don't you think?"

Mum made perfect sense. I hoped she was right.

Breakfast consisted of cereal and Pop-Tarts. Even Hal cringed at the thought of trying to feed eggs, bacon, and toast to eighteen people.

By the time everyone was up, fed, and dressed, it was nearly noon. Bambi and Tiffany took the younger kids to the movies, while Jodi and Kathleen and the older kids went to the mall. Elliott went down to the police station to bail out Ruthie. That left Hal, Mum, and me … and peace, blessed peace—that is, until Hal turned on the TV to watch football.

What is it with men that they can't stand to have silence for five minutes? Mum and I retired to the kitchen, where we fixed ourselves cups of tea.

Mum toyed with her teabag. "Well, kitten, did you and Hal get everything straightened out?"

"Mum," I said, "why is everything so complicated?"

"How do you mean, dear?"

"Well, I've read books and magazine articles on the differences between men and women, and the message always seems to be that men generally say pretty much what they mean, and it's the women who try to parse it

234

for subtext, dissect and analyze and read things into it, and so on. And women say things to men that they really don't mean, just to get a reaction, and it's the men who take it literally and react appropriately, instead of trying to analyze it like a woman would do."

"Yes, dear, I know." Mum squeezed her teabag against her spoon and placed it in her saucer. "Women write scripts, and the men don't learn their lines."

"So here's my husband, acting distant, and someone tells me about the existence of another female in his life, and that he was seen kissing said female. Therefore, I assume the worst, that he's having an affair—and furthermore, that it's somehow my fault. But when I ask him, he says it was nothing, and when I persist, he gets mad and tells me to get off his back about it, which I interpret to mean that he's just confirmed that he was indeed having an affair, and so I could proceed to have one of my own."

Mum sipped her tea. "Yes, my love, with the very available and horny Bernie Kincaid."

"Right. But in actual fact, Hal was telling me the absolute truth, that there was nothing going on, and he would have been highly offended that I didn't believe him. But being female, I found such a concept totally foreign."

"Mmm-hmm," Mum said. "It's a wonder we ever get together at all, isn't it?"

"So." I leaned my elbows on the table. "Suppose I'd gone ahead and had an affair with Bernie Kincaid, and suppose Hal had found out. He would have been outraged, and rightly so. But I would have felt that I had avenged myself and not had any idea that I had totally wronged him. I would have felt completely justified, wouldn't have even apologized. And if he had mentioned divorce to me, I would have divorced him first. Then he would have felt free to go ahead with his affair, and I would have too."

"Yes, dear," Mum said. "So, let's take this a step further and say that Hal started having sex with Bambi, not knowing who she was. Suppose she got pregnant? She would have been carrying Hal's *grandchild* as well as his child. When her pregnancy became common knowledge, the truth would come out that Hal had been fooling around with a student, which is bad enough but is also possibly statutory rape. How old is Bambi, anyway?"

"Nineteen, I think."

There sure was a lot of pregnancy going on, or so it seemed—all Jay's paramours, for example. Luckily for Jay, none of the women he'd impregnated were his own daughter. I shuddered. "Can you imagine what would have happened when Hal found out who Bambi's mother was and that he was actually Bambi's father and had been committing incest?"

I wasn't sure that qualified as a crime in the legal sense, but in the emotional sense, it would be a loaded loose cannon. The shit would fly far and wide.

"I would imagine," Mum said, "that Hal would certainly lose his job and probably be unable to get another at any college."

"Yes," I said, "and Bambi's parents would no doubt sue him, and the punitive damages would sink him without a trace. Wow. We dodged a bullet there, didn't we?" If we hadn't been divorced by then, I thought, I could have been so deep in the hole I'd be looking up to see bottom.

Doctor Deep-Pockets, just ripe for the picking.

I shifted my thoughts to what I imagined Hal and Bambi must be feeling about what could have happened and what did happen. Had they actually been in love with each other or just in lust? How would it feel to find out that the person around whom one's sexual fantasies had revolved was actually a person about whom such thoughts would be considered sinful?

I hoped they'd managed to talk it all out during the two days Hal had been gone.

"Darling," Mum said, "there's a lot of hoo-hah about the sanctity of marriage vows and committing adultery in your heart, don't you know, as if it's the exception rather than the rule. The truth is that men, married or not, will look at other women and think about what it would be like to have sex with them; and women, married or not, will look at other men, and do the same."

"I suppose you're right," I said.

"Of course I'm right," Mum said. "It's what they *do* about it that buggers everything up, don't you know."

"I suppose that if it weren't for that, there'd be no need for rules about it."

It's possible, I reflected, that right now what Hal and Bambi were feeling was mainly relief. I sure as hell was.

Hal came into the kitchen. "What are you two so deep in conversation about?"

"Just girl talk, Hal, dear," Mum said.

"Of course. You were talking about me. Anybody ready for something stronger than tea?" He took a glass from the cupboard and the scotch from the bar and sloshed some into his glass. "Toni?"

"Okay, I'll have some too."

He fixed me one and sat down. "Now. What's the subject under discussion? Besides me, that is."

"What makes you think we were talking about you, Hal, dear?" Mum asked.

He shrugged. "Because that's what women always do."

"Talk about men, you mean. Well, my dears," Mum said, "this is quite a rum situation we're in, isn't it?"

"That's one way of putting it," I agreed. "I wish I knew what's going on." Like, for instance, what the hell Mum was talking about now—the same subject or a new one?

"Well, you figured out that Ruthie had poisoned Kathleen and the kids, kitten."

"Well," I temporized, "I figured out that she could have. Whether she did or not is another thing."

"But the police arrested her," Mum pointed out.

"Yeah, for assaulting a police officer, not for poisoning anybody. All they wanted from her was a statement. If she hadn't punched Kincaid in the nose, she'd have been home last night."

"Well, then, who's setting the fires, dear?"

Chapter 24

I met a lady in the meads
Full beautiful, a faery's child;
Her hair was long, her foot was light,
And her eyes were wild.
—John Keats

"Up till now I assumed that the same person who did the poisoning set the fires, but that's impossible," I said. "If Ruthie did the poisoning, she couldn't have set the fires. At least she couldn't have set the fire last night because she was in jail."

"Well," Hal said, "by now the police have copies of both of Jay's wills, so there's no reason for the firebug to keep trying to destroy either one of them. So this attempt on Jodi and Elliott's house would have to be for some other reason."

"But what?" Mum asked. "What else could he possibly want?"

"Perhaps he was trying to kill the occupants," I said.

"What for, dear?"

"Okay," said Hal. "Let's suppose someone wanted to kill the occupants. Who were the occupants? In Kathleen's house, it was Kathleen and her family, Tiffany and her daughter. In Ruthie's house, it was the same plus Ruthie. In Lance's office, it was Tiffany and Lance. That makes no sense at all. Is there a common factor?"

"Yes," I said. "Tiffany."

"Who would want to harm Tiffany?" Hal asked. "And why?"

"Well, let's see," I said. "We have a choice of Lance or Kathleen. I think we can eliminate the children, don't you?" I rushed on without waiting for an answer. "Okay. Was it Lance? Why? Why bother to start a fire in the office that could endanger him as well as her when he could just fire her and be done with it? And then when Kathleen had a fire, he was in the hospital, and then he died."

"Kathleen makes more sense," Hal said, "because her husband was having an affair with Tiffany."

"But Hal, love, it can't be Kathleen," Mum said. "Why would she set fire to her own house and endanger her own children just to harm Tiffany? It's *daft*."

"Well, it's got to be related to Jay's murder, whatever it is," I argued. "I seriously doubt that a firebug is going around setting random fires which *just happen* to include Jay's office, his wife, his partner, and his partner's wife."

"It's got to be love or money," Hal said. "Or both. We've got all of Jay's lovers who might benefit from Jay's death. They might be trying to get rid of anyone else who might benefit from Jay's death, like his wife, his children, and his current lover, Tiffany."

"You think any of them would feel so strongly that they would kill Jay to prevent anyone else from having him?" I said. "The most likely candidate for that scenario would be Kathleen herself. The spouse is always the most likely suspect."

"Nonsense," Mum said. "If Kathleen killed Jay because she caught him in bed with Tiffany, one would expect her to simply shoot both of them on the spot and be done with it, rather than opt for slow poisoning."

"But then she would already be in jail, awaiting trial for a double murder," I objected. "The money wouldn't do her any good, except maybe to pay for a lawyer."

"Assuming she could actually be cold-blooded enough to poison him and leave him to die in his car on the interstate in the snow, where would Tiffany come in?" Hal asked. "Did she help Kathleen do it? Or did she even know that Kathleen did it? *If* Kathleen did it, that is. Or did Tiffany do it herself?"

"There were light-colored hairs on Jay's jacket," I said. "They certainly didn't come from Kathleen, but they could have come from Tiffany."

"Why would Tiffany want to kill Jay?" Hal asked. "Because he didn't take her with him when he left? Or maybe it was just for money. She knew that Jay had provided for her and Emily in his will, right?"

"How much money are we talking about here?" I argued. "How many other women would she have to share it with besides Kathleen and Mitzi? Is Tiffany trying to eliminate Kathleen and her family so that there'd be more for her? If so, how did she get her hands on the Lovenox? Did Lance keep a stash of it at the office, or what?"

"Surely, kitten," said Mum, "you aren't thinking that she actually *set* those fires, are you?"

"Well, no, I hadn't actually gotten that far," I said. "I was just wondering who was trying to harm whom, and it just occurred to me that she's the only one involved in all three fires, that's all. Although I suppose it's not impossible …"

"We really don't know anything about her, do we?" Hal said.

He and I stared at each other. I felt as sure I knew what he was thinking as if he had said it out loud. *Google her!*

"I'm on it," I said and headed for the stairs.

"Okay," said Hal, and he began clearing the table. As I climbed the stairs, I heard Mum say, "Whatever are you two on about?"

We're back, I thought happily as I fired up the computer and got on the Internet. I had just gotten Google up and had typed in *Tiffany Summers*, when Mum and Hal came into the office. Mum made herself comfortable in the recliner with her cup of tea, while Hal pulled his desk chair up to my desk and watched as I hit *Search*.

There were 2,580,000 references for Tiffany Summers, at least 2,579,995 of which were porn sites. Not that I actually went through all 2,580,000 of them; after the first few hundred, they began to repeat themselves. I did find a few for Tiffany with a different last name or Summers with a different first name, but I also found two rather poignant ones: a birth notice for a Tiffany Sue Summers, born July 3, 1978, in Duluth, Minnesota, and further down the page an obituary for the same Tiffany Sue Summers, born July 3, 1978 in Duluth, Minnesota, and deceased of leukemia March 29, 1981, at Mayo Clinic in Rochester, Minnesota. She was survived by her parents,

Marjorie and Eldon Summers, and an older sister, Brittany Jo.

This was obviously not our Tiffany Summers. I bookmarked them both on the computer. I wasn't sure why, but just in case we ever needed them again, they'd be easier to find.

I made a note to find out where our Tiffany was born.

"Poor thing," murmured Mum sympathetically. "Have you tried spelling it *Somers* or *Sommers*?"

I tried it, with similar results—except for the birth and death notices.

"Well, I guess that's that," Hal said, rising. But I stopped him.

"Wait. Summers is her married name. We should be looking under her maiden name."

"Do you know what it is?" Hal asked. "Because I have no idea."

"You could look for a marriage announcement," suggested Mum.

"Good idea," I said and turned back to the computer screen. "But I don't know what her husband's first name was."

"Maybe there's a divorce announcement," Hal suggested.

"Hmmm," I said. I typed in *magicvalley.com*, selected *Clarion*, and searched in vain for divorces for the last ten years, since I didn't expect that Tiffany had been a child bride, but no joy.

"I'm going to try one more thing," I said. I went back to Google and typed in *Emily Summers*.

Hal, looking over my shoulder, objected. "You're just gonna get more porn sites doing that. Go back to the *Clarion*, and maybe you'll find a birth announcement."

"What if she wasn't born here?" I objected, but I did what he said and hit pay dirt.

Emily was born September 3, 2005, at our hospital, to Tiffany and Eldon Summers of Twin Falls.

Tiffany and Eldon Summers?

Hal straightened up and stretched. "Well, we don't know any more about Tiffany, but at least we have her ex-husband's first name."

"But that's just weird!" I said.

"What's weird?"

"Her husband's name is Eldon Summers."

"So?"

"The father of the Tiffany Summers who died was Eldon Summers."

"Huh," said Hal. "You're right, that is weird. What do you suppose it means?"

"Surely it's just a coincidence," said Mum.

"You know what the Commander says about that?" I asked her.

"What, dear?"

"'First thing ya gotta learn about coincidences,' he says, 'is that there's no coincidences.'"

"Dear me," said Mum.

"What are you getting at, Toni?" Hal said.

"It's such a long shot," I said, "for our Tiffany Summers to be married to an Eldon Summers, when the father of this other Tiffany Summers who was born in Duluth and died in 1981 is also Eldon Summers."

"So let's look for a marriage announcement."

"Or a divorce announcement."

But we found neither.

I went back to Google and typed in *Eldon Summers*.

There were 1,690,000 entries. I tried to narrow them down by location. None of them were in Twin Falls or even in the Magic Valley. I threw up my hands in frustration. "I can't do this anymore. Why don't we just ask Tiffany where her ex-husband is?"

"Kitten, have I missed something?" inquired Mum. "Why do we need to know where her ex-husband is?"

Hal and I looked at each other. He turned his palms up. "I don't know. Why did we?"

I shrugged. "Maybe we don't. We needed his name to find a marriage announcement or divorce announcement. But we didn't find either."

"Not in the *Clarion*, anyway. All that means is that they were married and divorced somewhere else."

"What we were really doing," I pointed out, "is trying to find out something about Tiffany. Something. Anything. For what it's worth. Which may be nothing. I'm done here," I said, shutting down the computer. "I think I can get more information from the medical record than we can get here."

Mum and Hal, obviously bored out of their skulls just hanging around the house, insisted on accompanying me to my office. Such a parade would attract way too much attention on a weekday, but today, Sunday, the halls were deserted. Brenda was on duty in the lab, and I took my companions into the lab and introduced Brenda to my mother, telling her that Mum had never seen my office. I knew that if I had sneaked us into my office, she would hear us and come looking to see who was there and catch us violating HIPAA.

According to the medical record, Tiffany's date of birth was July 3, 1978, and her birthplace was Duluth, Minnesota.

And her middle name was Sue.

Hal and I looked at each other. Mum, pointing to the computer screen, said, "Isn't that the same as that birth announcement in Google?"

"Oh, now, that is just too weird," I said. "That baby died of leukemia at age three."

"Don't go off half-cocked," Hal cautioned. "It's not impossible that more than one Tiffany Summers was born in Duluth in 1978."

"Tiffany *Sue*? And on the *same day*?"

"Not impossible," Hal said.

"My loves, you're forgetting something," Mum pointed out. "Summers is Tiffany's *married* name. What's her maiden name?"

"It gets weirder," I said, scrolling down. "Tiffany's maiden name *is* Summers. She's listed here as divorced."

"But the birth announcement said Emily was born to Tiffany *and Eldon* Summers," Mum said.

"There's no husband given here," I pointed out. "It says 'father unknown'.

"Makes sense if Jay Braithwaite Burke is Emily's real father," Hal said.

"But she gave her ex-husband's name to the papers," I said.

Hal laughed. "You really wouldn't expect her to give *Jay's* name to the papers, would you?"

I continued to scroll down. "No, but look who she gave as next of kin. Parents, Marjorie and Eldon Summers, in Duluth, Minnesota!"

"Jesus," Hal said. "She gave her father's name as the father of her child. Why would she do that?"

"Maybe it was the first name that came to mind," Mum suggested. "Like you said, she couldn't give the real father's name to the papers, now, could she?"

"Can you print that?" Hal asked. "Just in case the police need it?"

"Sure," I said and hit the proper keys. "But you know the police will have to subpoena it, and they'd have to have probable cause … hang on, I'll be right back."

"Where are you going?" Hal asked.

"The printer's in the lab. I've got to get that before Brenda sees it."

I got the printout just as it came off the printer. Brenda was in another part of the lab and didn't see me. I folded the printout and stuffed it in my jeans pocket.

Back in my office, I shut down the computer. "Let's get out of here," I said.

It wasn't until we were climbing the steps to the front porch that I voiced what I was thinking.

"You know what? I think the real Tiffany Sue Summers died in 1981."

"Then who's this?" Hal said.

"I don't know," I replied, closing the front door behind us. "But I'll bet it isn't Tiffany Sue Summers."

"In that case," Mum said, "perhaps it would be best not to ask her who she really is, don't you know."

I agreed with her. "Not if we don't want to get burned."

I'd let the police do it; because if Tiffany had really stolen that child's identity, it was because she had something to hide.

Like a rap sheet, for instance.

In Duluth, Minnesota, maybe.

For arson, perhaps.

Elliott had gotten home with Ruthie by the time we got back; but it was not what anyone would call a joyous homecoming.

Ruthie lit into me before I had taken two steps into the living room. "How could you do that to me?" she yelled, her face less than a foot from mine. "How dare you accuse me of trying to poison Kathleen and the children! And my own husband? What kind of a monster do you take me for? For your information, I no longer have any of Lance's Lovenox; I threw it all away after he died. Only now I wish I hadn't. I wish I'd kept it to kill *you* with, you bitch."

"Ruthie, for God's sake, take it easy," Elliott remonstrated. "You shouldn't make threats like that. They'll come back to bite you in the freakin' butt someday."

"I don't give a flying fuck!" she shrieked at him. "I'm not staying here. I'm not going to spend another minute under this roof. Take me to a motel. Now!"

Elliott shrugged. "Whatever you say. Get your stuff."

With one final vitriolic look in my direction, she headed for the stairs. I looked at Elliott. "Now what?"

He shrugged. "She's out on bail. She can go anywhere she likes as long as she shows up in court when she's supposed to."

Ruthie came back downstairs with what remained of her earthly possessions in two grocery bags. "Ready," she said.

"Car's unlocked," he told her.

She opened the front door and turned to fire a final shot at me. "I swear to God, I am going to sue you for everything you've got."

"You already are," I reminded her. A look of confusion washed across her face, but she said nothing more before she went out the door.

"Did she really dispose of all Lance's Lovenox?" I asked Elliott.

"I don't know. Maybe it all burned up when her house burned."

Another thing to ask the police about.

Monday, December 22

Chapter 25

A billion here, a billion there, and pretty soon
you're talking about real money.
—Everett Dirksen

Good thing I was on vacation, because I hadn't slept worth a damn.

I'd lain awake most of the night, mulling over question after question while Hal slept peacefully beside me, snoring softly. Killer, on the floor next to the bed, did the same. Geraldine wedged herself into the small of my back as she always did, like a little furry heating pad.

I didn't know where Spook was and didn't care, as long as he wasn't in the linen closet.

Right away I dismissed Lance as having murdered Jay. He had no motive. But Kathleen, Tiffany, and Ruthie probably did, as well as the other women mentioned in Jay's will.

Although love was a perfectly good motive for murder, in this case it didn't help much. These weren't *crimes passionels*; they were clearly premeditated. I was

251

pretty sure it was all about money. Considering what Jay had been doing with his Ponzi scheme, money was a much more viable motive. Kathleen stood to inherit under both of Jay's wills, unless she was the murderer, of course. Tiffany stood to inherit under only one of the wills, the most recent and probably the legal one. But so did an unknown number of other women, including Mitzi Okamoto, assuming none of them had remarried or died. I didn't count Jodi. Not even Jay Braithwaite Burke would be brassy enough to make Elliott draft a will that had his own wife in it.

And if there was anything left to inherit, where would it be? In Jay's Swiss bank account?

I figured that it wouldn't be in a bank account or brokerage account anywhere in the United States, because if it was, Jay wouldn't have needed to declare bankruptcy. On the other hand, there was that doctor from Hawaii who had sued him for his lost million dollars. It was only then that Jay had declared bankruptcy. So if Jay had any money in a domestic account, he would have wasted no time getting it into an offshore entity to protect it.

I assumed that if offshore accounts were safe from the IRS and bankruptcy courts they were also safe from lawsuits filed in the United States.

How much did Kathleen know? Besides the Swiss bank account, had she set any of this up when she worked for Jay? Because their oldest son was born in 1995 and Jay had started the fund in 1990, Kathleen had to have been working for him during the first five years of the fund's existence. I wasn't sure why none of us had asked Kathleen these questions. Maybe we were all afraid that if she had killed Jay it would tip her off and she might retaliate by killing somebody else.

How was Tiffany involved?

We still knew nothing about her. She didn't look a day over twenty-five, but I supposed she could have been thirty. If she was born in 1978, how old would she have been in 1995? Seventeen. It might work, if she could show that she had graduated from high school. But if she was somebody else who'd stolen that baby's identity, all the information we'd gotten from her medical record was a pack of lies; so that was no help.

On the other hand, if she'd stolen the identity of someone born in 1978, she'd have to present herself as that age when applying for a job. If she'd started working for Jay in 1995, she would have been in the perfect position to replace Kathleen when Bryan was born—*in more ways than one*, I thought cattily.

What about Ruthie? She must have worked in that office too at that time, because she witnessed Jay's first will. So both Kathleen and Tiffany knew about both of Jay's wills, and possibly also knew where the money was. But how much did Ruthie know? Did she know about the second will? How much had Lance known, and how much had he told Ruthie?

Nothing, if he was smart. Anything Ruthie knew would be common knowledge by now. The woman had a mouth like a steel sieve. Or was that just an act? Maybe that gossipy exterior hid a multitude of secrets that nobody would suspect she knew.

Like what she had really done with Lance's Lovenox.

Unfortunately, any records had probably been destroyed in the fire that destroyed Jay and Lance's law office.

Or had they?

Had that fire been set to kill Lance and Tiffany or to destroy incriminating files?

In the morning, I sat blearily at the kitchen table with Mum, Hal, Jodi, and Elliott, trying to revive myself with vast quantities of coffee. Mum, disgustingly perky for that hour of the morning, inquired chirpily about everyone's plans for the day.

"I need to go to the police station," I said.

"What for?" Hal asked. I knew he was thinking about Bernie Kincaid and wished I could say something to allay his fears, but I couldn't think of anything. Bernie would either be there or he wouldn't, and there was nothing I could do about that.

"I need to find out if the fire department recovered anything from the law office, like safes or fireproof file cabinets, and see what's in them," I said.

"I'll go with her," Elliott said. "I need to see that stuff too. I'll just give them a call so we won't be wasting our time. Hand me the phone, would you, Shapiro?"

Hal handed him the handset. Elliott placed the call, and from the sounds of it, he had connected with the Commander. After a few pleasantries, Elliott put a hand over the mouthpiece. "He says they recovered two safes, but they don't know the combinations."

"I'll bet Kathleen does," Jodi said, "or maybe Tiffany. Want me to get them up?"

"Get who up?" Kathleen asked. None of us had heard her coming down the stairs.

"You," Jodi said. "Do you know the combinations to the safes in Jay's and Lance's offices?"

Kathleen looked surprised. "You mean they managed to save those? Wow. Let me see. Jeez, it's been such a long time." She thought for a minute and then said, "Got some paper and a pen? I'll write them down." Hal gave her a pad of Post-its and a pen, and she wrote down two combinations. "I think that's right," she said. "If that doesn't work, maybe Tiffany knows."

I wasn't altogether sure that Tiffany would give us the right combinations, even if she knew them, in light of what I now suspected about her. It was another item I planned to discuss with the police, but I didn't want to say so in front of Kathleen.

Elliott relayed the combinations to the Commander. "He's telling Pete. Pete's giving it a try. Hey, he's got one of them open … and the other. Great," he told the Commander. "Don't take anything out. I'll be right down."

Five minutes later, Elliott and I presented ourselves at the police station. The safes stood open on the floor, their contents visible. We pulled up a couple of chairs and got to work. The Commander, clipboard in hand and toothpick in mouth, parked one butt cheek on the corner of the desk. "Gotta make a list of the contents for evidence," he said.

The contents of Jay's safe included copies of both his wills, a copy of Kathleen's will, and a Banque Suisse statement dated November 30, 2008, showing a balance of just over five million dollars. "Wow," Elliott said. "Looks like there's something to inherit, all right."

The contents of Lance's safe included his will, Ruthie's will, and his First Cayman Bank Ltd. statement, also dated November 30, 2008, with a balance of eight million dollars. Elliott's response to that was a little more unconventional. "Holy freakin' shit," he said.

When I'd remarked that this case was swimming in money, I had no idea what I was talking about. This case was *drowning* in it.

Elliott handed Jay's original will to the Commander. "We don't need this one anymore," he said. "This is the one we want. Toni, want to take a look?"

I took it and skimmed the pages, looking for the names of the beneficiaries. Ruthie had mentioned some of them but not all of them. Jeannie Tracy wasn't there. Aside from Kathleen, Tiffany, and Mitzi, I didn't know any of the other women—except for one.

Rebecca Sorensen.

Tall, blonde, gorgeous Rebecca. Nice Rebecca. Pregnant Rebecca. Pregnant with her and Jeff's first child.

Poor guy. I hoped he'd never find out it was really Jay's child.

"Well?" Elliott asked. "Any surprises?"

"Only one," I said and told him about Rebecca.

Pete came in at that point. "We managed to locate all those other women," he said. "They've all remarried, so they won't inherit."

"Rebecca won't inherit either," I said. "So far, she's still married." Until Jeff finds out about his child's actual parentage, that is, and divorces her.

We moved on.

Kathleen's will divided her estate equally among her four children and Tiffany. In case of her death while the children were under eighteen, their shares of the money were to be held in trust, the trustee being her mother, Mary Reilly. Also not a surprise; it was pretty much what we thought.

However, a recent codicil stated that in the event of the deaths of all the children before age eighteen, all the money went to Mary Reilly outright. In the event of the death of any child after age eighteen who had not willed his (or her) money elsewhere, that share went to Tiffany.

But what if Mary Reilly died?

Well, there was a codicil for that also. Her estate went to Kathleen. If Kathleen predeceased her, it went equally to the four children, or however many of them were living at the time. If none of them were living, it all went to charities.

Mary Reilly had not left money to Tiffany; but if she predeceased Kathleen, Tiffany would eventually inherit one fifth of it, according to the terms of Kathleen's will.

"Does Tiffany know about the codicils?" I asked.

"I suspect not, unless Kathleen told her," Elliott said. "I drew those codicils Monday. She didn't say so, but I got the impression that she didn't altogether trust Tiffany."

"Huh," I said. "That's interesting. I wonder why?"

"Guess we'll have to ask her when we get home," Elliott replied.

Right. Sometime when Tiffany wasn't around, preferably.

Next, we looked at Lance's will, which looked pretty straightforward, at first.

Half of the eight million dollars went to Jay. In the event of Jay predeceasing Lance, it was divided between Ruthie and Kathleen. The explanation given in the will was that it represented the earnings from the law practice, and therefore was half Jay's anyway. In the event of Kathleen and her family predeceasing Lance, the entire eight million dollars went to Ruthie.

"Jesus freakin' Christ," Elliott said. "What a motive!"

"What motive?" the Commander asked.

Elliott told him. Ruthie still had a reason to murder the Burkes.

The Commander shifted the toothpick to the other side of his mouth. "Pete? We need to get Mrs. Brooks down here pronto."

"On it," Pete said. "I'll take Bernie with me."

And a catcher's mask, I thought to myself, in case Ruthie reacts poorly to a second visit to the police station. I hoped Elliott and I wouldn't still be there when she arrived.

Then we saw the rest of the story.

In the event of the demise of Kathleen and her family *after* Lance's death, the money also went to Ruthie. Motive squared.

After that, Ruthie's will was almost anticlimactic.

Almost.

Ruthie had left her entire estate to a Mrs. Mildred Atterbury, residing at 26 Princess Margaret Street, Bridgetown, Barbados.

Chapter 26

She never told her love,
But let concealment, like a worm i' the bud,
Feed upon her damask cheek: she pined in thought.
And with a green and yellow melancholy
She sat like patience on a monument,
Smiling at grief.
—Shakespeare, *Twelfth Night*

"Who the hell is Mrs. Mildred Atterbury?" Elliott asked.

"We'll ask Mrs. Brooks that when she comes in," the Commander replied. "In the meantime, maybe you two better skedaddle before she gets here."

"We will, but there's one more thing," I said.

Elliott looked surprised. "What are you talking about, Toni?"

"Did you find fingerprints on the gas cans at the fires?" I asked the Commander.

"Amazingly enough, we did," he said. "We ran them through AFIS, the FBI's national database, and there we found a match."

"Tiffany's prints are in AFIS?" I asked incredulously.

"Who said anything about Tiffany?"

"Now you've done it," Elliott said teasingly. "You better tell him all about it."

"Tell me about what?" the Commander said, clearly confused.

"Well," I said, "yesterday Hal and I figured out that the only person involved in all the fires is Tiffany, and we realized that we didn't really know her very well or know anything about her, so we decided to Google her, and this is what we found." I reached into my jeans pocket—luckily I was wearing the same ones—and hauled out a wad of folded paper. I separated out the one with the birth and death notices of Tiffany Sue Summers of Duluth, Minnesota.

The Commander stared at it, uncomprehending. "I don't get it," he said. "This person's dead."

"I know," I said. "So then we went onto the *Clarion*'s website and found this." I handed him the printout of Emily's birth notice.

"Okay," he said, still mystified.

"Then we went to the hospital, and I looked up Tiffany's medical record, and here it is." I handed him the last sheet, the printout of Tiffany's demographics, next of kin, and so on. "Notice anything?"

"Huh," the Commander said. "Looks like there's more to this young lady than meets the eye. Maybe we'd better get her down here too."

Elliott started the car. "Okay, now what?" he asked me. "Home? Or have you got more detecting to do?"

"I want to talk to Mitzi and Rebecca and find out if they know they're in Jay's will," I said.

"You want to know if either of them has a motive?" Elliott asked. "Are you sure? It might be dangerous. You really should leave that sort of thing to the police."

In your dreams. "Okay," I said meekly. "In that case, would you drop me off at the hospital? I want to get Lance's autopsy sections into the tissue processor." *And talk to Mitzi, if she's there.* Damn. What if she was off this week too? Well, then, I guessed I'd just have to go to her house.

Elliott agreed. As he pulled up by the entrance, he said, "I'm going down to my office for a while. Are you going to walk home?"

"Probably," I said. "See you later."

Mitzi was at work. I found her in her office in the dark, looking at digital images on her computer. A plateful of Christmas candy sat on her desk.

"Toni! I thought you were off this week."

"I am, but I wanted to finish up the autopsy on Lance Brooks, because his wife is suing us."

"Oh, for God's sake," she said. "What on earth for? Does she think you screwed it up or something?"

"Oh, she's not suing us for that," I explained. "She thinks the surgeons screwed up. But they didn't. At least there's nothing in the autopsy to suggest that."

261

"Oh, I see," she teased. "She'll sue you when she finds out the autopsy didn't show anything for her to sue us for."

"You could be right about that," I said. "Can I ask you some more questions about your experiences with that hedge fund?"

She shrugged. "Sure, why not?"

"Those loans that you were supposed to take instead of salary? Did anyone address where you were to get the money with which to pay those back? Since all your earnings went directly into the Grand Caymans bank?"

Mitzi shook her head.

"So at this point you still haven't paid any of the money back?"

"Not so far."

"How much do you figure you owe yourself at this point?"

"At least three million dollars."

"Does that include interest?"

"Oh, no. With interest, it's more like four point five million."

Jeez Louise. "How much of that do you owe taxes on?"

"Just the three million."

"So you and Dave owe … how much?"

"With interest and penalties, one point five million."

"Did you and Dave split that when you divorced?"

"Yes," Mitzi said. "We each owe seven hundred and fifty thousand. Plus I'm buying him out on the house, so I owe him two hundred and fifty thousand for that. I want Jeremy to be able to stay in the same house and be in the same school with his friends."

Wow, a million dollars in debt. Mitzi was as deep in the hole as I would have been if Hal's ex-wife sued him for punitive damages and won. Were Rebecca and Jeff in the same fix? Then I thought of Jodi and changed the subject.

"What did Jay say when you told him you were pregnant?" I asked.

"He dumped me," Mitzi said.

"Because he didn't need you anymore now that you were pregnant?"

Mitzi looked astonished. "How did you know?"

"He did the same thing to somebody else I know," I told her. "So did he make any provisions to support you and your child after you and Dave divorced?"

"Not that I know of," Mitzi said. "After all, I'm a doctor. I make plenty of money. I don't need his."

"So if it turns out that he put you in his will, you'd be surprised?"

"Very."

Back in my office, I looked up Jeff's home phone number and address, but before I could call, Mike stuck his head in. "Hey, what are y'all doing here?"

"I thought I'd finish up Lance's autopsy, since Ruthie is suing us," I said.

"Hell, I can do that," he said. "I can cut it in after I gross tonight."

"Don't you have enough to do with all the surgicals and frozens and bone marrows?"

"Well, yeah, I've been hammered big-time today."

"All right then. I can do it. And I've already cut it in. All you have to do is make sure the cassettes get processed tonight and the slides cut tomorrow, and I'll come in and read them and sign the case out."

Mike shrugged. "Okay. Y'all don't have to twist my arm."

He started back to his own office. I called him back. "Hey."

"What?"

"Which surgeons are working this week?"

"Sorensen and Jensen. Why?"

"Just curious."

After he was gone, I called Rebecca. She answered the phone, sounding breathless. "You sound like you've been running," I said.

"Oh, there was somebody at the door," she said. "Who's this?"

"Toni Day," I said. "I was just making my Christmas rounds, and I thought I'd bring you some Christmas cheer."

"Oh, how nice!" she said. "Do you know how to find us?" She gave me directions. I thanked her and hung up. Then I walked home to get the car.

"What for?" Hal asked. "Where are you going?"

"I've just got a last-minute errand to do," I explained. "You don't ask questions like that at this time of year, remember?"

"Oh, right, because it's Christmas."

"I won't be long," I assured him.

First, I went to the store and bought a bottle of nonalcoholic eggnog and a box of bakery cookies. Then I was ready for my mission.

The Sorensens lived in The Willows, a rather upscale gated community on the northwest side of town near the canyon. It was not so posh that I had to have my retinas scanned to get in, but I had to push a button for the address I wanted, and Rebecca had to buzz me in before the gate would open and let me drive in. The streets wound around each other, making it very easy to get lost. However, Rebecca's directions were easy to follow, and I pulled up in front of a large sand-colored house with white brick trim and at least two stories. There may have been more. There were so many gables and projections that it was hard to tell from the outside.

Rebecca met me at the door, dressed in black knit pants and a baggy pink sweater that hid her belly. "Oh, how nice," she said again when I gave her the eggnog and cookies. "I have such a sweet tooth, you wouldn't believe. This is nonalcoholic, I hope, because—"

"It is," I assured her.

"Well, how about we crack it open and have some right now," she suggested, "and some cookies too."

"Sounds good," I said. "Can I help?"

"Oh, no, I can do it," she said. "You just make yourself comfortable, and I'll be right back."

I amused myself by wandering around her living room, looking at the pictures on the walls. They were all black-and-white sketches. This was obviously the front room that never got used, because it was white. All white. The carpet was cream-colored, the wallpaper a subtle cream-on-white pinstripe, the upholstery of the formal chairs, couch, and love seat a subtle cream-on-white paisley pattern. White vases filled with white lilies, orchids, and daisies were scattered about on tables, and the coffee table was topped with a white marble slab. The only color came from the green of the flower stems and leaves. Even the Christmas tree was flocked with white and covered in white-and-silver ornaments. Probably had white lights on it too, I thought.

I couldn't help wondering whose idea of decorating that was. I hoped the rest of the house had some color, or else how the hell were they going to keep it clean with a new baby?

Rebecca returned with a silver tray upon which were two goblets filled with eggnog and two white plates containing a selection of cookies. She put it down on the coffee table and invited me to sit. I picked one of the white chairs.

"This is a lovely room," I said.

"Oh, thank you," she said. "I'm so glad you like it. My mother decorated it, and Jeff keeps bugging me about how hard it is to keep it clean."

I picked up my glass of eggnog and took a sip, wondering how to start this conversation.

Rebecca started it for me. "Jeff says when the baby starts crawling, we'll probably have to redecorate."

"When are you due?" I asked.

"May fifteenth."

"Do you know if it's a boy or a girl?"

"It's a boy," she said. "Jeff is so excited."

"Have you picked a name yet?"

She looked thoughtful. "Jeff wants to call him Brent Alexander after his father and grandfather, but I want to call him Jeffrey Allen Junior. What do you think, Toni?"

"I like Brent Alexander," I said. "I don't know, but I think if I were a boy, I'd really hate being called Junior all the time." Besides which, I really didn't like the idea of this baby, who wasn't even Jeff's, being called Jeff Junior. Should I mention that? Rebecca would probably throw me out bodily.

Oh, what the hell. Was I going to just sit here in this sterile room, eating Christmas cookies and getting crumbs all over it? "At least you're not going to call him Jay Junior."

She nearly choked on her eggnog. "*What* did you say?"

"Rebecca. I've seen Jay Braithwaite Burke's will. You're in it."

She stared at me, shell-shocked, and then burst into tears. "Please don't tell Jeff," she sobbed. "He'll divorce me, and then what will I do?"

"I'm not going to tell anybody," I said. "Did you not know you were in Jay's will?"

"I had no idea," she said. "Why would he *do* that?"

"In case Jeff did divorce you," I said. "Jay meant to see that you and your child were provided for."

"Well, what's Jeff going to say when I inherit money from Jay?" she demanded. "Did he ever think of that?"

"According to the provisions of the will, you won't inherit as long as you're married," I told her.

She wiped her eyes and blew her nose. "How much money are we talking about here?" she asked.

"It depends," I said, "on how many other women inherit. I really don't know how much your share would be."

"Would it be enough to live on if Jeff divorces me?" she asked.

"Probably," I said. "Like I said, I don't really know. I don't think you'd have to declare bankruptcy, anyway."

"Oh, that reminds me," she said. "I haven't talked to Kathleen since she moved out. How is she?"

"She's fine, as far as I know," I said. I didn't feel like getting into the saga of the Burke family with Rebecca. Kathleen could tell her all that herself, if she wanted to, but I didn't feel it was my place.

Well, that was the most interesting part of the conversation, until I drained my eggnog and stood up. "Well, I won't keep you," I said. "I should be getting home."

Rebecca saw me to the door, and from my vantage point on her doorstep I noticed a house a few doors down that looked as if it had been burned. "Whose house is that?" I asked.

"Lance and Ruthie Brooks," she said. "Such an awful thing. He died, and then she had a fire. The fire department said she couldn't stay there because it was unsafe. I don't know if she plans to try to salvage it or rebuild it."

"I'm so sorry," I said. "That *is* an awful thing, especially at this time of year. Where did she go, do you know?"

"She's staying at the Blue Lakes Inn," she said. "But she was here just this morning, making brownies in my kitchen. She said they were a Christmas gift for Kathleen and the kids."

Brownies full of rivaroxaban. Oh goody. Oh shit. I hoped I wasn't too late. I thanked Rebecca again for her hospitality and left.

"Well, you have a nice holiday," she called after me as I went down the walkway to the car.

"You too," I called back as I unlocked the door and got in. I pulled away from the curb and drove down the street toward Ruthie's house. I drove around the corner and parked out of sight of Rebecca's house, where I hauled out my cell phone and called home. Hal answered.

"Don't eat those brownies," I said without bothering to identify myself. "They're full of rivaroxaban."

"Toni?" Hal said. "What are you talking about? What brownies? We don't have any brownies."

"Oh, thank God."

"Where are you?"

I didn't tell him I was sitting around the corner from Ruthie's burned house. "I'll be home in a few," I said and hung up.

I got out of the car and walked back toward Ruthie's house, hoping Rebecca was busy in her kitchen instead of looking out the living room window.

Ruthie's house had originally been painted dark green, but most of the front was charred black. The corner facing Rebecca's house contained a gaping hole. Yellow caution tape circled the yard. I stood on the sidewalk, facing the house and wondering where one would hide a stash of Lovenox where the fire department wouldn't find it. That reminded me that I still didn't know if they'd found it or not. I sighed. So many loose ends.

Well, no point in trying to look around in there until I knew there was something to look for. I should come back after dark, anyway. No point in having inquisitive eyes watching my every move and tattling to the cops about it. I could do my own tattling, thank you very much.

I went home.

Chapter 27

The good die first,
And they whose hearts are dry as summer dust
Burn to the socket.
—William Wordsworth

The house seemed very empty when I got back: just Hal and the dogs. "Where is everybody?" I asked.

Hal got up to fix me a drink. "Kathleen decided to go spend the holidays in Boise with her mother, Fiona's taking a nap, Elliott's at work, and Jodi and Bambi took the kids to the mall."

"So, Kathleen and the kids and Tiffany are gone?"

"Yep. They left not too long after you and Elliott."

Wow, that was fast, I thought. They weren't even up when we left.

"The police wanted to talk to Tiffany," I said. "I gave them all that stuff we printed off the computer yesterday."

"Pete was here looking for her," Hal said. He handed me my drink. "But they were already gone. So what have you been doing all day?"

"Well, after the police, I went to the hospital and talked to Mitzi, and then I visited Rebecca Sorensen."

"What did you find out from the police?" he asked. "Pete was kind of in a hurry when he was here. He didn't say much."

"Didn't Elliott—"

"I haven't seen Elliott all day," he interrupted me. "So tell me, already."

I told him about going through the contents of the safes, and the provisions of the various wills, particularly Lance's and Ruthie's, with the Commander.

"Who the hell is Mildred Atterbury?"

"A relative?" I speculated. "A childhood best friend? A nanny? Or is it Ruthie herself—an alternate identity to slip into when this is all over and everybody else is dead?"

"Jesus, Toni, that's cold," Hal remarked.

"No colder than poisoning one's husband and seven other people," I defended myself. "Is it too much to surmise that Jay and Lance intended to do the same thing, with all that money in offshore accounts? If Jay hadn't come back here to get Kathleen and the kids, we'd never know anything about it. He couldn't stay here, not after his Ponzi scheme became common knowledge; he'd be facing a prison sentence at the very least. And he couldn't retire to a Caribbean island using his own identity, because the Russian Mafia would find him and kill him."

"You've got a point," Hal said. "He could be the late Mr. Atterbury."

"I suspect that the police are going to try to find out if there really is a Mrs. Mildred Atterbury living at that address," I said. "Problem is, if Jay has already bought that place as Mr. Atterbury, it'll look all legal and aboveboard. So that won't accomplish anything."

"But they have to check it anyway," Hal pointed out, "or their investigation will be incomplete."

"Well, whatever she calls herself," I said, "you can't get away from the fact that Ruthie is the only one who has Lovenox and rivaroxaban, and she's had experience with both of them. She knows how much to give and how long to give it in order to achieve the desired level of anticoagulation for her purposes."

"So what you're saying is …"

"She knows too damn much *not* to be the murderer."

"And according to the provisions of Lance's will," Hal said, "Ruthie still has a reason to kill the Burkes, even though Lance is already dead. Jesus. I wonder where she is."

"Pete and Bernie went after her while we were still there," I said. "But they weren't back when we left. I hope they've got her in custody."

"Me too," he said. "Now, what's all the hoo-hah about brownies?"

"Rebecca told me that Ruthie made brownies this morning in her kitchen and told her they were a gift for Kathleen and the kids."

"Oh, Jesus," Hal said. "But they didn't have any brownies when they left here."

"Are you sure?"

"Positive. I helped them pack up and load the car. I should know if there were brownies or not."

"Well, that's a relief," I said.

The doorbell rang. The dogs and I ran to answer it, and it was Pete. "Can I come in?"

"Of course." I swung the door wide. Pete bent to fondle Killer and Geraldine and then took a seat on the couch. Hal offered him a beer, which he declined. "I'm still on duty," he said.

I offered him a Coke, which he accepted.

At this point, Jodi, Bambi, and the Maynard kids returned from the mall. Bambi ran upstairs. Jodi made a beeline for the downstairs bathroom. The kids dumped the shopping bags full of already-wrapped presents out under the tree and turned on the TV while all talking at once. I threw up my hands in frustration. "Let's go in the kitchen," I suggested, "where we can hear ourselves think."

We arranged ourselves around the kitchen table.

Pete reached in his pocket and pulled out a folded sheet of paper and handed it to Hal.

"Holy shit," Hal said and handed it to me. It was a wanted poster from the St. Louis County, Minnesota, sheriff's office, showing a female (at least I think it was a female) with straggly dark hair framing a sullen face that looked nothing like Tiffany. Mary Bernadette Kowalski, it said, wanted on one count of arson and three counts of felony manslaughter in Duluth in 1995.

"Yikes," I commented. "I'd hate to run into *her* in a dark alley. This can't be the Tiffany we know. Can it?" I appealed to the room in general. Bambi had come back downstairs and was looking over Pete's shoulder. Mum came in and pulled up a chair next to me.

Jodi looked over my shoulder. "Oh, I don't know," she said. "She might clean up all right. If she bleached her hair, put a nice blonde rinse on it, and smiled ... maybe."

"She *is* a bottle blonde," Bambi said. "Couldn't you tell? I mean *really*, you could see her roots for *miles*."

Spoken with the complacency of a natural blonde who knew how fortunate she was.

Pete turned around, saw Bambi, and jumped to his feet. Their eyes met, and I could practically see sparks fly. "Hi," he said huskily, putting the entire spectrum of emotion into that one simple word. Bambi looked up at him, an expression of wonder on her face as she replied, "Hi, I'm Bambi."

"My daughter Barbara, known to all as Bambi," said Hal. "Bambi, this is Pete Vincent."

Pete, still staring, shell-shocked, at Bambi, repeated, "Hi."

"Down, boy," Hal said. "Pete? Earth to Pete?"

"Oh, sorry," Pete said. "Let me get you a chair." He got one from the dining room and put it next to his own chair. "Please, sit here."

Bambi sat, a secret smile on her lips.

"Pete, dear," said Mum, "are you saying that the person we know as Tiffany is actually a *criminal*? And that she stole that little girl's identity?"

"It's a good bet," Pete said. "At this point, we can't rule it out."

"Wait a minute," Bambi spoke up. "Wouldn't they have different Social Security numbers?"

Elliott fielded that one before Pete had a chance to. "Not necessarily. Kids didn't have to have Social Security numbers back then. The way the law was," he went on to explain, "a person could get a Social Security number at any age, but most didn't until they were old enough to get a job. But the Tax Reform Act of 1986 required Social Security numbers for all dependents over five years old. Then in 1990 it changed to one year old in order for their parents to deduct them on their income tax returns. As of 1996, kids get Social Security numbers at birth."

"Mary Bernadette Kowalski," Pete said, consulting his notes, "was born in 1972."

"That means that 'Tiffany' is actually thirty-six years old," Hal said.

"What you're saying is, the real Tiffany Sue Summers didn't have a Social Security number," I said. "So Mary Bernadette could just apply for one as Tiffany Sue, with no one the wiser."

"Right," said Pete. "As long as she had identification."

"So what happens now?" I asked. "Are you or the Boise police going to arrest her?"

"Hopefully they've already done that," Pete said. "Ray called as soon as we got back after we failed to find her here. She should be in custody by now."

"Should be?" Hal asked. "I'd sure feel better if I knew for sure."

"I'll check when I get back," Pete assured him.

"But what if, in the meantime, she sets fire to Kathleen's mother's house?" I asked. "She sets fires everywhere the Burkes go, and now they're on their way to Kathleen's mother's house."

"Right. Why wait?" Pete said. "I'll find out right now." He hauled out his cell and pressed a button. "Ray? Can you check with Boise and find out if they've intercepted the Burkes yet? These folks are real anxious to know if they've got Tiffany Summers in custody yet. They're afraid she's gonna burn down Mary Reilly's house. Call me back. I'll be right here. Thanks." He hung up. "That's the best I can do right now."

"Thank you, Pete, dear," Mum said.

"What about Ruthie?" I asked. "Is she in custody, or did you just ask her questions and let her go?"

"Oh, she's in custody," he said, "but I don't know for how long. She was screaming for her lawyer when I left, so I don't know what's gonna happen."

"Pete, dear," my mother said, "do you mean to say that both Ruthie and Tiffany might be at large after all this?"

"Mrs. Day, we do the best we can," Pete said. I could almost hear his teeth grinding. "Sometimes it just isn't good enough."

"It's the freakin' lawyers," Elliott said.

Pete smiled. "Couldn't have said it better myself."

Bambi saw Pete to the door, where, after a brief conversation that we couldn't hear, he left. Bambi came back to the table smiling, followed by taunts of "Bambi's got a boyfriend," from the peanut gallery in front of the TV.

"Got a date?" I asked her *sotto voce*.

She nodded. "Saturday night."

"Good girl."

Jodi clutched her head and put her elbows on the table. "What a mess," she moaned. "How do guys like

Jay Braithwaite Burke manage to bamboozle a bunch of doctors? You'd think they'd be smarter than that."

"Doctors are smart," I told her. "Just not about money."

"Do you include yourself in that assessment, kitten?" Mum asked. "I thought I brought you up better than that."

"You did, Mum," I assured her. "So far I haven't been suckered by anybody. But it's not for lack of trying. You wouldn't believe the phone calls I get at work from salesmen wanting me to invest in gas futures, or art, or diamonds, or cattle ranches, or oil wells."

"She gets them at home too," Hal said.

"So what do you do, dear?" asked Mum.

"Hang up on 'em," Hal said.

"What I usually do is tell them to send me the literature in the mail so I can go over it with my accountant, and I hang up when they try to argue with me."

"And I suppose the literature never arrives," Jodi said.

"Of course not, and I never buy their product, either. As far as I'm concerned, if I can't wear it, hang it on my wall, eat it, drink it, read it, drive it, or plant it in my garden, I'm not buying it, especially sight unseen over the phone."

"Attagirl," said Hal.

"Mitzi," I said, "is a million dollars in debt. Can you imagine? I can't. It boggles my mind. But she owes the IRS seven hundred and fifty thousand dollars and her ex-husband two hundred fifty thousand, and she's completely calm about it."

"Of course, this *is* Mitzi we're talking about," Hal said.

"Well, that's true."

"What do you mean by that, Hal, dear?" asked my mother.

"Mitzi doesn't show her emotions," I explained. "One can never tell what she's thinking just by looking at her."

"Unlike Toni, whose face is an open book," Hal said.

"Yes, kitten, you always were a terrible liar," Mum agreed.

"More's the pity," I said. "It's a real liability when trying to detect things. I wonder," I went on with a meaningful look at my mother, "who I inherited *that* from."

Mum smiled. "Yes, dear."

"But getting back to doctors and money," I said, "the banks just aid and abet by giving them huge mortgages so that they can buy huge, palatial mansions—just because they're doctors and have the earning potential to pay it off."

"Of course, now," Elliott said, "those houses aren't worth the amount owed on them."

"This one probably isn't worth what we paid for it thirteen years ago," I said. "But we've already paid it down enough that we could pay it off if we wanted to."

"But still," Jodi said, "you guys have handled your finances well and stayed away from scam artists."

"We aren't typical," I said. "Hal was used to living on a professor's salary, and Mum taught me well."

"But those other guys," Hal said, "you know the next time a shyster like Jay Braithwaite Burke comes along, they'll flock to throw their hard-earned money away on the latest tax-evasion scam, just like before. The learning curve never goes up."

Jodi and Elliott had sent Kevin and Renee to get fried chicken, potato salad, coleslaw, and whatever other fixings they wanted, and now, with full bellies and a cozy fire in the fireplace, I had just drifted off to sleep.

I didn't get to sleep long. Hal woke me and handed me the phone. I looked up at him uncomprehendingly. "What?" I said.

"It's for you. Some doctor in Boise."

"Why does a doctor in Boise want to talk to me?"

"Why don't you ask her?"

"You're not going to tell me, are you?"

Hal was clearly running out of patience. "Toni ..."

With resignation, I pulled myself up to a sitting position and took the phone. "Hello?"

"Dr. Day?" She sounded quite young.

"Yes," I said.

"This is Dr. Vicki Page in the Emergency Department at St. Luke's in Boise," she said, "and I was told that I needed to talk to you about some patients we have here, Kathleen Burke and several children."

"You've got them in your emergency room?" I asked in disbelief. I looked at my watch. To my astonishment, it was ten fifteen. I looked around. Kids in sleeping bags lay sprawled all over the floor, sound asleep.

"Yes, I do, and they're all bleeding."

"Really."

"They all have nosebleeds, and we can't get them stopped. Mrs. Burke asked me to call you."

"Hang on a second," I said and put my hand over the mouthpiece. "Where is everybody?"

"They've all gone to bed," Hal said. "I wasn't going to wake you, but then the phone rang."

"Okay." I removed my hand and said to Dr. Page, "Who exactly do you have there? Kathleen Burke and how many children?"

"Four," she answered. "Bryan, Robert, Megan, and Angela Burke."

"And no other adults?"

"No, should there be?"

Shit. Where the hell are Tiffany and Emily? "Not necessarily. Did you ask them what they've eaten?"

"Yes, and about medications too. But—"

"Have they eaten any brownies?"

"Brownies? What the hell …"

"Ask them if they've eaten brownies and ask where they got them. Please, it's important."

"Hang on."

I put my hand over the mouthpiece. "Tiffany and Emily aren't with them."

"Where are they?" Hal demanded.

"Shhh, keep your voice down."

Dr. Page's voice sounded in my ear. "Are you there?"

"Yes, what did they say?"

"Mrs. Burke says that a friend called and said she'd left a gift for them at the Blue Lakes Inn. They picked it up on the way out of town, and the children opened it and found it to be a box of brownies."

"Did they all eat them?"

"Hang on."

"They ate the brownies Ruthie made," I told Hal.

"Mrs. Burke said they all ate the brownies, but the kids ate more than she and Tiffany did," Dr. Page said. "Who is Tiffany?"

"Somebody who should be with them," I said. "She has a child too."

"Just a minute," she said.

I heard voices as Dr. Page spoke with someone. Then she was back. "The charge nurse says a blonde lady brought them in and then left. Now can you tell me what's going on?"

"I think it's possible that they've all been poisoned with an overdose of heparin, and this is not the first time it's happened."

"Really," she said, sounding skeptical. "Now who exactly are you?"

"I'm a pathologist at Perrine Memorial Hospital here in Twin Falls."

"And how do you know these people have been given heparin? Were they in the hospital there?"

"No, they didn't get it in the hospital."

"So, they're all taking Lovenox? Kids and all?" Now she sounded *really* skeptical.

"No, it was an oral form of heparin that I suspect was put in those brownies."

"Heparin doesn't come in an oral form," she told me severely. "Is this some kind of a joke? Because I don't have time for—"

"There *is* an oral form of heparin," I explained. "It's called rivaroxaban, and it's in clinical trials."

"Do you know the name of the patient it was prescribed for?" she asked, and I told her.

Next she asked for the prescription number so she could go online and check it out with the Board of Pharmacy. "I don't have it," I said, "but her doctor here is George Marshall."

"The gastroenterologist," she said.

"That's the one."

Then she asked me the really hard question. "Why were they poisoned?"

I told her that it was a very long, complicated story, that the woman for which it had been prescribed was suspected of poisoning other people, and that the police were involved, whereupon she thanked me and hung up.

"Can we go to bed now?" Hal asked.

"We'd better not," I said and told him what Dr. Page had told me. "What do you bet Tiffany and Emily are on their way back here in Kathleen's car?"

"To burn this house down? Why? The Burkes aren't here anymore."

"Do you want to take that chance?"

"No, of course not," Hal said. "In fact, I think I'd better call the police and let them know what's going on."

He did so. By the sounds of it, Darryl Curtis was on duty. "Do you know about Ruthie Brooks and Tiffany Summers?" he asked. "You do? Great." He filled Darryl in on what Dr. Page had told me. "We think Tiffany is on her way back here in Kathleen Burke's car. Maybe. I don't think we'll be getting much sleep tonight. Great. Thanks—what, Toni?" he asked.

"Ask him about Ruthie," I said.

He did so. "Oh jeez. Okay, thanks." He hung up.

"Don't tell me. Ruthie's out."

"Yep. Her lawyer got her out."

"I thought Elliott was her lawyer," I said, "but Elliott didn't bail her out this time. I wonder who this other lawyer is."

"No idea," Hal said. "I'll ask Elliott about that in the morning. I suppose we'd better sleep down here, just in case?"

I agreed. We stretched out in the recliners under afghans.

"What do they do to stop the bleeding?" Hal asked.

"The antidote for heparin is protamine sulfate in the same dose as the heparin they received."

"But how do they know how much heparin they received?"

"Huh. I guess they'll give it until their anti-Xa's are normal."

"Titrate them, in other words," Hal said.

My husband, the chemistry professor.

"Right. Only, now that I think of it, I'm not so sure that protamine neutralizes rivaroxaban. They might have to depend on fresh frozen plasma to replace clotting factors."

"Sounds like they might be in the hospital for a while."

"Yeah. Kathleen won't be needing her car for the duration," I said. "But I wonder about Tiffany and Emily. Kathleen told Dr. Page that they ate the brownies too."

"Maybe they weren't bleeding yet," Hal said sleepily.

Bet they will be by the time they get here, I thought.

The dogs woke me out of a sound sleep, barking and growling at the front door. I hauled myself out of my recliner and shook Hal.

"Wha—?" he said.

"Somebody's out there."

Chapter 28

Heat not a furnace for your foe so hot
That it do singe yourself.
—Shakespeare, *King Henry VIII*

"Where?"

"Outside. Don't you hear the dogs?"

Killer and Geraldine were becoming more frantic. They left the front door and raced around the living room, barking at the windows. I looked out the front window and saw nothing.

"Go wake up Elliott," Hal said. "I'll go see what's going on out there."

"The hell you will," I said. I ran upstairs and banged on the door of the room Jodi and Elliott were sleeping in. Elliott opened it, tousle-haired and bleary-eyed. "What the hell's all the freakin' commotion about," he growled and then seemed to regain full consciousness. "Are we on fire?"

"Not yet, but somebody's out there, and Hal told me to get you."

"Jesus, Mary, and Joseph. Jodi, you stay put until I call you." He followed me downstairs, grabbed his coat and boots out of the closet, and put them on. Then he dashed out the front door after Hal. The dogs were gone. I could hear them barking outside. Jodi came down the stairs as I was getting my coat and boots on. "What's going on?"

"Our firebug may be here," I told her. "Hal and Elliott are out there with the dogs."

"And you're going out there too? Not without me, you're not." She got her coat and boots too, and as soon as we got ourselves outfitted, we were out the door. By now, several of the children were also awake, and Kevin was preparing to follow us out the door as we left. Jodi closed it behind her to keep the children from getting cold.

Outside, it looked like a winter wonderland in the moonlight. I heard Hal's and Elliott's voices and saw their footprints leading from the porch and around the house to the garage. Kevin came out the front door. "Kevin!" I shouted. "Go out through the kitchen into the garage."

"Okay," he shouted back and went back inside.

"How'd she get here?" Jodi asked me. "I thought she was in Boise."

"She's got Kathleen's car. But I don't see it parked out here on the street, do you?"

"It might be around the corner," Jodi suggested. "Let's go see."

"It might be in the alley too," I said.

We ran around to the opposite side of the house from the garage. No cars. Then we got to the alley, where I took one look and grabbed Jodi's arm, pulling her back, finger to my lips. I put my mouth to her ear. "She's there," I whispered.

Kathleen's car was parked on the side street, just beyond the alley. The trunk was open, and Tiffany was lifting a gasoline can out of it. The dogs, who were inside the backyard fence, were making enough noise to wake the entire neighborhood.

As we watched, Tiffany unscrewed the top of the can and began to dribble its contents along the fence and the back door of the garage. As she did so, she kept wiping at her face with her coat sleeve. If she managed to set the fence on fire, it would quickly spread to the garage, and then to the house via the kitchen. It was all hundred-year-old wood.

"We've got to stop her before she lights that," Jodi whispered to me.

"Go find the boys," I whispered back. "I'll stay here and watch her."

"Okay." She disappeared into the shadows.

I stayed put until I saw Tiffany slosh what looked like the entire contents of the can onto the garage door and put it down. As she drew what looked like a butane lighter out of her coat pocket, I knew there was no more time. "No!" I yelled and ran toward her as fast as I could in snow boots.

She turned to look at me as I rapidly closed the gap between us. "You can't stop me," she said. "I'll burn you as soon as look at you." She pointed the lighter at me and lit it just as I crashed into her, knocking her flat. The butane lighter went flying, no longer a threat. But my coat sleeve was burning. I knew that if she managed to push me into the gasoline she'd spilled, it would ignite, and so would I.

That's what she was trying to do, all right—use me as a lighter. She grabbed my coat and tried to pull me into the spilled gasoline. I pulled in the opposite direction. Grabbing her by the hair with my burning arm, I managed to set it on fire. She screamed and let go of me long enough for me to tear off my coat and fling it over her head. With her vision obscured, she couldn't see where she was going when I pushed her into the fence on the opposite side of the alley. She fell to her knees, and I flung myself on top of her and hollered for Kevin, who, last I saw, was supposed to be heading into the garage from the kitchen.

Kevin opened the garage door just as Hal, Elliott, and Jodi came barreling around the corner into the alley to find me struggling to stay on top of Tiffany as she bucked like a bronco to throw me off. "Help me," I yelled. "I can't hold her much longer."

Both Hal and Elliott grabbed Tiffany and hauled her to her feet. While Kevin assisted his father, Hal pulled a cable tie out of his pocket and neatly secured her hands behind her. "Fiona's calling the cops," he said.

Jodi picked up my coat and was about to pick up the butane lighter when I hollered, "Stop! Leave it for the cops!"

That's when I saw the dark stains Tiffany had left in the snow, and I got my first good look at her face. Her nose was bleeding.

"What the hell do we do with her now?" Elliott asked. "I don't want to take her in the house with the kids there, but it's freezing out here."

"The police should be here any minute," Hal said, and at that moment Tiffany bent forward and threw up. Blood. I could smell it. Hot and coppery.

"Ugh. That does it," Elliott said. "*Definitely* not in the house."

"They're coming," Jodi said. "I hear sirens."

I heard them too. "Maybe we should have had them bring an ambulance too. She's going to need to be in the hospital."

I needn't have worried. A police cruiser, lights flashing, pulled into the alley, followed by an ambulance. Darryl Curtis and another officer I didn't recognize got out of the car.

"How did you know we'd need an ambulance?" I asked Darryl.

"Your mother asked for one," he said.

"Hey!" Jodi called. She was standing by Kathleen's car, looking in the window. "Look at this!"

We all ran over to the car and looked in.

Curled up in the back seat under a blanket was Emily.

But the car was locked. "Hey, Darryl," I called. "Does she have car keys in her pocket?"

By this time, Tiffany had been loaded into the ambulance, and the paramedics were closing the doors. Darryl went over and spoke to them. One of them opened the doors and climbed in, returning a few seconds later to hand something to Darryl. He came over to the car and unlocked it. "Who's this?"

"This is Tiffany's daughter Emily," I told him. He reached in and scooped her up in his arms. Emily woke up and began to cry, and that's when I noticed that her face was covered in blood too.

"I think she needs to go in that ambulance too," I said. Hal went over to the ambulance and pounded on the driver's window. He rolled it down. Darryl was right behind him with Emily in his arms. "Got another passenger here," he said. The paramedics piled out of the ambulance and opened the back doors yet again. One of them climbed inside, took Emily from Darryl, and placed her on the gurney next to Tiffany, who began to cry.

When we finally got back in the house, everybody was awake. Mum, aside from calling the police and reading my mind, had prepared a quantity of hot chocolate and allowed the children to drink their fill. The stuff she gave us to drink was heavily laced with Kahlua, and it wasn't long before we were warm again.

"How did you know we'd need an ambulance?" I asked her.

"Well, darling, all this talk about Ruthie and her brownies, and Tiffany and her fires … I just thought somebody might be either bleeding or burned or heaven knows what else," she said, "so I just suggested that they might need one. I assume they did?"

"They sure did," Hal said. "Tiffany and Emily were both bleeding."

"Emily? Tiffany brought *Emily* with her? Where are the Burkes?" Mum asked.

"In the hospital in Boise, bleeding," I said. "The emergency room doctor called earlier because Kathleen asked her to."

"Where was I?" my mother demanded.

"You'd already gone to bed," I replied.

"Tiffany dropped them off and then left," Hal said. "She took Kathleen's car. It's parked out back of the alley."

"Are the cops still out there?" Bambi asked.

"Yeah," I said. "They've got to gather evidence. Process the crime scene."

"Do you suppose they'd mind if I watched?"

"Bless your heart," I said, hugging her with one arm. "I'll go with you."

"You're going out there again?" Hal asked. "You're crazy."

"Guess we both are," I said.

Out in the alley, Darryl and his companion were prowling around with flashlights, looking for whatever they could spot. They'd encircled the area with yellow crime scene tape. The gasoline can had disappeared, and so had the butane lighter. Darryl looked up as we came around the corner into the alley. "Please stay outside the tape. This is a crime scene," he said automatically, and then he recognized me. "Oh, sorry, Toni. Didn't realize it was you."

I introduced Bambi. "She's Hal's daughter, and she's interested in forensic science," I said. "Would it be okay if she watches you guys?"

"Oh, sure. I know who you are," he said to her. "You're Pete's new squeeze. No problem. You just stick with me, kid, and I'll show you the ropes. No kidding," he added as he caught my eye. "We'll take good care of her."

I thanked him and went back in the house. The children were already asleep again, and everybody except Mum and Hal had gone back to bed.

"Well, I guess I know what to get you for Christmas now," Hal said. "A new coat."

"My goodness, kitten," Mum said. "I didn't realize that she'd actually *burned* you."

"Better my coat than our house," I told her. "Besides, I set her hair on fire."

"*Antoinette*! You didn't."

"Well, it *was* after she set my coat on fire, and I tried to put it out by throwing my coat over her head," I said. "I was just trying to keep her away from all the gasoline she'd spilled."

"Bloody hell," Mum said.

I yawned.

"Sweetie, go to bed," Hal said. "I'll stay up and wait for Bambi."

I kissed him. "Thank you. I believe I'll take you up on that."

As I climbed the stairs, I reflected that even though Ruthie was still at large, we were all safe as long as we didn't eat any of her brownies.

Now, what had she *really* done with Lance's Lovenox?

I still didn't know.

Tuesday, December 23

Chapter 29

We have scotch'd the snake, not kill'd it.
—Shakespeare, *Macbeth*

Tuesday morning I woke early and walked down to Jim Bob's for a couple of boxes of doughnuts. By the time I got back, everybody was up, drinking coffee and talking about the previous day.

I poured myself a cup of coffee, draining the pot. I sighed in resignation. In my house, the rule was that whoever emptied the pot set up a new one. So I did, and I started it brewing; and I thought about getting one of those big stainless steel urns that makes thirty cups. We might need one if we were going make a habit of accommodating multiple families in the future.

Mum said, "Kitten, could I trouble you for a cup of tea while you're up?"

"No prob," I said. I put a cup of water in the microwave and rummaged around in my tea canister for an Earl Gray teabag while it heated.

"What's the occasion for the doughnuts?" asked Elliott, helping himself to an apple fritter.

"Not cooking breakfast for eleven people," I said, handing Mum her cup of boiling water with a teabag in it and a spoon. "And because we caught Tiffany trying burn our house down, and she's under arrest, so we don't need to worry about that anymore."

Mum pushed the teabag down to the bottom of the cup with the spoon. "Barbaric," she snapped. "Why you don't have a proper teapot, I cannot imagine. Have I taught you *nothing*?"

She always said that. Every time she visited us, she said that, and I'd resolve to get one; but then she'd go home and I'd forget all about it, until the next time. So I ignored her and sat down with my cup of coffee, reaching for a glazed doughnut as I did so.

"I don't get it," Jodi complained. "What would be the point?"

Bambi chose this moment to make her appearance. "The point of what?" she asked, reaching for a doughnut.

"Burning down our house," Jodi said. "Or Ruthie's, for that matter. I mean, Lance's office and Kathleen's house, that was one thing, but now we know it wasn't that."

Bambi looked bewildered. "Wasn't what?"

"The wills," said Jodi.

"What wills?"

"Jay Braithwaite Burke's wills," Hal said.

"You might as well tell her the whole freakin' thing, Shapiro," Elliott said, "because it's not over by a long shot."

"I defer to my wife," Hal said. "After all, it started with an autopsy."

"Not exactly," I said. "It started in 1990."

Bambi tossed her hair in frustration. "*What* started in 1990?"

I gave her the *Reader's Digest* condensed version of the saga of Jay Braithwaite Burke's hedge fund.

Bambi interrupted. "What's a hedge fund?"

"It's a superfund," I explained, "that contains different types of mutual funds, some of which go down when the market goes down and some go up. It also has mechanisms that will sell shares if it drops too far and buy them when the market goes up. It's meant to protect the investor from losing too much."

"Darling," said Mum, "you sound positively erudite on the subject."

"Fred takes good care of us," I said.

"That's our broker," Hal said baldly, "who told us to stay the hell away from Jay Braithwaite Burke."

I looked around and saw that the children were absorbed in the early morning cartoons on TV and were not listening to us. Kevin and Renee were tending to the fire.

"So then what happened?" Bambi asked.

"It turned out to be a Ponzi scheme," I told her. "Everybody lost their money."

"The freakin' economy collapsed," Elliott said. "The investors started taking money out to pay their bills, and the whole thing collapsed. That's when the freakin' IRS caught him."

"And all those doctors wound up owing the IRS hundreds of thousands in back taxes, interest, and penalties," I said. Thinking of Mitzi, I added, "Millions, some of them."

"Wow," said Bambi. "I bet they were pissed."

"I'm sure they were," I said, "and one of them sued him, but he declared bankruptcy and disappeared."

"And then he showed up dead," said Hal. "Hence the autopsy."

Bambi appeared fascinated. She leaned forward, arms on the table. "What killed him?"

"An overdose of heparin," I told her. "That's a drug used to prevent blood from clotting in people with heart valves, or in people who have had heart attacks or strokes or deep vein thrombosis. Apparently Jay had a history of DVT."

"Did Ruthie kill him too?" Bambi asked.

"More than likely," I replied.

After breakfast I went to work and read out Lance's autopsy slides. As I suspected, the tumor in Lance's liver and pancreas was pancreatic cancer, specifically a pancreatic ductal adenocarcinoma. Besides the liver, the lymph nodes in the vicinity of the pancreas were also involved, and there were implants in the peritoneum throughout the abdominal cavity and on the surfaces of the small bowel and colon.

The liver, apart from the tumor nodules, showed necrosis around the portal triads—strands of fibrous tissue containing branches of the hepatic artery, hepatic veins, and bile ducts. Many small hepatic veins were thrombosed. This explained why Lance was in liver failure. The bile ducts and the liver cells themselves contained obvious bile plugs, which explained the deep-green, gross appearance of the liver.

There was no evidence of tumor in any of the other tissues.

Lance's lungs, besides being full of blood, also showed an acute change called diffuse alveolar damage, with areas of reactive fibrosis surrounding collections of black, granular material and the beginnings of hyaline membranes, signaling the onset of adult respiratory distress syndrome.

This is similar to hyaline membrane disease in newborns and is frequently the final insult that carries off seriously ill patients. It had nearly carried off Hal three years ago. It can start with a bacterial or viral pneumonia, or aspiration pneumonia, or any other insult to the lungs—in Lance's case, smoke inhalation.

It was a toss-up what got Lance first: the lungs, the liver, or the blood loss. His carboxyhemoglobin was only eighteen percent, about double what a heavy smoker would walk around with on a daily basis; but it was not quite toxic, let alone lethal.

I dictated the microscopic description of the slides, the clinical pathologic correlation, the significance of the special studies, and final diagnosis. Cause of death: homicide by poisoning with heparin.

Someone would type it later today, and I would sign it out on the morrow.

I walked home.

The Commander stood in the middle of my living room, hat in hand, looking around at the mess on the floor.

"This is the first I've seen of what's been going on here," he said. "I've been hearing from Kincaid and Vincent about all these fires, but dang! Until I came up this street, I had no idea of the damage involved." He gestured toward the front window. "Now I can see that the Burkes' house is a total loss and how badly young Elliott's house is damaged—and the effect it's had on all your lives."

That was quite a speech for the Commander, but he'd been hit with it all at once. We'd kind of gotten used to looking across the street at the blackened heap that used to be Kathleen's house. And stepping over all the piles of clothing, toys, and sleeping bags on the living room floor had become second nature. It reminded me of the flood scenes in *The Nine Tailors* by Dorothy Sayers in which the entire village sets up housekeeping in the church until the floodwaters recede and they can go back to their ruined farms and start over.

"This is nothing," I told him. "You should have seen it when all the Burkes were here too."

He sat down on the couch next to me and put his briefcase on the floor. He opened it and extracted a handful of papers. "That's what I wanted to talk to you about," he said. "Now, I understand they're in Boise?" He fished a toothpick out of his shirt pocket and stuck it in his mouth.

"Last we heard," Hal said from his recliner, "they were in the hospital." He was obliged to raise his voice to be heard over the TV, and I asked the kids to turn it down so we could talk.

Bambi came over and sat on the couch on the other side of me. The Commander looked up and took the toothpick out of his mouth. "Who's this lovely young lady?"

"Hal's daughter Bambi," I said. "She's interested in police work. Bambi, this is Commander Ray Harris of the Twin Falls Police Department."

"Happy to meet you, Commander," she said. "Is it okay if I listen?"

"If the doc says it's okay, it's okay," he said. He stuck the toothpick back in his mouth and spread the papers out on the coffee table. I noticed that one of them was a wanted poster. "See this picture here," he said, the toothpick bobbing up and down as he spoke. "Mary Bernadette Kowalski, her name is. Here's an article from the Duluth *News Tribune* from back in 1995 about the fire she's supposed to have started. And this here is an obituary you might be interested in," he said, handing it to me. It was headed "Family Perishes in House Fire" and identified the three bodies found therein as having been Eldon, Marjorie, and Brittany Jo Summers, who had been predeceased by their older daughter, Tiffany Sue. The article was dated June 15, 1995.

"My God," I breathed. "That's right about when Tiffany came here."

"Wow, she killed her whole family," Bambi said.

"Not *her* family," I said. "That's Tiffany Sue's family—the family of the child whose identity she supposedly stole."

"I'm glad you said that, Doc," said the Commander, moving the toothpick to the other side of his mouth, "because until we match Tiffany's fingerprints to those we found on the gas cans and those in AFIS, we don't have absolute proof that the person you know as Tiffany Summers is actually Mary Bernadette Kowalski."

"You mean to tell me that you haven't fingerprinted her yet? She's in the hospital, right over there across the street and down the block," I said. "Why didn't Darryl do that when he arrested her? Don't tell me you didn't put her under guard in the hospital, either?"

My outburst had to do with the specter of Tiffany escaping and coming back to our house to finish the job she started last night, but the Commander interrupted me. "Now, Doc, that isn't what I said. We have her fingerprints. We just haven't matched them yet. We should get that later today. And she is under guard. What I wanted from you is some idea about how long she'd be in the hospital. Pete and Bernie went over there this morning, but the doctor was doing some kind of a procedure on her, so they didn't have a chance to talk to him. I figured that, you being a doctor yourself, you could give me some idea what's gonna happen."

"Have you called St. Luke's in Boise to find out how the Burkes are doing?" I asked. "That should give you some idea about how Tiffany and Emily are going to do, because they were all poisoned with the brownies that Ruthie made yesterday for them to take to Boise with them. In fact, there might be some brownies left that could be tested. They might be in Kathleen's car, in which case you've already got them, or they may be at Kathleen's mother's house, and—oh jeez, I hope Mary Reilly hasn't eaten any of them, because if she did she'll be in the hospital too."

The Commander shifted the toothpick to the other side of his mouth. "Assuming those fingerprints match, we can hold Tiffany for attempted arson, and with the fingerprints from the other fires, we can hold her on those too. And if we can show that she is actually Mary Bernadette Kowalski, who is wanted for that arson in Duluth thirteen years ago in which three people died, we can see that she's put away for life. But what about the child? What's gonna happen to her?"

I couldn't even begin to answer that question.

Bambi tried. "Oh, my God, we can't let her end up in foster care. Surely somebody will adopt her." She looked beseechingly at me.

Yikes. Was she suggesting that Hal and I adopt Emily? Surely Kathleen would adopt her. She already had four children, and Tiffany and Emily had lived with her ever since Jay had disappeared. She'd be inheriting millions of dollars, so money shouldn't be an issue. But if Kathleen didn't want to, how about Jodi and Elliott? Problem with them would be that they were older. Elliott was pushing fifty. Would they want to add a sixth child to their family, one that was only three years old? Or would she end up in foster care if Hal and I didn't adopt her?

Would this be my chance to give Hal his immortality?

It was a rhetorical question, because he might not want it anymore. He was six years older than Elliott.

I looked at Hal. He wasn't looking back at me. He was absorbed in the newspaper, which I was sure he had memorized by now. "Hal?" I said. "Are you listening to all this?"

"Not on purpose," he said, not taking his gaze off the newspaper. I stared at him as if my gaze could penetrate his skull and make him look at me. It didn't work.

Bambi took matters into her own hands. "Hal? Couldn't you and Toni adopt Emily?"

Hal put down the newspaper. "Bambi, I don't want to discuss it right now. Tell you what. If Jodi and Elliott don't want to adopt her, and Kathleen doesn't want to adopt her, Toni and I will talk about it. But not right now. Got it?"

Bambi sighed. "Okay. Whatever you say. *Dad.*"

Hal rolled his eyes, rustled the newspaper pointedly, and went back to reading it. As far as he was concerned, the discussion was over.

"Well, I reckon you folks will figure something out."

I'd forgotten the Commander was still there, I'd gotten so wrapped up in the adoption discussion. He'd gotten to his feet and zipped up his parka, preparing to leave. "I'll see what I can find out about the Burkes—and Mary Reilly too," he said. Then he was gone.

I felt at loose ends, feeling that I needed to be doing something but having no idea what. I hated that feeling. It made me want to eat something, and that just pissed me off, because I was one of those people who gained weight just looking at food, just smelling food, just *thinking* about food. It wasn't fair.

I looked in the refrigerator; nothing there appealed to me. I looked in the pantry; everything there required preparation. I stood in the middle of the kitchen, looking around. A flash of something shiny caught my attention. There on the kitchen counter, nearly hidden behind the toaster oven, stood a clear glass cookie jar, half full of Christmas cookies and tied with a shiny red ribbon.

Hmm. Where had that come from? I picked it up. It was covered by a thin coating of dust, in which I could see smudgy fingerprints. Okay, I know I'm not the best housekeeper, but surely I'd wiped that counter more recently than that. Or maybe not. With all these people in the house, routines went out the window. Perhaps that counter had been wiped off by someone else, like Jodi. Or Mum.

At that time in the early afternoon, everybody was busy doing their own thing. Jodi and Elliott were both at work, the kids had gone to the mall again, and Hal had gone off on an errand—I didn't know what and didn't ask, not at this time of year. Perhaps he'd gone shopping for my new coat. Anyway, only Mum and I remained at home, so I asked her about the cookie jar.

"I think it's Jodi's," she said. "Or maybe Kathleen's, but she probably would have taken it with her to Boise, so it's probably Jodi's."

Just as long as it wasn't Ruthie's. Obviously someone had eaten some of them, and nobody here had gotten sick, so I decided that they were safe. I reached in and grabbed a handful. "Mum? Want some cookies?" I asked.

"No, kitten, I'm fine," she replied.

So I settled down on the couch with a book, made short work of the cookies, and before I knew it, I had fallen asleep, to be awakened by the commotion when everybody arrived home in time for cocktail hour.

Hal and Elliott prepared drinks for everyone, while the kids spread out on the floor in front of the TV, watching *The Grinch Who Stole Christmas*. Hal prepared lasagna, using our largest baking dish, while I sliced up a loaf of French bread and filled a cookie sheet full of garlic bread.

While the lasagna was baking, I began to prepare a salad. I assembled tomatoes, an onion, a head of lettuce, and a cucumber on the cutting board, and then proceeded to slice the tip of my thumb almost completely off. Only a flap remained attached by a thread of skin.

I stared in disbelief as blood welled up and began to drip on the cutting board. Then it began to hurt—a lot. I gritted my teeth and grabbed a wad of paper towels to stanch the flow.

Hal noticed. "Sweetie? Are you okay?"

"I cut myself," I said through my teeth. "Get me some ice? Please?"

Mum came into the kitchen. "I'll get it, Hal, dear," she said and created a compress out of more paper towels and ice, which she applied to my thumb, discarding the used towels that were already soaked through.

It wasn't long before the new ones were too. I took the compress off and looked at the tip of my thumb. Nothing had changed. Blood continued to well up just as merrily as before and actually pulsated. As I stared at it, I began to feel queasy and light-headed.

"Mum, I think I need to lie down," I said. I took two steps toward the living room and fainted.

Chapter 30

It may seem a strange principle to enunciate
as the very first requirement in a Hospital
that it should do the sick no harm.
—Florence Nightingale

I woke up on the couch with Hal applying a wet cloth to my forehead and Mum putting a new compress on my thumb. I felt no better.

"Hal, dear," she said worriedly, "I don't think it's going to stop."

"Maybe I should take her to the emergency room," Hal said. "Toni? Can you sit up?"

I did so. The room was spinning, so I closed my eyes and lay back down. "No way," I told him. "I'm afraid I'll be sick if I do."

"No, you won't. Come on, honey. We're going to take you to the emergency room and get that stitched up. You'll feel better once it stops bleeding. Fiona, can you take her other arm, and we'll get her out to the car?"

"I'll do it," Jodi said. Mum went back in the kitchen, and Hal and Jodi assisted me through the door and into the garage. Hal drove, and Jodi kept pressure on my thumb, which was now wrapped in a hand towel as well as another change of paper towels and the ice pack.

I sat with my head tipped back and my eyes closed, praying that I wouldn't throw up in the car. *Shit*, I thought, *what the hell's going on here? Blood shouldn't bother me. I'm a doctor, for God's sake, and I was a med tech before that. I deal with blood all the time. It's usually not mine, though, and not usually pouring out of me so fast.*

The towel was already showing patches of red by the time we got there. By the time they got me into a cubicle, it was soaked through.

Jodi looked worried. "Toni, you don't usually get sick at the sight of blood. What have you eaten today?"

"Breakfast," I said.

"How about after that? Lunch?"

"I ate some of your cookies," I replied.

"My cookies? What are you talking about?"

"That cookie jar in the kitchen. Isn't that yours?"

Her face cleared. "Oh, that isn't mine. It's Kathleen's."

"How the hell did a cookie jar make it through three fires and end up at our house?" Hal asked. "That's not the type of thing that generally gets rescued in case of fire."

"Where'd Kathleen get it?" I asked. "Did she make the cookies?" All this talk about cookies was making me even more nauseated. I took deep breaths.

"I think Ruthie gave it to her," Jodi said. "You know Ruthie, always baking things to give to people."

Yeah, right. Things spiked with rivaroxaban. I groaned dismally.

"Well, that didn't sound very good." My colleague, Dave Martin, MD, Family Medicine, came in, removed the towels, and said, "Whoa. What'd you do, Toni, cut an artery?"

"Not on purpose," I said faintly.

He peered at me. "You don't look so good. Don't tell me you faint at the sight of blood, you of all people!"

"Not until today," I whispered and threw up.

Everybody jumped back. Dave stepped outside the cubicle and asked somebody to call Housekeeping, and then he looked down at the mess on the floor. "That's got blood in it," he observed.

I lay back and wiped my mouth. "My thumb probably dripped on the floor." One could only hope. *Cleopatra, Queen of Denial.*

Dave said, "Not that much." He threw a towel on the floor to cover up the vomit and then removed the new ice pack he had put on my thumb. It was soaked with blood.

"I can't sew that up until the bleeding stops," he said, "but I can at least anesthetize it." He injected some Xylocaine, which hurt more than the cut did for the first few minutes. The bleeding continued unabated. Dave shook his head.

"I'm gonna try something here, Toni, that's contraindicated, but I don't know what else to do. I'm gonna shoot some Xylocaine with epinephrine in here. I know we don't usually do that in the extremities, but despite the risk of gangrene, it looks like we could use some vasoconstriction right about now."

I nodded without speaking. I would have done the same thing in his place.

It worked. The bleeding stopped. Dave stitched the skin flap back onto the tip of my thumb, wrapped it in a huge bandage that went all the way around my hand and looped around my wrist, and told me to elevate it and keep ice on it.

At this point I expected him to get up and leave, but he didn't. He just sat there, looking worried. Finally he spoke.

"Toni, have you ever had a bleeding problem before?"

"No."

"Anybody in your family?"

"No."

"You're not on any anticoagulants, are you?"

"It's possible," I said. "I ate some cookies earlier that might have rivaroxaban in them."

"Rivaroxaban?"

"It's an oral form of heparin that's in clinical trials."

"Oh, yeah," he said. "I think George actually has a patient that's on it. And you think it's in the cookies you ate?"

"If you get an anti-Xa on me," I said, "and it comes back positive, you'll know."

"Huh. Who the hell would put rivaroxaban in a batch of cookies?" he wondered aloud.

"Someone who wants to kill the people who eat them," I said. "I think you need to call the police."

"You got it," he said abruptly, rising from the stool he was sitting on. "And after that I'm gonna get the lab down here and draw some blood, and by that time the cops should be here."

"Hal," I began.

"I know," he said. He hauled out his cell phone. "I need to make sure nobody else eats those cookies."

"Also make sure nobody touches that cookie jar. It's got fingerprints on it, and they're not all mine."

"Fiona?" Hal said. "Don't let anybody eat those cookies. They're what made Toni bleed. Yes, apparently Ruthie made them and gave them to Kathleen. No, don't touch it. The police will want to test it for fingerprints. Yes, that would be a good place for it. Wear gloves and try not to smudge it. Thanks. No, she's not bleeding any more. I don't know. She might have to stay here tonight. You'll know as soon as I do. Bye." He closed the phone and looked at me. "What do you suppose he's gonna test you for?"

"Probably a pro-time and a PTT, maybe a d-dimer to see if I've got DIC, and the anti-Xa."

Hal nodded, but Jodi asked, "What's DIC?"

"Disseminated intravascular coagulation," I said. "It's a condition where blood clots in the blood vessels and uses up all the clotting factors and platelets so that the blood can't clot any more. The d-dimer is a breakdown product of fibrin that shows up in DIC."

"Wow," Jodi said. "What causes it?"

"Trauma or surgery, especially if some kind of cancer is involved."

"You did have trauma," Hal commented.

I snorted. "This is nothing; I'm talking about *major* trauma, like a car accident, with crushed organs and broken bones and stuff like that."

Someone from Housekeeping came in and mopped up the floor. As she left, Brenda came in. "Doctor! What are you doing here?"

"Bleeding," I said economically, and Hal added, "She cut herself, and it wouldn't stop bleeding."

"Oh," she said. "That explains it."

"Explains what?"

"He's ordered a CBC, pro-time, PTT, fibrinogen, d-dimer, and anti-Xa," she said. She gave me a long look. "Is this related to all those other anti-Xa's?"

"You got it."

Efficiently, she drew my blood. "Someday you're gonna tell me all about this, right?"

After she left, a nurse came in and started an IV. She put an ice pack on my hand. She adjusted the bed and put another pillow behind my head. "Is there anything else you need, Dr. Day?"

I ran my tongue around my mouth. It tasted awful. Vomit's bad enough without decomposing blood, which doesn't taste any better than it smells. "Could I brush my teeth?"

She brought me a little kit that contained a toothbrush, a tiny tube of toothpaste, a tiny bottle of mouthwash, and a wipe, along with an emesis basin and a glass of water—all of which I accepted gratefully. While I was brushing my teeth, Dave came back in.

"The police are on the way. Also, I think I should admit you, at least for overnight, in case you bleed anymore. When the labs come back, we'll know what to do next. While I was out there, I took the opportunity to look up rivaroxaban, and apparently protamine doesn't work for that as well as it does with Lovenox or unfractionated heparin, and they recommend prothrombin complex concentrates instead. They can get that from the pharmacy. So once they get you all neutralized and you don't have any adverse reactions, you'll be good to go in the morning."

"Who's gonna take care of me up there?" I asked.

"Jeannie's on call, but I called George too, since he's the one who knows the most about rivaroxaban."

Hal stood up. "I guess we might as well go home, then. Do you want me to bring you anything?"

"Oh, a couple of books—the one I'm reading and that new Dick Francis. And a ChapStick."

"You got it."

"Oh, and some Kleenex."

"There's some Kleenex right here," Jodi said. She handed me the box. Hal kissed me good-bye, and Jodi hugged me. Then they were gone.

I grabbed a couple of tissues and blew my nose. Bloody. *Terrific.*

"Toni? Are you decent?" A familiar voice called from outside the curtain screening my cubicle.

"Come in, Bernie."

Kincaid peered around the curtain as if to check that out for himself and then came in. He pulled up the chair that Dave had used and sat down, pulling out a notebook. He looked up at me just as I was trying to plug up a nostril with tissue to keep it from dripping. "Nosebleed?"

"Nosebleed, upper GI bleed, and stitches in my finger, which I cut while making salad," I told him.

"Dr. Martin said something about poisoned cookies."

"Yes. I ate six of them. Then I found out that Ruthie made them."

"When did you find that out?" he asked.

"Just a few minutes ago," I replied. "I thought they were Jodi's, but Jodi told me just now that Ruthie had made them and given them to Kathleen."

"So you're in here because you're bleeding?" he asked.

"I'm in here because I cut my finger and it wouldn't stop bleeding. Then when I got here, I threw up blood. Now my nose is bleeding. I'm going to be admitted overnight so they can give me an antidote so I won't bleed anymore."

"So, Ruthie Brooks strikes again," he said. "She seems to have it in for you, doesn't she?"

"Well, I am the one who tattled on her to the police," I said, "but this time I think I was an innocent bystander. Those cookies were meant for the Burkes, who apparently had already eaten some."

"How do you know that?"

"They were in a big glass cookie jar, and it was half empty. Nobody else has gotten sick, so it had to be the Burkes who ate them. Then they ate the brownies too and ended up in the hospital. Have you heard anything about how they're doing?"

"I think they're still there, but stable," Bernie said. "They might get out in time for Christmas dinner, who knows?"

"What about Ruthie?" I asked. "Are you going to arrest her again?"

"I wish we could," he said with a sigh, "but all the evidence we have is circumstantial. That lawyer of hers would be all over us like a dirty shirt if we go after her again, suing us for false arrest and stuff like that. We're practically gonna have to catch her in the act, like you caught Tiffany."

Damn. "Who is her lawyer, anyway?"

"Some big shot from Boise, name of Chaim Rabinowitz."

Chaim Rabinowitz? Jesus. Hal was gonna love that.

Bernie stood. "Well, I'll be going over to your house now to collect that cookie jar. Hope you can manage to get some sleep. You look like you need it."

I looked up at him, thinking it was marginally better than being told I looked like dog meat, when he leaned over quickly and kissed my cheek. "Good luck, Toni."

"Thanks," I said, and then I thought of something. "Bernie!"

"What?" He peeked around the curtain again.

"Did the fire department ever find any Lovenox in Ruthie's house?"

"Nope, and we didn't either."

After he was gone, I wondered what my chances would be of finding something after both the fire department and the police department had failed to.

A snowball's chance in hell? A needle in a haystack? A fart in a windstorm?

Nevertheless, if I ever got out of here, I resolved, I would look anyway. Sometime when Ruthie wasn't around. Now when would that be? Now that the police couldn't get her off the streets, I'd have to think of something to distract her for an hour or two. Maybe I could get Mum to take her to church on Christmas Eve or Christmas morning or—wait a minute. Lance's funeral! When was Lance's funeral? It had to be the day after Christmas at the earliest. They wouldn't have a funeral on Christmas Eve or Christmas Day.

A young girl in a royal blue polo shirt with *Transport* over the breast pocket interrupted my train of thought. She looked barely old enough to even be in puberty. "I've come to take you upstairs," she said. "You're going to ICU."

ICU? Was I that sick? Did anybody ever get to go home the morning after a night in ICU? I didn't think so. Suddenly I felt like a prisoner, like I'd been kidnapped, like some evil mad scientist was going to use me for medical experiments.

To my dismay, that's just about what happened that night.

Jeannie came in about five minutes after I'd been settled into my ICU bed and had been hooked up to monitors and an IVAC to regulate the flow of my IV. She took a fairly exhaustive history, which consisted mostly of negatives, since I'd never actually been sick before—except for the car accident three years earlier, which was in my chart already, and a physical exam that was, in her words, disgustingly normal. "Except for the fact that you've got a nosebleed, a cut finger, and hematemesis," she said. "We need to get some more labs, because we need to know your electrolytes and your renal function. Your other labs should be back any time."

She went to the nursing station and made a phone call.

When she came back, she said, "I'm getting you typed and screened, just in case we need to transfuse, and we'll probably give you some fresh frozen plasma to replace your clotting factors. If your PTT is too high, we'll have

315

to consider protamine sulfate to neutralize the heparin in your blood."

"No, no, no, no protamine," George declaimed, Gnarly Finger in the air as he swept into ICU and screeched to a halt at my bedside. "This isn't heparin as you and I know it, Jeannie. This is rivaroxaban, which is still in clinical trials, essentially an experimental drug. Protamine doesn't work on it."

"Well, how about FFP?" Jeannie asked.

"We can use FFP," George said, "but PCCs would be better."

"PCCs?" Jeannie asked.

"Prothrombin complex concentrates," George lectured. The man was a walking differential diagnosis and never missed an opportunity to teach. "They contain prothrombin and factors VII, IX, and X, as well as proteins C and S—and a little heparin to prevent activation of the other clotting factors so you won't get DVTs. We don't want to go too far in the other direction, now, do we?"

"I guess not," I said.

"Have we got any labs back?" George asked Jeannie, and she shook her head. Then she turned her head and looked toward the nursing station, where someone was trying to get her attention. "Oh. Maybe that's them now," and she took off at practically a dead run.

George stood looking after her and shook his head. "Where does she get all that energy?" *Easy*, I thought. *She's half your age.* But I didn't say it.

Jeannie came back with a printout in her hand. "Well, Toni, your white count's normal, and your hemoglobin is thirteen-point-four, so I guess you don't need transfusion quite yet. PTT's only twenty-eight seconds, but the *pro-time* is elevated. INR is three-point-five. That's weird."

"Not really," George said. "The two tests recommended for following rivaroxaban are the pro-time and the anti-Xa. Did Dave order one of those?" He peered nearsightedly at the printout. The lighting around the beds was not especially conducive to reading computer printouts at the best of times.

"Yes," I said. George looked at me in surprise. "I asked him to. What was it?"

Jeannie said, "Holy shit. Eight-point-five. Reference range zero-point-four to one-point-one." She looked shell-shocked.

George did too. "Toni. How did you know to ask Dave for an anti-Xa?"

I had to laugh. "Hello. I'm a pathologist. We've had the anti-Xa available in the lab for a year for you guys to monitor heparin with, and you keep ordering PTTs. That wouldn't have done you much good here tonight, would it?"

Brenda came back to draw my blood for the other tests George and Jeannie had ordered, and before long I was receiving FFP through my IV. Four units dropped my anti-Xa down to five-something.

A little later I complained of nausea, and the nurse told me she had orders to put a nasogastric tube down if that happened. The drainage from the NG tube was bloody, and George decided to endoscope me. Right there in my bed. The nurse anesthetist on call came and gave me Versed, so I knew nothing until I woke up and the procedure was done.

The nurse, Leslie, came over and peered into my face. "She's awake, Doctor," she said, and George loomed over me. "Well, I'll tell you what we found, Toni, even though I'm gonna have to tell you again in the morning because you won't remember. You're bleeding from the stomach and the colon, but I found no specific bleeding spot anywhere to embolize or cauterize. Some of that blood might even be swallowed blood from your nose. Anyway, the FFP helped some, but I'm gonna give you some PCC now, and then we'll see. If we need to, we'll give some more in the morning, but I don't want to give more than that because all the clotting factors have different half-lives. Factor VII has only six hours, but prothrombin has sixty to seventy-two hours, and so it tends to build up and cause DVTs."

Jeez, I thought. I was damned if I did and damned if I didn't.

Wednesday, December 24

Chapter 31

Home is the place where, when you have to go there,
they have to take you in.
—Robert Frost

In the morning my anti-Xa was down to two-point-seven.

After the second unit of PCC, it dropped to one-point-two, just above the upper limit of the therapeutic range. I got discharged shortly after lunch. Hal and Mum came to take me home.

It started snowing shortly thereafter and continued for the rest of the day. The wind howled around the corners of the house and in the chimney. The kids didn't want to go outside. Actually, nobody wanted to go outside. It was just the kind of day that simply cried out for a roaring fire and wassail, and that is exactly what we did. We gathered around the TV, the kids and Killer on the floor with pillows and throws, and me snuggled under my afghan with Geraldine on the couch, drinking wassail or hot chocolate and watching our favorite Christmas DVDs: *It's a Wonderful Life*, *The Bishop's Wife*, *Miracle on 34th Street* (two versions), *National Lampoon's Christmas Vacation*, *A Christmas Story*, *White Christmas*, and so on.

Hal had gone out and gotten quantities of hot wings, and that was our supper, along with chips and dips, crudités, nuts, and candy—none of it prepared by Ruthie.

Then we turned off all the lights—in order to better enjoy the ambiance of the Christmas tree lights and candles—and watched the old black-and-white version of Dickens's *A Christmas Carol* on DVD, which was just as deliciously scary as it had been when I was little.

Grandma and Grandpa Day would turn off all but the Christmas lights, and we would gather around the old black-and-white TV with a big bowl of nuts, still in their shells. Grandma would hold me in her lap while Mum and Grandpa cracked shells and passed nuts around. With Grandma's arms around me, I could wallow in the scariness knowing that nothing bad would happen to me.

But now I knew that wasn't true. Scary things like murder and fire *could* happen to me. They'd been happening all around me, to people close to me. It had only been a matter of time before they happened to me.

Thursday, December 25

Chapter 32

Some hae meat and canna eat,
And some would eat that want it;
But we hae meat, and we can eat,
Sae let the Lord be thankit.
—Robert Burns

Christmas morning the younger kids were up before daybreak. They came trooping upstairs and pounded on all the doors. Elliott told them with dire threats to leave the freakin' presents alone until everybody was up, but it was too late, and the ensuing racket got all of us up.

Bambi and Kevin had played Santa Claus, handing out presents, and the kids made short work of them. I brewed coffee, Elliott made his famous eggnog, and Jodi made pumpkin pancakes. Then the kids went out and built a snow family in the front yard, while Jodi and I hauled a trash can in from the garage and cleaned up all the wrapping paper and trash.

Hal gave me a tiny digital camera, small enough to put in my pocket; so that's where I put it. My new coat was a wool peacoat like the old one, except it was black instead of navy blue and had gold buttons. It made me look thinner than the old one too.

The kids watched more Christmas movies on TV, and then Hal and Elliott and the kids watched football. Jodi and I read. A lot of napping got done. All in all, the day passed pleasantly.

Mum had been busy in the kitchen most of the day and wouldn't let anybody help. It was supposed to be a surprise.

Later she served up a celebratory feast of standing rib roast and Yorkshire pudding, with trifle for dessert, and nobody said much while chowing down on that awesome repast. It took me right back to the first Christmas dinner I could remember, when I was three. It had been my first Christmas in the United States, at Grandma and Grandpa Day's house, where I lived until I married Hal—where Mum still lived.

But Mum put an abrupt end to the nostalgia.

"What on earth is going to happen to that poor child?" she asked the group at large over coffee and dessert. "It's not a rhetorical question, my dears. Don't you think we should do something about her so she doesn't end up in foster care and turn into a drug addict or a street person or, God forbid, end up in jail like her mother?"

Truth or consequences time; I could avoid it no longer. "Hal, what should we do?"

Hal looked at me as if I'd punched him in the stomach. "What do you mean 'we'? Are you suggesting … I mean, don't you think I'm a little old to be raising a child now? By the time she's in high school, I'll be an old man!"

Christ on a crutch. Hal was panicking even more than I was.

"Hal, calm down," Jodi said.

"Easy for you to say," Hal began, but Jodi laid a hand on his arm.

"What I'm trying to say is that you don't have to do anything about Emily," she said.

"We don't?"

"What Jodi is trying somewhat clumsily to say is that we've decided we want to adopt Emily," Elliott said.

"Are you sure?" I asked, startled. "I mean, you already have five kids. What about them?"

"What about us?" Kevin said. "We all talked about it. We're all okay with it, right, guys?" he asked, looking around at the others. "I mean, she knows us and we know her, and she's lived with us."

"Yeah," Renee put in. "We don't want her to go to some nasty old foster home where she doesn't know anybody."

"Emily's been through a lot of bad shit lately ..." Jason began and then caught his mother's eye. "Stuff," he amended hastily. "She's been through a lot of bad *stuff*— all those fires, and Kathleen and all the kids moving to Boise, and her mom going to prison and all. She needs to be with people she knows."

This was beginning to sound rehearsed. Maybe it was. But the kids all sounded sincere.

"We got kind of used to having her around," Cody added. "So now we get to have her back, and I don't have to be the youngest anymore."

"I get to have a little sister," Julie said.

"Wow," Hal said, looping an arm around me. "Sounds like you guys have got it all figured out."

"Wait a minute," I said. "Has anyone talked to Kathleen? I sort of assumed that she'd adopt Emily."

"I talked to her," Jodi said. "I thought that too. But she doesn't want to. Her kids teased Emily unmercifully, and she was always upset. I saw that when they were staying with us. Tiffany stuck up for her, but Tiffany isn't going to be around anymore, and that's going to be traumatic for her. She seemed a lot more comfortable around our kids, and our kids really took to her."

"Huh," Hal said. "Who'd 'a thunk it?"

"Wait a minute," I said. "Aren't there a lot of hoops to jump through before you can actually bring her home?"

"Not to worry," Elliott said. "I'm a lawyer, remember? We've already applied to be her foster parents. That way she'll be living right here while we deal with the complexities of the system."

"Huh," I said. "What if you don't get to be her foster parents? What happens then?"

"Fritz Baumgartner," Elliott assured me, "has friends in high places. He says it's a done deal."

Lawyers. They think there's nothing they can't do. In this case, however, I sincerely hoped it was true. "Well, good," I said. "I'm glad she's got a home."

Bambi put her arms around both of us. "Me too," she said. "After I thought about it, I realized that it was unfair to you and Hal to expect you to adopt a three-year-old at your ages after you'd never had children and had no experience taking care of one. You know," she continued, "people aren't born knowing how to take care of a child. You have to know what you're doing, and you have to *want* children. People who don't want them don't take good care of them."

I pulled back to look her in the face. "My, aren't we the authority on child rearing," I teased her. "Where'd all that come from?"

Her face was serious. "My mom never seemed to like me as much as my brothers," she said. "It's kind of hard to describe, and she never said so, but I knew. She was always kind of cold and impatient with me, even before the boys came along."

"What about your dad?" I asked. "Marty, I mean."

"He's okay," she said, "but he's not home much. I mean, he's always at the dealership, or at some meeting, or playing golf, or something. He and Mom don't spend much time together anymore."

I had to bite my lips to keep from saying that Marty was probably having an affair.

"But you guys," Bambi continued, "didn't even know me. You didn't even know I existed until I showed up here, and you just accepted me as if I'd always been part of your family."

"Of course we did," I said. "What else would we do? You *are* part of our family."

"See, that's what I mean. What I'm trying to say is that I really feel loved here."

"Well, that's good," I said, wondering where this was going.

"What I'm saying is that, given a choice of living here or living with Mom and Dad, I'd rather live here," she said. "If you want me, that is."

"Darling child," I said, "of course we do."

God bless us all, every one.

Friday, December 26

Chapter 33

The best-laid schemes o' mice and men
Gang aft a-gley;
And leave us naught but grief and pain
For promised joy.
—Robert Burns

L ance's funeral was scheduled for two o'clock on Friday afternoon at the Episcopal Church, to be followed by interment at Sunset Park, the cemetery out on Kimberly Road at the south end of town.

Hal would rather have his fingernails pulled out one by one with a pair of pliers than go to a funeral, so he and Mum stayed home while the rest of us went to the church. I never objected to Hal staying in the house during a funeral, because I knew that houses sometimes got robbed by folks who cased the obituaries and death notices for that very reason.

Ruthie sat alone in the front pew, all in black with a veil over her face, holding a black lace-edged handkerchief to her mouth. I walked straight up to her with Jodi and

Elliott right behind me. I sat next to her and put my arm around her. "Ruthie, I'm so sorry for your loss," I said, trying to appear sympathetic.

Ruthie wasn't having any. She turned her head and gave me an angry glare. "I'll just bet you are."

I squeezed her shoulder. "No, really. Aside from all that, I am really sorry that Lance died. I don't think any of us realized how sick he really was."

She shrugged off my arm and turned away, stifling sobs. Jodi, on the other side of her, replaced my arm with hers. I got up and walked slowly toward the back of the church and saw the Burke family coming toward me. None of them looked particularly full of piss and vinegar, but Kathleen looked awful. She had visibly lost weight, her hair looked dull, and her normally rosy face was ashen. I wondered how much blood she had lost.

She hugged me. "We heard about Tiffany and Emily," she said. "I can't believe it. Does this mean that she tried to kill all of us by setting fires to whatever house we were staying in? Why? What was the point?"

I merely shook my head. This wasn't the time or place for a complicated discussion of wills and inheritance, and if Kathleen still didn't realize that Ruthie had been poisoning them all along, this wasn't the time or place for her to find that out.

Kathleen took my face between her gloved hands and looked at me closely. "Toni, you don't look so good. Are you okay?"

"I am now, but I was in the hospital too. I ate some of those cookies you left behind." Well, okay, she'd figure it out now for sure.

"We'll talk later," she promised. "Come along, kids. Let's go give Aunt Ruthie our condolences."

Aunt Ruthie? Seriously? Oh, jeez.

I continued on toward the back of the church to where I knew the restrooms were located. I ducked into the ladies room, pulled my jeans and L.L.Bean snow sneakers out of my capacious purse, and changed my clothes. I slipped out a side door and peered around the side of the church. When it looked like everybody who was coming had come, I dashed across the street to the parking lot and drove to Ruthie's house.

I parked around the corner, out of sight of Rebecca's house, as I had before. I probably didn't need to worry about that, because Rebecca was probably at the funeral, but it didn't hurt to be careful.

I left my purse in the car but put my cell phone in my coat pocket on vibrate. I put my flashlight in the other coat pocket. My Christmas camera was still in the pocket of my jeans. I put my car keys in the other pocket, buttoned up my coat, looked around to make sure nobody was around, and started down the alley between the houses.

Ruthie's was the third house down from the corner. The backyards of all the houses were hemmed in by six-foot fences. I looked for gates. The third gate I came to was securely latched, but it had a broken board, part of which was missing. I peered through. The house was painted dark green with white window trim. The back porch was also painted white, and recently too. It seemed to be in much better shape than the fence, which leaned into the backyard and had several loose boards. I wiggled them all experimentally. A dog started barking. I jumped and backed off. I didn't know Ruthie had a dog. *Shit.*

Then I came to my senses and realized that if Ruthie wasn't staying in the house, her dog shouldn't be here either. If she had one, she would have had a neighbor take it or boarded it in a kennel. I didn't think the Blue Lakes Inn allowed pets. In any case, the barking dog was in somebody else's yard.

I wiggled boards some more. One seemed looser than the others. I continued to wiggle it, and it got looser still. Eventually it loosened enough that I could push it into the backyard. It left a six-inch gap. Could I squeeze myself through a six-inch space? It would be asking a lot of my hips to compress themselves *that* much. It would also be asking for trouble. What if I got stuck?

Maybe if I took my coat off. I hung it on one of the loose but still attached boards and experimentally put a leg through the space. My thigh fit. If my thigh fit, could my butt? Slowly and carefully, I started to wiggle one butt cheek into the space. Too tight. Maybe if I tensed up my gluteus maximus. A little better. One butt cheek slipped through. Now I had a splintery one-by-six wedged into my butt crack.

Oh God, please don't let anybody come along right now. I was neither in nor out. I put a shoulder through. No problem, but my boobs got stuck. I hunched my back. I was still stuck. With my hands, I pulled my boobs to each side and managed to slide my upper body through, although my cashmere pullover would never be the same. I tensed up my other glute and tried to slide the other butt cheek in, but my jeans got hung up on a splinter that was threatening to come right on through into my butt. Was I going to have to sacrifice my jeans, or worse, my skin? I managed to get myself unhooked from the splinter by pushing my butt cheek back out through the space and then pulling my butt fat sideways with my left hand. I was in.

Whew. Better not count on that as an escape route, should I need one.

I retrieved my coat, but I'd worked up too much of a sweat to put it back on. I looked at my watch. Twenty minutes had gone by. *Damn.* The funeral surely wouldn't take more than an hour, and the funeral procession out to Sunset Park and the burial service might give me another hour; but I really had to get moving if I was going to be done before Ruthie was free and aware that I was no longer among the mourners.

I surveyed Ruthie's backyard. I couldn't see much of it. In front of me stood a barberry hedge about four feet high, overgrown and impenetrable. Barberries have thorns. Lots of them. Too bad I hadn't thought to bring a pair of gardening shears. I could see only one solution. I wrapped my coat around my head, shoulders, and arms and forced my way through. Thorns ripped at my jeans, making pincushions of my thighs, and my brand-new coat would never be the same. Hal wouldn't be happy about that.

Thirty minutes had gone by. I extracted the worst of the barberry twigs and thorns from my coat and put it on. I crossed the backyard and mounted the back porch steps, testing each one before settling my weight on it. They held, and so did the porch itself. But the back door was locked. *Oh, hell.*

Or maybe not. Around the side of the house was the gaping hole I had seen from the street. For God's sake, what was I doing *kvetching* about a locked door when there was a hole big enough to drive a truck through right around the corner? Of course, it was all charred and possibly unsafe, and I'd get soot all over me, but my clothes were already trashed, so why should I care about that now?

Anyway, the only reason I had chosen to enter Ruthie's house from the back was to avoid being seen going in the front. As I turned away from the back door, I noticed a trapdoor in the floor of the back porch and wondered what it was for. Getting into the crawlspace, maybe? If I didn't find anything inside the house, I'd check it out.

So I went around the side of the house, being careful to avoid being seen from the neighbor's windows, and went in through the gap in the wall.

Inside, it was totally black. What little light came in from the outside barely penetrated the gloom. The pervasive odor of smoke and gasoline burned my eyes and made me cough. I tried not to breathe too deeply.

I turned on my flashlight and looked around. It became immediately apparent that nothing in this space had survived the fire. No point in looking for Lovenox here. I kept going, hoping to come out into something, anything, unburned, hoping the floor would hold me and I wouldn't go crashing through into the basement or crawl space. This dank, black, smoky void seemed to go on forever.

Eventually I came to a wall. It had a window in it. The glass was shattered. Through it I could see the neighbor's house on the side opposite Rebecca's. I turned the flashlight off. Enough light came in through the window that I could see without it.

I continued along the wall and eventually came to the kitchen. The appliances were still there but blackened. I looked inside the stove and saw nothing. The refrigerator contained food that was clearly way past its expiration date, and the stench made me gag. I closed the door hastily. I saw a light switch next to the sink. I flipped it and jumped back, expecting sparks, but nothing happened. I flipped it off again. I supposed that electricity was too much to hope for. The woodwork had been destroyed, and the contents of the drawers and cabinets had avalanched out across the kitchen floor, shattered and twisted. Apparently the entire inside of the ground floor had been gutted, and the walls and most of the floor were all that remained.

No Lovenox there. I kept going. I came to a staircase. The banister was gone, but the treads looked amazingly intact. Did I dare risk it? I shone the flashlight on my watch. Forty-five minutes had passed. *It's now or never*, I figured, and I put one foot on the lower tread, testing it. It held, and so did the other treads. Soon I was on the second floor, and it seemed even smokier and blacker than the ground floor had been. Small wonder, since heat rises. I could see holes in the floor where the light from below shone through them. I flipped the flashlight back on. The second floor looked in slightly better shape than the ground floor had—except for the floor itself. That looked decidedly unsafe.

There were four bedrooms and a bathroom up here with lots of places to hide things: in drawers and closets and under mattresses. Unfortunately I could see no way to get to them and search them without breaking through the floor. Maybe I could distribute my weight by crawling on my belly. *Christ on a crutch.* This was going to take for-friggin'-ever.

It occurred to me that if the furniture hadn't broken through the floor, then maybe my weight wouldn't either. On the other hand, it could be the straw that broke the camel's back—and my back as well, if I fell through. So I started with the largest bedroom and moved carefully around the perimeter, looking in drawers and closets and under beds, feeling between mattresses. I even checked the drawers in the bathroom and looked inside the toilet tank. Then I eased my way back down the stairs.

No Lovenox there either. I checked my watch again. An hour and fifteen minutes had passed. I felt a pang of dread. I was running out of time. If I had a brain in my head, I'd get my ass the hell out of here. But I hadn't looked in the garage or the crawl space. I was getting discouraged, but I reminded myself that the police and fire department hadn't found anything either.

But I guess I didn't have a brain in my head, because suddenly I felt really sure that the crawl space was the hiding place. Ruthie's garage was little more than a carport, surprising for such a large house in such an expensive neighborhood. And there was no storage space there. So that left the crawl space.

In my house, the entrance to the crawlspace was a trapdoor in the closet that held the water heater, but it could also be in the kitchen or laundry room.

In Ruthie's house, it was in none of those places. It had to be the trapdoor on the back porch.

I unlocked the back door, looked around, and saw nobody. But it was getting late. Days are short in December, and it's dark by five. In another hour or so, people would start coming home from work, and there'd be more neighbors around. I found a ring set into the floor and pulled up on it. It took all my strength, but I got it open. I shone my flashlight around and saw a ladder leading from the trapdoor down into the blackness below. *Here goes nothing*, I thought and lowered myself through the hole. The crawl space was about six feet deep where I stood, but I could see that in some places it was much shallower than that. I could also see a small amount of light coming in through openings in the sides that were covered by latticework. That wouldn't last much longer.

The furnace stood right behind the ladder on a concrete pad, directly under the kitchen floor. Nothing was hidden where I was standing; I saw nothing but dirt. So I started toward the front of the house, around the side of the furnace. The space was shallower there, and I was obliged to bend my head in order to stand up straight. Within the maze of pipes and hoses that led away from the back of the furnace, I saw something pale. Something that wasn't a pipe or a hose. I crept closer. I reached for it. I grabbed it and worked it free.

Bingo.

Inside a plastic grocery bag, I found several unopened boxes of Lovenox, ten syringes to a box, as I found when I opened one. All the boxes bore pharmacy stickers with Lance's name on them: "One syringe, 40 mg (4000 IU) to be injected subcutaneously in the abdomen daily, alternating left and right sides."

With my breath coming in short bursts and my heart threatening to pound its way out of my chest, I worked my camera out of my jeans pocket. Too late I wished I'd spent more time learning how to use it, but I remembered that

I had taken pictures of the kids opening their presents. I had used the flash, and I didn't think I'd changed any of the settings.

I hadn't. The flash worked. Kneeling on the cold concrete and trying to still my shaking hands, I photographed the boxes inside the bag and out. I photographed the contents of an open box of syringes, took a close-up of the label, closed the box, put it back in the bag, and replaced it where I'd found it. I shoved the camera back into my pocket.

Now all I had to do was get out of here before Ruthie—

Too late.

Chapter 34

The female of the species is more deadly than the male.
—Rudyard Kipling

Whang! Something whistled through the air and crashed into the furnace just above my head. I must have been subliminally aware of air movement because I had ducked reflexively. Otherwise the blow would have landed on my head.

My evasive move had knocked me off balance. I tumbled off the concrete pad onto my back in the dirt. Ruthie stood over me, something long, shiny, and metallic in her hands, ready for a second try. She'd changed out of her funeral clothes into black pants and a black sweatshirt with the hood up, looking like a fat ninja. Her eyes were distended, teeth showing in a grimace, face distorted with such malevolence that I hardly recognized her. This was not the bubbly, cuddly Ruthie we all knew. This was a raving madwoman.

I tried to scramble to my feet. Ruthie swung again. I heard the whistle through the air before her weapon caught me in the right side. The pain knocked me off balance. I fell over onto my back. Ruthie swung again. Her breath rattled harshly in her throat. I rolled to the side, and the weapon caught me again in the right side. I rolled back onto my back to minimize the force of the blow, and she got me again in the abdomen. *Jesus. What the hell is that thing?* I rolled onto my side, the breath knocked out of me. With a strength born of murderous rage, Ruthie finished me off by stomping me in the ribs. I felt them crack.

I curled myself into a ball, trying to protect my soft parts and get some air back into my lungs, but my newly broken ribs made that a *really* painful process. Ruthie discarded her weapon, tossing it behind her where I couldn't reach it, and hauled a roll of silver duct tape out of her pocket. Roughly, she rolled me over on my stomach, and jerked my arms behind me. I tried to resist, but she placed a knee right in the middle of my back and put her full weight on it. Oh my God, could she possibly have chosen anything more painful to do to someone with broken ribs? Obviously she didn't care. I tried to buck her off, but it hurt too much. She taped my wrists together behind my back. I felt her lift her weight off me, and I tried to roll back onto my back and kick her, but she evaded me. She forced me back on my stomach and taped my ankles together too. Then she crawled around behind me and managed to drag me, in short painful jerks accompanied by a great deal of huffing and puffing, into an upright position against the side of the furnace.

The pain was unbelievable. Every tortured breath produced a knifelike agony.

I was done.

Once she got me where she wanted me, she collapsed on the dirt, gasping for air. It couldn't have been easy, dragging someone who weighed the same as she did across a dirt floor, and I'd done nothing to help. Not that I had anything left with which to fight her; I'd simply let myself be dead weight.

I watched in a miasma of pain as she caught her breath and crawled around behind the furnace again, reemerging with a flashlight in her hand. She crawled over to where she had discarded her weapon and returned to sit right in front of me. Now I could see that the weapon of my destruction was a golf club, a five iron, unless I missed my guess—probably one of those new, lightweight titanium ones that were supposed to hit a ball fifty yards farther than the old ones did. No wonder it hurt so much on impact. If I survived this, my side and abdomen would be a glorious shade of purple.

"Doctor Toni Day Shapiro," she said, laying the golf club across her knees. "You think you're so smart. Look at you. Bet you don't feel so smart now, do you?"

Did she think I was going to play twenty questions now? Not hardly. I occupied myself with continuing to breathe.

"So who's the smart one now?" Ruthie taunted me. "Sorry I had to hit you like that, but I couldn't have you running off to the cops with my Lovenox, could I?"

She crawled around me, and I heard her fumbling around in back of the furnace. I felt my cell phone buzz in my coat pocket. I was practically lying on it. If only I could reach it with one hand, I could flip it open. But my hands were tied, literally. I attempted to twist my body so that my bound hands reached my pocket, but oh my God,

341

it hurt. I gritted my teeth and attempted to rearrange myself so that my fingers slipped into my pocket. I held my breath while struggling to flip my phone open inside my pocket, which would automatically answer it. I heard Hal's voice and prayed that Ruthie hadn't heard it too. I attempted to cover it up by talking.

"Ruthie, what the hell do you think you're doing? You'll never get away with it."

Christ on a crutch. In a truss. It even hurt to talk.

Apparently it worked. She was busy back there doing something that rustled, and she gave no sign that she'd heard Hal's voice. She came back out with the grocery sack and emptied it a few feet from me. "I bet you're wondering what I'm doing, aren't you," she said conversationally. "I meant to get rid of these boxes earlier," she went on, "but then I had the fire, and I had to leave, and the fire department said I couldn't come back here. But I had to dispose of all this Lovenox before the police found it."

There were five boxes of syringes there. Ruthie began opening them. "But now I'm glad I didn't have a chance to get rid of them, because now I've got the perfect place to put them."

Once she had all the boxes opened, she crawled over to me and pulled on my feet until she had me flat on my back. I was lying on my bound hands, which was damned uncomfortable, but not nearly as uncomfortable as what Ruthie had in mind. Surely she wasn't going to do what I thought she was.

She was. She unbuttoned my coat and spread it out. She pushed my shirt up over my boobs. Then she uncapped one of the syringes and shot the contents into my abdomen. *Ouch.* But Ruthie wasn't done. Ten syringes to a box. Fifty syringes in all. One by one, she shot all of them into me, while I rolled around and struggled as much as I could with broken ribs. But eventually she managed to discharge all fifty syringes into some portion of my anatomy, mostly into my abdomen, which meant that I had received fifty times the recommended dosage of Lovenox in a matter of ten minutes or so.

I wasn't just going to bleed; I was going to *dissolve*.

Ruthie glanced over. "Now I'm gonna burn these boxes and these syringes, and gee, it might spread to the rest of the house, so you'll burn or die of smoke inhalation—if you don't bleed to death first."

The syringes wouldn't burn. They were glass. If Ruthie burned down the remains of her house and I died in the fire, they'd still be here as a silent testimony to how I'd really died. Small comfort.

"So, since I'm gonna die anyway, why don't you tell me the whole story," I suggested. Maybe, if my cell phone battery hadn't died and the connection was still open, Hal could tell the police. Maybe while she was talking and bragging on how smart she'd been, somebody would miss me and come looking. Just call me Scheherazade.

No, wait; Ruthie was Scheherazade. I was Camille.

She hauled a butane lighter out of her coat pocket and pointed it at the pile of refuse. But she didn't light it. "Why not?" she said. "I've never watched anyone bleed to death before. It might be fun. So here goes."

"Start at the beginning with the Ponzi scheme," I suggested.

"Jay and Lance were both in on that Ponzi scheme," she said obediently. "While Jay sold it to the doctors, Lance managed both his and Jay's money in a legitimate, offshore Swiss bank account, which I set up myself. But neither one of them invested a dime into the Ponzi scheme after the first investment. They weren't as stupid as all those doctors. When they took the first payment, it went straight into the Swiss account, which was invested in all sorts of blue chip stocks that went through the roof.

"You know, Jay and I were lovers long before he got involved with any of those other women," Ruthie said. "Before I married Lance, as a matter of fact. Jay got me pregnant too. But it almost killed me, and I lost the baby."

"Gee, that's too bad," I said.

She inclined her head. "Thank you for your sympathy. Even I know you don't really mean it," she said. "Jay and I were going to leave our families and retire to a Caribbean island under new identities with all the money. We'd even picked the names. We were going to be Mr. and Mrs. Alastair Montgomery Atterbury." She sighed dreamily. "I was going to be Mrs. Mildred Atterbury. We had fake passports and everything. Everything was going great until the economy crashed.

You could pick any name you wanted and Mildred is the name you picked?!

"But Jay knew just what to do. He took Tiffany home and had sex with her in his bed on an afternoon that he knew Kathleen would be home early, so she'd catch them, and he knew her well enough to know she'd divorce him. That way he wouldn't have to divorce her and go through all the explanations and recriminations and stuff. Then, when that doctor sued him, he declared bankruptcy, flew to Grand Cayman, took his money out of the bank there, transferred it to a bank in Barbados under his new name, and got credit cards and a driver's license. Then he flew to Barbados and bought a house and a car using his new identity too."

I closed my eyes and prayed that my cell phone battery would last and that I hadn't accidentally turned it off. With any luck, Hal would have called the police by now. Ruthie ignored me. "He had everything in place. The only thing we had to do was get rid of our families. Then, finally, we could be together."

By now it had gotten too dark to see clearly. Ruthie got up on her hands and knees and crawled over to me. She shone her flashlight in my face, and her expression turned mean—meaner than before, if that were possible. She gazed into my face through slitted eyes. Now what, I wondered. What was she going to do to me now? Hadn't she done enough? No, probably not; she hadn't killed me yet.

"Only one problem," she hissed. "The son of a bitch changed his mind. He decided to take his family with him. Instead of me. After all I'd done for him too. So I killed him."

"And how did you do that?"

"Need you ask, Miss Smartass? I thought you had it all figured out."

"I want to hear all the details," I said, thinking of Rebecca. "Come on, Ruthie, I'm already dead. You've got nothing to lose."

She seemed only too happy to oblige. "Well. When Jay came back, he flew into Boise, checked into the Red Lion Riverside under his new name, and called me. I went to Boise to pick him up, driving his car. We spent three days in Boise. I put rivaroxaban in his drinks and his food, and he got sicker and sicker, and finally started vomiting blood."

"My goodness gracious," I said.

"That was when I decided to bring him home. But I couldn't get him out of the hotel and into the car by myself, so I called Lance, and he drove up to Boise to help. By that time Jay was so weak he couldn't walk or dress himself, so we dressed him and carried him out the back way when it got dark and nobody was around. You ever been to the Red Lion?"

"Downtown or Riverside?" I asked. Like it mattered.

"Riverside. You know how the wings are all stretched out end to end, so you have to walk a mile to get to the dining room? Well, our room was in the furthest wing on the far end."

"Good choice."

"We laid him out in the back seat of his car with one of those big forty-five-gallon lawn-and-leaf bags under him and towels under his head and on the floor in case he bled any more. Then we left without bothering to check out or clean up the room."

"That wasn't very nice," I said. "Weren't you afraid of leaving Jay's DNA all over the place?"

"Why should I care? The room was registered to Alastair Atterbury, not Jay Braithwaite Burke."

"So then what happened?"

"I drove Jay's car, and Lance followed me in our car. It started to snow. By the time we got to Jerome, the roads were snow-covered and slick. We saw cars off the road all over the place, but we managed to stay on the road until we passed exit 165 for Jerome, and then I slid off the road into the median, and Lance pulled over and stopped to help me. We both thought Jay was dead by then.

"So we put him in the driver's seat, turned off the lights, left the engine running, and disposed of the plastic bags and towels in the nearest Dumpster when we got to Twin."

"So much for Mr. and Mrs. Alastair Montgomery Atterbury," I commented. "Was he going to call himself Monty or Al?"

"Oh, very funny," she sneered. "Where do you get off making fun of me?"

"You've already killed me, *Millie*," I pointed out. "I can do anything I want." *Where the hell were the police? When was all this Lovenox going to take effect? And how? Nosebleed? Hematemesis? Bloody diarrhea? Were my broken ribs bleeding into my chest?*

She turned and crawled away from me. When she turned back around and sat, her eyes glistened with tears. "I couldn't let him do that to me. I couldn't! So I decided that if I couldn't have him, I'd get the next best thing: the money."

"Let me guess. Next you had to kill Lance," I said.

"Don't you dare tell me what I did next! This is *my* story."

"Sorry. Who'd you kill next?"

"I had to kill Lance," she said.

"Told you so."

She glared at me furiously. "You shut up and let me talk! Or I'll—"

"Ruthie, get on with it, would you?" If I could have done it without poking my ribs out through my chest, I'd have sighed. "I'm probably running out of time."

"I will if you quit interrupting."

I would have held my hands up in surrender if they hadn't been tied behind me. "Please proceed."

"I put rivaroxaban in his food. It was supposed to make him bleed, but he got jaundiced instead and stopped eating. So I took him to the hospital."

"That's because he had pancreatic cancer."

"That's what Dr. Marshall said. So I took extra Lovenox in my purse and put it in his IV when nobody was looking."

"How clever of you."

"You're making fun of me again," she accused.

I shook my head. My nose started running. I must have shaken something loose in there. I sniffed mightily, or at least as much as my ribs would allow. "Never. Please continue."

She smiled. "You're bleeding. It won't be long now."

I tried to turn my head and wipe my nose on my shoulder, but it didn't seem to help.

She continued. "I also had to get rid of Kathleen and the kids. I put rivaroxaban in the lasagna and in the cookies and the brownies. If they hadn't gone to Boise, I could have finished them off too."

She crawled back to me and leaned over. It was completely dark now, and her face was outlined only by the flashlight beams. I couldn't read her expression, but I was pretty sure it wasn't all sweetness and light. It didn't really matter, did it? "Now I can go be Mrs. Mildred Atterbury," she said, "and live in a villa in Barbados, overlooking the ocean, with all that lovely money. Have a nice death."

She pointed the butane lighter at the trash pile and lit it. The cardboard flared up nicely, and the sudden warmth actually felt rather pleasant. She looked at it dispassionately. "Gosh," she said, "that really is a sorry little pile of trash, isn't it? That'll never catch. I guess I'd better help it along." With that, she directed the butane lighter at the floor above her. Then I became aware of the sounds above my head. The house above me was already burning merrily; I could hear the wood crackling. No wonder Ruthie got so mad at me for interrupting and slowing her down; I was keeping her from getting out before the floor caved in. Isn't that just like me, always wanting to be the center of attention?

Ruthie put the butane lighter back in her pocket and pulled a cloth out of her pocket. She shoved it into my mouth and covered my mouth with duct tape. She wrapped the duct tape all the way around my head. "Maybe that will shut you up, Doctor Smarty Pants. That sucker's not coming off any time soon. I'm out of here."

"Ciao," I tried to say, my voice muffled. My nose was running down the back of my throat. If I kept swallowing all that blood, it was going to make me …

Suddenly I knew I was going to vomit. I couldn't help it. Maybe if I could direct it out my nose instead of my mouth, I could keep from choking. Retching, I rolled back onto my side and forced the vomit out my nose. So far so good. Another spasm. Out the nose. Another spasm, and another. Then I realized that my nether region was soaked too. *Oh, shit.* Literally. I could smell it.

"Ugh," Ruthie said. "That's gross. I'm glad I don't have to stay around and watch. It was bad enough watching Jay do that, and he wasn't even gagged." She turned and crawled away from me. By the light of the flashlight she carried, I saw her get to her feet, straighten up, and climb back up the ladder to the back porch. I heard the trapdoor fall back into place, leaving me alone with the bonfire.

With my clothes soaked, I felt colder than ever. My belly felt like it had doubled in size, and it hurt. It was getting really hard to take a decent breath without pain. I tried to breathe in little, shallow breaths, which helped a bit. Maybe lying on the other side would be more comfortable. But no, it wasn't. It felt like the time I fell off the teeter-totter in the first grade and landed right smack across the iron frame on my stomach, knocking the wind out of myself.

But now I hadn't had the wind knocked out of me. I took another breath to demonstrate that to myself, and it *gurgled*. Why would that be? I coughed. That hurt my belly. It hurt my chest too. Which was worse? I couldn't tell. Liquid ran out of my nose, and I couldn't wipe it because my hands were restrained. Warm wetness soaked my gag. It was better wet than dry, but it tasted like blood.

You know, being a doctor, I always think the worst. *It's perfectly obvious,* I told myself. *I've got broken ribs, and they've punctured my lung, and that's why I'm coughing up blood. There's a word for that:* hemoptysis. *I'm having hemoptysis. Sure I am, and Hal will tease me about it, like he always does when I say things like that.*

I was now shivering so violently that my muscles were cramping. My abdominal muscles in particular. I had never experienced such pain. My entire belly seemed knotted, making it even harder to breathe.

And now there were cramps in my lower pelvic region too. *Oh, no, you've got to be kidding*, I thought. *What a rotten time to be getting my period. But it never fails. Hal and I plan a trip, and I get my period. That time we went camping in Montana with bears around, I got my period. Swimming in the ocean off Huntington Beach, I got my period, announcing, "Come and get it!" to any sharks that might be cruising by.*

So naturally, I end up tied up in a crawlspace with broken ribs and hemoptysis, and I get my period. Stands to reason.

Damn it. Where were the police? My cell phone battery must have died. I couldn't think of any other reason why Hal hadn't called them. If he had called them, why weren't they here? "Help!" I yelled, or attempted to. I couldn't get much sound past that gag; plus it hurt. It kept getting harder to breathe, and everything smelled like blood. The gag in my mouth tasted disgusting. A sudden cold breeze blew the smell away, but it came back.

Eventually I noticed that I had stopped shivering. My muscles weren't hurting so much. I was getting sleepy. *I guess I'll just go to sleep*, I thought, *and when I wake up it'll be morning.*

Wait a minute! I screamed at myself in sudden realization. *I can't go to sleep! If I do, I'll never wake up. This is hypothermia. I need to keep moving and stay awake or I'll die.* A new bout of abdominal cramping seized me, and with it came the nausea. I vomited again, remembering to force it out my nose, but I couldn't vomit and control my bowels at the same time. Oh God, what a mess. The renewed odor of fresh, warm blood assailed my nostrils, mixed with a strong fecal smell, a stench reminiscent of the contents of Jay Braithwaite Burke's gastrointestinal tract that had sent Bernie Kincaid out of the room, hand over mouth. *Holy shit*, I thought, *at this rate I'll bleed to death before morning.*

Somebody should be missing me by now, I thought. Surely Hal has reported me missing. Even if he didn't hear Ruthie's confession over my cell phone. Somebody should show up soon.

And what was it with the crawl spaces, anyway? When Hal had been kidnapped three years ago, he'd been trapped in a crawl space. Now I was trapped in a crawl space. Both times in the dead of winter. Some originality was definitely called for here. On the other hand, black widow spiders were unlikely to be down here at this time of year. I failed to derive much comfort from that, though, under the circumstances.

Maybe, I thought, if I could roll until I hit an outside wall, I could get to one of those spaces with the lattice work. It was just lath. Surely I could break it and get out. I tried. Too bad I had to keep stopping because it hurt so fucking much. But you know, it pretty much hurt all the time, so I figured I could just as well suck it up and keep on rolling.

No doubt it would force the ends of my broken ribs right out through my skin, resulting in a comminuted compound rib fracture. Was there such a thing? Perhaps it'd be reportable. Perhaps they'd name it after me: Shapiro's fracture.

Such a phenomenon would also let air into my chest cavity, resulting in that bane of emergency room physicians everywhere, the Sucking Chest Wound—and possibly also the dreaded Flail Chest.

After about five revolutions, I came up against a wall. The effort left me breathing hard, or trying to. Each breath felt like a knife in my chest. My belly cramped up again, and then there was a huge wave of nausea. I vomited again, which resulted in more fecal incontinence and more pain. *If this keeps up much longer*, I thought, *I'll die and be glad of it.*

*Hell used to be hot. But now, post-*Exorcist*, it's supposed to be cold and smell like shit. Maybe I'm already dead and gone to hell.*

Okay, what did I do to deserve that? I didn't actually commit adultery, although it was a close thing. It must have been all that taking the Lord's name in vain. Shit. I'm here in hell, doing time on a cussing rap.

I'm trapped in the crawlspace of a house that's on fire. Well, at least I'll be warm for a while, before it all falls in on me or I die of smoke inhalation, whichever comes first.

The smoke smell got stronger. I began to hear a crackling noise—a really *loud* crackling noise. And then a crash.

The fire, having burned through the floor, dropped a chunk of burning material into the crawl space several feet from me, possibly right where I had been lying before I started rolling. It provided enough light that I could see my surroundings. I saw a gap in the wall, and I saw flames through it. *Shit! Wouldn't you know my escape hatch would be surrounded by flames!* I quickly ran through the options open to me: stay put and die of smoke inhalation, exsanguination, or having the burning floor cave in on me, whichever came first; or force my way through the opening and hope that my blood-soaked clothing and the snow outside would protect me from the flames.

Well, that's a no-brainer, I thought.

Gritting my figurative teeth—since I couldn't actually grit my real ones around the fucking gag—I rolled toward the gap, feet first. I thrust my feet and legs through the hole, which tore at my clothing. There was a sharp metal edge of something that gleamed in the firelight. *Ha! Maybe it's sharp enough to cut my bonds,* I thought.

I worked myself painfully into position and began rubbing my wrists against the metal edge. It wasn't easy since they were tied behind me. *It'd be a lot easier if they were in front—hey!* I had seen someone on TV curl his body and slide it between his arms and get his bound wrists in front of him. Well, I'd always been pretty limber—at least without a sore belly.

I worked my butt through my arms, then my thighs, endeavoring to ignore the excruciating pain in my chest and belly. I felt a new and even more painful sensation of something ripping inside my chest, undoubtedly more rib action. *Oh goody,* I thought, *a new place to bleed from.*

Finally, I got my wrists in front and started sawing. After what seemed like an eternity, the duct tape tore and my wrists were free. They were also bleeding profusely from cuts and scrapes. *Terrific,* I snarled to myself, yet another source of blood loss; just what I needed.

That baseball mitt of a bandage on my thumb hadn't been much help. In fact, I had cut through some essential part of it that held it onto my hand and was in imminent danger of losing it. *If it isn't one thing, it's ten others.*

Toni, for God's sake, quit bitching and get your butt through that hole before the floor caves in. I stuck my head out the hole. The metal edge caught on the duct tape holding my gag in place. I reached back to free it and found that it was already nearly cut through. With energy dredged up from I-knew-not-where, I ripped it the rest of the way and spat the blood-soaked rag out onto the snow. Now I could vomit through my mouth like a normal person for a change.

Okay, now start by breaking off some rotten boards, make the hole bigger. Then put my head and an arm through, then the other arm, push with my still-bound feet, get both shoulders through. Now for the hips—oh God, wouldn't it be a bitch if I got stuck now. Wait a minute, it was my coat that was bunching up. If I could just take it off—but no, I couldn't. What if I just slid back in until it was looser and then pulled my coat up around my waist? There, that was better. Without the folds of the heavy wool coat, my hips slid out easily, and I rolled as fast as I could away from the house and toward the street, trying to ignore the pain in my chest that was making it harder and harder to breathe.

Not a minute too soon, either. Behind me, the house collapsed with a roar and a spray of sparks and burning embers, some of which landed on me. I kept rolling and thanking God for the snow, the blessed snow that quenched all the sizzling embers and sparks that kept landing around and on me.

When I judged that I was far enough from what was left of the house to be safe, I stopped and rolled over on my back, arms spread out on the snow, looking up at the sky and all the beautiful stars. I felt imbued with a lovely sense of warmth and well-being, which I knew was the beginning of the end, but I didn't seem to care. I coughed and blood ran out of my mouth. *Bloody hell*, I thought with my last remnant of consciousness, *I really* have *punctured my lung.*

Saturday, December 27

Chapter 35

Who shall decide when doctors disagree,
And soundest casuists doubt, like you and me?
—Samuel Pope

Next time I woke up, I was in the hospital, snug and warm, with lights and a nice dry bed—one that was, at the very least, softer than the packed dirt of Ruthie's crawlspace—and people tending to me who weren't brandishing butane lighters or five irons.

I looked up and saw clustered bags of clear fluid hanging overhead, and a bag of blood, nearly empty. My hands were restrained but attached to the bed rails this time, not behind me, so I wasn't lying on them, and there were no intravenous lines attached to my hands or my arms. Both my wrists were bandaged. My thumb bandage had been replaced too. So where the hell were all those intravenous lines going?

I had a tube in my throat and another one in my nose. A machine was breathing for me. I heard it behind me. My chest still hurt, but it seemed to be a dull ache rather than the unbearable ripping, tearing, stabbing pain it had been before. The clicking I heard next to me came from the IVAC, which was regulating how fast the IV fluids were running into me. I couldn't turn my head on account of the endotracheal tube, but I could roll my eyes and see it. Next to it was a morphine pump, or at least I assumed it contained morphine, with a button I could push if I needed more—that is, I could if I wasn't restrained. I guessed I'd need to address that at some point, but not now.

I supposed too that I'd need to move at some point, but I was unwilling to face the pain that would undoubtedly ensue if I tried. At least I was warm—at least I thought I was, until the first of many rigors shook me. They had me wrapped in a Bair Hugger, which was a kind of super-heavy electric blanket. I knew they used those in the Recovery Room—or as they call it these days, PACU, or Post-Anesthesia Care Unit—for that very reason. Those post-anesthesia shakes were not pleasant, particularly considering the state of my abdominal area, and because I was having them, I deduced that I'd had some kind of surgery.

I tried to raise my head and look down at myself, but I couldn't raise it much because of the endotracheal tube, not to mention my sore belly. The intravenous tubes seemed to lead under my hospital gown, so I deduced that I had a PICC line or Port-a-Cath or some other kind of central venous access. There was a nasogastric tube in my nose, and a chest tube was leading out of my right side. The tube had bloody fluid in it. The nasogastric tube did too.

It was all too much. Drained of energy, I let my head flop back on the pillow.

Two nurses came to my bedside with a new blood bag and went through a ritualistic review of the information on the blood bag, the paperwork attached to it, and my hospital wristband before they hung it and took the old one away. I was fuzzily gratified that they had correctly performed the transfusion patient identification procedure required by the College of American Pathologists, which accredited our lab, and hoped that they weren't just doing it for my benefit. Idly I wondered how many of those I'd gone through. Had I broken Lance's record yet?

Conveniently, and just in time to answer that question, Jeff Sorensen appeared and lifted up my gown to check my dressing. It was a big one, reaching from my right chest all the way around to my back, or at least to where I could no longer see it. Apparently I'd had a thoracotomy. Below the dressing my entire abdomen was almost black with hemorrhage. No wonder it hurt.

"How many does that make?" Jeff asked the nurse, whose name I knew was June, as he picked up the clipboard hanging on the bedrail.

"Ten," she answered, "and eight of fresh frozen plasma."

"And the last hemoglobin?"

"Eight point five, Doctor."

Yikes, I thought. *Ten units of blood and my hemoglobin's only eight point five? That sucks.*

"How's the I&O?"

"Fifteen eighty-five in, twenty-five forty out."

"Hang another liter of Ringer's and two more units packed cells, and check the hemoglobin again after thirty minutes."

"Okay, Doctor."

Jeff left without saying anything to me. No doubt he hadn't even noticed I was awake and listening to every word he said. *Surgeons! I ask you …*

George Marshall, on the other hand, noticed right away. "Toni? Oh good, you're awake. You really had us hopping there for a while. Did you know you'd nearly bled out? You've got three broken ribs, and one of them really did a number on your lung. That jug's nearly full, June. How long since it's been changed?"

"Four hours, Doctor."

"That's not good," George said. "She's still bleeding from the stomach. How's the hemoglobin?"

"Eight point five, Doctor," June said.

"That's all? How many units packed cells?"

"Ten. And eight FFP."

"And the anti-Xa?"

"About the same, Doctor."

"Damn," George said. "It's all going right out that chest tube."

"Doctor," June said, "do you want more FFP?"

"Sure," George said. "One more unit of packed cells and another FFP. Then check the hemoglobin again."

"Dr. Sorensen said the same thing, Doctor."

"This doesn't make any sense," George said. "She's had an exchange transfusion and then some. How about the platelets? Only thirty thousand? Okay, another ten platelet packs as well. How's the urine look?"

"Bloody."

"I guess that figures. Keep on with the antibiotics."

"Yes, Doctor."

He patted me on the shoulder. "I'll stop by this afternoon, Toni. Hang in there. We'll get it figured out; don't you worry. Try to get some rest." And he was gone.

Well, that was encouraging, I thought. *The blood's pouring out of me as fast as it's going in, but it shouldn't be. And I only have thirty thousand platelets, when I should have about two hundred thousand. Was it just dilutional from the ten units of blood, or did I have DIC? Why wasn't all that fresh frozen plasma replacing my clotting factors like it should? I suppose one reason was that it was pouring out of me right along with the blood transfusions.*

Bottom line: until the bleeding stopped, nothing they gave me was going to stop the bleeding.

What we have here is a Catch-22 of life-threatening proportions.

Now what? Was I supposed to just lie here and be nothing more than a conduit for gallons of blood, FFP, Ringer's lactate, platelet packs, antibiotics, and whatever else they chose to pour into my PICC line? None of it was doing me any good; it was just passing through, waving bye-bye on its way to the big jugs on the floor. *See ya later, alligator.*

I wished I could ask all these questions, but I couldn't talk with an endotracheal tube in place, and I couldn't write notes with my hands restrained. I couldn't even ask for a pad and pencil in sign language.

Maybe when Hal came, he could ask the questions for me. Only, how was I going to tell him what they were?

I was at this point more frightened than I'd been in Ruthie's crawl space. At least then I'd had some hope that I'd be rescued, taken to the hospital, and treated, and then everything would be all right.

But it didn't sound like everything was going to be all right. In fact, it sounded pretty damn hopeless. I knew that this state of affairs couldn't continue indefinitely. Eventually I'd develop pneumonia or adult respiratory distress syndrome or sepsis—and finally, multiorgan failure.

Poor Hal. How was he going to deal with watching me slowly deteriorate day by day? Seeing my life's blood running out through tubes into those jugs on the floor, with no end in sight? How would he handle the hopelessness of knowing that no matter what anybody did, he would eventually lose me? It would be like having terminal cancer.

How would I handle seeing the pain in his eyes, the tears, and the despair—and my inability to comfort him? If I was unable to hold him, unable to even talk to him— this man I loved with all my heart—how was I going to even tell him how much I loved him? How could I say good-bye to him? I was going to die, and I wouldn't see him again until he died too, because I did believe in an afterlife where I would eventually be reunited with all my loved ones.

But Hal was Jewish and didn't believe in an afterlife, so he didn't even have that comfort. He couldn't know that he would be with me again someday. And at the utter hopelessness of that thought, tears came to my eyes, ran down my face, and I began to sob—not an easy thing to do with an endotracheal tube in place. I gasped and fought the ventilator, pulling at my restraints, and an alarm started beeping. My chest and belly were killing me, but I couldn't stop.

June rushed back in. She looked at my face and gasped, "Dr. Day, Toni, what's wrong? Are you in pain? What hurts?" As if I could tell her. *What hurts? Everything. My chest, my belly, my throat from the fucking ET tube, my nose from the fucking NG tube, and my breaking heart.* All I could do was cry and struggle against my restraints, and all she could do was check to make sure that all the tubes were in place, that I hadn't managed to pull anything out, and that my restraints were secure but not too tight. She checked my incision and replaced the dressing. She checked to make sure my Foley catheter was properly taped to my leg and not under any tension and that it was draining properly. She checked to make sure I hadn't soiled myself. Then she injected something into the PICC line.

"There now," she said solicitously, "that should feel better soon, and then you can just take a nice nap." She patted my arm and left.

Obviously Jeff or George or somebody had left orders for sedation in case the patient threw a tantrum. Time out. Bedtime for Bonzo.

Sunday, December 28

Chapter 36

Surgeons must be very careful
When they take the knife
Underneath their fine incisions
Stirs the culprit ... life!
—Emily Dickinson

I awoke to see Hal and Mum standing at my bedside. They were deep in conversation and didn't notice at first that I was awake.

"Fiona," Hal was saying, "she's asleep. She can't hear you."

"I was just making conversation, Hal, dear," Mum replied. "Just because her eyes are closed doesn't mean she can't hear me."

"Well, she can't answer you," Hal countered, "so it's not a conversation. Whoever heard of a one-way conversation? It's a monologue, is what it is."

For the love of God, I screamed, but of course no sound came out. *Why are the two of you carrying on this stupid, pointless conversation about having a conversation, when I'm lying here dying and I can't even tell you or say good-bye or how I love the both of you more than life itself—which seems ironic since life itself is what's at stake here?*

Of course my agitation caused the monitor to go crazy and make much more interesting lines and patterns than before, while every alarm in the place went off.

A nurse, whose name I knew was Leslie, tore the curtain aside. "What's going on in here?"

"I don't know," Hal said, shrugging. "All of a sudden she just started struggling and …"

Jeff Sorensen materialized behind him. "How's our patient doing?"

Hal turned to look at him. "She seems upset."

"Well, let's check." Jeff moved in closer and Hal moved aside. Jeff lifted up my gown to check my incision, and apparently Hal and Mum were seeing it and my belly for the first time, because they both stared at it as if a snake had just crawled out and stuck out its tongue at them.

"What the hell happened here?" Hal demanded. "Is all that hemorrhage from surgery?"

Jeff stopped in the middle of removing my dressing and stared at Hal. "No, it's not from surgery. It looked like this when she came in. It's actually a little better today." He went back to the dressing. "Looks pretty good. Nice and pink, no sign of infection. Awful lot of drainage, though. Looks like it hasn't stopped bleeding. Better put a thicker pad on it next time, Les."

"Yes, Doctor."

"How's the hemoglobin this morning?"

"Eight-point-three, Doctor."

Jeff straightened up and stared at her. "That's less than it was last night! And after—how many units of blood since then?"

"Four, Doctor, and two fresh frozen plasma and ten platelet packs. And by the way, her platelet count is only twenty-five thousand."

Jeff ripped off his latex gloves and clutched his forehead. "Jesus. I don't get it. I don't get it! We've poured in, what, ten, no, *fourteen* units of blood, twenty platelet packs, at least ten units of fresh frozen plasma, and where's it going?"

Hal backed up and looked down at the floor. "Into those bottles, I'm thinking."

"I'm sorry, Doctor," Mum said, "I'm sure I don't mean to interfere, but you do realize that my daughter can hear everything you've said, don't you? Look at her face! She's scared to death, and with good reason. Could we possibly discuss this elsewhere?"

Jeff glanced at me. I opened my eyes wide and glared at him so fiercely that I'm sure the whites showed all the way around. I rattled my bed rails and tried to make a writing motion with my right hand, the one that wasn't bandaged. He gave me a slightly panicked look and then vanished around the curtain after Mum and Hal.

He was replaced almost immediately by George Marshall, who jerked a thumb in the general direction of where Mum and Hal and Jeff had gone and looked at me. "What's the hoo-hah all about?"

Was he expecting me to tell him? How? I rattled the bed rails again and tried to convey to him that I wanted a pencil and paper to write on. I couldn't very well talk with a fucking ET tube in my mouth.

Leslie spoke up. "Dr. Sorensen's upset because the bleeding hasn't stopped or even slowed down. She's had fourteen units of blood, twenty platelet packs, and ten of FFP, and her hemoglobin is eight-point-three and platelets twenty-five thousand."

I rattled the bed rails again. Leslie put her hand over mine to still it, but I wasn't having any. I had something to say, goddamnit, and I couldn't get it across to anybody. I rattled the rail harder. I tried to vocalize. The ventilator didn't like it. The monitors reacted and alarms went off again.

"Toni, stop it," George snapped. "You're not doing yourself any good doing that."

I opened my eyes wide and looked at my right hand, then back at George and back at my hand. I rattled just the right bed rail this time. Leslie removed her hand and looked hard at my fingers.

"Doctor Marshall?"

George looked up from my chart with annoyance. "What, Leslie?"

"I think she's trying to tell us something. I think she wants to write something."

George looked at my hand and then my face. "Is that what you want, Toni? To write something?"

I nodded as much as I could with the damn tube in my way.

"Well, Les, go get her a notepad and a pen," George said, "and we'll see what this is all about."

I relaxed back onto my pillows with a sigh of relief, and the ventilator didn't like that either. Leslie disappeared and came back with a notepad and a pen. She untied the restraint on my right wrist and gave me the pen. "Here, Dr. Day, can you hold this? I'll hold the pad for you."

I flexed my fingers and took the pen. With great difficulty, I wrote, as legibly as I could, "cell saver?"

Leslie held the pad out to George. "Cell saver?" he said, puzzled. "I'm sure they used it in surgery, but …"

At that point Jeff, Mum, and Hal came back in. "We did," Jeff said. "We'd have gone through twice the blood if we hadn't. What's this all about?"

I reached out for the pad. George gave it back to me. While Leslie held it for me, I wrote, "chest tube wash out Lovenox give back RBC."

Jeff looked at the pad and then at me. "You want us to run your chest tube drainage through the cell saver and wash your red cells and give them back to you, and you think that'll wash the Lovenox out of your blood?"

I wrote, "yes."

Hal looked over Jeff's shoulder. "Would that work?"

George shrugged. "It might be worth a try. What do you think, Jeff?"

"It'd help if we had some idea how much Lovenox she got," Jeff said. "The cell saver can wash about five hundred cc's at a time, but it's gonna take a while to wash her whole blood volume. Maybe plasmapheresis would be faster."

"Why don't you ask her?" Mum suggested.

I wrote, "50x."

"What's that?" asked George.

"She says she got fifty doses," Hal said.

"Jesus," Jeff said. "No wonder she's still bleeding. She's basically gotten an exchange transfusion already, but her anti-Xa is still sky-high. We can't just keep running bank blood through her. But we don't have the wherewithal to do plasmapheresis here. She'd have to go to Boise or Salt Lake for that, and she's not stable enough to transfer, except by Life-Flight."

I wrote, "ask BB or RC".

"BB?" Mum asked. "RC? What are those?"

"Blood Bank and Red Cross," Hal said. "Doesn't the Red Cross have a mobile donor setup in a van that they use to go to smaller towns? Maybe they have a plasmapheresis unit."

"Well," Jeff said, rubbing his hands together, "let's ask the blood bank. Maybe they can get the Red Cross to let us use it."

They left, talking animatedly.

I was elated. Maybe now things would begin to turn around. Maybe they'd turn around in time to keep me from bleeding into my brain, because that was the only thing that hadn't bled yet, which was—you should pardon the expression—a bloody miracle.

Hal leaned over and kissed me on the cheek. "Gotta go, sweetie. Love you."

Mum kissed my other cheek. "We're going to go and let your doctors get on with it, kitten. We'll be back later."

Leslie retied my restraint. "Looks like I've got my work cut out for me," she told me, and she too vanished. I heard her talking to the patient in the next cubicle. I figured I may as well go back to sleep, since there wasn't anything else to do, and that was a mistake.

I dreamed that I was back in Ruthie's crawl space, where she chased me around with a butane lighter and a large knife, threatening to cut my wrists and my throat. She came closer and closer and finally caught up with me behind the furnace, where she pulled the hoses loose and wound them around me, immobilizing me. She plunged the knife into both of my wrists, pinning them to the ground, and then held the knife to my throat, while I screamed and struggled futilely until everything faded to black.

I didn't know how she managed to have the knife in two places at once, but it was a dream, and as such, didn't have to make sense.

"June, give me a hand here. She's gonna pull everything out if she keeps this up. Hey! Toni! Wake up! You're having a bad dream!"

I opened my eyes. *Oh, thank God. That was bloody awful.* I never thought I'd be so glad to find myself in a hospital bed—although, in the dream I could move my arms and talk, and now I couldn't. I guess you can't have everything.

My cubicle was full of people. June was holding my legs down. George and Jeff were each holding down a shoulder. When they saw that I was awake and no longer struggling, they let up on the pressure. George and Jeff looked at each other across my body. "So what do you think?" Jeff asked.

"About what?" George returned.

"This is the third time in twenty-four hours that she's had an episode like this. Do you think we need to paralyze her?" I knew that they were talking about giving me a shot of succinylcholine or something so that I wouldn't fight the ventilator, but I wasn't having any truck with that. *Paralyze me? I don't fucking think so!*

So I shook my head vigorously from side to side in an emphatic negative and tried to yell, "No!" which put me once again at odds with the vent and resulted in yet another cacophony of alarms.

"Oh for God's sake," Jeff yelled. "Toni, stop it. You're not doing yourself any good, struggling like this."

George pulled at his moustache. "I think she's trying to tell us she doesn't want to be paralyzed."

Jack Allen put his head around the curtain. "Hey, do you guys mind? All this noise is disturbing the other patients."

"Sorry," George said. "We were discussing whether or not we should paralyze Toni to keep her from fighting the vent, and she objected rather violently."

Jack looked at my face for the first time and recognized me with a start. Then he checked the pulse oximeter. "How much O2 you got her on?"

"Forty percent," Jeff said. "Why?"

"Well," Jack said, "this looks pretty good. How bad do you think she needs to be on the vent?"

Jeff sighed impatiently. "She had a thoracotomy day before yesterday. She's got three broken ribs, and one of them tore her lung up pretty bad. She's still bleeding from her chest and her stomach. What do you think?" He didn't really sound as if he were asking for Jack's opinion, but he got it anyway.

Jack said, "Can I try something?" and not waiting for an answer, he turned the ventilator off. "Toni? Can you take a breath for me?"

I did so. It hurt, but no more than before. I took another. And another. Jack said, "What's the pulse oximeter say now?"

"Ninety percent," George said.

"And that's on room air," Jack said. "Look. She's breathing just fine on her own. Toni? Are you getting enough air?"

I nodded.

"How about it, guys? We let her breathe on her own for about, say, twenty minutes? June, keep checking that pulse oximeter. If she drops below eighty-seven, get Respiratory to hook up a bypass at forty percent. Then, if she can keep her pO2 above ninety, we can take that tube out and use a nasal cannula. Would you like that, Toni?"

This time I nodded as vigorously as I had previously shaken my head. Had I possessed a tail, I would have wagged it.

"You know," Jack said, "she's had that tube in for nearly two days, and after three days she'd have to have a tracheostomy so the tube won't wear holes in her larynx."

George pulled at his moustache some more. It seemed to help him think. "Well, you're the pulmonary guy," he conceded. "If you think she can do without the tube, who am I to argue? Seems to me, the sooner we get that out, the better."

"Okay with me," Jeff said.

Okay with me too. Last thing I need is another scar. Assuming I survive long enough, that is.

"I'll write the orders," Jack said and disappeared around the curtain.

"Toni, in case you haven't noticed," Jeff said, "you're having plasmapheresis as we speak. Actually, it's more like a plasma exchange. That's why you've got lines in both wrists, so we're a little concerned that you don't struggle. Okay?"

I looked around. Sure enough, there was another machine next to my bed. A familiar figure sat in a chair next to it, checking the lines and bags hanging from it. She smiled at me. "Do you remember me, Dr. Day?" she asked. "I'm Sherry McKinstry. I used to be a nurse anesthetist here. Now I'm a trained perfusionist for the American Red Cross in Boise. I do plateletpheresis and make fresh frozen plasma."

I nodded. I did remember her. Years before, a patient had died on the operating table, and I'd done the autopsy. The findings had absolved Sherry from any wrongdoing.

Now she was the one who took donor blood and ran it through her machine, removing platelets and plasma and returning the red cells to the donor. One plateletpheresis pack was equivalent to ten or twelve single platelet packs removed from single units of blood. She was basically doing the same thing to me, removing my blood, taking away the plasma containing the Lovenox, and replacing it with albumin and fresh frozen plasma, and returning the red cells to me. No doubt I'd have to receive more platelets too, since they got removed along with the plasma.

"I've never forgotten what you did for me," she continued. "Now I have a chance to do something for you."

I tried to smile, but it was hard to manage it around the ET tube. I lay back on my pillows and tried to relax. If I could keep my O2 up like a good little girl, I could lose the dratted thing.

"Don't stop breathing," Jeff advised with a grin. "You don't want to piss Jack off."

He left.

I heaved a huge sigh of relief, ribs permitting. No alarms went off, and I lay there smiling right out loud. So to speak.

.

Chapter 37

Talk of your science! After all is said,
There is nothing like a bare and shiny head.
Age lends the graces that are sure to please,
Folks want their doctors mouldy, like their cheese.
—Oliver Wendell Holmes

The Torture Toni Club returned right around six. At least that's what they said; I couldn't see a clock from where I was, and I had not a friggin' clue where my watch might have gotten to. Sherry and her machine were still there, pumping my blood round and round as before.

A change of shift had occurred at three o'clock, and this time my nurse was Julie. She bustled in right after the doctors and informed them that my pO2 had remained above ninety percent on room air and that Respiratory Therapy hadn't had to put bypass oxygen on my ET tube.

"Right you are, then," said Jack, "out it comes. Ready, Toni?"

I was born ready. I nodded.

Without further ado, Jack ripped away the tape and hauled that sucker right up out of my throat. I gagged and retched and then began to cough. *Oh, God, that hurt. Christ on a friggin' crutch.* I would have wrapped my arms around myself if it hadn't been for the goddamn restraints. Bloody mucus came up. The nurse held an emesis basin under my chin to catch it and wiped my mouth. Jack beamed at me. "There. How does that feel?"

"How the hell do you think it feels?" I whispered rustily. Thank God Hal and Mum hadn't had to witness *that* performance.

"Check another blood gas in an hour and call me," he said to Julie, and then he was gone.

She put some more ointment on my lips and around my nostrils and then put an oxygen mask on me, since a nasal cannula would fight with the NG tube, and then checked the pulse oximeter on my finger. "Ninety-five, good," she said, writing something on the clipboard, and then she was gone.

Jeff and George came in and noted happily that the volume of bloody drainage from their respective tubes was significantly decreased and that sometime in the foreseeable future I could look forward to losing them as well.

"Well," Sherry said, "it looks like this is working, Doctor. Just one more hour should do it, and then I'll be getting back to Boise."

"Tonight?" I whispered. "On these roads?"

"Shouldn't be too bad," she said. "It hasn't snowed in two days, and the interstate is plowed and sanded."

Mum and Hal appeared. Hal said, "Hi, sweetie, how are you doing?" before he got a good look at me.

"On the whole, I'd rather be in Philadelphia," I rasped.

Hal jumped and gasped. "Fiona! Her tube's out! She can talk!"

"Yes, dear," Mum said placidly. "I was wondering when you'd notice." She kissed my cheek. "It feels better, doesn't it, kitten?"

No shit, Sherlock. "Sure does," I whispered.

Hal took the hand without the pulse oximeter and squeezed it. "Thank God. How do you feel, sweetie?"

How the hell did he think I felt, all tied down and full of tubes? He'd been there; he should know. "Fine," I said huskily.

"We almost lost you," he said.

"So I hear."

He leaned over and kissed my forehead. "I love you," he said and left.

Mum took over. "Antoinette, my darling, you scared us all to death! Don't you ever do anything like that again, do you hear me?"

"Sorry," I whispered.

"Your Hal was a right basket case," she went on. "We all thought we were going to lose you."

"He didn't stay long," I complained.

"Well, there's a man for you," she said briskly. "He didn't want you to see him cry."

"Oh."

She indicated the plasmapheresis unit and Sherry. "What's all this, kitten?"

"Plasmapheresis," I said huskily. "Sherry is washing out my blood."

"Oh, is this the machine from the Red Cross? I'm surprised it got here so quickly."

"We don't normally do this," Sherry said, "especially on weekends, but when I heard it was Dr. Day, I came right away. She got me out of a lot of trouble once. This is my way of repaying her."

"How wonderful. Hal, dear, did you hear that?"

Hal came back to my bedside. "I sure did. So this is Sherry? I remember that autopsy," he said. "I'm glad to finally meet you. I can't thank you enough."

"My pleasure," Sherry said. "I think it worked. The doctors were saying there's less drainage now."

Julie poked her head around the curtain. "Doctor, there's a couple of policemen out here to see you."

"Send them in," I said.

Kincaid and the Commander appeared and greeted Hal and Mum. Hal appeared to be less upset by the presence of Bernie Kincaid than he had been before. They ignored me; maybe they thought I was still intubated. So I spoke up. "Hey, you two. Over here. Patient talking here."

"Toni!" Kincaid said. "You look …" He obviously didn't know what to say. I probably didn't look especially good, and he probably didn't want to say I looked awful, so I helped him out.

"Extubated?"

"Well …"

"Doc, you're a sight for sore eyes," the Commander said. "We just wanted to bring you up to date on things. We caught Ruthie, by the way. We got her trying to dispose of her bloody clothes in the Dumpster behind the Blue Lakes Inn. Her neighbor, Mrs. Sorensen, was the one who called them. She saw the flames out of her living room window."

"Who called you?" I asked.

"Your husband. He heard the whole thing on the phone."

"I turned the answering machine on as soon as I heard you and Ruthie talking," Hal said.

"So we basically have her whole confession on tape," the Commander said. "How did you manage that anyway, Doc?"

"I had my cell phone in my coat pocket, and my coat was all bunched up so I could reach it when it rang," I said. "I had it on vibrate, so Ruthie didn't hear it when Hal called me, and she didn't see me trying to open it, either. That was just plain lucky."

"My buddy Roy Cobb said that when they investigated the crawl space they found forty or fifty glass syringes, or parts of them," Kincaid said. "Did she inject all of that into you?"

"There were five boxes of ten syringes," I said. "She shot them all into me. And she didn't care about giving me hematomas, either. You should see my belly."

The Commander raised a hand. "That's okay. We'll pass."

"Who found me?" I asked.

"One of the firemen," Kincaid said. "They didn't know who you were, but I did. So I swung by and picked up Hal on the way to the hospital, since I couldn't call him, on account of his line was busy."

Yeah, right. All my fault.

"Not to mention that her fingerprints," the Commander said, trying not to smile, "were on the duct tape she used on you."

"So where is she now?" I asked.

"In jail, of course," the Commander said. "On two counts of first-degree murder and seven counts of attempted murder. She's not going anywhere."

Not getting out on a technicality, for instance, to creep into my hospital room in the dead of night with a few syringes of Lovenox to squirt into my IV.

Not that killing me would help her now. Too many people knew about her; she couldn't possibly get rid of all of them.

"You should have seen Jeff's face when I told him you'd been shot full of Lovenox," Hal said.

"Did he tell you to go pee up a rope?" I asked. That was one of Jeff's more colorful expressions.

"Not with two cops there to back him up," the Commander said, "and tell him that the person responsible had killed two people that way and had tried to kill seven others."

"What about Tiffany and Emily?" I asked.

"Tiffany's been discharged," Kincaid said, "and she's in jail. Emily's still here."

"She has pneumonia," Mum said. "Poor little thing. Jodi's been here checking on her every day."

Julie put her head around the curtain again. "I'm sorry, but you folks are going to have to leave now," she said. "You're disturbing the other patients, and I'm sure Dr. Day is tired. And Dr. Sorensen's here."

They all said good-night and left, Mum and Hal kissing me good-bye. "See you in the morning, kitten," Mum said.

I heard a brief conversation in the hall, and then Jeff came in, accompanied by Julie, who carried a sterile tray.

"What is this, Grand Central Patient?" I grumbled.

Apparently Jeff didn't hear me. Preoccupied, he checked the clipboard and put the head of the bed down so that I lay flat. He pulled up my gown.

"Hey," I reminded him. "I'm over here. You know, the patient?"

He stopped what he was doing and stared at me, uncomprehending.

"I'm not just a belly," I said.

"Oh. Sorry. Hi, Toni. I'm just checking your dressing. Okay?"

Surgeons. What are you gonna do? "Yes, Jeff. Thank you."

He palpated my belly. I raised my head and looked. It was now a really ugly mixture of purple, green, and yellow and was not nearly as tender as before. Gently he removed my dressing, and he and Julie changed it. "This is healing nicely. Not much drainage. No sign of infection. Your anti-Xa is down in the therapeutic range, and I think we'll keep it there for now. Don't want you to have DVTs or throw an embolus."

I glanced around. Somehow, with all the commotion around my bed earlier, Sherry and her machine had vanished. I mentally said a brief prayer that she'd get back to Boise safely.

"I think, if nothing else happens," Jeff said, "we can take these tubes out tomorrow and let you go home on Wednesday. How about that?"

Epilogue

I celebrated New Year's Eve and New Year's Day in my own home, tucked up on the couch by the fire with a book and my loved ones around me.

Killer lay on the floor by the couch. Geraldine didn't much like being banished from my lap, but she grumpily made do with forcing herself in between me and the back of the couch and digging her pointy little feet into my thigh.

Everyone reacted with horror to my description of the ordeal in Ruthie's basement, particularly being beaten to a bloody pulp with a golf club by a madwoman.

"You were lucky," Hal said, "that you didn't also have a ruptured spleen."

He was right. I wouldn't have survived that, even without the Lovenox.

"That's for sure," I remarked. "If she'd hit me from the left side instead of the right, I'd be sitting here dead."

Jodi shook her head. "I've known Ruthie for twenty years," she said. "I never would have guessed she could

385

go off the deep end like that. What's going to happen to her?"

"Life without parole," Elliott said, "in the state penitentiary."

"What about Tiffany?" Bambi asked.

Elliott shrugged. "Probably the same, depending on what kind of a deal her lawyers work out with the State of Minnesota. Don't forget, she killed three people there."

"And Emily should be out of the hospital next week," Jodi said happily.

"Then she gets to come home with us," Cody said.

"She'll come here first," Hal said. "Until your house is livable again."

"Are you sure?" Jodi asked doubtfully. "We could go to a motel."

I looked at Hal and shook my head. "No way. Once everybody's back to work and the kids are back to school, it won't seem nearly so crowded here."

"Mike never did get the rest of his Christmas vacation, did he?" Hal asked.

"Unfortunately, no," I replied. "He'll have to take a week off some other time. But next year I'll let *him* have the first week off, and I'll take the second."

"When do you think you'll go back to work, dear?" Mum asked me.

"I'm thinking the nineteenth," I said. "That's when Hal has to go back to work, and Bambi goes back to school."

"But that's only three weeks away," Mum objected. "Isn't that going to be too soon?"

"I don't think so," I said. "The Great Deductible Race will be over, and things should have calmed down considerably. I should be okay."

"How long do you want me to stay, kitten?"

Mum's question took me by surprise. I'd assumed she'd stay until I was back on my feet, or until I went back to work. "Mum, I want you to stay as long as you want to stay," I said—I hoped—tactfully. "How long do you want to stay?"

"I'll stay as long as you need me to, darling. But I am getting rather anxious to get back home. I've been here much longer than I planned to be."

Odd. I'd never known my mother to be anxious to leave before. She'd always gotten a little teary-eyed when she left me. Now she was anxious to go home?

I looked at her narrowly. Did I see what I thought I saw?

Omigod. My mother was blushing!

"Mum. What are you not telling me?"

"Why, whatever do you mean, dear?" Mum looked me straight in the eye without flinching.

I started to laugh—carefully, as it still hurt. "Now I know where I get it," I told her. "Mum, you're a worse liar than I am!"

"Antoinette, *really!*"

"It's a man, isn't it?"

"Don't be silly."

"Come on, Mother," I teased.

But she wouldn't tell me, no matter how much I hinted and badgered her about it. "All in good time," she kept saying. I knew my Mum; she wouldn't tell me anything until she was good and ready.

She was a lousy liar, but she was really, really good at keeping secrets. The only problem was that when she had one, everybody knew it.

"I've got a secret too," Bambi said, "but I'm going to tell you what it is. Pete and I are engaged."

"Engaged!" Hal said. "How the hell can you be engaged? You just met!"

"We love each other," Bambi said. "I knew it the minute I saw him, and he did too."

"But this is preposterous," Hal insisted. "You've only known each other a *week*."

"Two," Bambi said. She pulled the silver chain around her neck up out of her shirt and showed us the ring hanging on it.

"Darling!" Mum said. "It's absolutely perfect."

I looked at it next. It was a simple solitaire in white gold and must have been nearly a full carat. "Can Pete afford this?" I asked.

"He paid cash," Bambi said, "so I guess so."

I reached out and tried to hug her without ripping my stitches. "Congratulations."

"When do you plan to break the news to Shawna?" Hal asked.

"We thought we'd go down and spend the rest of Christmas break in Newport Beach," Bambi said. "Pete has a week's vacation coming up."

"Boy, I'd like to be a mouse in the wall when she hears that news," Hal went on. "You'll never convince her that Pete's a nice Jewish boy." Then he started to laugh. "And that's nothing compared to what my *mother* will say. She doesn't even know that she has a granddaughter yet, let alone one who's marrying a *goy*!"

She'd say that the apple doesn't fall far from the tree, I thought. "Hal. You haven't told your *parents* yet?" I pretended outrage, but I had a hard time not laughing too. For once Ida Shapiro would have somebody else to *kvetch* at besides me.

"We thought we'd have the wedding in July," Bambi went on. "That way we can have it in the backyard, if that's okay."

"Not if you want a Jewish wedding," Hal said. "There's no synagogue here and no rabbi, either. You'd better have it at your mother's, don't you think?"

"Why not have two?" I asked. "One here, one there. That way everyone can come."

"Are you two going to be able to make it on a policeman's salary?" Hal asked, ever practical.

"Pete is a detective sergeant," Bambi said, "and he's up for promotion. He's passed the lieutenant exam already. And I'll be working too, don't forget. I've already enrolled in my forensic science classes for the spring semester."

"Good girl," I said.

"Just think, Toni," she enthused, "next time you get involved in a case, I can really help you!"

I hated to discourage her, but I really hoped there wouldn't be another case. This one had involved way too much blood for my taste—and way too much of it mine.

Mazel tov!

About the Author

Jane Bennett Munro, MD, is a hospital-based pathologist who has been involved in several forensic cases over the course of her thirty-three-year career. Now semiretired, she lives in Twin Falls, Idaho, where she enjoys music, gardening, and skiing. She is the author of *Murder under the Microscope.*

Made in the USA
Coppell, TX
06 June 2020

27130798R10236